A broken MELODY

SAMANTHA BUTTERFIELD

A BROKEN MELODY
THE MELODIVERSE BOOK TWO

SAMANTHA BUTTERFIELD

Copyright © 2026 by Samantha Butterfield

All rights reserved.

No part of this book may be reproduced, distributed, or transmitted in any form or by any means, including photocopying, recording, or other electronic or mechanical methods, without the prior written permission of the author, except in the case of brief quotations used in reviews and certain other noncommercial uses permitted by copyright law.

This is a work of fiction. Names, characters, places, and events are either the product of the author's imagination or used fictitiously. Any resemblance to actual persons, living or dead, or actual events, is purely coincidental.

A Broken Melody

First Edition

ISBN: 979-8-9999886-2-1

Cover design, Interior Formatting and Interior Images/Icons by K. Jaspersen @ K. Jaspersen Designs

Edited by Ramona Mihai

There was no AI used in the making of this book.

THE MELODIVERSE

Every book in The Melodiverse follows a different member tied to Veritas Records. From musicians, producers, and corporate figureheads, there isn't a soul untouched by heartache. The glamour of fame can only do so much to hide the pain, the cracks are always there when the lights go out.

A Broken Melody is the second standalone story in this interconnected series. There is no need to read any other books to get the complete feel for this story, but you are more than welcome to.

If you would like to see Ben and Haunting Memories first introduction, you can read A Dark Melody, but it is not necessary for the plot.

CONTENT WARNINGS

A Broken Melody is a dark romance. It focuses heavily on the trauma both main characters endured and endure, with many scenes that might make people feel uncomfortable and/or trigger some unwanted memories.

Please read with caution. Please put your well-being first.

You can find a list of warnings below.

(Please note that the list may include some spoilers. I highly recommend you read it regardless to avoid any unwanted trauma.)

<u>Content Warnings:</u>

- Rape (talked about mildly described)
- Sexual Assault (talked about, mildly described)
- Sexual Abuse (talked about, mildly described)
- Family Sexual Abuse (Talked about, mildly described)
- Parental Abuse (on page)
- Verbal Abuse (on page)
- Physical Violence (on page)

CONTENT WARNINGS

- Knife & Gun Violence (on page)
- Trauma Sharing
- Talks of Self-harm
- Talks of Death
- Talks of Suicide
- Talks of Drug Use/Addiction
- Drinking
- Detailed Sex Scenes (open door)
- Kidnapping
- Name Calling
- Hospital/Medical Talk

Please note there might be a few things that I may have missed. I apologize in advance if that happened. If you find anything missing that should be listed, please feel free to message me on any social media platform or my email which can be found on my website, so I can apologize directly and update the list.

-Samantha

A BROKEN PLAYLIST

Blame it on Bad Luck- Bayside
Brick By Boring Brick- Paramore
Desire- Palaye Royale
bad decisions- Bad Omens
Nothing Good Happens After 2am- MOTHICA
Like That- Sleep Token
Bad Man- Coheed and Cambria
Irresistible- Fall Out Boy
Aqua Regia- Sleep Token
Damaged- In This Moment & Ice Nine Kills
Save Yourself- KALEO
Bulletproof Heart- My Chemical Romance
Emergency Contact-Pierce the Veil
Follow You- Bring Me the Horizon

To the broken, may you find the harmony in healing.

"A broken sound can still be beautiful." - unknown

ONE

Ben

WES IS IN LOVE, AND I'M AN ASSHOLE.

Don't get me wrong, I'm happy for him. Truly, fucking ecstatic. Abbey Dark is definitely a catch. No one in their right mind can blame him for falling in love with her. Unfortunately for him, she isn't an easy person to love.

Abbey has her issues. The media eats her up, and in turn she decided not to eat at all. She picked hiding from her problems with drugs, drinking, and dating horrible men. Can't fully judge her for all that, but until Wes came along, she was headed for rock bottom.

She seems to be getting better, with his help of course. Still, Wes has his hands full with her. They weren't even together when he nearly killed a man over her. Not that I hold that against him. The guy deserved it. Drugging and trying to rape Abbey earned him the beatdown Wes delivered. I would've finished the job for him if the security guard hadn't shown up.

Despite what that piece of trash had done, Wes still received six months of probation for nearly killing him. The assault was considered excessive. It's the lightest sentence they could've given him, but still a load of crap.

Now our band, Haunting Memories, is forced to take a break

from touring. Veritas Records was kind enough not to drop us from the label completely. Since we are one of the more popular bands, they didn't want to lose out on all the money we make for them. From albums, merch, and ticket sales, we do pretty well. And if we do well, they do even better.

Of course, they are expecting us to do some work during this break. We are supposed to be working on a new album. My bandmates are taking their time with that, however. They aren't in any rush to get to the studio.

We've been going strong for almost five years with Veritas. Put out three amazing albums that topped the charts. Done quite a few sold-out tours. Mostly as second acts, though we have headlined a few too. We've been working hard to keep the spotlight on us. So now the guys think a little break has been earned.

I know better. A break would give the next great band a chance to come in and steal our spot in the limelight. It's not like I care about being famous, but I don't want to lose our spot as one of the label's top dogs.

If we fall out of favor, we risk getting moved down to opening acts. Maybe even given fewer spots on tours in general. Or worse, we could get dropped from Veritas completely. Everyone knows getting dropped from Veritas is a death sentence in the music world.

Wes has been writing songs, which is good. A bunch of crappy love songs about Abbey, but they are better than the sad shit he put out after his last girlfriend cheated on him.

Thank the lord that relationship ended.

Wes is far too loyal for his own good. That fact has helped me out countless times, but it leads to him doing stupid shit for people who don't deserve his kindness.

Now he is spending all his effort helping Abbey conquer her demons. I can't fault him for that. He has helped me fight mine more times than he knows, but it leaves me with far too much free time on my hands.

I'm not too upset about it. What I am, however, is fucking bored.

It's that boredom that has me perched on a stool at one of Los Angeles's infamous rock clubs, The Recluse, on a random Monday night. It's barely eight,, and the bar is mostly empty.

I'm currently on my third glass of whiskey and trying to ignore the fact that none of my bandmates responded when I asked them to hang out. They are far too busy doing their own thing these days.

We have a close relationship. A tight-knit group, that all come from a small town in Utah. Over the years we've become a family. I'd do anything for any of them, and they tolerate me.

In the beginning, hardly a day went by without us hanging out. If not all of us, at least two or three of us would be out and about together. I lived with a few of them from time to time. We did everything together. Enjoyed each other's company. Helped each other pick up girls. Now they all have their own lives, and I feel left out.

Over the last year and a half when we weren't touring or recording an album, it could be weeks before I managed to convince one of them to hang out with me.

Before Abbey, I could count on Wes to answer his phone and entertain me most nights. Even with his last few girlfriends, he would still come out with me every so often. Maybe he would drag his girlfriend along, but it would still be good fun. With Abbey it's different, though.

She comes first now. He lives and breathes for that girl. Every fucking song he writes is about her and how head over heels he is for her now.

I'm losing him. No. I've already lost him.

Again, I can't fault him for falling for her, but ditching your friends for a girl is so high school.

I could never do that again. Love is not on my agenda. I have no use for the drama. Commitment is overrated. Devoting yourself to anyone is just setting yourself up for pain. I want nothing to do with all of that. I'll take my one-night stands over that misery.

I haven't been in a relationship for five years. Back then I was twenty and trying to figure life out. Trying to figure myself out. To be honest, I'm not sure it even counts. I was committed to Janet, but I highly doubt it went both ways. She was an older, drug-fueled mess that loved to drag me into her problems.

Nearly got me addicted to drugs too. I came way too close to losing myself in her chaos. Not because I cared about her, but because it was easier to jump into her downfall than deal with my own issues.

Damn near got myself kicked out of the band right before our big interview with Veritas. I was so strung out on heroin the day we were set to fly out to LA, I couldn't get through airport security.

Wes pulled me out of the darkness, like always. Got us another flight to LA. Forced me to get my shit together. Made sure I never saw her again.

Perhaps it's the guitarist in me or the rock star status, but I don't see any point in having a girlfriend now. When there are so many women who are dying for a night with me, why should I settle for one girl? Sure, it leads to nights like these where I have no one to keep me company, but it's better than dealing with someone else's problems.

Some people believe in love. I get it. They meet someone, become obsessed, devote themselves to them and try to live happily ever after.

I'm just the odd man out because I don't believe in that crap. Why should I when I have countless girls throwing themselves at me?

I might be a little skinny, but I have the whole bad-boy image down. The blond hair and blue eyes used to fool people, but the black skinny jeans, flannel shirts, and cigarettes clear up any doubts. I am not the guy you bring home to meet your mother. I'm the guy she warns you about. I'm an asshole, and it's been well established. Yet, for some reason, the girls look past all that and still find me attractive.

It helps that I also know how to play guitar better than almost anyone else in the scene. Whenever I have a guitar in my hands, I'm strumming along to a tune. Whether it's one from the radio or one in my head. I stroke the strings with ease.

I'm not like the other guitarists. I don't care if I'm playing on a huge stage to a sold-out crowd or simply sitting in an empty room by myself. The setting doesn't matter. I just love playing music. I'm practically addicted to it.

Which makes not touring or recording an album extremely difficult. I feel the ache in my chest. Not that I don't find a reason to pick up my guitar every chance I get, but it isn't enough to just strum for a few minutes. Once it became a job, it gave me purpose. I crave the purpose. The reason to play. Without it, I feel like I'm just aimlessly wandering through life.

"Another?" the bartender asks as I spin the empty glass on the bar counter.

"Nah. Just the bill."

This place is dead. It's not helping me feel any better about myself.

I pay my tab, pull up my hood, and step out into the streets of LA. It's Monday, and while very few people are out at the bars or clubs, it's still lively out. People walk around in a constant rush because one mile takes 20 minutes of travel time. In this city, everyone has somewhere to be.

Except me. I have nowhere to be. No one expecting me.

I skim my phone, hoping to find someone to spend my night with. I'd take a past hookup or some lame band guy, who only wants to hang out for a shot at fame. I'm that desperate for entertainment at this point. I'm so bored I may actually go insane.

A message from Oscar Muniz, a drummer I toured with last year, gives me some hope. He is inviting me to some house party a few neighborhoods over.

I barely know the guy, so I'm sure inviting me is just a way for him to look cool. I often get asked to parties by smaller bands as a way for them to come across as more famous than they are. Lucky for him, I'm just bored enough not to care. If it's fun and there is alcohol, I'm in.

Sending him a reply, I smoke a cigarette before ordering myself a car.

I'm not fond of going to a random person's house, but beggars can't be choosers, and tonight I'm a beggar. I just need something to keep me busy. Anything at all.

When the car drops me off at the address Oscar gave me, I'm pleasantly surprised to see a large mansion overflowing with people. The street is littered with parked cars, from people who probably shouldn't get behind the wheel. Music floods through open windows. Groups gather here and there, smoking, talking, and drinking.

House parties aren't really my thing. I go to some parties thrown by the label that happen to be in houses, but they are far less wild than this. It fills me with memories of shitty house parties back in Utah. High school days, when I only dreamt of being as famous as I am today.

It fills me with pride to walk up the walkway and have people do a double take. They know me. They know my band. The fact that I'm here is shocking. I should be out in the VIP section of some club, hanging out with models, rock stars, and other famous people. Yet, I'm here at the same party as them.

I can hear them whispering among themselves. That doesn't bother me in the slightest. I've learned how to deal with the whispers, the rumors, the gossip. Being a famous rock star has its perks. If the only downside is people talking crap about me, I'll take that in good stride. Let them talk. Sell their stories. All it does is create a bigger buzz about me.

"Ben!" someone calls out. "You came!"

My head whips around to find a face I sort of recall. It could be Oscar or someone else from his band or another band entirely. Who knows. I don't honestly care. If someone is bold enough to call me over, I'm going to go. Might as well have a partner in my crimes tonight. A wingman, if you will.

The guy looks a little younger than me. Probably in his early twenties. Caramel brown waves sit on his head. A round, boyish face, with a button nose and light blue eyes, watches me as I move closer. The sleeves of his red flannel are pushed up, revealing a few random tattoos on his light tan forearms, and a band tee underneath lets me know he has good taste in music.

I weave through the crowd, catching a few stunned faces with jaws dropped in recognition.

"Oscar said he invited you. I didn't think you'd actually show, though." He laughs. "Is Wes with you?"

"No." I shake my head.

Wes is who people really want to meet. They consider him the genius behind the music we make. The lead singer always gets all the glory, and Wes deserves it. He does a lot of the work to earn it too. I write a good portion of the music, but the lyrics are mostly his. My guitar riffs are always my own. Maybe built off his input, but I do my own little tweaks to make it fit my vibe.

Most people drool over the lyrics, though. And Wes is mighty fine with a pen. The guy is a bleeding heart of hope and despair. I can't wait for people to hear the new stuff. I wonder whether a whole album of love songs will sell.

"Ah. Right, he probably isn't allowed to party since he is on probation."

"And on Abbey," I add with a laugh.

"Not sure I'd want to party if my other option was Abbey, either." He smiles. "You probably don't remember me, huh?"

"Vaguely. I have a shitty memory."

"Cameron Ward. I'm the lead guitarist for Great Falls. We did the tour with you guys last summer."

"Right. Hard to forget a band like Great Falls."

I'm not lying, even if the face he makes shows he doesn't buy it. Great Falls is a pretty decent band. I remember a few of his guitar riffs impressing me quite a bit. Their self-produced album is downloaded on my phone, but I'm not here to stroke the guy's ego.

"Want a drink?"

We weave our way through the massive crowd of people throughout the house. Every corner is stuffed with people. Hot girls are mixed in with your average wannabe band guys. Music makes talking hard, but not impossible. The air is heavy with booze, weed, and a hint of cigarettes.

I let Cameron lead me through the swarm of people to the giant dining room. The table is covered with bottles of every kind of alcohol you could want. It looks like a liquor store threw up in here.

"Help yourself."

I pick up a bottle of whiskey, filling up a plastic cup halfway. I want to get my buzz back, but I don't need to get fucked up tonight. I'd much rather find a willing girl to take home.

"Whose party is this?" I ask as he pours himself a drink.

"Calvin Loudman. He is just renting the place. Every few weeks he throws a huge party at a rental. Shit gets wild, but it's all good fun."

"Cam," a voice cuts in. "You left me again."

I glance over to see an attractive girl standing to our side. She glares daggers at Cameron, and I'd assume she is his girlfriend if it weren't for the fact that she is almost a carbon copy of him. Just slightly shorter, with great tits and longer hair. Not long hair, just longer than his. Her caramel hair sits just at her shoulders.

She wears a tight tan turtleneck that sticks to her chest like latex. A short brown skirt highlights the curves of her hips, while the dark tights covering her legs stick to her like a second skin.

Her lips are pouty under the pink gloss she wears. Simple eyeshadow rests over her light blue eyes that look so much like Cameron's it's almost eerie. Only her eyes are far less friendly. There is a rage resting behind them, and I'm very tempted to see what would happen if I fanned the flame.

There is a light brown mark sitting at the corner of one eye. It hints that she might be more trouble than she is worth.

She clearly tried to cover up a bruise, and while the idea of someone laying hands on a woman makes me ill, that is not the kind of drama I need in my life. Her honor is not mine to defend, so I'll kindly stay out of it.

"I just went out for a smoke and ran into Ben here. Chill, sis."

"I specifically asked you not to leave me alone," she says sharply. "You know..." Her eyes roam over to me as if she suddenly realized that Cameron mentioned someone else being here.

"Why did you come then?" He chuckles. "Stop being so uptight, Prue. Have a drink and try to have some fun." He passes her a bottle of vodka.

She eyes me before glancing at the bottle in her hands.

"This is Ben." Cameron motions to me. "From Haunting Memories."

"I know who he is." She raises an eyebrow, letting her eyes dart back to me. "You look different in person."

"Do I?" I smile. I could show her a whole world of different in person, but I resist the urge to stick my dick in her. Whatever trouble stems from the bruise on her face is not worth whatever pleasure she could bring my cock.

Instead, I let my eyes drift to a group of girls off toward the stairs. They giggle among themselves, glancing my way. Clearly, they know who I am, which will make it a whole lot easier to fuck them.

"What are you doing here?"

I shrug.

"Slumming it." Cameron laughs. "Reminding us lesser guys what the dream is."

"And trying to get lucky." I laugh, nodding to the other girls.

Prue rolls her eyes, lifting the bottle to her lips. She takes a gulp, and I try not to laugh when her face twists in disgust from the burn.

"Why do people drink this stuff?"

"To have fun. You should try it," Cameron replies. "Have a few more sips and try to make some new friends. Ben and I are going to go try to make some of our own, okay?"

"Please don't abandon me," Prue pleads softly.

"I'm not abandoning you. I will be around. Relax and try to have a good time, okay? I won't be far."

She nods, taking another sip.

I follow Cameron as he ducks around a few people toward the girls by the stairs.

"Sorry about her. She's had a rough couple of months. I'm just trying to show her life can be fun, you know?"

"Yeah." I nod, ignoring the part of me that would like to show her how fun I could be.

The call of chaos is one I've learned to ignore after Janet. No girl is ever worth the trouble. Least of all some stuck-up girl with a bruise under her eye.

TWO

Ben

Cameron and I chat up different girls. Eventually we bump into Oscar, who has a girl hanging onto his arm. I continue to drink myself stupid as the idea of leaving with any of the girls seems unnecessary when there are plenty of empty rooms.

I sneak off with two different girls throughout the night.

I fuck one in a tub big enough for the both of us. She will surely brag to her friends about the job I did with limited room. I let her put her number in my phone even though I have no plans of ever calling her. I made it clear it was just a hookup, but some girls never heed my warnings.

I fuck the second one in a bedroom upstairs.

We leave the blankets disheveled, not bothering to make up the bed when we are done. I toss my used condom in a drawer on the side table as she fixes her makeup using the mirror on the dresser. This isn't my house, nor am I responsible for renting the place, so the mess is the least of my concerns.

She invites me back to her place for round two, but I know that will just lead to her wanting to have breakfast with me. That is not something I want to deal with, so I politely decline and join back up with Cameron and Oscar.

Cameron silently tracks some girl throughout the night. He is trying to play it off, but I've seen that look far too many times. The way the eyes zero in on someone. It's a dead giveaway that a guy has the hots for a girl.

I have no idea who she is to him, but he watches with fascination as she dances with other guys, while drinking like a fish. I don't bother pointing it out. We aren't friends, though if we were, I'd tell him not to waste his time.

That girl is wild, and he is trying to make it big. He does not need her getting in the way of his dreams.

His sister, Prue, comes up to us from time to time. Asking how much longer he plans on staying. He suggests she gets herself a ride home, but she always says no. I guess sticking around to bug her brother is more fun than going home alone.

It's mildly annoying, but I don't address it. Whatever hard time she is having has apparently earned her the right to interfere in Cameron's fun. I don't know their family dynamics well enough to know if that's fair or not. Being an only child has gifted me the ability to never have to care about someone else.

Of course, over the years Wes has become more like a brother to me than a friend. I'm pretty sure my parents liked him more than me. He did a better job of comforting my mother after my father died than I did. I'm pretty sure he talks to her more often too. I know for a fact they have breakfast at least once a month.

My mom is just crazy about Abbey Dark. I figure she thinks if they get married, she may actually have a chance of being a grandmother, maybe not by blood, but Wes would give her that title over his own mother any day.

That's not happening, though. Abbey would not do well being pregnant, and I do not plan on having kids myself, so she is going to be robbed of that chance.

I'd feel bad, but as my mother, she has come to expect disappointment. I try not to lose sleep over it anymore. She stopped trying to change me or raise me at an early age. Instead, my saint of a mother has taken to offering me forgiveness that I don't ask for, and acceptance I don't deserve.

She offers the same things to Wes, and he eats it up. His home life was not great, and every chance he had, he was at my house enjoying the comforts two loving parents could give. What I didn't want, he did, and it worked out for the both of us.

He got a family, and I got the burden of being a good child off my back. Plus, we both got each other. A win for everyone.

So, I try to ignore Cameron's needy sister when she comes around, because just like my family isn't typical, I can only assume theirs isn't either. Even though it is becoming increasingly obvious, they are well off.

In fact, most of these people seem to come from wealthy families. I overhear conversations about cruises and trips on yachts. Vacation houses and travel plans are all these people care about. That, and designer clothes.

Still, I'm having a decent night. While some of them are rich, none were necessarily famous. They were the outcasts of the elite, the wannabe rock stars among the soon-to-be lawyers and doctors. I am a big fish, and this is a small pond.

That doesn't seem to faze them, though. They are happy to see me, but they don't trip over themselves to try to get my attention. I get shown respect and admiration, but they treat me like I'm one of them.

It's been far too long since I felt like I belonged somewhere. It's almost sad that I feel more at home with these people I barely know than I have with my band lately.

Oddly, in the larger scene, I've been feeling a little lost. It's hard when you get to the top. You never know who you can trust. Everyone is out to find a way to steal the spotlight. Jealousy runs rampant among the top dogs. You either bite or get chewed on.

Despite constantly touring with other bands, I haven't made nearly as many friends as you'd expect. As a band, we learned early on to only trust each other. We are nice enough to the other bands in the scene and on the label, but we don't consider them friends.

Now, as we all start to get older, our lives are starting to go in different directions. They are forming other relationships. Starting to think about the distant future. Making plans to better their lives while I'm just floating by.

I miss the days in the beginning when we were just stupid kids. There was no future, just the present. We'd waste our time doing stupid shit. Getting drunk. Tattooing our bodies. Living life to the fullest, with no thoughts about what tomorrow would bring.

Even then I was the odd man out. I knew early on that Dennis, Arron, and Nicolas didn't care about me the same way Wes did. They put up with me because of Wes. Over the years they grew to like me, but if it came down to it, they would easily cast me to the side to save their own skin. I could only count on them so much. They'd back me in a fight, but they wouldn't lay down their lives for me.

We are a family, but a family with limits. And those limits are starting to be tested.

I am starting to become a loose end for them to tie up.

One day, probably soon, they will ditch me and move on with their lives. I'll become an abandoned has-been.

It's extremely pathetic to think about.

"Hey," Cameron says into my ear. "I'm going to disappear for a bit. If you see Prue, can you let her know I didn't leave without her?"

I nod as he slinks off with a pretty girl.

I have no plans of running into the fun sucker. Doesn't matter how hot she is, needy girls are not worth the headache.

Wandering my way through the crowd in desperate need of a cigarette and a moment of silence, I actively try not to spot Prue among the people.

I'm hoping the fresh air will help me sober up a little. The low feelings are starting to make my mood dip, and I'm bound to do something stupid if I don't regain a sense of sobriety.

Glancing through a window, I find a tiny corner of the front porch not overflowing with people and make my way there.

Once outside, I let the cool winter air hit me. Glancing off to the side for a moment, I notice the short light brown hair that has been plaguing me all night.

Prue sits on the ledge of the porch. Her legs dangle over the railing, and the bottle of vodka from earlier sits to the side of her. Barely anything is gone from it, which isn't surprising. She doesn't seem like the type to let herself have any fun or get drunk.

I sigh softly, hoping she doesn't hear me. Pulling out a cigarette, I light it carefully. I don't need her bothering me, asking where Cameron is. I'd deliver the message, but I'm not in the mood to deal with any kind of bullshit tonight. Not even from a sexy girl.

Judging by the bruise on her face and the things Cameron has said about her, I just know letting myself get involved would lead to an altercation. It's not in my nature to be okay with people being abused. While fist fights are a thing of my past, I'd easily kick the ass of whoever hurt her. But you can't fight with your hands when you need them to play guitar for a living, so I try to avoid getting myself into those situations these days.

The sound of my lighter attracts her attention, though. Her head whips in my direction for a moment. Eyes scanning over me, before turning forward again. She wipes at the corner of her eyes. It's a dick move not to check on her, but I don't move, inhaling on my cigarette instead.

Silence surrounds us for a moment. Just the sound of me smoking and the sad vibes radiating off her fill the air.

Cursing under my breath, I take a step in her direction.

"Cameron wanted me to let you know he didn't leave without you."

"Good to know." Her voice is full of annoyance.

I'm not nearly sober enough to deal with her attitude. Despite the loneliness that is creeping up on me, I've been having a good night. I'm not about to let her ruin it. I don't care what she has been through. She has no right to bring everyone down with her.

"You can't fault the guy for wanting to have a good night."

"I don't," she snaps, her head turning back to me.

"Good."

"Do you come to these parties to feel better about yourself?"

"What?" I almost laugh at the question.

I have no idea who she thinks she is, but crying or not, I'm not putting up with crap from anyone. Ever. Did enough of that through my youth. No way am I doing it with some girl I barely know.

Even if she is clearly nearing a total mental breakdown. And wearing a very short skirt.

"Do you hang out with the smaller bands so you can show off what a big shot you are?"

"No." I chuckle. It's not every day a girl insults me back.

"Oh. I just assumed." She slides off the porch rail, turning to face me. "You could be at the big clubs hanging out in the VIP section. Or throwing a party of your own for all your famous rock star friends. Instead, you're here."

"I like these people." I take a drag off my cigarette. "They aren't half bad. Maybe you should take a fucking chill pill, get off your high horse, and try to get to know them."

She looks stunned by my comment. Part of me hopes it stung a little. Don't care how well off her family is, or what she went through. She doesn't get to judge anyone else.

"I don't think I'm better than them," she snaps. "I'm not some stuck-up bitch."

"No?" I let the corner of my lips curl up, eyeing her up and down. Drinking in the short-pleated skirt, that shows off just enough leg to pass as sexy, but still conservative. The turtleneck covers her top half, but sticks to her like glue, leaving little to imagination. Teasing in all the right ways, but letting every guy know she doesn't sleep around. "Could've fooled me."

Her mouth opens but no words come out. Quickly she snaps

it shut, staring at me like she can't believe what I just said. Her hands squeeze into fists, as she shakes her head in frustration.

"God!" she exclaims. "Guys like you are such assholes."

"Spoken like a stuck-up bitch." I laugh.

Her mouth drops open again, but then she is marching up to me. The glare on her face makes my cock throb. Her light blue eyes remind me of the clear sky before a storm. A part of me is tempted to let that storm consume me for the night.

But that would be a bad idea. Unless...

"You don't even know me," she fires back. "I am not stuck up."

She is fuming and it shouldn't make me happy to have gotten under her skin, but I can't fight the grin that comes over my face. I'm in trouble and the self-destructive addict that lives inside me is excited to see where it takes us.

"Maybe stuck-up isn't the word, but I bet a good chunk of change on the bitch part being true."

"Why?" Her question comes out in a grumble. Trembling with rage. It shouldn't make me happy, but it does.

I'm digging myself into a hole here. I'm just drunk enough not to care if she goes and sells the story of how Ben Parker is an asshole. It's a badge of honor to me at this point. I do like her brother's band, though. I would like to tour with them again. So, the right thing to do would be to walk away.

But my feet stay planted. An arrogant smile plastered on my face as I stare down at this very angry hot chick, trying not to get an erection.

"Your brother lets you tag along to a fun party, and you spend the whole night trying to make his life a living hell, while sulking around like a stuck-up bitch."

Her eyes go wide, and her lips tremble, despite being too stunned to speak.

"I mean, I get it. This isn't your scene. Obviously." I glance down at her brown and cream outfit. "But for your brother's sake, you could at least pretend to have a good time. These parties lead to connections. This kind of thing could be great for his career, but instead of being supportive, you keep nagging him. That's pretty selfish. And very bitchy."

In a fraction of a second, her clenched fist opens, and her hand collides with my face. There is a good amount of force behind it, but it barely leaves behind a sting. The act of it takes me by surprise, though. I didn't expect physical violence from her, but I don't hate it.

I laugh when she pulls her hand back. My hand rubs over the spot she hit. I'm in shock and my cock is now officially partly hard.

"Not helping your case, Prue."

"No?" She reaches forward, taking my cigarette from between my fingers. Dropping it to the ground, she stomps it out. "Why don't you go on then. Tell me how awful I am, despite the fact you don't even know me. List off more ways I suck, while you sit on your own high horse. Pretending you are some rock god. Fucking all the girls you want, and then never calling them back. Trust me, nothing you say can hurt me. I know how guys like you are. Been with a bigger asshole than you. Nothing you say can hurt me."

"Okay." I shrug. "I think you could go much further in life if you learned how to fucking relax. It must be so exhausting to do nothing but nag and complain all the time. I'd say remove whatever is stuck up your ass, but we both know you would never let anyone touch that hole." I smirk.

She rolls her eyes.

"Though anal is probably a fitting word for you, huh?" I continue. "I bet you love being in control of everything. You just scream neat and tidy. Bet your closet is organized down to the fucking shade. I imagine fucking you would be like having sex with a corpse. You look like the kind of girl who would just lay there and let the man do all the work. You drip of high maintenance and neediness. All your ex-boyfriends probably leaped for joy when you finally cut them free. They only stayed because you look good on their arms and promised one day you'd put it in your mouth, even though you never had any intent on following through on it. You are just a bitch dressed up as a pretty girl."

I don't really believe half the stuff I'm saying. Most of it is just word vomit to piss her off more. She picked the wrong night to cross paths with me. I'm just low enough to want to ruin someone else or throw myself into her chaos.

"And you are never the main character," she counters. "I mean, come on, look at you." She gestures up and down. "You are the side character, living in the shadow of everyone around you. Even here, you don't stand out. Why did you end up here tonight, Ben? Could it be all your other friends got tired of you? Maybe they outgrew you." Her hands rest on her hips as she goes off, pushing her chest out. I try not to let my gaze drop to her tits. "You are falling to the waste side. And hanging out with smaller people won't help people not notice how tiny you are." She glares. "And I bet tiny is a word you are very used to hearing, huh?"

"Is that a joke about my dick size?" I laugh.

"If the condom doesn't fit." She smirks. "And for your information, I actually enjoy sucking dick." Fuck me if that statement doesn't make me harder. "I'm actually really good in bed."

"Jesus, Prue." Cameron's voice comes from behind me. "Too much information, sis."

"Can we go now?" Prue pleads. "Please?"

"Yeah. Fine. Let me get my shit," Cameron says, turning around and walking back into the house.

"What's your number?" I ask, pulling out my phone.

"What?" Her eyes widen again. I could get used to the way shock lights up her features.

"Obviously I went a little too far. Let me make it up to you. How about coffee? My treat." I grin at her.

"No thanks," she snaps, marching past me.

I laugh and follow her down the porch steps. Trailing behind her as she walks down the driveway, I let my eyes fall to her ass. Round and mouthwatering.

I shouldn't be asking for her number, but the way she looked when she was telling me off was too fucking hot. Sure, she struck a few nerves, but when a girl isn't afraid to admit she likes sucking cock, you don't turn down the chance to see if it's true.

"Come on. It's just coffee."

"Go fuck yourself," she says, glancing back at me.

"I could. Or you could." I smirk. "You can show me just how good in bed you are, and I could prove that my cock isn't tiny in the slightest."

"Oh my God," she groans. "You are a real piece of work, you know that, right? How stupid do you think I am?"

"I never once called you stupid. Stuck-up and bitchy, yes, but never stupid."

"Does this often work for you? Calling girls bitches and then asking them out?"

"First time for everything." I shrug with a smile on my face.

"I'm never going anywhere with you. You're an asshole."

"Ouch. Prue. That hurts." I smirk.

"Sure." She rolls her eyes.

"Trust me, I am worth the headache."

"Doubtful."

"I called us a car," Cameron says, walking up. "Ben, it was fun hanging with you tonight."

"Yeah." I nod. "Good seeing you. When we get back to touring, I'll hit Oscar and you up. Maybe we could bring you guys back out with us."

"Dude, that would be awesome."

"I'm going to be sick," Prue mumbles, rolling her eyes again.

"Did someone have too much to drink?" Cameron asks with a chuckle.

"No." She sighs, looking over at me. "Clearly not enough."

"Goodnight," I say, shooting her one last smirk.

Part of me is glad she didn't give me her number. No matter how bored I've been, I don't need to invite trouble into my life. Wes would be proud of me for not getting her number. He'd be disappointed in all the other crap I said, but hey, he knows how big of an asshole I am.

Still, another part of me is disappointed I may never see Prue again. She was hot and even sexier when she was glaring at me like I was the worse person she ever met.

Perhaps if Haunting Memories ever goes back on tour, I'd drag her brother along and get the chance to fuck her. Hopefully when there are no bruises on her face and far less drama in her life.

THREE

Prue

STARING INTO THE MIRROR I FIND MY REFLECTION doesn't match who I used to be. The fading bruise under my left eye reminds me that I'm no longer that girl. She died a few weeks ago, at the hands of a man I thought I was going to marry.

I may only be twenty-two, but my whole life has been planned out for years. Since meeting Charles in my sophomore year of high school, all our families could talk about was us getting married one day. They didn't care that we were only kids. Our families had a goal in mind and were more than willing to let us be the path to get it.

My parents didn't pick him out for me. It's not like they forced him on me. I could've ended up with any of the sons of their chosen families. But when Charles showed interest in me, they were thrilled, and I just went with it. I'd do anything to make them happy. Anything to keep the focus off Cameron and tensions low.

The Davenports are one of the more well-off families. They have old money, and for whatever reason decided my family and our newer money was worth their time. Our families spent a lot of time together. Even before Charles expressed interest in me. My father was always golfing with his. Our mothers had brunch together a few times a month. They liked us and my family loved that fact.

It may not have been as arranged as marriages were back in the medieval times, but I still felt like I was a cow being sold to the highest bidder. And Charles' family was about as high of a bidder as I could land.

So, I entered a relationship with him. It wasn't bad. Not at first. He was charming. Bought me gifts, took me out on dates. I was arm candy to him. A prize possession that he loved to show off at the club houses our families went to.

The sex wasn't bad. In the beginning it was even a little wild. But I knew he was getting bored. We were young and stuck together due to family obligations. I tried to spice things up, but he didn't like any of the same things as I did. He wanted his dick sucked and my pussy to fuck.

He was boring in other ways too. Couldn't hold a conversation if it wasn't about sports, drinking, or being mean. He only passed classes because he paid someone to do his assignments.

Charles was a piece of trash that I was unfortunate enough to get stuck with, but I let myself pretend it was what I wanted. Went to the same college as him. Let everyone think we were a happy couple, while ignoring my own unhappiness.

I accepted my fate a long time ago. I didn't get to have passions or goals. I was just supposed to be a dotting girlfriend, supporting him however he needed, until we got married. Then I'd get to become one of those wives who never had to cook or clean. That hosted functions for charities and never got mad about anything.

As I carefully apply cover up over one of the remaining bruises, I'm reminded that I broke that last rule.

I let myself get mad. After finding out he cheated on me, I chewed him out. Called him every name I could think of. I always knew he would do it. The men in the society I was born in don't stay faithful. They are normally more discreet about it. I could've handled being cheated on but having everyone know it was happening stung. All while I was expected to stay loyal to him and his subpar bedroom skills. It wasn't fair.

So, I got angry. Then he got angrier. And well, now I'm covering up bruises with makeup and turtlenecks in a shared bathroom at my brother's apartment.

The pain he inflicted was horrible. I'm lucky to not have any scars from the way he busted my cheek open. The doctor my parents sent me to was very skilled. He made sure I wouldn't have any lasting marks. Couldn't do much about the bruises or cracked ribs, other than give me advice on how to help them heal.

As I study myself over in the mirror, I feel broken. My short brown hair hangs to my shoulders. Light blue eyes full of fury and sadness. Makeup only does so much to hide the fact I took a beating. Dressed in a gray turtleneck and a dark beige skirt. Most of my fair skin covered up to hide the evidence of his damage and my low iron, it's hard to pretend that isn't true.

I force myself to remember that it won't last.

No. I'll never be the girl I was before. She was weak, naïve, and pathetic.

Ben's voice from last night replays in my head. He may be a famous guitarist in a huge band, but most of what he said was untrue. I have never been stuck up or a bitch. I can't help but wonder if it would've saved me a world of hurt if I had been.

Is it too late for me to become the girl he tried to paint me as? Could I be a bitch? Learn how to manipulate guys? Start to use them for a change. Have the upper hand for once in my life. Be something more than a pawn for them to use?

The idea is appealing.

"Come on, Prue." Cameron's voice from the other side of the door makes me jump. "I knew you were going to hog the bathroom."

Cameron's voice reminds me I'm not completely alone.

Gathering my stuff, I head out of the bathroom.

"Sorry."

"It's fine." He smiles, but there is that look in his eyes he has had since he picked me up from the hospital that day. Guilt, concern, and pity. "Have a good day at school, sis."

"Thanks."

We are twins. He was born first, but I always felt like that was a mistake. I am more of an older sister than he has ever been an older brother to me. I guess five minutes isn't that much older, but still, I've been taking care of him for as long as I can remember.

He is the wild child. Obsessed with everything that our parents despised. Tattoos, rock music, partying, and rebelling. From the day he came across rock music on the TV, he was hooked.

Taught himself how to play guitar by age 10 and has never stopped since. He poured his heart and soul into the music. In some ways I'm jealous of him. He has passion, something I've never had. I wish I had an ounce of it to put into a hobby or interest, but all I ever craved was praise and pleasing people.

So, I took on the role of being the well-behaved daughter. Every time my parents zeroed in on Cameron, trying to reign him in, I stepped in to show them they didn't need to try to hinder him. They had me to parade around. I would do my job and his. Make the family look good.

It took a few years, but eventually they gave up on him completely. Put all their efforts into making sure I played my part right. Getting with Charles only helped take the spotlight off Cameron.

I give Cameron the freedom and support our parents couldn't and he gives me a purpose. It is an unspoken agreement between us. We never talked it out, never mention it now. I know he knows what I've done for him. He is grateful for it. I see it every time he lands a spot on a tour for some bigger band. Every time he tells me about an interview with a record label. I see the thankfulness in his eyes.

Now I'm the grateful one.

When I ended up in the hospital after Charles' assault,

Cameron was the first person I called. I knew I could count on him to not judge, not question and offer me somewhere to hide.

His two-bedroom apartment isn't the kind of place our parents would approve of, but he is rather proud of it. It's in the area around the college I go to, simply because it's cheap and it kept us close. He was able to get it at eighteen, moving out on graduation day. While our parents were watching me walk across the stage, unaware he had dropped out a few weeks prior, he packed up and left.

For the most part he pays for it on his own. Works two jobs and plays shows at local venues whenever he can. I help too. Slipping him some money when he has to quit his day jobs to go on tour. I treat him to dinners and buy him presents, like his dream car.

When our parents disowned him, they did it with grace. Cut him off for the most part, which was fine by him. He didn't want to live on their dime longer than he had to. They don't acknowledge him to their friends, but he gets invited to private family events. He rarely shows, but occasionally I ask him to come, and he does. They barely talk to or about him, and whenever I bring him up, they only pretend to hear what I have to say.

It probably hurts me more than him. He is important to me. I envy his freedom and confidence. Getting to see him make something of his life is rewarding to me. Watching him throw himself into his dream is the greatest thing in the world.

If I don't get to have control of my life at least knowing he does gets me through the day.

I can give up everything just for him to have a chance to make his dreams come true.

Though all that changed the minute Charles hurt me. Now I'm hiding out here, far away from my parents. Slowly becoming just as disgraced as he is.

He doesn't seem bothered by it, though. He encourages me to embrace the freedom, but I know it doesn't last.

Our parents keep begging me to return home. They didn't

mind Charles and me taking some time apart, but I know they expect us to reconcile.

Cameron is fully against that. Telling me to stay a few more days every time I even bring it up. Bringing me along to all his parties and shows.

The guilt is hidden in his eyes, a carbon copy of mine. He escaped first, leaving me to my own devices, which led to my own demise. Now he feels like he has the chance to save me.

And maybe he is right. Maybe it is time I become someone new. Leave the old me behind.

Become the bitch Ben Parker claimed I was.

Gathering up my textbooks and stuffing them into my tote bag, I realize I'm running short on time. Luckily, Cameron's apartment is within walking distance, because driving and finding parking would probably take far longer.

If I leave now, I might even have time to stop by and grab a coffee from The Mug Life. It's a small hole in the wall coffee shop just off campus, that all the students go to.

Going to an Ivy League college was the plan my parents had for me, but when Charles picked some smaller college, they allowed me to follow him. Anything to keep us together. It's not like I would have a use for a degree once we got married. It was just something for me to do. Another way for me to look good to their friends.

Charles didn't want to go to an Ivy League school. He wanted to stay in LA, and because of that, he picked some small, but still upper-class college. Most of our friends followed suit too. They wouldn't risk going to another school and losing their connection to the Davenports. The Davenports are the kind of family you want to stay close to. Old money holds more weight than gold these days.

Which is why I shouldn't have been surprised when all our friends took Charles' side. They were so quick to turn on me. Not that I was really close with any of them, but they treated me well enough since I was dating Charles.

I missed almost two weeks of classes after what happened. Partly because I was in a lot of pain, but mostly because I looked awful. Even my parents were shocked by the state of my face.

When I finally went back to school, no one talked to me. Even with the stitches still in place and the swelling noticeable, no one said a word. They all just pretended I didn't exist. Or worse, whispered behind my back.

Charles told everyone that I made up the attack. He claimed I was so upset about his cheating, that I wanted to make his life a living hell. Said I lied about him laying a hand on me.

Even with the evidence of what he did on my body, people bought his story. He spun a story that I did it to myself and people just went along with it.

They know he is lying, but no one wants to call him out. No one cares enough about me to address it. They just go along with whatever he says, because of how powerful his family is.

Which is exactly why I didn't press charges. That, and my parents told me not to.

I'm pathetic. So desperate not to rock the boat that I don't even get justice for what he did to me. Not that my parents would've let me anyways. They were happy to just cover it all up. It is better that we don't acknowledge what happened.

I'm not surprised that was their take on it, but it still hurts. They didn't want to ruin their friendship with his family, even if it meant covering up his abuse of their own daughter.

The sad part is I would've stayed with him. He cheated on me and I would've stayed. I just wanted him to grovel a little. Beg for forgiveness. At least pretend to feel bad about it.

Instead, he hurt me. I can't go back to that. I won't.

When I step into The Mug Life, I groan at the sight of only one person behind the counter and four people waiting in line.

I should just turn around and leave. I risk being late to class if I stay, but if I don't get some caffeine in my system, I may go insane.

I barely even got buzzed last night, but the vodka messed with my head a little. Mix in the whole conversation with Ben, and I ended up barely getting any sleep.

When the line moves, I take a step forward. Class can wait. I have a full day of them and being five minutes late is better than falling asleep in my seat.

"Prue." A voice takes me out of my head. "Hello."

The voice is easy to place. My body is trained to place it. Before, I'd plaster a smile on my face at the sound of it. Now I try not to scream as my heart begins to pound in my chest. My whole body tenses, and my mouth goes dry. I don't turn to look at him. I don't plan on acknowledging him at all.

I stand there, feeling every second passing by. My mind knows the person at the counter is talking to the next customer. I can faintly hear the voices that fill the coffee shop, but it's all background noise.

Somewhere in my mind I hear myself crying as I'm thrown around. The sound of glass crashing and the thud I made when I hit the ground makes tears fill my eyes. I taste bile as I remember the searing pain of him removing my jeans.

"Not going to say hi back? That's a little rude, isn't it?" The hint of amusement in his voice makes my blood boil. Charles always did like to rub salt in the wound, I just never expected to be on the receiving end of it.

"Rude?" I snap. "I think rude would be letting you come face to face with the damage you inflicted." The words spill from my lips in a harsh whisper. My eyes are pinned on the back of the head of the person in front of me.

Causing a scene is not the smartest thing for me to do. If I want to be someone different though, someone new, I can't just let him get away with talking to me like he didn't do a thing.

Greasy black hair is all my vision lets me see. It's what is keeping me from turning around and ripping out Charles' throat. The nameless head in front of me is enduring my glare as I wait and hope Charles walks away.

"I have no idea what you are talking about." Charles' laugh makes the hair on my neck stand up.

Memories of him laughing as I sobbed underneath him make my knees weak, but I stand firm. I will not let him get to me. Never again will he cause me pain.

My parents are pushing hard for me to take him back. Get the plan back on track. Both our parents have practically been planning the wedding since we turned eighteen. They all think we can just move past this, as does Charles.

I think the fact I have stayed away for almost two months is a surprise to all of them. I highly doubt Charles even considered the possibility I wouldn't go straight back to him after leaving the hospital. The day I gathered my things from his place, he was stunned. Even so, I saw it on his face.

He believed I'd be back. Everyone believes I will go back.

But I am not going back. I won't marry Charles. I repeat the line that has been my mantra since the day he assaulted me.

"But you were always a little crazy," he continues. "It's okay, your amazing body can distract me from the insanity. Seems Cameron and you are more alike than anyone thought. Both a little mentally unstable."

My body shakes with a rage I didn't know I could possess. He wants to pretend I made it all up, fine. I don't care if all our friends play along, but bringing my brother up is a step too far. He knows that, which is why he said it.

"I saw you come in. Jason and I were just over there enjoying our coffee." He moves closer, stepping into my line of sight. "It's been a while since we last spoke. Too long." The sight of him makes me ill. Tears fill my eyes again and I try to keep them from spilling out. "I have to admit, the whole turtlenecks and skirts are starting to grow on me. Maybe we can play teacher and student sometime." He smirks. "Whenever you decide to stop being such a filthy little liar, that is."

"We could play that game." I nod, glaring at him. "But then I'd have to report you to the dean, and you'd get to rot in the jail cell you belong in."

My words must be funny to him, because he throws his head back in a laugh. Something inside me is breaking because as his laugh echoes in my ears, all I can see is my hands around his throat, squeezing until his stupid, smug face turns blue.

He hasn't spoken to me since the day I picked up my stuff from his place. I know he has been keeping tabs on me. I've felt his eyes on me often, but he's kept his distance until now. I don't know what changed, but I don't like it. I want him to leave me alone.

I need him to understand he crossed a line. Because of what he did, I'm not going to be his again. The mean comments I could've taken. I could've played the role of pretty, dutiful lover, until the day I died, but I draw the line at violence.

I will not stay with someone who thinks they can put their hands on me. If I stay now, it will just keep happening. I know that. He thinks he is untouchable, and for the most part he is. The law probably would've done nothing but given him a slap on the wrist and a pat on the shoulder for taking up any of his time, but I can do more.

Show him not everyone in this fucked up world will bow to his wishes. Not everyone will obey his every command. He had that control on me before, but not anymore.

"I see you still want to stick to that story. I understand. Being cheated on must have stung. You feel the need to punish me, with this whole story about me hurting you. Don't you think that's going a little too far, though?"

"Story?" I scoff. "I have the fucking bruises too..."

"You are just dramatic enough to try to sell the story." He cuts me off, shaking his head. "It's your family's name getting dragged through the mud, Prue, not mine. You should know the longer you keep this up, the harder it will be to come crawling back."

"Go. To. Hell," I whisper just loud enough for him to hear.

"Have a good day." He smiles before leaning forward and planting a kiss on my cheek, just below the bruise under my eye.

I hear his feet walking away. Hear his voice speaking to someone else from the corner. My body shakes, too fired up from the exchange.

Turning around, I march out of the coffee shop. My sight is blurred as the tears I've been holding back threaten to break free. Biting the inside of my lip, I dart down the alley way nearby.

The air burns as my lungs seize up. Resting my head against the building, I slam my foot against the bottom part of the wall. If it hurts, I don't feel it. I'm too high on anger. Too blinded by hatred.

"Jesus," someone says. "What did the building do to you?"

My foot stops mid kick. I drop it to the ground, hoping whoever is standing there just walks away. It's bad enough I have to go to school with these people, but if any of them witness me falling apart, I don't think I'll survive the rest of the semester.

"I know I said you were a bitch, but isn't this taking it a little too far?" My head glances over to see light blond hair. Blinking out a few tears, I let Ben's soft features come into focus. "Are you okay?" he asks, raising an eyebrow.

"Go away," I groan.

Ben isn't the last person I want to see right now, but he isn't high on the list either.

"Who was the guy?" His head jerks back toward the coffee shop. "Ex-boyfriend?"

"Please," I mutter. "Just leave me alone."

"I could kick his ass." He steps closer to me. "Judging by your reaction to whatever he had to say, and the bruise under your eye, he probably deserves a good ass kicking."

I sigh, taking a step back from the building. Wiping under my eyes, I study Ben.

Last night wasn't the first time I've seen him. My brother toured with him and dragged me along to a few of the dates. He seems different compared to then. Maybe it was all the lights and rock and roll setting, but he looked tougher then. Now, in the light of day, I can see just how skinny he is.

His blond hair shags down in small waves. Not long, but in a tussle messed, nonetheless. His blue eyes are dark, like sapphires. Fair skin and a boyish face make him seem far younger than I know he is. Up close like this, when he is wearing dark jeans and a hoodie with some design on it, he doesn't look like the famous guy I see in magazine or on TV. Or like the guy I saw backstage flirting with girls. He looks like your average young adult now. Just your standard guy, who is offering to defend me.

It's a tempting offer. One that no one else has made. Why would he? It makes no sense, but part of me considers letting him hurt Charles. Give Charles a taste of what he dished out on me. Only, I know Ben probably doesn't mean it. Even if he does, I can't let him get involved. That will only cause more problems for me down the road.

"I have no clue what you are talking about," I counter after a moment. "What are you even doing here anyways? Dropping off some college girl you fucked?"

He chuckles. "I was meeting my mother for coffee before her class."

"Your mother?" It's hard to picture him as anyone's son, but now that he mentioned her, and the fact she has a class, I can clearly picture her. Like vividly. "Is your mother Joan Parker?" I ask.

"Yes." He nods.

"I took her class last semester."

Now that I know this, the resemblance seems almost uncanny. He looks a lot like her, down to the small nose and rounded cheeks. His jaw is sharper, and his eyes darker blue, but I can see her in him.

"How was it? Wait. Don't answer that. I don't want the illusion I have of her to be ruined."

"She was great."

"Can you believe she raised me?" He laughs, running his hands through his hair. "She moved out here a little after I got signed, hoping to be closer to me after my father died, but I'm always touring."

"You should spend more time with her. She really cares about you." I try to keep the bitterness from my voice. Mrs. Parker talked fondly of her son in class. Never mentioned he was a famous rock star, but nonetheless she did mention him.

"Probably," he agrees. "Are you okay?" His eyes roam over my face.

"Just peachy," I respond. "But I'm about to be late for class."

"Ditch." His lips curve into a sly smile. "We could get that coffee we talked about last night."

"What would your mother say about you telling one of her students to ditch school?"

"Ex-student," he counters with a smirk. "And look at me, do you really think she would expect anything else from me? I don't really scream good influence, do I?"

"You must have given her such a hard time as a kid."

"Oh, you can only imagine. I don't think she has slept a full night since the day I was born."

"Poor woman."

"Join me for coffee. We can make that ex of yours jealous."

"No thanks," I say, walking past him.

I expect him to stay put or go his own way, but he surprises me by falling in stride beside me.

"Was he the one who hurt you?"

"No." I shake my head. I've come to terms with the fact that lying about it is better than talking about it. New people didn't need to know the truth. It was better they didn't see me as pathetic as I am.

"No?" he presses.

"Does it matter?"

"To me, yes."

"Why?"

"I'm an asshole, but even I know to never put hands on a woman. There is a line and if a guy crosses it, I have no problems ridding the world of them."

"Listen, Ben, I'm sorry about last night, okay? I was just..."

"No, you aren't," he cuts me off.

"Yes I am."

"You seemed to rather enjoy going off on me last night. You even went so far as to slap me."

"You called me a bitch!" I stop walking and turn toward him. The anger I'd felt toward Charles moments ago begins to surface again. This time, though, it feels safer to direct it at Ben.

"And you aren't sorry." The corners of his mouth turn up. My eyes are drawn to his lips. They are a light pink, and I'm reminded of the theory that a man's lip color matches the tip of his dick. I wonder if that's true.

It was about Charles and the ex I had before him, and if it's true about Ben, I'm not sure I would mind having his cock in my mouth. I meant what I told him last night. I enjoy sucking dick. I am not some boring girl in bed, I've just not had the liberty of getting to fuck as many people as him.

God. I need to get laid. I'm going insane.

"Fine. I'm not sorry. In fact, I kind of want to do it again." I fold my arms over my chest as I start walking again.

Matching my pace again, he keeps up with me.

"Yeah?" He raises an eyebrow as if challenging me.

"But I won't. Now if you don't mind, I have a class to get to," I say firmly as we step onto campus.

"Lead the way." He waves his hand forward.

"What?"

"Lead the way," he repeats himself.

"You don't go here."

"Some kids ditch, others drop in for a free class." He shrugs.

"Why are you bothering me?" I groan.

"It's not every night an attractive woman slaps you in the face and says your dick is tiny." He smirks. "Hurt my ego. Now I'm forced to bother you until you let me prove how wrong you were."

"Okay." I stop walking outside of a restroom door. "Prove it. Let's go in here and you can whip your dick out. Show me just how not tiny it is."

His eyes light up. The blue darkens as his jaw locks shut. His Adam's apple tenses up as he stares at me. I watch as he processes what I just said. Tilting his head to the side, so the door to the bathroom is in his line of sight. Though his eyes don't completely move from me.

It feels strange to have his eyes on me. A little intense, but I refuse to be the first one to look away.

"No?" I press, rising an eyebrow. "What's the matter, Ben? Worried in the light of day your cock won't measure up to the game you're talking?"

"Oh, no. It will measure up just fine." He grins.

"So?"

"So." He nods, breaking eye contact to really take in the door behind me. "Ladies first."

I step into the bathroom, leaning against the sink as he walks in after me. He locks the door behind me before stepping in front of me.

"I didn't take you for a dirty girl." He glances around. "Did you ever fuck your ex in here?" His eyes drift back to me.

"No. And if you could stop mentioning him that would be great. Thanks."

"Yes. Of course." He nods. "I mean, once you see my cock,

I'm sure you'll forget all about him. This may be cathartic for you."

I roll my eyes, and he smirks in response.

We stand there, just staring at each other for a moment. His eyes are zoned in on me, as if he isn't sure whether he hates me or wants to fuck me.

I've seen that look before. My throat seizes up. I grip the edge of the counter behind me as my eyes fill with tears.

I blink. The feeling of my body being tossed around like a rag doll makes my lungs throb, behind the rib cage that is still sore. I see Charles standing over me, with a look of pure hatred and power.

Another blink and instead of dark hair and tan skin towering over me, I see Ben's light hair and soft features studying me.

I try to even my breath, hoping Ben doesn't notice me freaking out.

I'm not her anymore. I'm different now. Stronger. A bitch. I have the power now. There is a famous rock star standing in front of me, ready to show me his dick.

"Prue? Are you okay?"

"Yeah," I snap, folding my arms over my chest. "Are you going to show me or not?"

His eyes dart down for a moment, taking in my arms pressed against my breasts. I'm not well endowed there, but they are perky enough to be something men have stared at from time to time.

When his eyes glance back up to me, I can't help the warm feeling that settles in my stomach. His ocean eyes are full of waves of lust.

"Where did you go?" he asks, instead of doing what we came in here to do.

"What do you mean?" I pull away from the sink, straightening my back. "I was giving you a moment to pull your dick out." I shrug.

"Sure." His lips curve up slightly, as he takes another step toward me. "You know my band, right?" I nod. "And you know of Wes, the lead singer?"

"Yes, who doesn't? He is talented and handsome and extremely nice."

He chuckles. "Then you know that his girl, Abbey, was attacked recently, right?"

"Yeah, and?"

"She does that sometimes now."

"Does what?"

"Disappears inside her head."

"I didn't disappear."

"No?" he presses, taking another step closer. "Didn't get flooded with flashbacks?"

"No." I shake my head.

I have no idea why he is suddenly so interested in me. Last night he was such an asshole, but right now, he is kind of acting like a decent person. Like someone capable of caring. I don't like it. I don't need him to care about me. Assholes are easier to deal with. The idea that a nice person might live inside the cocky exterior of Ben Parker shatters the illusion I have of rock stars in general.

Besides Wes. Everyone in the world knows Wes is a great guy. Nearly killed the guy who attacked Abbey Dark. Them getting together is the closest the world will get to peace. They deserve each other. Abbey deserves to be loved by a nice guy for a chance. They both have earned the right to be happy. To be together. To be loved. All things I'll probably never get.

"Liar," he says softly.

"Can you just show me your dick, so I can get to class?"

"Tell me," he says, reaching down to the front of his jeans. My eyes watch as he undoes the top button. I force my eyes to drift back up to his face. "Do you often inspect men's cocks?"

"No."

My heart is racing in my chest. His eyes are so full of desire. I've never been looked at like this before. I'm not a prude by any means, but I've only been with two men. They both claimed to find me very attractive, but they never looked at me the way Ben is right now.

"I want you to get a good look at it, Prue." He goes on, tugging down his zipper. "Touch it if you must." His hand slips into his pants. I can't look away as he shifts his hips. "Do whatever you have to, to make sure you're able to form a good opinion of it. I want to know exactly what you think about it. Maybe you can leave me a review or type me up an essay, since you seem to be such a good student."

Pulling his cock out, my eyes widen. To say it's not tiny is not doing it justice. The thing is thick, and long. I wouldn't say it's dangerously long, but long enough to make a girl feel slightly uneasy. But my God, the girth of the thing is overwhelming.

Ben isn't thick anywhere else, which makes his dick look even larger. He probably has a BMI in the single digits, but whatever his muscle mass is, his cock probably accounts for most of it.

I can't think straight, as his hand strokes over it. It hardens even more as his hand slowly strokes it.

My core reacts with complete lust. My sex life wasn't bad. I'm open in the bedroom. I'd try almost anything just to see what it feels like, and my libido is off the charts. When it comes to sex, I can be a little wild, in fact. I don't mind if things get a little rough there, it's only when it spilled outside the bedroom that it became a problem.

Not that Charles or my boyfriend before him was anything exciting in bed. They were so caught up on their own pleasure, they didn't even care to ask if I enjoyed myself. I had to take to getting myself off in private. God forbid I ever tried to ask for anything outside of what they wanted.

His hand works over his cock. Focusing on how it has a slight curve and a big vein running down it, I feel myself getting wet.

I shouldn't be turned on right now. Not after everything that happened just a few weeks ago. Yet, the sight of his giant cock has me dripping. The thing would split me open. It's the biggest thing I've ever seen, besides a gag gift dildo. How did he ever manage to fit that in a woman and not kill her?

"See?" His voice is low, heavy with lust. "Not so tiny."

I'd roll my eyes at his cockiness, but he's kind of earned the right to be.

I was extremely wrong. Ben Parker's cock is not tiny.

FOUR

Ben

Prue doesn't speak a word as my hands stroke over my cock. Her eyes are like saucers as she watches me jerk off. It makes me grow harder, to the point it almost hurts.

"You can get closer," I say with a smirk, not that she can see it. Her eyes are fixated on my dick. "It doesn't bite."

Without a word, she drops to her knees. That's a sight within itself. Beautiful Prue, in her pleated skirt and tight turtleneck, on her knees before me is an amazing sight.

Her caramel hair falls forward as she brings her head level with my cock. Licking at her glossy lips, I can almost feel her breath on the tip.

My strokes increase in speed. I'd much rather have her touching it, but I'm not about to push the girl who seems to be recovering from domestic violence. I'm not that big of an asshole.

Bumping into her so soon after last night was not my plan. After my mother ran off to her class, I stayed put, drinking my coffee tucked in a corner. The universe just happened to deliver Prue to my feet.

I noticed her asshole of an ex and his friend early on. They oozed a level of smugness that made me instantly hate them. Frat boys who had daddy's money to piss away.

I have a problem with elitist men like them. They walk around like their shit doesn't stink and their cocks are larger than they ever are. Counting on their family's money to buy them whatever they need and getting them out of anything. It's frustrating we must live in a world where they get to be the top dog and piss on everything around them. It gives them a sense of entitlement and turns them into assholes.

Sure, I'm an asshole too, but I have the cock to back it up. I don't dress up my bad behavior as something it isn't. I own the fact I'm a terrible person, not act like I'm the greatest thing since sliced bread.

When she walked in, I didn't believe my luck. It took a great amount of focus for me to stay sitting. She is trouble. I smelt it on her last night, and when she walked in, in another short skirt and tight shirt, I knew it wouldn't be wise of me to talk to her.

She is chaos and destruction. Whatever drama she is involved in is not healthy for me. Years of doing stupid shit has taught me to ignore the urge to walk into the eye of a storm, but with her, it feels impossible not to get sucked up into it.

Watching that jerk approach her made me uneasy. I could feel the rage rolling off her and his smug attitude left a sour taste in my mouth. When she tensed up at the sound of his voice, it took the thought of Wes's disappointment to keep me grounded.

I wanted to intervene. The image of his smug smile dropping when he realized I knew her filled me with glee. But I remembered the bruise on her face and if he was the one to cause it, there was a good chance I'd kick his ass right there with far too many witnesses.

I shouldn't have gone out after her, but I was concerned. I owed it to Cameron at the very least, to see if she was okay. Or at least that was going to be my excuse.

Then she got annoyed by my mere presence and I couldn't resist the temptation to get under her skin. Her attitude is almost addictive. Watching her eyes roll excites me. It shouldn't, but it's like two globes of sky twirling, pulling me in. The snide comments that seem to always follow, sting in the best ways.

She knows exactly what to say back. Holding her weight against my witty remarks turns me on more than it should. I'm not used to someone matching my energy in such a way.

It's intoxicating. I want more of it. More of her.

I don't normally chase girls. Don't normally need to, but with her, I'm willing to.

That is probably a bad sign, but as her hand lifts toward my cock, I find I don't care. Not even Wes's voice in my head, screaming that this is only going to end badly can get me to walk away right now.

I need her to touch me.

"May I?" she asks. Her voice is low, so soft and seductive. Her eyes look up, peering up at me for a moment, before dropping back to my cock, that is just fractions of an inch from her hand now.

"Sure."

I don't know what I'm giving her permission to do right now, nor do I care. I'd let her do just about anything to me. She has no idea how much power she has over me at this exact moment.

She pulls her hand away, and I bite my lip to keep back the protest that wants to slip out.

Then she spits on her hand, lifting it back toward my cock. I grip the base of it, holding it steady as she wraps her soft, wet hand around the middle.

"Oh." She gasps, letting her hand slide up toward the tip.

"Oh?"

"It's heavy."

"Heavy?"

She nods her head, working her hand back down toward where mine is.

"What does that mean?"

"I don't know." Her eyes glance up at me. "It's thick, but I didn't expect it to feel so heavy."

"Is that a bad thing?"

No woman has ever mentioned the weight of my cock before, and I'm not sure if it's a complaint or a compliment. No way of knowing if I should be insulted or proud.

"No. I don't think so," she whispers.

Leaning her head forward, she opens her mouth, allowing spit to dribble between her lips onto my cock. I barely hold back the groan that threatens to escape my mouth.

She works her hand over it, and I let go of my grip, allowing her to fully get acquainted with it. Spitting into her other hand, she adds it to the mix. Both her hands work up and down my shaft, slowly, almost painfully slow.

My balls ache and she must be able to tell because she lets one hand drop down to them. Squeezing them with her palm, she lets her fingers rub the area they meet my cock.

I've been with more women than I care to count. Hand jobs and ball squeezing are nothing new to me. I even let a girl put a finger in my ass once and didn't hate it, but right now I'd let Prue peg me if she wanted. Her hands feel that good.

Gripping both my balls and cock tighter, her eyes dart up to me. Pale blue eyes stare into mine. She isn't angry or full of rage right now. I think she is more turned on than me at this moment.

"Is this okay?"

"Yes. God yes." I nod my head eagerly.

"You like my hands on your cock and balls?"

"I can't imagine any man wouldn't like it."

"But are you any man?" She smirks up at me.

"No," I admit. "I'm just an asshole with a fat cock."

"Yes," she nearly moans in agreement.

"I want to fuck you," I mutter. "Can I please fuck you, Prue?"

"No." She shakes her head, letting her short locks wave through the air. "No way that's happening. I'm just examining it, remember?" She shifts back, releasing my balls. Her grip loosens on my cock, and I groan.

"Wait," I say quickly. Panic is kicking in. She is about to leave me with blue balls and I'm in no mood to have to work to find another girl to take care of it. "Okay. Just. Fuck." I mutter, unable to think straight, as her strokes grow even slower. It's teasingly pleasurable.

"Maybe," she says, grinning up at me. "Since I'm supposed to be getting a real honest impression of the thing, I should taste it."

"Yes. You should."

"But I suppose the point has been made. I was wrong. You do not have a tiny dick."

"Prue," I mumble. "I'm at your mercy here. Please don't stop."

I'm normally above begging, but something about this girl is fucking with my head. Blame it on my need to self-destruct or maybe it's just how good her hands feel. Who knows, all I know is I need her to keep touching me.

"Did you mean it?" she asks as she tightens her grip again.

"Mean what?"

"That you would kick his ass?"

"Yes." I nod. "You finish me off and I will track him down and bash his fucking skull in."

"So violent." She smiles up at me.

"Do you like that?"

"A little. You were wrong about me being a bitch, but I think I could get used to being one if it means I get to have control over powerful men."

"Oh no, baby." I laugh. "I'm afraid it doesn't work like that."

"No?" Her other hand grabs my balls again. A groan falls from my mouth as my eyes flutter. "I think it might."

"Sure. Yeah. Whatever you want, just please..." My voice trails off as she quickens her strokes.

"Do you want me to suck it?"

"Yes. Fuck. Please. Whatever you want, just wrap those pretty little lips around my fat cock and make me cum."

"Anything I want?"

"Yes." I peer down at her.

"I'm going to hold you to that, Ben," she says softly, before letting her lips wrap around the head of my cock.

Her jaw slacks open as she slowly devours it. Letting her hand grip the base as she eases her way down, she lets her other hand gently play with my balls.

Water fills her eyes as I fill up her mouth. Girls rarely take more than a third of it in their mouths. I might not have the longest cock in the world, but the thickness can be a little overwhelming.

I've had to master the art of oral sex and foreplay to make sure girls were turned on enough to step up to the challenge of taking it. Once they got used to feeling me stretching them, they tend to find themselves addicted to it.

But blow jobs weren't often given. Or at least not for long. They'd barely be able to take the thing, tapping out before I could get off. I can't complain, I enjoy sex more anyways.

So as Prue pushes her head further down my dick, taking over half of it in her tight little mouth I realize I was also wrong. She does know how to please a man.

"Jesus," I groan as the tip of my cock presses against the back of her throat. She gags for a moment, pulling back a bit, before pressing forward again.

She lets me slip down her throat and I moan. I could explode right now if I wanted. Have I ever been this far down a woman's throat before? I highly doubt it, at least not since before puberty, but I don't allow myself to think that far back right now.

Her eyes flicker up to mine as I let my thoughts come back to the present moment.

"Guess I was wrong too. You do know how to suck cock."

Her blue-sky eyes sparkle, looking up at me. Allowing me to slip down her throat even more, her hand drops from the base of my cock. Suddenly her lips are pressed against my groin, and I'm seeing speckles of blue dance in a sea of darkness.

"Fuck," I hiss as her cheeks flex. She pauses before slowly easing back so just half my cock is in her mouth. Then just as quickly as she does that, she has the whole thing back in her mouth. "Okay. Fuck. Baby. I don't know if I can..." My voice trails off as I moan.

She bobs her head a few more times, making me moan almost nonstop. The feeling is out of this world. I'm not sure I'll be able to recover from this. No girl's mouth will ever compare. Prue has ruined blow jobs for me.

It's perfectly on point. She is a bitch but fuck if she hasn't earned that right.

Her eyes glance up at me. Glazed over with lust that probably mirror my own.

"I'm going to cum. Jesus," I mutter. The pleasure overwhelms me.

Her lips press against my groin again, as she flexes her cheeks. Her hold on my balls tightens and I explode down her throat.

A fury of moans pour from my mouth, echoing off the walls of the bathroom. I can feel her throat constricting as my load slides down it. She doesn't release me until my cock starts to go limp.

Pulling back, she sucks in a deep breath, as drool coats her chin and lips.

"Thank you," I mumble like an idiot as I try to catch my breath.

She smiles at me. Pride and lust mixing in a way that makes my soft cock throb.

"You get an A on size alone, but I'm giving you a C on duration. I barely started sucking, and you blew your load." She laughs lightly, rising to her feet.

"I apologize for that." I tuck my cock back into my boxers, doing up my pants. "I just can't recall the last time a girl has deep throated my cock."

"Oh." Her smile widens. "Does that mean I get an A as well?"

"Oh yes. You earned yourself an A plus and gold stars to match." I smirk. "Now why don't you prop yourself on that counter and let me examine you?"

She shakes her head. "I'm late for class." She runs her hands through her hair before spinning around to face the mirror. She wipes drool off her face.

"Ditch it. I have a feeling the things I could teach you are far more beneficial for you than any class here."

"Ha." She glances back at me. "Are you implying I'm only good for one thing?"

"Not at all. You have three holes." I smirk.

Rolling her eyes, she strolls to the door of the bathroom. "See you around, Ben." She unlocks the door. "Or hopefully not." Shrugging, she walks out.

The door slams shut behind her, and I freeze for just a moment. Wes's voice babbles away in the corner of my mind, warning me not to go after her. I ignore it, sprinting out the bathroom.

For once I want a girl's number. I need more of her. If her mouth feels that good, I can only imagine the things she could do with her other holes.

She is speed walking toward a building. I jog to try to catch up to her, nearly stumbling into random people. I don't pause to let them recognize me. Don't need any fans bothering me right now. I need the girl who doesn't want me, in good ole Ben Parker fashion.

"Prue?" I call out as I enter the building.

I lose sight of her. The halls are mostly empty. Dozens of doors line the hallway. I have no idea which one she is in, or if she just used this building to cut through to get to her classroom, while trying to lose me.

This is my opportunity to come to my senses. I could just turn around and walk away. Go out tonight and try to find another girl to distract myself with. Call Wes and have him remind me why getting involved with chaotic women is bad. Instead, I start peeking into classroom windows.

I spot her caramel hair in the fifth room I check. She sits in the middle section, a few seats in.

I let the door thud loudly behind me as I enter it. Eyes glance toward me. The teacher looks up but doesn't stop talking. He must assume I'm a student. I try not to let that hurt my rock star ego.

Prue doesn't look back, but it doesn't matter. The whispers behind her must tell her who I am, because she ducks her head down.

Making my way to her, I squeeze past a few other students. I ignore their groans as I make my way down the row she sits in. Lucky for me the seat beside her is empty. I plop down into it. She still refuses to look in my direction.

"Hello," I whisper. "You tried to escape me." I wag my finger at her, like she is a bad dog. Or a bitch if you would. "That was very rude."

"First, I'm a bitch, now I'm rude?" she whispers back. Irritation laces her voice and makes me irrationally happy.

"And in between you had my cock down your throat."

The faintest shade of pink takes over her fair skin as her head turns toward me. Her blue eyes sparkle as if recalling what just happened minutes ago.

"What was I then?"

"Fucking fantastic."

"Good to know." Her head turns back toward the teacher.

"Give me your number."

"Shh... I'm trying to pay attention."

"Write your number down." I tap her open notebook, right over little doodles that show she hasn't been paying attention at all.

"No."

"I will make a scene," I warn. Her head snaps to me. Her eyes turn into daggers. "I will do it. I have nothing to lose here. This is your school, your class, and I am a famous rock star. Someone starts recording and we make a splash on all the gossip sites. You'll never be able to escape my glorious shadow."

"If I give you my number, I won't be able to escape either."

"Not true. Once I get what I want, I get bored quickly."

Her eyes do loops as she shakes her head. "Was a blow job not enough?"

"No. Not by a long shot."

The whispering behind us grows louder as more people start to place me. She glances back for a moment.

"Seems we already started to attract attention." She shrugs. "Maybe I don't care about losing anything this place holds." Her eyes rest on the back of the head of some guy. The glare she gives him is far worse than any time she glared at me. I quickly piece together that he is her shitty ex from the coffee shop.

"Okay." I nod. "But remember I warned you." She looks back at me. I smirk as I push myself to my feet. "Hey," I yell out. Eyes turn to me, and the teacher pauses, looking my way.

"Yes?" the teacher asks.

"What class is this?" I ask, glancing down at Prue as her face starts to turn pink.

"Shouldn't you know that?" the teacher questions. Clearly, he is annoyed already. Sadly for Prue and him, I'm just getting started.

"Fuck it." I shrug. "I'm not a student here. I lost the need for books once music entered my life, but then I met Prue." I motion at her, and she rolls her eyes for the hundredth time. "Prue, you have stolen my heart. I can't take another second of not being with you. I want to spend the rest of my life with you. Please make me the happiest rock star on the planet and marry me."

Once again, her eyes spin. I glance around to see a bunch of eyes glued to us, including her ex-boyfriend. I smile at him, while he stares on, stunned.

"Can you take this outside?" the teacher remarks.

"No. I'm not leaving until she answers me. Think of the baby, Prue," I add, watching her eyes widen. "We could be a family."

"It isn't yours," she replies, without missing a beat.

"I'll raise a bastard," I reply quickly, as the corner of her lips curve up. "Be a better father than that jackass of an ex of yours could ever be. You know I'm so much better in bed than that limp dick mother fucker."

"That's enough!" the teacher yells. "Leave this classroom right now or I will call security."

"I'm not scared of campus security. Nothing scares me but being without Prue."

The teacher rushed out of the classroom, probably to go find campus security.

Out of the corner of my eye, I see people pulling out their phones. Prue glares at me, though there's a flicker of amusement beneath her fury.

"Prue, what the fuck is going on?" Her ex stands at the end of the row we are in. He is fuming, and it makes me even more determined to get her phone number. Can't leave her to fend for herself against the bastard. Especially after causing this scene.

"Listen, dick, you might not want to come any closer," I snap at him.

"And why is that?" He smiles smugly. "You think I won't press charges if you lay a finger on me? I got better lawyers than some loser guitar player."

"I think I'd pay good money to get my hands on you," I reply, turning back to Prue. "Number. Please." I tap her notebook again.

She studies me and I meet her eyes straight on. I can feel movement behind me. Pretty sure her ex is coming closer despite my warning. What an idiot.

I wouldn't mind beating his ass, but I'd rather not end up in prison. He seems to be aware of who I am. His threat of having better lawyers is meaningless when he'd have witnesses to prove what I did was not warranted.

"What the fuck is going on here, Prue? Have you been screwing him this whole time?"

"No," she replies loudly, but I don't think it's to his question. "I'm not giving you my number, but I will take yours." She holds her pen out to me. "And if you're lucky, I'll call you."

Behind me her ex makes some comment, but I ignore it for the sake of not ending up in prison for beating his ass. Instead, I grab the pen from her hand, bending forward to scribble my number in her notebook.

"You have two days to call me before I come and hunt you down. And Prue, you don't want me to have to hunt you."

"And why is that?" she asks with a smile.

"Because if you thought this was a scene, you have no idea what I'm capable when left waiting for too long." I smirk, backing up. I purposely make a point of bumping into her ex behind me. "And you," I say, without even facing him, "better keep your distance. You don't want to find out what I do to pieces of shit like you."

"Is that a threat?"

"No. That's not a threat at all." I smile, squeezing past him. I climb up the stairs toward the door I entered, just as security enters the room from below.

Ducking into the hallway, I stroll casually out the building before anyone can think of following me.

I have no idea what I just got myself into, but boredom has led me to worse places than a pretty girl with great deep throating skills.

FIVE

Prue

I'M SURE I'M GOING TO LOSE POINTS OFF MY GRADE FOR Ben's little outburst, but it was kind of fun. Him being interested in me makes me feel a little better about myself. I know it will be short-lived, but I'm going to enjoy his attention while I have it.

Sucking him off in the bathroom wasn't part of my plan, but the size of his cock fried my brain. I forgot about everything else as he revealed it. When I touched it, it removed all logic from my mind. Suddenly, all I wanted was to make him feel good. To prove I wasn't some stuck-up bitch, but some girl who knows a thing or two about making a guy cum.

When he offered to return the favor, that's when reality came crashing back down. I haven't let anyone touch me, not even myself since Charles attacked me. It's been a long few weeks since I had an orgasm, a new record for me. I'm used to getting off almost every day, mostly from myself, or after some lousy sex with Charles, where I'd sneak off to the bathroom to finish what he couldn't.

It's not that my body didn't want it. Despite everything I endured, my body still craves sexual pleasure. I just can't find the will to do it. I'm afraid of what it will be like now.

It's not that Charles and I didn't have sex often. I gave him blow jobs and sex pretty much daily. If he wanted it, I gave it. There was no reason for him to cheat, other than his desire to be with someone else. I didn't withhold sex, even when he stopped being able to get me off.

Missionary and no foreplay just didn't do it for me. I'd ask for more and he'd promise to try something different, but when the next time rolled around, he'd just pretend to forget.

With Ben it felt different. I didn't get to be on the receiving end of anything he had to offer, but the fact he offered was more than I'm used to.

Having his cock in my mouth and his eyes on me, lit a fire in me. My pussy has been throbbing since.

I felt powerful, even as I knelt before him. I felt like I could've asked him for anything, and he'd give it to me. Cupping his balls and taking him down my throat made me feel sexy and desirable.

I know he has been with countless women. The great tales of Ben Parker have been posted on quite a few sites. Stories I didn't read until the night after the bathroom incident. According to the posts about him, he goes out of his way to please the women he takes to bed. No one sugar coats what kind of asshole he is after, but during, he is good.

I try not to think about the fact everyone else he has been with brags about how good he made them feel. It was my choice to tell him no, so I try not to be jealous that they all got to cum on his giant cock and I didn't.

None of them talk about him after the sex. No one says anything about him chasing them down and causing a scene over them. I hold on to the hope that maybe I impressed him a little. Perhaps I still have a chance to experience the mind-blowing sex they all brag about.

I know once he has me, I'll be tossed aside like all the other girls. It's just after everything I've been through, I feel like I deserve a fling. And if I'm going to have meaningless sex, why not have it with a man that has a history of delivering a good time?

I study myself in the mirror again. Completely naked. For the most part all traces of the damage Charles did are gone. There is a light bruise under my eyes. It grows less noticeable each day. A bruise on my collar bone that is a mixture of his thumb pressing into my neck and his teeth biting into me. A few more light marks still trail over my body. Mostly my thighs.

Knowing he cheated on me, then had the nerve to beat and rape me when I got angry about it, made me violently ill those first few nights. Now it just leaves me feeling pathetic.

Ben eased those feelings. Knowing someone still wanted me, that I could still get someone off, made me feel less bad for a little while.

Charles witnessing the scene Ben caused didn't turn out too well for me. He didn't report it back to my parents, but he has left me countless text messages. Keeps asking what is going on between Ben and me. I don't bother replying. He doesn't get to know. I'm not his girlfriend anymore. Never will be.

I stare at Ben's number in my phone. It's been two days since he gave it to me. I don't doubt he'd come looking for me if I don't text him soon. I enjoyed him being willing to go to such extremes to get my number, but I worry what happens next time.

I don't think he is capable of hurting me physically. He didn't scream abusive, but I'm sure he could cause a lot of chaos if he wanted to. I'm not sure anything could be worse than what Charles did, but I also don't need any more drama in my life right now.

My parents still text me daily, begging me to come home or encouraging me to reach out to Charles. I always make up an excuse. I know if I go over there, they won't let me leave, or Charles will be waiting for me so we can all talk it out, like this is something that we can all move past.

I shouldn't go seeking out Ben at this point. If my parents found out, they would probably disown me just like they did Cameron. Charles would probably kill Ben and I both if he even knew about what happened in the bathroom.

Inviting Ben into this situation is selfish of me, but I could use the distraction. I desperately want to feel good right now. Though I don't know if I could even have sex with him at this point. If I reach out to Ben, he is going to expect sex.

The bruises on my body aren't all Charles did. When he raped me, he was very rough, tore me a little. The sting from that has faded, but I've been too scared to see if I felt any different from it.

The idea of sex is overwhelming. Ben might have hinted that I gave him a great blow job, but would that be enough for the man every other girl has claimed to have gotten the best orgasm from? Doubtful.

Still, I text him.

ME

Hello, not so tiny dickhead.

I type out and hit send before I can second guess myself.

Time drags on slowly after. It's Thursday night and I can't imagine he is doing much of anything. I mean he is a rock star, and I did meet him at a random house party on a Monday, so maybe he is busy. Still, as the hours go by, I can't help but feel like I waited too long.

I shouldn't be surprised. We didn't meet on good terms. I'm not at my best right now. He seemed unfazed by Charles the other day, but maybe with some time to think about it he realized he didn't want to get caught up in my drama.

I highly doubt I'm worth it to him. Or to anyone.

I shouldn't have even messaged him. Bringing him into my life would not end well for either of us.

I should just go back to my parents. Try to make them see why I can't marry Charles. They have to understand my reasons. Knowing what he did to me, seeing the aftermath, they couldn't really want me to be with a man like that. I know it would be good for business, but deep down, my parents have to love me. They have to want what's best for me.

I'd marry anyone else they wanted, just not someone who hurts me. There has to be a line somewhere. That has to be the line, and they can't expect me to cross it. Not for any amount of money in the world.

I've done my part. I do everything I can to make them happy, to look good to all their friends, just this once they have to let me have a say.

For years I played the role they needed me to. Took the classes they wanted me to take, volunteered when they needed me to. Dressed up for the parties they went to. Helped with the events they put together. Made sure to get good grades. Stayed out of trouble. Followed the rules. I never complained about the pressure. Never pushed back against anything they wanted.

Just this one time. This has been the only time. And it's justified.

They have to see that. I need them to see that.

If they accept that I can't take Charles back, I'll go back home. I'll be the daughter they have come to expect. Date whoever else they want. Be the person I was before.

I thought I could use this as a way to reinvent myself. Become someone strong, someone capable of holding power. I wanted to be the person Ben saw. Tough. Bitchy. Confident.

But it's not possible. I will always be the weak, fragile, people-pleasing Prue.

That person would disgust Ben. He clearly had a thing for girls who could challenge him. If he knew who I was before, he wouldn't be interested at all.

Though as the night goes on, it appears he isn't even interested in the version of me I showed him.

He did tell me he gets bored easily. I bet that was the most honest thing he has ever said to a girl. He got bored waiting for me. I thought I could drag it out. Put it off. Talk myself into it, but it didn't work.

Two days of trying to convince myself to enjoy whatever fun Ben could offer ended up costing me my chance at it. The bitter irony would be amusing if I wasn't so broken.

I told myself if I got one night with Ben, I could go back to my parents and feel better about becoming the old Prue again. I went back and forth with the idea. Part of me didn't want to give myself another taste of freedom. To never fuck Ben so I wouldn't know what I'm missing out on. But a bigger part of me wanted to gift myself one chance at a good time.

I know my future is going to be full of lack luster sex and a cheating husband. I deserve one fling. One little memory to hold on to for the rest of my life.

But talking myself into the idea of sex was hard. Even now, as I lie curled up in bed, hoping Ben replies, I feel sick to my stomach at the thought of doing it. The only reason I'm willing to try with Ben is due to the countless testimonies on how good he is. It helps that he seemed to find me attractive even after having a vague idea of what I went through.

If I end up not being able to do it, I highly doubt he would be mad. He would simply walk away. It would be embarrassing, sure, but I'd never have to see him again. Never have to be reminded of it.

The silence lets me know that I messed up, though. He wasn't really interested in me. Probably found some other girl who didn't make him work for it. That didn't call him names or push his buttons.

Some girl who trips over herself to fan his ego. Doesn't call him an asshole. Worships the ground he walks on. And doesn't have an ex-boyfriend that hurt them.

I lost my only chance at a good time. Now I have no choice but to go crawling back to my parents. Beg them not to make me take Charles back. Go back to being the girl everyone expects me to be.

The thought makes tears well up in my eyes. My chest tightens. The room seems to grow or maybe I'm shrinking. I feel like I'm being swallowed by the darkness around me.

I feel incredibly small. Always have been. Just a tiny piece in a large puzzle someone else controls. I have no say in my life. No agency in my own wellbeing. Only put on this Earth to be a pawn for my parents.

I thought I had accepted that. Thought I came to terms with it years ago. But Charles shattered my acceptance with his fists. Broke my will to quietly accept my fate when he pinned me to the ground and raped me.

Ben gave me a taste of freedom. Now there is a hunger inside me that wants to be freed. A need for freedom and expression. Burying it might kill me, but I know Ben isn't going to text back. He lost interest already. I'll never get the chance to feed the beast inside me.

I just have to let it be smothered with the expectations everyone has of me. Find a way to bury it deep inside. Accept that I am never going to be the Prue that Ben thought I was.

Tomorrow, I go back to being pathetic little Prue.

SIX

Ben

It's Thursday night and I'm sitting at a table across from Wes at some fancy restaurant. Abbey sits beside him, playing with the straw in her drink and studying her food like at any moment it's going to come alive and attack her.

"This is nice," Wes says, looking around the table.

I glance around as well. Nicolas sits next to some smoking hot blond girl, whose name I never bothered to learn. They've been dating for a few months, but every time I see her, I can't help but be shocked he kept her around. She screams groupie. They met at some club and the sex must have been good, because he has been hooked ever since.

Can't blame him. She is a beauty. Always wearing these tight-fitting dresses that hugs all the right spots. Her make up is done up like a model and her hair teased to all hell.

I know very little about her personality as I tend to zone out whenever her high pitch voice starts talking. Don't care about anything she has to say. I guess as long as she is making my friend happy, my annoyance with her is a moot point.

Aaron nurses a drink while his fiancée, Stacy, pretends to sip from the same drink she had from before they joined us at the table. She raises it to her lips but never takes a sip. The thing is almost overflowing as the ice melts.

The idea she might be pregnant fills my soul with dread. I don't want to have to find another rhythm guitarist. Aaron balances me out well. We have good energy on the stage. Replacing him would suck. I don't want to have to get used to someone new.

Dennis keeps checking his phone. Texting back urgently whenever it buzzes. I'm sure he's chatting up his latest true love. The guy is worse than me when it comes to commitment. He can never stick with someone longer than a week.

He is always claiming to find the one, just to find something he doesn't like about her. Or letting some petty problem tear them apart. I've tried to tell him it's better to be single than deal with all that, but he is determined to find the love of his life.

Poor guy still believes in that crap.

"Yeah." Nicolas nods. "It really is."

"I've been thinking," Aaron says, glancing at Stacy. "Maybe we should extend the break, you know? Take a whole year off. We could take our time with recording. Really make this next album our best yet."

Stacy nods and straightens up. Her swollen tits press forward, rounder than ever before. I paid enough attention in biology class to know what that is a sign of. Fuck my life.

"Jesus fuck," I mutter. The eyes around the table all snap to me. "When is the baby due?"

"What?" Dennis glances up from his phone, looking at Aaron.

"Stacy is obviously pregnant."

"You are such an asshole," Aaron snaps.

"How did you know?" Stacy's expression is shocked, but she doesn't deny it.

"You haven't touched your drink. Your face is glowing, and your tits are about two size bigger."

"Asshole," Aaron snaps again. "Stop looking at my fiancée's tits."

"I'm not fucking blind." I shrug.

"You're pregnant?" Abbey asks Stacy.

"Yes," Stacy says, smiling. "Going to have to push the wedding back."

"Congratulations," Nicolas's girlfriend says. She seems genuine about her reaction, but her high pitch voice makes me want to stab myself in the ears.

"Wow. Aaron is going to be a father." Dennis laughs. "That's some crazy shit."

"We can't take a whole fucking year off," I say. "Six months is bad enough, but a whole year? We run the risk of losing fans and falling out of favor."

I can feel Wes's glare without even looking at him. He is not happy that I outed the news. Probably less happy about my reaction. Mentioning that six months was bad enough will probably cause Abbey to spiral with guilt as well.

I just turned a pleasant night into a bad one.

"I'm sure that won't happen," Abbey says softly. I glance at her and her eyes are staring up at Wes. "You guys are too great to lose any favor."

"What happens when the baby is born? Are you going to bring it along? The road is no place for a child. Or do you plan on leaving Stacy alone for weeks at a time to raise it alone?"

"Dude," Nicolas snaps. "Can you just take a second and be happy for them?"

"I'm so fucking happy they are happy. Fucking bouncing off the walls with glee because they are a happy fucking couple with a baby on the way, but what about me?" I down the last bit of my drink. "You all barely talk to me these days. Ignore my texts. Don't take my calls. I haven't seen any of you for weeks. We take a whole year off and I won't even know you guys when we go back on tour."

"Shit, dude," Aaron says. "It's nothing personal. We just have our own lives."

I watch as the faces around me drop as the words leave his mouth.

"Yeah. I got that much." I nod, pushing myself from the table. "Great to know I'm not a part of them." I push myself to my feet.

I make my way outside, desperate to be as far away from my so-called band mates as possible. Here I thought we were like family, but they just confirmed that they don't feel the same.

"Ben," Wes calls after me. "Shit. Wait up."

If he hadn't saved my life a few dozen times, I'd continue on my way. But I can't ignore him even if I wanted to, so I freeze.

"Ben," he repeats my name, catching up to me. "He didn't mean it like that. You know that. You just reacted poorly to his good news, and it made him mad."

"Yeah. Okay." I glance over at Wes. "Doesn't make it any less true."

"I get it. We've all been a little wrapped up in our own worlds. I'm sorry."

"Don't be." I pull out my pack of cigarettes. Wes doesn't owe me an apology. He has been the only person outside of my parents who ever truly cared about me. The only one of them that gets a pass. "It's life. It happens. I'm happy you are all happy." I nod, lighting my cigarette.

"Do you ever think about getting a girlfriend? Or a boyfriend. You know I don't judge." His face tugs up in a smile.

Wes always has a way at disarming me. I hate it. The guy makes it impossible for me to stay angry.

"If I didn't go gay for Dennis' luscious locks, I'm not going gay for anyone." I laugh.

"They were pretty sexy." He chuckles. "Come back to the restaurant. We will figure the band stuff out later, but for now, let's celebrate our wins."

"No thanks," I say. "I'll apologize later, but right now I kind of just want to be alone."

"Ben." He studies me over, looking for any signs he needs to be concerned about my well-being. I'm used to that look. I've seen it far too many times. "You know if you ever really needed me, I'd be there in a heartbeat."

"I know." I nod. "And same to you. And them."

"It was good seeing you." He sighs.

"Yeah." I nod back toward the restaurant. "You better get back to your girl before she loses a fight with her dinner."

"Yeah." He nods, glancing toward the building. I can almost hear his thoughts. For him this is a rock and a hard place. Does he go back and save Abbey or stay and rescue me? The choice is far too easy for him. I watch as it kills him to make it. "See you soon, okay?"

"Yeah. See you soon."

I stand on the sidewalk, smoking my cigarette and watching Wes head back to the restaurant. He keeps his head down as he walks, probably stressing about what dumb decision I'm going to make because of this.

I've already made plenty of dumb decisions this week. Ones he would frown upon and lose sleep over, like letting Prue suck my dick in a college bathroom and making a scene in her classroom.

I've spent the last two days trying not to think about it to be honest. Each hour she didn't contact me felt like a blessing disguised as utter agony. I tried to distract myself. Went out, flirted with girls, but never took one home.

Hard to want to fuck someone else when the girl who gave you the best blow job of your life could text you at any moment. I wanted to be free when she finally reached out. Didn't want to miss the chance of knowing how good her other talents could be.

When she texted me just before dinner I chose not to respond, though. It killed me. Sitting at that table, with people I thought were my best friends, itching to message her back, but not wanting to pass up on the chance to have a good time with them.

Prue might be the only pussy I want to fuck right now, but no pussy is worth missing out on the rare occasion my friends actually want to see me.

Now I wish I blew them off to see her. Would've saved me a lot of misery.

Deep down I already knew how they felt, but hearing it, seeing it, really sucked. The reality that I'm losing them is starting to sink in.

Aaron is going to have a baby. Wes is going to stay with Abbey until one or both of them dies. Who knows when Nicolas will lock down whatever his girl's name is. Dennis will eventually find that dream girl he keeps looking for. All of them will go make themselves a new life, one where they don't need me.

I ponder these thoughts in a state of pity as I walk the streets of LA. Set on finding me some hole in the wall bar where I can drink myself stupid.

Tonight, I don't want anyone's company. I want to drink until I can't see straight as I accept that my whole world is crumbling. My dreams are becoming ruins and the family I thought I had has outgrown me, just like Prue said.

I'm falling to the waste side, just as she predicted the night we met.

"You aren't driving, are you?" the bartender asks, setting another double of whiskey in front of me.

"No. If you keep pouring until closing, I promise to leave you the biggest tip of your life."

He nods before walking to the other side of the bar.

I'm sitting at some small dive bar, with classic rock songs playing way too loud. I've had about three double of whiskeys as I sit on a stool toward the end of the bar. There is a nice exit nearby, where I can step out to smoke a cigarette from time to time.

Some bikers sit at a table eating and chugging beers. An older couple are perched on a high top in the opposite corner, drinking like this is the highlight of their miserable week.

The bartender is working a solo shift and nodding along to eighties rock music.

Here I don't have to worry about some girl trying to flirt with me. No one knows or cares that I'm a famous guitarist in a big band. I can just sit here and get shit faced.

Let myself get absolutely wrecked. All by myself. Completely alone as I wallow in self-pity. Drown in it even. Let the loneliness consume me.

It's probably not healthy. Wes wouldn't approve. My mother would be disappointed. I have a habit of letting myself return to my self-destructive habits, time and time again. Why should now be any different? Learning no one wants to spend their time with me is worthy of a dose of alcohol poisoning, right?

I've done enough bad shit to earn all this, but it doesn't mean it doesn't sting. I don't have to accept what karma dealt me with a smile on my face. Much rather be face first in a puddle of my own vomit as I accept defeat than in the presence of people who don't give a damn about me.

That's why I still haven't text Prue back. I'm borderline drunk and more than a little turned on at the memory of the way her throat felt. But she is the last person I want to see me like this.

My pity party is not something she gets to attend.

She would gloat if she saw what went down tonight. I can just imagine the way she would've glared at me after I spilled the beans about Stacy being pregnant. Her blue eyes would've sliced me open right there for them all to see.

I bet her eyes would've fallen out of their sockets from rolling so much as I pissed and moaned about taking time off from touring. I can just hear her saying 'I told you so' after Aaron made it a point that I was the only one not doing anything with their life.

I shouldn't even be thinking about her right now. I'm drunk and miserable. Yet a part of me craves her company. When was the last time I craved a specific girl's company? Never. I mean, I've drooled over hot girls before, but once I put my cock in them, I was done.

I've never wanted a girl outside of her body before. Still don't. Not really. I just want more of Prue's body.

She has the perfect body. She hides it under those turtlenecks and tights. Not normally my type. I like edgy girls, not prim and proper, but the idea of ruining her neat demeanor excites me.

She is also bitchy in the best ways. Not afraid to hurt my feelings, even enjoying it a bit. She doesn't bite her tongue with me. Doesn't hold back. She's completely unimpressed with me. It's refreshing. I enjoy someone who isn't afraid to push back.

I don't think she likes me. The part of me that craves misery enjoys that. I don't need her to like me. I'd prefer her to hate me. It's what I deserve.

I try not to dwell on the other girls I've been with. They are just a blur of memories. Good times were had with each of them, but they never did more than scratch an itch. I used them for sex. Had them warm my bed, got them off, and let them return the favor.

The rock star life has always been sex, drugs, and rock and roll. I can't do the drugs anymore, so I double take in the sex part.

I make everyone I sleep with aware that I'm not in it for a relationship. Many have tried to change my mind regardless of my warning. I'm not opposed to letting them try, particularly if they are a good fuck. I won't say no to fucking the same girl twice, but I'm never going to be the guy to buy them chocolate or meet their parents.

Prue knows that. She isn't stupid. She has a rock star for a brother, she knows the deal. Plus, I'm not her type. She apparently likes rich, frat boys with tiny dicks.

She is just using me to make that ex of hers jealous. Or maybe she really did just like having a cock in her mouth and didn't care who it belonged to. Doesn't matter much to me. I just want to return the favor.

I desperately want to taste her. Fuck I would've had her spread her legs in that classroom if I could. The desire to let her know how good I could make her feel is overwhelming.

Always is. It's like after everything that happened in my life, I'm now programmed to please women. I need to be the best they ever had. Make them cum and leave them with the memory of a great time.

I would love to do that with Prue. I bet after she experiences my tongue and fingers, that attitude of hers would wane. Maybe not forever, but a few doses of my cock and I might be able to tame her.

Oh, fuck it. I don't want to tame her, it's just the fun of trying. I think taming Prue would be robbing the world of a masterpiece. We need more bitchy girls who aren't afraid to call people out.

She said that wasn't who she is, but I see it differently. Maybe she pretends to be coy and sweet, but I bring out a layer of bitch in her that makes her shine. I bet with the right coaching the girl could light the world on fire.

Judging by her asshole of an ex, she deserves to do it. Let her get some revenge for whatever she's been through. I don't need to know the details to know she earned her vengeance.

I'd be happy to help. Cheer her on as she burns this whole planet to the ground. I've never been able to do it. Never had the strength to get revenge, get even, or destroy anyone else but myself.

I would gladly let Prue ruin me as practice.

I don't know why, but I think I would enjoy it too. Something about her is a welcome change. I'm not going to be her boyfriend, maybe not even her friend, but I wouldn't say no to a small fling with her.

We'd both know where we stood. She could hate me but get off while doing so. I could self-destruct with my cock in her.

They say misery loves company, and clearly, we are both miserable right now. Together, we could find a semblance of comfort. Rebel in the chaos. Enjoy the destruction. One of us taking, and the other giving.

Staring at her message in my phone, now way more intoxicated than I should be, I wonder if bringing her into my pathetic life is wise. She deserves better, she doesn't know it, but she does.

I'm just a giant asshole. Even if I could teach her how to embrace her inner bitch, she doesn't need me ruining her life.

Yet as the bartender ushers me out of the bar into the chilly winter night, I decide fuck it. Let Prue decide my fate. Let her make the decision.

And so, I call her.

SEVEN

Prue

At some point the loneliness becomes panic, and the panic makes me pass out. It's only when my phone buzzes that I snap out of the semi lucid dream state I've become accustomed to since the attack.

I groan, trying to ignore it. It's probably Charles. I don't want to deal with him right now. Or ever. When it continues to buzz, I grab it, tempted to break it into tiny pieces.

It's only when I see Ben's name that I pause. There is a saying, nothing good happens after 2 a.m., and it's currently 2:15. A piece of my mind tells me to go back to sleep, but something louder screams to answer it.

"What?" I snap into the phone. A mumble on the other end of the phone takes me by surprise. "Ben?"

"I…" He laughs. "Fuck. I need you." His words are slightly slurred. I'm not sure I heard him right, or that he has the right number. "I'm a fraction of a second from spending the night in jail. Can you come get me?"

For a moment I stay silent as I debate what I should do. He has more than enough money to order a car home. He has countless other friends he could call, but he called me.

This is the definition of a booty call. He called me to fuck me.

I wanted this, right? But could I do it? Would it be easier if he was drunk?

"Prue. Please," he groans.

"Where the hell are you?" I sigh. It's worth a try. If this fails, I'm no worse off than I was before.

"I'll text you the place. Then you come get me."

"Fine. If only so you don't end up dead in a ditch somewhere."

"You care if I die? How pathetic." He laughs.

My jaw drops open. Why is he such an asshole? I should leave him to fend for himself, but I need to try. It's now or never.

The line goes dead and then a moment later I get a notification that he shared his location with me.

Ben Parker just shared his location with me. What the hell has my life become?

Climbing out of bed, I throw on a pair of sweatpants and tug one of Cameron's oversized hoodies over my head.

Even though he is an asshole, I'm not going to let him get arrested or die. I tell myself it's because I wouldn't want someone to leave my brother drunk and stranded, but there is more to it.

A little part of me is happy that he called me.

When I pull up outside of the bar Ben's location indicated, I find him sitting on the curb. His legs are sticking out into the street. His hands rest on the ground, causing his neck to hang back, even as his head slumps forward.

The neighborhood isn't one of the best and I'm worried about both of our safety at this point. Does the guy have a death wish or something?

I park and get out of the car. He stares up at me when I walk up beside him.

"You really came?" he mumbles. He smells like liquor and cigarettes. "Jesus, you are more pathetic than me."

"Really? I'm a bitch, rude, and now you're adding pathetic to the list?"

He laughs. "You forgot fucking fantastic. At least when your mouth is doing something besides being bitchy." His lips curve up into a stupid smile.

I'm tempted to get into my car and drive away, but his eyelids droop reminding me that he is extremely drunk. I should take everything he says with a grain of salt, only, he is saying the same stuff he has said since the moment I met him.

"Let's get you home." I reach my hand forward, ready to help him up.

"No. Not yet. Sit with me for a bit." He pats the curb beside him.

"Ben, it is almost 3 in the morning. You're drunk and I have class in the morning. Let's get you home."

"School is stupid. It doesn't teach you shit."

"I'm sure your mom would just love hearing you say that. Plus, a degree gets you a better job."

"Great tits also help. You got those, so no need for a degree."

I roll my eyes but take a seat beside him. He smiles over at me like he just won some kind of game. I glare back at him, but that only makes him smile more.

For a moment neither of us speaks. I stare at his side profile from the corner of my eyes. His hoodie covers up most of his tattoo, but a few peak out on his neck and hands.

He looks just as broken as I feel. Makes no sense to me. He has his dream career, is famous, and could have any girl he wanted. Including me.

"What made you call me? No other girl wanted to fuck the drunk idiot?" I ask after a few minutes.

"I came to this bar. Do I look like I wanted to fuck someone tonight?" He laughs. "I was celebrating."

"Celebrating what exactly?" I ask, glancing back at the locked up-front door of a tiny dive bar that makes me question when I need to get my next tetanus shot.

"How pathetic I am." He grins, bumping his shoulder against mine. "But you had that figured out in one night. Pinned me down to a T." He makes a little t with his fingers. I try not to smile at the silliness of the drunk idiot beside me. "All my friends are out growing me. I'm completely alone. God, how fucking sad is that? I guess all the fame doesn't mean shit."

"Make new friends." I shrug.

"Is that what you're doing?" He eyes me. "I heard those kids whisper in class the other day. They don't seem to like you very much."

"Accuse the popular guy of hurting you and watch the shitty people drop like flies."

"Let's key his car."

"Let's not." I laugh.

"Set his house on fire?"

"Pretty sure you'd go up in flames if you got anywhere close to an open flame right now."

"Two birds. One stone."

"Ben, come on. Let's get you home."

"Fine." He pushes himself to his feet, nearly falling over as I watch in horror. I'm hoping I don't have to carry him home. He may be skinny, but he is still taller than me by a few inches and I'm not very strong. "Take me home."

I help him get into the car. He instantly takes over my sound system putting on some music as I start the car.

"Where do you live?" I ask, pulling away from the curb.

"I'm not giving you that information." He laughs. "I don't trust you not to sell it on the internet."

"Really?"

"As revenge for the scene in the classroom."

"Okay? So where am I supposed to take you then?"

"Home. Your home." He smirks.

"No. That is not happening. I'm staying with Cameron. If I

bring you there, he will never shut up about it." If Cameron even knew I had Ben in my car, he wouldn't stop grilling me for details. If he ever finds out about the classroom scene, he would lose it. It's not normal for me to hang out with any other rock star but him.

"Fine then," he groans, pressing his hands into his eyes. "Take me to a hotel. Make it a Hilton."

"Just tell me where you live. I promise not to sell it on the internet."

"God," he mutters, pulling his hands from his face and turning to look at me. "If you take me there, I will slit my wrists open."

"Okay. Got it. So straight to a mental hospital it is."

"Jesus. Can you just stop being a bitch for one second?"

"Call me a bitch one more time and I'll slit your wrists for you," I snap.

Here I am doing something nice for the guy, and he has the nerve to continue to insult me? I don't know what kind of night he had, but nothing about his life could be worse than mine right now.

Out of the corner of my eye, I see his lips curving up into a wide grin.

"Bitch." His voice is full of amusement. I glance over to see him holding his wrists out toward me.

Pulling over, I unlock the car doors as I whip my head toward him. "Get out."

"Make me. Bitch." He smirks.

"Asshole."

"I claim that with pride, baby. You're going to have to try harder than that if you want to hurt my feelings."

"Pathetic." I shoot back.

"I've already admitted that. Try again."

I press my lips together, studying him. He is asking for it. He deserves it even. Since meeting him, he has done very little to earn my respect. Called me a bitch from night one, and hasn't stopped, even after I gave him an amazing blow job.

Still, I shouldn't sink to his level. He is clearly going through something. Having a bad night. And he did offer to kick Charles' ass for me.

"Got nothing?" He raises an eyebrow, his lips almost dropping into a frown.

"You are a sad little boy," I say. If he wants to be hurt, why should I deny him? I have more than enough reasons to inflict some pain for a change. "I'm so sorry your band is growing up and your mother loves you so much she moved here to be closer to you. You have a wonderful life and you take it for granted. It's beyond pathetic. You just want to waste your life fucking girls and playing shitty guitar."

"*Shitty guitar?*" His eyes widen, full of disbelief. "You think I play shitty guitar? Have you not listened to any of our albums? You can insult every other part of my personality. Hell, tell me my cock is small compared to your piece of shit ex's, but you cannot insult my guitar skills."

"No? Why not? It's not all that impressive." I shrug. It's a lie. He is a very skilled guitar player. Cameron's goal is to be as good as him, and he is getting there. Ben has a level of skill very few can obtain. But if he is going to call me names, I'm going to push his buttons right back. "I don't even like Haunting Memories," I lie again. I've seen them live a few times, even when Cameron wasn't on tour with them. I own a few albums and shirts. You don't have a brother in a band and not learn to like the bands he likes too.

"You are such a lying bitch." He laughs.

"Takes one to know one."

"Nice come back. Did you learn that on the playground?"

"Did you learn to play guitar from the bands on the radio?"

"Oh God. That's the meanest thing anyone has ever said to me."

"Good."

"Jesus. You win. I will never call you a bitch again."

"Liar."

"Takes one to know one." He smirks back. "Just take me home."

Sighing, I let him put his address into my phone and begin to drive toward his house.

He doesn't speak the rest of the ride. Neither do I. I don't really know what I should say. What happens when I get him back to his place? Is he expecting me to go in and have sex with him? Was it just desperation that had him calling me tonight?

I glance over at him occasionally. He keeps his head forward but leaning against the window. His fingers grip at the edge of his shirt around his neck. He looks small like this. Harmless even. Like he wouldn't be able to hurt a fly. Of course, I know better.

I thought the same thing about Charles. Knew he was a jerk but didn't think he would ever hurt me like he did. Ben has already proven he is an asshole, with a razor of a tongue, one he likes using on me. It stands to reason he could hurt me if he wanted to.

Still, as angry as Ben makes me, he also has a way of making me feel oddly comfortable. I'd go so far to say that he made me feel good. Confident. Unafraid. Strong.

Something about the way he throws insults at me and calls me names is kind of fun. I have no way of knowing if he really thinks I'm a bitch or not, but getting to hurl insults back at him is different, enjoyable even.

When I pull into a parking space in front of his condo, he undoes his seatbelt and reaches for the door handle. Doesn't bother saying thank you or bye, just slips from the car. I watch as he wobbles on his feet, back hunched over.

I can't let him climb up the steps of the building alone. He will fall to his death trying to make it to his door without any help.

Groaning, I turn off my car and slide out of my seat, catching up to him as he grips the rail of the steps. His eyes drift over to me, questioning me with a raised eyebrow.

"I'm not leaving you to try to get to your place alone. You'll die."

"And you would just hate that, huh?" He laughs.

"Lead the way." I roll my eyes.

I follow him to his fourth-floor condo. I stand and watch as he fumbles with his keys, cursing under his breath as he tries to slide it into the hole, then pushing the door open.

It thuds against the wall as he swings open. He flicks on his lights. Standing in the doorway, I glance around the place.

He has a black couch that is big and plushy. Black probably wasn't the best color choice. I'm surprised the thing isn't covered in sex stains. I'm sure a black light would turn the whole thing blue.

There is a black coffee table sitting in front of a black stand where a large TV sits. Black bookshelves line the other wall. He has far more books than I imagined he would have, but mixed in are little trinkets I can't quite make out.

A few awards hang on his walls, with posters of his band and others.

Off to the side is a square dining table with some chairs around it. He has an open kitchen, twice the size of Cameron's kitchen. A hallway is off to the side leading to more doors.

Glancing back to him, I see he has pulled his hoodie over his head. It lays discarded on the dark wooden floor. His shirt gets tossed onto the black shaggy rug under the coffee table.

"Am I bigger?" he asks, as he kicks off his shoes.

"What?"

"Than your ex."

"Are you seriously asking me that right now?"

"Yes." He smiles, unzipping his jeans. I glance behind me. The hallway is empty, and it's late, but the fact he is unbothered getting undressed with the door wide open and me standing here is bold.

I just stare at him as he pushes down his jeans. His black boxers hug at his hips. Despite being skinny, there is a slight outline of muscles on his body. His stomach is toned. Tattoos cover his skin. Nothing like a sleeve or anything, just random little designs here and there. A ghost, a flower, a stick figure. Many other things I can't quite make out.

"So, am I bigger?" he asks again. My eyes drift up, meeting his, as he stares at me.

"Yes." I roll my eyes. "By a lot."

"Do I have the biggest cock you've ever seen?" He tilts his head to the side, mouth curved up in a knowing smile.

It's hard to hate him for being cocky about his dick when it's as impressive as it is.

"Yes. Happy?"

"Oh yeah. I'm just fucking ecstatic."

He strolls to the couch, plopping down on it and reaching for the remote.

That should be my sign to leave. I did my good deed. Picked him up, got his drunk ass home, and stroked his ego. There is no reason for me to stay any longer, but I don't move.

"How many girls have you fucked?" I ask, taking a step inside.

"I'd tell you, but then you'd never let me fuck you." He laughs, looking over at me.

"That comment alone makes me not want to fuck you." I scoff back.

"Sure." He smiles. "Sit. Make yourself at home." He puts on a TV channel with music videos playing.

I eye the couch, then glance back at the door.

"I should probably go."

"Okay." His face drops into a small frown.

"You're going to be okay, right?"

"I guess we will find out. Maybe I make the morning news. Rock star kills himself after throwing himself a pity party at a local bar and bothering a pretty girl to take him home." He laughs. "Well, I'm sure it would be a few days before anyone bothered to check on me." His voice dips.

Groaning, I shut the door and sink into the other side of the couch. I kick off my shoes, tucking my feet under my knees.

"You feel sorry for me now." He grins.

"Always have." I smirk back at him.

"I swear I wasn't always this pathetic. I mean I think I've always been sad, but not like this." His eyes drift toward the bookshelves for a moment. I can't be sure what exactly he is looking at, but then he quickly looks back at the TV.

"Why are you like this now?"

"Everything I love is slipping from my hands. The people I thought would always be there for me are abandoning me. They have become someone to someone else. Someone who isn't a piece of shit like me. I will have nothing and no one soon."

"Have you ever thought about doing the same? Finding someone to settle down with?"

"Never. Love is a soul sucking disease."

"Yeah," I say softly.

"Tell me about it."

"About what?"

"Your ex. What did he do? When? Did he do it before?"

"I rather not talk about it."

"I'll tell you mine if you tell me yours."

"Oh yeah. I'm sure you've been abused so many times." I cross my hands over my chest, rolling my eyes. Part of me wants to march out of his stupid condo and go home, but I find myself unable to move. His misery is comforting.

"Maybe not the same way, but I have been abused too." His eyes sweep over to me. Dark blue waves of agony stare back at me. "And I'm not talking some silly girl stomping on my heart. I'm talking about real, illegal kind of abuse."

"By who?"

"Nah uh." He wags his finger at me. "You don't get that information without agreeing to the terms."

"Fine." I shrug. "I rather not know about your tragic past anyways."

It's only partly untrue. I'd be curious to hear about whatever abuse he went through, but it's probably best I don't know. The less I know about Ben the better. I don't want to be his friend. I barely want to be around him at all. I'd take the great sex he is rumored to give, but I don't need anything more from him.

"No? Afraid you might think differently of me if you knew?"

"No. Whatever happened to you could've turned you into a better person. You could've grown from it, instead you use it as an excuse to justify becoming this." I wave, gesturing to his body. "My tragic event is going to make me stronger."

Or at least I'm going to pretend it will.

"You are so naïve." He chuckles, shaking his hair. Blond strands fly in every direction before he stills. "The abuse lives inside your bones now. You will never be able to escape it. I bet it eats you alive at night, huh? Seeing his face must make you sick. You can pretend, act so well he never knows, but you'll know and that's all that matters."

I press my lips together, processing his words as tears fill my eyes. Part of me knows he is probably right. Even as my mind tries to tell me it's just the words of a silly boy who has no idea how to deal with the real world. But I'm terrified he is right. What if I can never move past it?

"That's what I thought," he says lightly. "So, tell me, Prue, what do you plan to do with your demons? I tried every way possible to drown mine. Music has been the most helpful, but that is slipping through my fingertips now. What will you do?"

"Maybe I'll become a serial killer," I snap, wiping at my eyes. I refuse to let his words get to me.

He laughs loudly, hugging his chest as his laugh fills the room. I feel my lips curve up, the sound and sight of him laughing making me feel a little warm inside. I try to cover it by glaring at him, but I can tell he sees right through it because he laughs harder.

"Who would you kill first? Him or me?"

"Neither. Only rookies kill someone they know. You need to

pick someone random, someone you have no ties to. It has to happen in a place you frequent often so if they happen to find evidence of you in the area it makes sense. Getting rid of the weapon is important. So often people get caught because they have the weapon on them. They think it's safer to have it, but it's not."

"Holy shit." He laughs again, as I grin at him. "You've put a lot of thought into this."

"No. I just listen to a lot of podcasts."

"Not music?"

"I listen to music too." I shrug.

"My band?"

"Yes. I've even been to a few of your concerts. I was backstage a few times when Cameron toured with you guys."

"And somehow I didn't notice you."

"You had a girl on both arms. I don't think you felt the need to look anywhere else." I laugh. "Plus, I had a boyfriend."

"Are you younger than Cameron?"

"Yes."

"By how much?" His eyes widen, as if he is trying to do the math. "Please tell me I didn't let a fucking teenager suck my cock. That would be a low I don't think I could live with."

"Five minutes. We are twins."

"Jesus. Thank the lord." He rubs his head. "Do you have any idea how many teenagers try to fuck me? It's terrifying."

"You need to start checking ID."

"I should." He laughs. "You must be 21 and up to ride this ride."

I let myself laugh again.

Ben might be a giant asshole, but he could be a good distraction.

Maybe he could numb my pain.

EIGHT

Ben

I KNOW WHEN I SOBER UP, I'M GOING TO REGRET calling Prue, but as she sits on the other end of my couch, I feel an odd sense of peace. At least when it's a known fact someone hates you, you don't need to hide any parts of you. I can be my true self with her. I'm always an asshole, but with her I can be pathetic as well.

We have fallen into a calm silence, watching music videos play on TV. My vision is growing clearer with every passing moment. The hangover is just on the horizon, though. Whenever I finally go to sleep, I'll wake up feeling worse, but for a moment it feels good to give into the misery. Let future Ben deal with the fall out of me trying to keep from blowing my brains out.

She eyes me now and then. Either trying to see my reaction to the music video on the screen or seeing if I've fallen asleep. I can't know for sure, but I don't let on that I'm aware of her eyes on me. I'm not in the mood for one of her snide comments.

"You should sleep," she finally says. "And I should go."

"No," I protest, turning to face her. "Stay the night."

"No." She laughs, shaking her head. "I don't think that's a good idea."

"I'm not asking to fuck you. I'm afraid I couldn't get it up if you wanted me to." I smirk. "Just stay, as a friend."

"A friend?" Her eyebrow lifts, challenging that idea.

"We could pretend for the night."

"It's technically morning."

"Jesus Christ, Prue, why are you so difficult?"

"Trying to live up to the names you keep calling me." She smiles, and suddenly I don't mind how difficult she is being. That smile is too fucking good to see. I could get used to that smile. "I have class in the morning and if I'm not getting lucky, what's the point in staying with a man who keeps insulting me."

My eyes light up at the idea of her getting lucky. I could make her feel real lucky. I want to do that more than anything honestly. The alcohol in my system might pose a challenge, but I have more tools than just my giant cock.

"That's a fair point." I nod. "I do owe you an orgasm. I'm a big fan of tit for tat." Her eyes sparkle for a moment, as if the idea of an orgasm from me is the best thing she ever heard. It makes my limp cock tense. Maybe I could get it up for her. "I'll make you a deal."

"A deal?"

"Let me get you off and if I fail, I'll let you leave and never call you again."

"You just said you were too drunk to get it up," she counters, a smug little smile on her face.

"I play guitar for a living, Prue, but I know how to strum a pussy better."

She doesn't say anything for a long moment. Wheels are turning behind the sky that is her eyes. A layer of desire sits in them, as she chews on her lip for a moment.

"No," she says softly. "But I will counter your deal."

"With?"

"Let me suck your cock again. If you can cum, I'll stay."

Well fuck me. That's not the offer I was expecting. My cock is slow to stiffen but still stiffens at the memory of how good her mouth felt.

"Do you have an oral fixation or something?"

"I just like a good challenge."

I ponder that idea for a moment. The idea of her mouth around my cock is tempting. It has me slowly growing hard already, but I much rather make her cum. I want to see what that looks like. Those eyes that do loops whenever I annoy her and try to slice me open every time I insult her must look glorious when she is coming undone. But even as my cock stiffens, it doesn't harden completely.

I'm not sure I can get fully hard right now. That happening in front of her is a level of embarrassment I'm not sure I can handle right now.

"I only accept your terms if you get naked first."

"No," she says quickly, eyes darting to look at the floor in front of her.

"Why not? You aren't exactly hiding anything with those tight turtlenecks and skirts you've been wearing."

"I am too," she whispers.

Oh. I'm a fucking idiot. That shitty ex of hers hurt more than just her face. Those turtlenecks are hiding more bruises.

That idea makes my blood boil with rage. I no longer want her mouth wrapped around my dick. I want his teeth in the gutter. His head on a pike in the middle of that college of hers, full of idiots who side with an abusive punk over her.

"Okay," I say softly. "Go home, Prue."

She doesn't need me making her life any harder than it seems to be right now. There is a pain inside her and I'm not about to intensify it. The best thing I can do is leave her alone.

Her head turns back to me, eyes zeroing in on with a look of pure evil. I shouldn't like it. It shouldn't turn me on, but it does anyways.

"That afraid you won't be able to get it up?" She smirks, sliding closer to me. A layer of pain rests behind those evil eyes. I know she thinks she can use me to bury it, only because I want to bury mine inside her too. "Am I not hot enough for you, Ben?"

"No. It's not that," I say softly. "I think I'm trying to do the right thing for the first time in my life."

"The right thing?" she questions.

"You don't need me making your life any harder."

She laughs. "You think awfully high of yourself, don't you? There is no way you can make my life any harder than it has been. You don't have that kind of power over me." Dropping to the floor in front of me, she grins up at me. "I've made you cum before. Quite quickly if I recall. We both know, between the two of us, I hold all the power, don't I, Ben?"

I don't know what part of the situation unfolding in front of me does it, but my cock hardens to full mass.

She stares at the bulge in my boxers, licking her lips and sealing my fate like a fucking envelope. I can't do the right thing now. Not with her on her knees in front of me, taunting me.

If she wants to use me to bury her misery, she can.

"You really believe that, don't you?" I smile down at her, reaching into my boxers and pulling out my cock. Stroking it, I watch her eyes move with my movement. "You only have as much power as I allow. You'd do well to remember that. The day you finally let me touch you, I will ruin you, Prue. No other man will ever make you feel as good as I will."

"We will see about that." She smirks up, her eyes peering up at me.

"Go on then. Show me all that power you are talking about." I motion to my cock.

She bends her head toward it, letting her hands grip my thighs. Parting her lips, she lets spit dribble onto my length. I use my hand to work her spit down my shaft.

Her tongue licks at the tip. I'm getting harder by the second. Her eyes become saucers again. Fixated on my cock. It almost makes me self-conscious, but I barely get a chance to think about it before she takes me in her mouth.

"God," I groan. My hand touches the back of her head, needing her to take me deeper. The way only she can. She flinches, reminding me I'm handling a fragile girl who could bolt at any moment. "Don't," I say softly, letting my hand drop back to the couch. "Don't think about that. Stay here with me, baby."

Her eyes glance up at me as she sinks her mouth lower, taking more of me into her mouth.

"You are so fucking good at this. Too fucking good." I dig my nails into my couch, trying to ground myself in the moment.

I wonder if all the bitching she does has helped her with her dick sucking skills. Maybe all that complaining and moaning she does, makes her able to suck cock better. If that's the case, I'll never complain about it again.

My eyes shut as she lets me slide down her throat. Her hands rest on my thighs, digging her nails into the flesh. The little bit of pain sends a shock straight to my balls.

I know the minute she lets me return the favor I will have the upper hand but for now, she is right. She holds all the power, and I don't think I give a single fuck at this moment. Let her have complete control if it means I get to feel like this.

"Prue," I groan. "I hope you don't have any tests today, because it's clear you aren't going to school today."

She chuckles around my cock, and I feel it in the base of my cock.

"You don't care though, do you? Isn't this better than anything school could teach you?"

She nods, letting her eyes sit on mine for a moment. I barely know this girl, but I can see the lust inked into her light blue eyes. She is enjoying this just as much as I am.

"Yeah. You'd rather have my cock down your throat than sit in a boring classroom."

Thrusting my hips a little, even though she has me as deep as she can possibly go, I groan as she quickens her pace. Flexing her cheeks as she breathes around my cock.

"It's nice to know your mouth is multi-talented. You can suck cock just as well as you can bitch and moan."

Her mouth leaves my cock shocking me for a moment.

"You have no idea how good I can moan." She smirks, licking her lips.

"I hope to find out one day. Now please, get back to it."

She grins. "And if I don't?"

"If you don't, I'm pretty sure I'll combust into a million little pieces."

"So, I do have power over you?"

"Jesus. Yes. Okay? You have a modicum of power over me, Prue. Now please, keep sucking my cock."

Her mouth widens, as her eyes light up. Quickly, she takes me back in her mouth, pushing forward until she has it all inside of her. Her tongue rubs against the underside as she sucks me harder than before.

She is far too good at this. I doubt I'll ever enjoy another blow job in my life. Before, they barely did the trick as it is, but now, knowing what she is capable of, they will never compare.

It would be a shame if it wasn't so fucking good.

I let her go on for a few minutes, fighting back my release to savor it. The desire to show her I'm not some loser who finishes in two minutes every time keeping me from blowing my load. Bad enough I did that the first time.

She moans around my cock at some point, digging her nails deeper into my thighs and I nearly explode. My control is slipping. I'm not going to last much longer.

"Fuck. Prue," I moan. "You're going to make me cum, baby." Once again, she looks up at me. The lust in her eyes sends me over the edge. The minute I start cumming she pulls back a little, allowing me to fill her mouth. I almost prefer this feeling compared to cumming down her throat like last time.

She grins when I finish, pulling her mouth off my softening cock. Shifting forward she opens her mouth, showing me my cum sitting on her tongue.

"Jesus," I moan, my cock already flexing again.

Grinning, she shuts her mouth, and I watch her throat as she swallows my load.

How could anyone hurt this girl? All I want to do is make her feel a fraction as good as she makes me feel. She is so fucking hot. A little vixen of lust covered in prim and proper attire. It's the fucking male fantasy. Girl next door, slut in the sheets.

I reach forward, gripping her face. She melts into my hold, relaxing as I let my thumb stroke her jaw. I press my forehead against hers, trying to memorize the way her eyes look at this moment. It's a picture I wouldn't mind adding to my collection of tattoos. But I highly doubt I could draw it well enough.

I let my lips dip to hers. My tongue sweeps across her plump bottom lip before she presses it against mine. I let her think she is leading, as our lips dance together. Her hands wrap around my neck, pulling me closer. I slip off the couch, pushing her onto her back.

She is too caught up in the kiss to care that I'm hovering over her body. I doubt she even notices the parallel position we are in right now.

My hand moves to unzip the hoodie she is wearing. It smells like another man, but I don't care. Shouldn't care. Whoever it belongs to isn't about to make her feel as good as I am. By the time I'm done with her, she won't even remember them.

When her tongue pokes against my lips, I let it in. She explores my mouth with urgency, as my hands begin to slip up her shirt. I want to know what her tits feel like in my hands. Her flesh alone feels like heaven. Smooth and soft. Cold as fucking ice, and the desire to warm it up with my own overcomes me.

I let my fingers stroke her hip bone and she gasps into my mouth. Her little body thrusting up against mine. I fight which direction to let my hand go. I want to touch every part of her, but what part first?

Letting my hand side up her flat, taunt stomach, I let it rest just under her tit for a moment as she continues to let her tongue dart in and out of my mouth.

When I shift slightly, letting my hand rests against her rib, she gasps again, jerking away from me.

"Ow," she mutters.

"I'm sorry," I blurt out, not aware I had applied any pressure.

"Get off me." She pushes at my chest.

I snap backwards, creating space. Her voice tells me she is no longer present in this moment, but somewhere in her head. She is fighting a memory right now. I'm not sure what set her off, but I want to find out so I can avoid that in the future.

"I'm sorry," I repeat. "What did I do wrong?"

"Nothing," she snaps, sitting up. She tugs the zipper of her hoodie back up. "I have to go."

"Wait. We had a deal," I say. She crawls to her shoes, sitting on her ass and quickly putting them on. "Prue. Wait. What happened?"

"I have to go," she says, pushing herself to her feet. I stand up too. She stares at me, a mixture of sadness and fear dances behind her eyes. I fucked up. I knew this wasn't the right thing to do, but I did it anyways. "Please?" she whispers.

"I'm not holding you hostage. You are free to go."

She stares at me, then lets her eyes dart to the door. I see her trying to map out a route there. I think the beating she took from her shitty ex was far worse than just a few bruises.

Taking a step between me and the couch, she freezes when I take a step back.

"Don't call me again," she snaps. "Okay? Just leave me alone." Her voice is trembling, and tears fill her eyes.

"Prue." I move slightly in front of her, and panic flashes across her face. "Hey." I place my hands on her shoulders. She tries to jerk away, but I grip them, holding her in place. "Look at me."

Her eyes downcast at my order.

"You are freaking the fuck out."

"That's rich coming from you." She shoves at my chest. "Move. Let me go."

"I will. I'm going to let you leave, but I need you to calm down before I let you drive home. Okay? I know a panic attack when I see one. You aren't safe to drive right now."

"A panic attack?" she snaps, glaring up at me. "This isn't a fucking panic attack. I just want nothing to do with you. Like ever."

I laugh. I don't mean to. This isn't funny at all, but it's like her flight or fight response has somehow morphed into one.

"Move," she yells.

"Okay." I release my hold on her, stepping to the side. "For the record, I'm really sorry, Prue."

She marches to my front door. "Whatever," she mumbles. Swinging the door open, she doesn't even glance back as she steps out, letting it slam behind her.

I sink back into my couch, shutting my eyes.

I didn't mean to cause her any more pain. Didn't want to take her back to that moment. I thought I could be a distraction. Be something for her to use to escape the memories, but obviously I'm no good for her.

I'm no good for anyone. That much is becoming apparent. The need to self-destruct is poison to everyone around me. No wonder no one wants anything to do with me. Can't embrace being an asshole without accepting that people are going to want nothing to do with you because of it.

The damage done to my soul is beyond repairing. That's why I cover myself in a blanket of cockiness and put on the face of a jerk. I never want people to see the brokenness inside of me. The only person I thought might accept it was Prue, but that was selfish of me. She didn't need my pain. She has enough of her own.

Dropping to my side on the couch, I let my body curl up in a ball. My eyes pressed tightly together, I let the darkness swallow me. The faint memories of fingertips caressing over my body makes bile climb up my throat.

The memories mix together. A figure haunts me in the darkness. Taking advantage of the loneliness like always. Reminding me, if it was wrong, it wouldn't feel this good.

But it is wrong. So wrong.

Feeling good doesn't change that fact. It taints it. And this is the same thing.

Prue might feel good, but using her to cover my wounds when she has her own is wrong.

The best thing I can do is honor her wishes. I'll leave her alone. Never contact her again. Try to forget about how good her body felt beneath me.

She deserves to get better, and I'd only get in the way of that.

So, I'll delete her number in the morning, and never see her again.

NINE

Prue

Tears fall down my face in a steady stream as I drive back to Cameron's place. Ugly, snot filled, sobs fall from my lips, and I try not to wreck my car.

The idea that Charles has fucked me up so much that another man can't touch me without causing me to think about him is too much. I'm not sure how I'm supposed to survive in this world alone, but apparently, I don't have a choice.

After everything that happened to me, I shouldn't be surprised that I couldn't go through with it. I knew it was a possibility. It was the fear I had this whole time. I thought I could get past it. Thought I'd be able to block the memories out.

Ben is hot, gorgeous even. That kiss was the best I've ever had. The way his lips guided over mine, leading just slightly, but allowing me some semblance of control, made my whole-body melt. For just a moment, his lips were on mine, and it felt good. Everything else faded away.

He wanted me. I wanted him too. His cock in my mouth is not enough. I crave more. I knew he would deliver pleasure beyond what I've been used to. I could feel it just from the kiss, but then he touched my ribs.

The spark of pain was small, but reminded me of what Charles did. Suddenly, I couldn't do it. I couldn't let Ben keep touching me while my mind was being flooded with memories of pain.

I'm sure it didn't matter. Even if the pain in my ribs didn't surface, something else would've taken me back to that night. Ben is right. What Charles did to me will live with me for the rest of my life.

Charles broke more than my skin, cracked more than just my ribs. He destroyed my spirit too.

Once back at Cameron's, I crawl into bed. Pulling the blankets over my head, I curl into a ball and fall apart even more.

I have to get up in a few hours for my first class, but maybe Ben is right about that too. School is pointless when you don't have any goal in mind. I should just drop out. There is no point in trying to live up to my parents' standards anymore. Whatever guy they have me marry is going to want sex and when I can't do it, there is going to be problems.

Problems I'm not sure I want to deal with. It's better if I just disappear. Letting down my parents isn't going to go over well. They will disown me, and then I won't be able to afford school anyways. Or life. Or anything.

I'm better off getting a crappy job somewhere and trying to get by on my own.

But old habits die hard. As I stand in the bathroom, staring at the redness in my eyes and bags underneath them, and Cameron knocks, complaining once again about how long I'm taking in the bathroom, I'm reminded of the truth.

I'm not trying to make my parents happy for myself. I'm doing it for Cameron. I'm doing it to keep the pressure off him. Everything I endure is so he can achieve his dream.

I know he wouldn't want me to continue. Not with how bad things have gotten. If I stay on their good side though, I get to reap the benefits that come with being the Ward's only golden child. Getting back on their good side would allow me to share some of those benefits with Cameron.

Sighing, I accept the fact I don't have a choice. I will go to class today, play the part once again. Then ultimately, I will go back to the life I had before.

Opening the door, Cameron greets me with a small smile. When he sees my face, it fades.

"Are you okay?" he asks. Being twins means he can read me almost better than anyone. It's the fact we have the same eyes. It's always been hard to keep things from him. One look into my eyes and he just knows when something is up.

"I'm fine." I offer him a smile back. "Or I will be," I lie.

"You know, Prue, we don't need them. We never did."

"It's not about needing, Cam. They're our parents."

"No." He shakes his head. "They just happen to be two people who are responsible for unleashing us onto the world. They stopped being our parents when they decided we were nothing but stock options."

"I still have to go back."

"No, you don't. They don't care that Charles..."

"Cam, if I don't go back, we both suffer the consequences."

"I've been managing just fine. And you're smarter than me, so you will be even better."

"I won't go back unless they agree that I don't have to marry him."

"They will just pick someone worse."

"Doubt they could find anyone worse than him." I fake a grin. "I'll be fine, Cam. I promise."

"Yeah." He nods, brows scrunched up as he stares at the bathroom door. "Just promise me you'll tell me before you leave."

"I will. Now I have to get ready for class."

"Have a good day." He nods, stepping into the bathroom.

I change quickly. Putting on a cute dark brown skirt and a beige turtleneck. I'm used to the skirts, but I normally wear low-cut shirts. Charles liked when I showed off my skin, which is ironic given how he made it impossible for me to show any for weeks.

I lace up brown boots and grab my textbooks off the desk. Stuffing them into my tote bag, I slide in headphones before heading out the door. Turning on Haunting Memories, I find myself trying to isolate Ben's parts.

After last night, I know I shouldn't be thinking about his lips on me, but I can't help it. They felt so good. His hands on me may have brought back my own haunting memories, but for a second, it was nice.

Walking into class I ignore the whispers that follow. You'd think after a few weeks they would've found something else to talk about, but no. I think the scene Ben caused just added fuel to the fire.

The idea I had the guts to leave Charles is probably the highlight of the circle. There has always been a layer of toxic behavior in our group, but no one brought attention to it. There would be some talk about so and so having an eating disorder or drug problem, but for the most part we kept things lowkey.

You learn in these groups it's best not to cast stones. All our houses are made of glass. The more attention you put on someone else, the brighter the light gets put on you.

We are supposed to have each other's back, but of course there is always one person you don't cross in the group. The leader. The glue keeping us all on top. I crossed him and now I have to face the fall out.

Since leaving Charles, school has been harder. I can almost physically see my grades dropping. I was allowed to take two weeks off, but those weeks put me behind. Plus, it's hard to focus on class when I share half of them with Charles. There is at least one person from his friend group in every one of my classes. The whispers are distracting. Knowing they all know what happened but pretend I'm the crazy one eats away at me. I find myself doodling or spacing out.

I make my way to my normal seat, pretending not to hear

someone whisper slut at me. Another rumor Charles has added to the list after Ben's scene is that I cheated on him first. Can't be surprised he would use that to sway even more sympathy his way.

I freeze when I see Charles sitting in my spot. I glance around, trying to find somewhere else to sit, even as he spots me at the end of the row and smiles.

"Prue." He beckons me. For some reason, my feet carry me to him. It's like I have a death wish or something. His voice never made me feel good, but it never felt like razor blades cutting at my ear drums until after, until now. "No Ben today?"

"It's not what you think." I sigh, pulling out a single headphone. "He was just messing with me."

"Yeah?" He raises an eyebrow as his eyes fill with a fury I've only had directed at me once before.

"Not like that."

"You just keep digging yourself a deeper hole, you know that, right?" He shakes his head. "Anyways, I have a thing tonight and I just happened to put your name down as my plus one before everything happened between us."

I stare at him blankly. There is no reason for him to be telling me this. Surely, he could go alone, bring one of his friends or find some other girl to take. No one would question it. You don't question a change when it comes from the Davenports.

"So, I'll pick you up at 7."

"Excuse me?" I don't mask the shock in my voice. He has to know better than to think I would go anywhere with him.

"Don't be difficult, Prue. Maybe this could be our second chance. We can put all this behind us. You can admit you were just hurt. It would be in your best interest to finally apologize so we could move on."

"What would I apologize for exactly?"

"Listen, my parents like your family. They think we'd make good babies and shit. They are willing to look past all this. It's good for business. For both of our families."

"Then why did you do it?"

"Prue," he says sharply, "be ready at 7. You're staying with Cameron, right?"

"I'm not going anywhere with you. Ever again."

"Yes." He stands up, towering over me. His head bends to the side of my face. I can't move as my heart pounds in my chest. "You fucking are." The threat is webbed into his words.

"Fine," I say softly.

"See, that wasn't so hard, was it?" He smiles, pressing a kiss to my cheek, before walking to his normal seat.

I'm not going with him, but I know if I push it now, I will pay the cost the moment he can get me alone. Best to let him think I'll go along. When he shows up at Cameron's tonight, I won't be there for him to collect, though.

"Cameron?" I call out as I enter the apartment. Dropping my bag to the floor, I walk throughout the apartment trying to find any sign of him.

I need him to be home. He will take me out somewhere, keep me safe. Deal with Charles if he had to. I'll be okay in his company.

Only he isn't home. I'm all alone with only two hours until Charles is supposed to show up.

I pull out my phone, calling him.

"Hey sis," he answers after a few rings.

"Where are you?"

"I'm in San Diego for a show this weekend, remember?"

"Oh. Right. I forgot."

"What's wrong?"

"Nothing." I sigh. "Have fun."

"Prue?" He pushes.

Cameron can read me like an open book. I remember when I called him to pick me up from the hospital, I barely had to tell him anything. He knew from the sound of my voice that something was wrong. His first question was what hospital.

It's probably a twin thing, but regardless, it is what it is. Even if he doesn't seek out revenge for me, he'd protect me in a heartbeat. If I told him what was going on he would rush back, probably not in time, but he would try.

"I'm fine. Just thought we could have dinner or something. Go have fun. Play great."

"Okay," he says. "Are you sure?"

"Yeah. Go rock your ass off."

"If you need anything just call. I'll be back Sunday."

"See you then." Only I worry I won't be here when he gets home.

I pace the house as tears threaten to spill from my eyes. I don't want to be this girl. I can't be the weak girl who goes back to the man who beat her. Though I fear if I don't things will end up worse. That thought claws at my chest, slicing open my heart.

People really expect me to just take him back. My own parents even.

Sighing, I unlock my phone, scrolling through my contacts. So many names, but no one I trust to not hand my location to Charles just to get on his good side.

Pausing, I stare at the only person I know who isn't scared of my ex. Who just a few days stood up to him even. My one last chance, but I doubt he wants to hear from me after my freak out at his apartment this morning.

It's the only chance I have, though.

So I click on 'not so tiny dickhead' and type a single word text message. If he replies to it, I know not all hope is lost. If he doesn't, I'll accept my fate.

ME
Hey.

I crouch on the floor of the living room, gripping my phone tightly in my hand. From where I am, I can see the time on the microwave.

Time seems to slow down as I stare at the green glowing numbers. Slowly it changes six times. With each new number my chest tightens. Am I really going to let my fate be in the hands of an asshole who could find countless girls to entertain him?

Still, last night he called me. He wanted me.

Another three minutes pass before my phone buzzes in my hand.

The screen flashes with an incoming call from 'not so tiny dickhead.'

I pause. I told him to never contact me again just a few hours ago, and one text has him calling me. Given the circumstances, I shouldn't be fighting back a smile, but I am. It's nice to know my outburst didn't entirely turn him off.

I answer it, unsure what to say though, I don't speak for a moment.

"Hello? Prue?"

"What are you doing tonight?" I blurt out.

He laughs on the other side of the phone. "You are fucking crazy."

"You are so mean," I groan.

"Yes, and yet you messaged me."

"You called me last night," I counter. This was a terrible idea. He is so frustrating.

"I was drunk. What's your excuse?"

"I can't stay in this apartment," I say softly.

"Your brother annoying you or something?"

"No. He is out of town."

"Are you scared of being alone?" he asks, genuine concern laces his voice, for the second time in less than 24 hours. The thought of how pathetic I must seem to him makes my stomach tense for a moment. "Are you okay?" he asks after a moment. The layer of concern in his voice doubles, making my throat tighten. He doesn't really care, does he?

"No," I snap. "Just... never mind. Forget I called."

"Prue. Wait. Just tell me what's going on, okay? I know I'm an asshole, but if you need something..." His voice trails off like he doesn't know how to finish that statement.

"My ex asked me to go to this thing with him tonight. He wouldn't take no for an answer. Now he is coming here at 7 to pick me up. I can't be here when he shows up and Cameron is out of town. If I'm home, I don't think things will end well for..."

"Text me your address. I'll pick you up, but there are conditions."

"Conditions?" Leave it to Ben to save me on his terms.

"You have to go out with me."

"Out? Like a date."

"It will look like a date," he says. "Put on your best turtleneck and a cute little skirt. We are going to grab some food and drinks while we make all kinds of headlines."

"He won't like that."

"Prue, do you think I give two shits what he likes?"

"No. But..."

"And I know you don't think very highly of me, but do you think for one second I'd let him hurt you?"

"After you're gone..."

"Never," he says plainly. "If I grow bored of you and think he is still a threat to your safety I will end him."

I don't exactly know how Ben plans on ending him, but the idea stirs more emotions in me than I expect. He sounds willing to do more to protect me than my own parents. That hurts, but fills me with an excitement I can't explain.

"Okay."

"See you soon, Prue," he says, hanging up.

After texting Ben Cameron's address, I quickly strip off my

clothes. Using the full-length mirror on the closet, I examine my body. The tiniest bruise sits on my collarbone, matching the one under my eye. It's barely noticeable but still makes me feel uneasy. Sighing, I pull a black turtleneck over my head, hoping soon there will be nothing left to cover up.

I slip on a short plaid skirt, adding black boots to the outfit. I almost look like the kind of girl who would go out with a guy like Ben. I rush to the bathroom to throw on some make up. Light cover up, a Smokey layer of eyeshadow, and a red lip gloss complete the look.

Running my hands through my light brown hair, I tussle it so the layers stand out a little. I'm not as edgy as most the girls Ben has been with, but tonight I at least look less prim and proper. Maybe no one will even be able to tell who I am if the paparazzi does get pictures of us.

I grab a black cross body purse packing it with my wallet and lip gloss for touch ups, then I check my phone.

The anxiety grows with each passing moment, as the time gets closer to six now. I know Charles said he would be here at 7, but my gut tells me he'd show up early just to make sure I'm wearing something he approves of.

I pace the living room, doing circles around the couch and coffee table, willing LA traffic not to keep Ben from getting here soon.

At 6:30 my phone buzzes. Glancing at it makes my stomach sink.

> **CHARLES**
> Wear that tight little blue dress you wore to the Christmas party my parents threw.

I don't bother replying, just stare at the clock again. Hoping Ben gets here before Charles does.

Five minutes pass before Ben calls me.

"Hello," I answer.

"Hello. Would you like me to come up and get you?" he asks

on the other side of the phone. The faintest sound of music fills up the background.

"No. I'll be right down."

"Sounds good."

Sighing, I take a deep breath before walking to the door, feeling like I just escaped a fate worse than death. I swing open the door just for my heart to sink.

TEN

Ben

I'M PARKED IN A SPOT RIGHT OUTSIDE THE ENTRANCE to Cameron's apartment building, smoking a cigarette, waiting for Prue to join me.

I spent most of the day sleeping to starve off a hangover. It worked well enough that I decided to go out again tonight. My plan was to either throw myself another pity party or find some girl to take mercy on me.

Honestly, after Prue's freak out, I was left feeling pretty low. I shouldn't complain, the girl got me off. Maybe not in my preferred way, but cumming down her throat is nothing to whine about.

I felt bad for pushing her to her breaking point. I wish I knew what I did wrong. Instead, I tried to respect her wishes to be left alone. I didn't bother her for an answer.

I needed to find myself some other girl to distract me from Prue. That's what I told myself as I was getting ready to go comb through my regular bars. Just needed to find a girl who was the opposite of her. Maybe a blond with dark eyes. Or someone with jet-black hair and brown eyes. Someone who'd fawn over me. Make me feel like the famous rock star I am, not the asshole I also happen to be.

Then she messaged me.

I really did try to stick to my plan. Spent a good few minutes trying to remind myself why getting involved with her was a bad idea. I even texted Wes to see if he had a minute to chat. Hoping he could remind me why girls with drama are a bad idea for a guy like me. When he didn't reply, my resolve broke.

I called her, because if her voice sounded too pained, I thought it would remind me why I wasn't good for her. Remind me the broken can't save the broken. However, once I heard her voice, the opposite happened. Even when she got annoyed with me, there was a layer of fear in her voice that made my heart ache. Left me no choice but to run to her rescue.

She needed someone and called me. Clearly her circle of friends is very limited, if she is reduced to relying on me. I couldn't deny her help.

If it came down to needing to kill her shitty ex, I'm not sure I wouldn't capitalize on the opportunity. It's not like I have a lot to lose, and being Prue's knight in shining armor seemed like a fitting way to end my miserable existence.

The idea of spending the night with her didn't sound so bad either. Whisking her away to safety, filling her up on good food and drinks, sounds like a lot of fun. I can't wait to have her insulting me in the most painful ways. It's a nice mixture of a fun time and a pity party all in one.

I think I've gotten addicted to her licks. Not just the ones that traced my cock, but the venom in her words. They sting so good. It feels good to have someone else hurting me for a change. She doesn't know none of what she says can compare to the things I tell myself every day, but I do enjoy watching her try to break me.

I get down to the end of the cigarette before realizing it's been a decent amount of time since I heard from her. I'm aware she is a girl. Girls have a problem with getting ready on time but given the circumstances and her lack of desire to impress me, I think she would be down by now.

I call her phone, but it just rings twice before going to voice mail.

Nothing about this feels right. Cursing LA traffic under my breath, I climb out of my car.

Marching to the door of the building, I glance around the lobby through the glass door. I spot some guy in a suit leaning against the wall by the stairs. He looks far too much like some jerk who would hang around with her ex.

I pull out my phone, grateful she included the apartment number in her text message.

Pulling the door open, I let it slam shut behind me. The guy in the suit glances at me, eyeing me up and down. He must not have a good taste in music, because he doesn't seem to know who I am or consider me a threat. He glances down rather quickly.

Little does he know I fight much better than it would seem.

Walking past him, I decide to take the stairs to get a better lay of the land. I stroll up the maze of stairs and hallways until I'm at the third floor. Reading numbers of doors that make no sense to me. I finally see apartment 310, which is closer to 314 than I've been.

It's then that I hear a crash a few doors up and across the hall. I speed walk toward it. I know it's not a good thing to hear given the situation. Dread crawls up my neck.

The door reads 314, which happens to be the one she sent me. It's shut, so I tap on it. The low shouting on the other side isn't aimed at me, leaving me no choice.

Closing my eyes and cracking my neck, I suck in a deep breath. A lawsuit is the last thing I need right now, but there is no way in hell I'm just walking away from a woman in need. So much for not getting involved. Past Ben would be annoyed, and unfortunately for future Ben, he has a right to be.

I grip the handle and shove the door open, my eyes sweeping over the scene before me. He has her pinned against the wall, her wrists trapped above her head, his face inches from hers as he murmurs words I don't bother trying to catch. My gaze drops to the scratch on his cheek. Looks like she tried to fight back.

Good girl. Not that she is any match for him. I'm barely a match for him. He is tall and bulky. He has the money for steroids and endless bottles of prework out powder.

"Hello," I say, shutting the door behind me. I don't need witnesses.

Both heads snap in my direction. Her eyes widen, even as they spill tears.

"Listen, dude, this doesn't involve you," he says to me. "You shouldn't be messing with another guy's girl anyways."

"I'm not your..." He cuts her off by slamming his hand over her mouth.

Any chance of leaving without blood on my hands is dwindling.

"She is just angry with me, but we are going to work that out." he continues. There is a threat laced in his voice.

"Yeah. I don't think so," I say, taking a step closer. He doesn't like my movement, tensing up, and forcing that tension against Prue.

More tears drip down Prue's face. It shifts something inside of me. I haven't been the nicest to her, but seeing her cry like this, with another person's hands on her, fills me with a rage I didn't think I had in me.

Though as much as I want to kill this fucking prick right now, I know Prue doesn't need to see more violence, especially from me. I don't want her to associate me with violence. I'd much rather she associates me with pleasure.

But in my gut, I know she isn't going to handle the fact I've witnessed this very well. She wants to be strong and brave. She likes to act like she is the things I called her that first night. Enjoys the idea she holds some power over me, even if it's just from the fact she sucks dick better than anyone else I've come across. Now that I'm seeing her vulnerable and weak, she is going to try to push me away even harder. The insults she is going to hurl after this are going to hurt, but the price of my pain is nothing compared to saving her from this jackass.

"Dude, just leave," he snaps at me. I kind of wish I knew his name right now, but it's probably best I don't. I'd be bound to track him down and ruin his whole existence if I knew it.

"No. I think *you* should leave," I counter.

"Me? I'm her fucking boyfriend. You're just a guy in a semi famous band who her parents would be ashamed to hear she fucked."

"Ha." I laugh. I half wish his words were true. Not sure I'm going to be able to fuck her after this. "Please take your hands off her."

"This doesn't involve you, man," he groans.

"It kind of does."

"Why? Cause you fucked her? She's just a slut, and while I can't say I blame you for hitting it, you need to let it go. She is going to be my wife one day."

"I highly doubt that." I slide closer. I don't want to spook him too much, but I want to get closer to her. "Also, to be fair, I haven't fucked her. Not yet anyways, but when I do, she won't ever think about you again." I smirk when his eyes pop out at my comment.

His hands fall from her body, as he turns toward me. The point was to get his attention on me so Prue could get away, but she doesn't move. She stays pressed to the wall. Her eyes haven't left me, but they are miles away. I doubt she is aware of what is happening around her.

Disassociating is probably the best thing for her to do right now. Let her mind block out this situation with something pleasant. I know firsthand how helpful that can be. If you block out the hell around you, it makes it easier to pretend it didn't happen in the first place.

"Do you really want her that bad? You have access to models, porn stars, fucking Abbey Dark."

"Abbey is Wes's girl." I shrug.

"Like you don't share." He rolls his eyes. "Why are you so into what's mine?"

"Prue isn't yours." I laugh. "And what can I say, I like a good challenge."

"I'll give you that much. Prue is a fucking challenge, that's for sure." His eyes dart back to her. I use this moment to move closer. "But she is mine."

"No. She isn't. I really think you should leave now."

"I'm not leaving until she puts on that fucking dress and comes with me," he yells into her face. She flinches, but her eyes don't stray from me.

"Okay," I say, moving even closer. I'm right next to her now. Her ex glares at her, nostrils flaring, as she continues not to look at him. "Hey, Prue?" I speak softly. Her eyes regain focus at the sound of my voice saying her name. "Can you go put on that dress for me?" She blinks, processing my words. "I'm going to have a nice chat with this prick and make sure he knows better than to ever lay a finger on you again, okay? So go put on that dress while we talk?"

Her body doesn't move, but her lips tremble. Tears begin to drip down her face again. I wish I could let her know I'm lying. That there is no way I'm letting her go anywhere with this guy ever. That I just want her far away from this situation. I need her out of harm's way. But I can't really say that. I just hope she knows me better than that.

"Prue!" he shouts, slamming his fist into the wall beside her head.

I can't stop myself. I jump forward. Grabbing his shoulder, I push him backwards, before slipping into the space I create between Prue and him.

His body mass is a little intimidating, I'm not going to lie. All that bulk is hard muscle. It makes my body ache prematurely. The rage is vibrating off him right now and I'm reminded that he hurt her. Just by touching him, I know he is a serious threat to my wellbeing. He must have done quite a number on her. That thought makes my anger double.

"You don't want to defend her. She isn't worth it."

"Listen, fuck face. I'd defend any woman from the likes of you. It's just a matter of if I kill you or just castrate."

"I'd like to see you try." He shoves me.

The force sends me back against Prue. I can feel her jerk as she hits the wall behind her. A small gasp escapes her lips and my hands ball into fists on pure instinct.

When my fist connects with the prick's face, just below the cheek bone, he is stunned. Stepping back, creating some much-needed distance between him and Prue. I don't think he expected that much force from someone my size.

I reach behind me, gently moving Prue to the side, urging her toward the nearest door. She sticks to the wall, not moving. Her eyes are no longer on me. Instead, she looks at him with a level of fear I really don't like.

He rubs his cheek, glaring at me. I keep my composure calm, but my heart is pounding in my chest. I'm not happy about this situation. Part of me wants to hit him again. Then not stop until he is a fraction of the man he thinks he is.

Taking a step toward me, he flexes his own fists, as if he is trying to intimidate me. Outwardly I act unimpressed, but I'm aware that any hit he lands is going to hurt. But being hurt has never stopped me before. Getting my ass kicked was once a daily occurrence. My body has learned how to take a beating, and I'd be damned to die at the hands of a guy like him.

I raise my fists, letting him know I'm not about to back down.

His lips curve up, as the glare turns into amusement.

"You're going to regret that." His eyes drift toward Prue, but I move, staying in his line of sight. He doesn't get to look at her.

"Not likely," I reply.

"Fine," he shouts, causing Prue to flinch behind me. "But you should know this isn't going to end well for either of you. All you had to do, Prue, was join me for an evening of fun. Instead, you want to run around with this piece of shit." His hand waves to me, as if his insult could even bother me. "You will both live to regret this."

"Touch her again and I will fucking end you."

He laughs, shoving his hands in his pockets. Strolling toward the door, he holds his head up high, like he somehow won the fight when I was the only one who landed a punch. When the door slams shut behind him, the walls rattle from the force. I turn to look at Prue.

Her eyes are zeroed in on the door, as if she is waiting for him to return. The look on her face reminds me, once again, that I'm dealing with a broken girl. She can pretend all she wants, but whatever he did, hurt her far worse than she cares to let on.

"Prue," I say, reaching forward to touch her. She doesn't react to my touch. That's either a sign she trusts me or a sign she is too deep in her head to notice. I let my hand stroke the back of her head, checking for any signs of damage from when she hit the wall. "Are you okay?"

Her eyes blink, softening a bit as if she is slowly slipping back to the real world. Her eyes zone in on me. She stares at me for a second before pressing her lips against mine.

I'm dazed for just a moment as her lips move against mine. I just let it happen, even letting my lips move back, before I snap to my senses.

"Prue," I mumble, pulling my lips back just slightly. They are still touching. She follows the movement of my words, letting her tongue slip into my mouth. Her tongue grazes my teeth as she explores my mouth.

This is not good. I know she isn't in the right frame of mind to be kissing me like this, but her lips feel so soft against mine. Her mouth is so warm and inviting. There is a part of me that just wants to get lost in the moment. Maybe this would be good for her. Break whatever spell he has over her.

But if I let this continue, I'm no better than him. She needs time to process what just happened.

I try to pull away. Maybe not with as much force as I should, but I'm trying not to hurt her fragile mental state.

She nips at my bottom lip as I try to slip away. Following my step backwards, she lets her teeth clamp down on my bottom lip.

"Fuck," I groan, finally breaking free from her. My tongue runs over the area she bit, checking for blood. "Prue. What the fuck?"

"I'm sorry," she mumbles, pressing her hands into her face as a sob escapes her lips.

That probably wasn't the best reaction on my part, but it took me by surprise. I sigh, walking up to her. My hands take ahold of her shoulders. This time she tries to jerk away. I don't let her slip from my hold.

"Prue. It's okay. I'm sorry. It just took me by surprise." I keep my voice as soothing as I can. "Can you look at me, baby?" She shakes her head. "Please?" I press, letting one hand touch her chin, tilting her head up.

Her eyes open. Sky blue hues peek up at me, as a few tears trickle down her face.

"I'm sorry I yelled."

"I'm sorry I bit you." Her voice is so low it nearly breaks my heart.

"That's okay." I offer her a smile. "It was kind of hot, to be honest."

Her eyes roll, even though they are still filled with tears.

"I'm sorry," she says again. "That you had to deal with him."

"No. I'm sorry *you* had to deal with him," I correct her, letting my thumb stroke her cheek. Her skin is so soft compared to my calloused fingers. Years of strumming the guitar made my fingers rough. Never bothered me before, but now I wish they were soft enough to offer her comfort.

"Thank you." She nods.

"Are you okay?"

"No." She laughs. "Not at all."

"I mean are you physically hurt?"

"I'm fine." She shrugs. "You should go. I feel bad for ruining your night."

"There is not a chance in hell I'm leaving you here alone," I say as she steps away from me.

"He has some event to go to. He isn't coming back. I'll be fine."

"That is not a risk I'm willing to take."

"I'm not your responsibility, Ben."

"I know that," I say, though at this moment she kind of feels like my responsibility. And I don't mind it as much as I thought I would. I'm sure somewhere Wes is getting the sense of my impending doom. "But I owe you for last night."

"I really just want to be alone."

"Yeah, see... I don't think that's a good idea." I smile. "And frankly I'm just a big enough asshole to not care about what you want. Why don't we still go out? We'll grab some food, hit up a few bars, and I'll crash on the couch after."

She sighs, folding her arms over her chest. Her hip sticks out as she studies me. She is probably trying to decide what mean thing to say next. What name will she hurl at me? What insult can she throw at me? And how bad will it hurt?

I try to hide how excited I am to hear whatever she is thinking about saying. I don't want her to know I secretly enjoy the verbal abuse. That would just make her want to be nice to me. She is evil like that. A little vixen that has been put in my life to help me self-destruct.

"You still want to hang out with me?" she asks. It takes me a moment to accept she isn't going to add a kick to the balls at the end of that question.

"Yeah?" I shrug. "Why wouldn't I?"

"You call me a bitch, among other things. You keep saying how difficult I am. Then there is the little matter of my freak out this morning, and you literally just had to assault my ex to keep him from hurting me. Why the hell would you still want to be around me?"

"You're the best cock sucker in town." I smirk. Her eyes roll, even as her lips curve up into a small smile. "Please, Prue. Just come out with me, okay? I promise to be less of an asshole."

"Is that even possible?"

"I think I can manage being a decent person for one night."

"I'm not holding my breath." She laughs, shaking her head.

"So?"

"Okay. Just give me a few minutes to fix my makeup."

"I'll wait right here." I grin at her.

When she disappears into the room, I pull out my phone. I glance through the notifications. Seeing two missed calls from Wes should be a reminder that getting involved with Prue is a bad idea. All I have to do is call him. I know he would talk some sense into me. Remind me of what is on the line if I let myself get caught up in a girl's chaos again.

But it's far too late for him to save me. I'm fully sucked into the storm that surrounds Prue now. There is no turning back if I wanted to, but I don't want to.

That should be the ultimate sign that things are going to end poorly, but I have a habit of ignoring red flashing signs. All the No Smoking, Emergency Exit, and No Crowd Surfing signs never stopped me. They mean nothing to me. I embrace the chaos, just like I am with Prue, now.

ELEVEN

Prue

Once again, I find myself staring into the bathroom mirror. My face is blotchy from crying. I apply a cold cloth to it, hoping to soothe some of it away. I also try to fix my makeup. If I'm going to go out with Ben, I don't want to look like the sad girl I've seemed to become.

I can't believe I let Charles put his hands on me again. When I opened the door and saw him standing there, I was too stunned to scream. Even when he pushed me inside and began berating me for trying to skip out on going with him, I couldn't find it in myself to scream.

I only tried to escape when he pushed me against the wall. Slapping him resulted in him shoving me harder. From that moment all fight left my body.

Even when Ben came walking in, I didn't have the strength to try to remove myself from the situation. I couldn't. My mind wandered back to being a little kid and getting put in time out because I spilled my juice on my mother's rug. From there it was like an endless trip through memory lane as I tried to figure out how my life got to this point.

Where did I go wrong? I simply don't know.

Having Ben defend me made me feel worse. It shouldn't. I

know that. He saved me from another beating. I should be grateful, but I never wanted him to see me vulnerable again. This morning was bad enough, but having him step in to save me from Charles' fury was not what I wanted to happen. Just having him come whisk me away was bad, this showed him just how broken I truly am.

Kissing him added a layer to this nightmare I wasn't expecting. I already knew what his lips felt like, but in the moment, they felt like safety. This morning it was all lust, but just moments ago, it was different.

I don't know why my mind snapped. A self-preservation attempt to cover up the fact I was almost a victim yet again, I guess. But Ben pulled away. Something I'm both grateful for and a little hurt by. I know why he did it. Now it's apparent that under that asshole exterior Ben Parker has a heart. He has a limit to his cruelty, and a moral compass that far out reaches the people I'm used to having in my life.

I can't deny the fact that seeing that side of him did something to me. I had planned on using Ben as a distraction. I just wanted to have sex with him and never see him again. That idea is slipping from my grasps now. No longer do I think I'll be able to get rid of him without feeling the loss in my gut.

The guy has been far nicer to me than anyone in my life, besides Cameron. He may call me names and make fun of me, but he does it in a way that makes me feel good. Like nothing he says is supposed to hurt me. In a way, it doesn't. Not one word he said has caused me any level of pain comparable to what my own parents have said.

I'm afraid I'm starting to like Ben and that's not something I can afford. Especially knowing I don't have much say in my future. Just convincing my parents to not make me marry Charles is going to be hard enough. Asking them to let me even talk to Ben would be a miracle.

Plus, it's not like Ben is offering me anything permanent. I'm not entirely sure why he keeps coming around. I'm certain given enough time that ends. He is still an asshole, a morally sound one, but an asshole, nonetheless.

When I'm done touching up my makeup, I throw on a leather jacket, then I head back to the living room.

Ben is lounging on the couch. His lanky legs are outstretched on the coffee table as he mindlessly scrolls through his phone. Music plays softly from his phone. Some song I don't know, but he seems to as he hums along to it.

"Ready?" I ask.

He glances up at me, locking his phone. His eyes roam over my body, as if he hasn't already seen me tonight. Resting on my face, as he pushes himself to his feet.

"If you are." The music stops on his phone as he slides it into his pockets. "You look really good in a plaid skirt. Giving me all kinds of high school flashbacks." He smirks.

"Are you driving?"

"I had planned on it, yeah."

"But you plan on drinking tonight."

"Yes. But not a lot."

"What do you consider a lot?"

"Last night comes close."

"That was a little more than a lot in my book."

"Yeah? Would you feel more comfortable if I ordered us a car?"

"Yes."

"I'm insulted that you'd think I'd risk your life, but fine."

"I don't think you'd see it as a risk until it ended badly, but with our combine finances there is no reason to drink and drive."

"Okay." He rolls his eyes. "I'll call us a car then."

"I can pay."

"I don't need your money, Prue." He grins. "But I do need a cigarette, so why don't we wait outside."

The air is chilly tonight, and I pull my leather jacket tightly around my body, ignoring the soreness in my back from when Charles shoved me into the wall. I try to push all thoughts of him out of my mind as Ben inhales his cigarette, staring off toward the street.

I can't take my eyes off him. It's halfway past seven. All the streetlights have turned on, even though the sun isn't completely down. They illuminate Ben and me. For some reason they make him look way too hot for his own good.

It's not like I didn't already know what girls saw in him, but after everything that has happened tonight, watching him smoke a cigarette in the evening night just makes him look... *attractive*.

His black denim jacket is unbuttoned, showing off a black band tee of some band I never heard up. Tight black skinny jeans hug his body, tucked into black doc martens. His blond hair is a mess like always. Strands blowing every way in the light breeze.

I never got to picture myself with anyone other than stuck up rich guys. The tiny taste of freedom I have right now, has me wondering if I could be a rock star's girlfriend. Not that that would be Ben. I don't think he is the commitment type.

"You shouldn't smoke." I cut through the silence.

"Why not?" His eyes dart to me.

"It's bad for you."

"I think a lot of what I do is bad for me."

"But smoking is a like really bad. It leads to lung cancer and taints the tips of your fingers."

"It's not that bad, compared to the other things I have put in my body."

"Like?"

"Heroin," he says, so nonchalantly, it takes me a second to process his words.

"Heroin?"

"Yeah." He shrugs. "I've done heroin a few times. Meth too but not nearly as much."

"When."

"Years ago. I wasn't addicted or anything, but you know, I think smoking isn't nearly as bad as those things."

"Yeah." I nod, studying him. What in the world could've

made him do heroin? He isn't stupid. It's not some big secret how those drugs could mess up your whole life. Why would he do it? What would make him risk his whole world for drugs?

"Have you ever done any drugs?"

"Pot. Once when I was like thirteen."

"Jesus, Prue." He laughs. "You are way too fucking good for me."

"For..."

"Car is here." He motions to a black car pulling up before I have a chance to ask what he means by his statement.

He holds open the door, ushering me in. He lets me slide to the other side before climbing in after me. I do my seat belt up, eyeing him until he does the same.

"Where are we going?" I ask, as the car pulls away from the curb.

"My favorite burger joint. You do eat meat, right?"

"Yes."

"Wasn't sure since you are so fucking pale."

"I have low iron, asshole." I push his shoulder with my hand.

"You don't say?" He grins at me.

"I thought you said you wouldn't be an asshole tonight?"

"And I thought you knew I was a liar."

"God," I groan. "What did I get myself into?"

"A good time. Relax." His hand falls to my thigh.

My eyes stare down at where his hand touches me. I don't seem to mind the physical contact, but it's a strange gesture. I don't know how to feel about it. He quickly pulls his hand back, pulling his phone from his pocket.

I watch as he scrolls through his phone a bit, curious what he is looking at. Maybe he is on some dating site looking for a girl to ditch me for. Or looking for the next party to go to where he can get lucky.

"Have you ever had a girlfriend?" I ask after a few minutes of silence.

"Yeah. One or two, but it's been years. Commitment is hard in my line of work."

"Or just for you." I challenge back with a laugh.

"That's probably part of it. I'm not very good at being tied down."

"No?" I raise an eyebrow at him with a sly smile on my face.

"Not like that." He laughs. "Though, I've never tried that before."

"Would you let me tie you down?"

"Yes," he says far quicker than I thought he would. It makes my stomach flutter, more so when his eyes stare into mine. Lust fills his eyes and for some reason that has my pussy throbbing. He still wants me after everything he witnessed. "I'm not sure there is much I wouldn't let you do to me."

"Oh. I'm sure I could find something." I grin at him. "I could put a finger in your ass."

"I'm not a huge fan of that, but if you want to try it, by all means." He shrugs, a smirk tugging at his lips.

"You've done that before?"

"I've had a lot of sex, Prue. There isn't much I haven't done."

"Hmm." I tap my chin, trying to hide my shock. I know for a fact he has tried a lot of things. The gossip sites didn't skip out on the details, but hearing he is willing to let me do things to him has me craving to break him. If only to say I did. I want to find the thing that makes Ben crack.

"Keep thinking. I'm sure you'll find my line at some point. If not, I look forward to you trying." He laughs, scrolling through his phone some more.

"What are you looking at?"

"Bands."

"Bands?"

"There is this list of bands that have a need for a guitarist. I'm seeing if there are any good ones out there."

"Why? Don't you have a band?"

"For now." He shrugs. "Aaron is having a baby. Wes is on

probation, and I highly doubt he will ever do a tour without Abbey. That's going to limit us."

"You think your band is going to break up?"

"I don't know, but I want to be prepared if it does."

"You could do that? Just jump to another band?"

"I don't want to, but I need music. It's hard for me to not be playing. These last two months have been hell for me. Every one of them have been enjoying the break, but it's killing me." He runs his hand through his hair, looking out the window. "Obviously, I would pick playing with them if I could, but if they don't want to do it anymore, what else can I do?"

I shrug.

I didn't realize how much music meant to him. I've been around band guys a bit, given my brother's passion for music. A lot of them just enjoy the fame that comes with being a rock star. Sure, they liked music, but I think if they could be famous, make good money and rarely have to play the music, they'd be just as happy.

Not Ben. He seems to crave it. Maybe he can't do commitment because he is too committed to music.

"What are you going to school for?" He glances at me.

"Nothing really. I never really had a passion. I'm just trying to get my AA while deciding what to major in. I think Cameron got all the passion in the family. I go to school, get good grades, and stay out of trouble so our parents don't make a big deal about him wanting to be a rock star."

"That's very sad."

"What?" My jaw drops at the nerve of him. I think it's pretty nice of me, not sad.

"You have nothing you are passionate about? Nothing at all? There isn't a single thing that brings you joy?"

"I guess at some point I gave up all my dreams so Cameron could live out his."

"What did you want to be when you were a kid?"

"The same as any other kid. A teacher, a vet, president. I did like art when I was younger. I'm not very good at it, but I do like to draw and paint when I have free time."

"See! That's something. Why don't you do something with that?"

"I'm not good at it." I shrug. "Plus, it's not like my parents would pay for art school. They want me to have a useful degree."

"What do they consider useful?"

"Honestly, something that looks good on paper. I don't think they expect me to have a career."

"What's the plan for you after college then? Marry that dick and pop out a few kids? Be some wine drunk housewife?"

"Pretty much. That's what they expect of me."

"Fuck that," he says. "You should do what you want to do, Prue. You don't owe them anything. What do you want to do with your life?"

"Not be the golden child anymore," I say softly. "I want to do something stupid and not have to worry about what people will say or how much it will disappoint my parents."

"Okay. We can work with that. What did you have in mind?"

"I don't know. I guess I'm open to suggestions."

"I think a sex tape could be a good start." He smirks, and I roll my eyes. "No? Hmm. What about nipple piercings?"

"Sounds painful. Plus, I could easily hide those."

"Not if you made a sex tape after."

"I'm not making a sex tape." I laugh.

"It was worth a try." He laughs.

"A tattoo," I say, grinning at him. "I could get a tattoo."

"Oh right. Tattoos are frowned upon by some people. I tend to forget that." He glances down at his body. Even as it is covered in a jacket, a few peek out on his wrists and neck.

"Does it hurt?"

"Depends on who you ask." He shrugs. "I find it very relaxing, but I know others who hate the feeling."

"Do you regret any of yours?"

"Most, but at the same time, not really. They all meant something to me in the moment. They each come with a memory I rather have than not."

I nod.

"Prue. Do you want to get a tattoo tonight? I know a guy who owes me a favor. One text and it's done."

"No." I shake my head. My parents would be mortified if I came back with a tattoo. While being rebellious is the reasoning behind the idea, I can't risk getting on their bad side any more than I will be when I demand to not marry Charles. "I'm not trying to end up with an infection."

"He is legit. Has a shop a few blocks from the restaurant."

"I can't get a tattoo. That's Cameron's thing. My parents would freak out if they knew I got one too."

"Is that not the point?" he asks, as the car comes to a stop.

"No." I sigh.

He slides out of the car, offering his hand out to me. I take it, letting him help me out of the car. Pulling me close for a moment, his ocean eyes sparkle with a glint of desire. My heart skips a beat, as time seems to freeze for a moment.

His lips tug up into a smile. My head bends forward just slightly, desperate to feel his soft lips against mine again.

"I bet a tattoo would look great on you. I think underneath the prim and proper outfit you put on, is a very wild girl who wants to rebel. And you know what, Prue? I'd love to meet her."

I laugh. "You are insane. There isn't a single part of me that is rebellious. That's all Cameron."

"The way you deep throated my cock tells a different story." He smirks.

I shove him and he releases his hold on me with a laugh.

"Can you not say that so loud?" I roll my eyes.

He just laughs again, leading me to the front of a restaurant, holding the door open for me. It's small, but the décor screams that it's high class. I see some kind of award pinned to the wall behind the hostess. For some reason I assumed it would be a dirty hole in the wall when he mentioned burgers, not an actual restaurant.

He strides up to the hostess and I follow behind him.

"Table for two."

The lady looks up from the screen she was staring at. She must know him because her lips scrunch up as her eyes turn into daggers. I almost want to check to see if I'm bleeding even though they aren't pointed at me.

"Ben," she says his name like it's poison.

"Hello, Sherry. I'd prefer a booth in the back, but whatever is available is fine. Who's cooking tonight? Paul or Stan?"

"We don't serve your kind here," she snaps.

Ben chuckles and she intensifies her glare. "I highly doubt Victor would approve of you talking to such a loyal customer that way. And in front of a guest, no less. Tsk tsk." He shakes a finger at her. "Now there is no need to get your panties in a bunch, if you are wearing any, that is. I made it perfectly clear it was a one-time thing."

"You failed to mention you also fucked Claire."

"That wasn't my information to share." He shrugs. "There is no need to be hurt. She wasn't nearly as much fun as you."

"Is she as much fun as me?" Sherry nods in my direction.

"No. She isn't fun at all." Ben flashes me a grin. "She is an old stick in the mud, but I think I can loosen her up."

"Run," Sherry says to me before grabbing two menus. "Follow me," she huffs over her shoulders.

"You are terrible," I whisper to Ben.

"Yes. Yes, I am." He smiles at me.

I didn't need further proof that Ben was a playboy. Though seeing it in person reminds me, I may have his attention right now, but that's not going to last.

I should be grateful, but I only find myself disappointed. I could get used to having him around.

TWELVE

Sherry tosses the menus on the table, shooting me one more glare before walking away.

I'd feel bad, but she knew who she was sleeping with. It's not like it's some big secret. I was up front about it.

"She seems nice," Prue says with a smirk. She slides into one side of the booth.

"It's not my fault girls think they can tame me." I shrug, sliding into the booth across from her. "I'm unattainable and untamable."

Rolling her eyes, she picks up the menu, studying it like there is going to be a test. I've been here enough times that I don't need to look at a menu. I get the same thing almost every time. I take to just watching her make faces as she reads it.

It's cute. Her forehead scrunches up. Her head tilts to the side. She nods to herself, occasionally, tapping parts of the page. Her eyes glance up at me, annoyance flashing across her face.

I shouldn't like the way she looks at me like I'm the most frustrating guy on the planet, but it makes me happy.

"Have you been watching me this whole time?"

"Yes. Because you are so fucking fascinating."

Her eyes spin in circles for the billion time since meeting me. I wonder how much longer until the things fall out of their sockets. They must have been acrobats in a past life, the way they do loops all the time.

"What are you getting?"

"A BBQ bacon double cheeseburger and a large fry. You?"

"A junior cheeseburger."

"That's why you have low iron. A junior-fucking-cheeseburger? Fucking hell. No. You are not getting a junior cheeseburger, or they will think I'm on a date with a minor."

"It's not a date," she challenges.

"Doesn't mean shit what it is, it's about how it looks." I grab the menu from her hands. Skimming it for the first time in months, I try to find something she might like. "Okay. You'll get a glam burger with fries."

"You can't just decide what I'm going to eat. That's extremely rude." She folds her arms over her chest. "I can't eat that much food."

"So don't finish it." I shrug, tossing the menu on the table. "But you are not ordering a junior cheeseburger on my watch."

"Fine." Her eyes roll again. "If you're going to force me to indulge, I also want a strawberry milkshake."

"Would you like that with a cherry on top?" I grin.

"Yes," she shoots back.

After we order, she takes to glancing around the restaurant. Lavish Royal is one of my favorite restaurants. Its simple food is done classy. It's won many awards for taste alone, yet the vibe is a mix of upscale and edgy.

When I found this place, I swore I'd never sleep with anyone who works here. Didn't want to risk being thrown out, but after getting to know the owner, and the plenty of hot women he hired, that went right out the window.

He would pick keeping me as a customer than any girl who decided to throw a fit over me sleeping with them and never calling them back. Not sure he will ever make boss of the year like that, but with food as good as his cooks serve, it doesn't matter.

I also swore I'd never bring a girl here. I didn't need one of my hook ups finding out about this place. They might want to return. While I'm sure Victor would kick them out over me, I don't want to make him do that.

So as Prue studies the place, to avoid looking at me, I sit with the fact I'm breaking a lot of my rules for her. I don't like it. I don't like the way she makes me feel at all.

I'm not stupid. It's not like I haven't liked a girl before. I know what a crush feels like. Couldn't be immune to that if I wanted. It's human nature to feel drawn to people, especially pretty girls, but it's never been like *this*.

I normally entertain a girl for a few hours, sleep with her, and move on to the next. With Prue I find myself not ready to move on yet. That might change when I actually fuck her, but until then I'm forced to sit with these warm, fuzzy feelings.

And I hate them.

"Where are we going after this?" she finally asks, resting her eyes on me.

"We are going to get you a tattoo."

"I'm not getting a tattoo." She tucks a strand of her short hair behind her ear.

"Oh. Yes, you are. It's now my job to bring out the rebellious girl trapped inside of you. I owe it to the world."

She laughs. "It was just a fun idea, Ben. I can't really get a tattoo. Unless…"

"Unless?" I question. I can tell by the tone in her voice that I'm not going to like whatever answer she gives. Her evilness knows no bounds when it comes to me. She is trouble, and I'm addicted to it.

"Unless you get one too." She grins. "And I get to pick what you get."

"Okay." I shrug. If that is her master plan to try to get out of getting a tattoo, she has no idea who she is messing with. I'm damn near out of space, at least anywhere visible, but she doesn't seem to realize that I have very little shame. "I accept your terms and conditions. We will both get tattoos."

"I hope your guy is familiar with the male appendage." She smirks.

"Probably not as familiar as you." She sticks her tongue out at me, as her eyes light up. "Don't tease."

"I almost got my tongue pierced once. It was a dare, but I chickened out."

"What a shame."

"That was the closest I've ever been to being drunk."

"Oh fuck, Prue. Really? You don't drink?" I groan, resting my head on the table. This girl has no idea what fun is, and I'm going to suffer trying to teach her how to have it.

"I drink. A little. A glass of wine here and there. I like cosmos." She shrugs, as I peer up at her. "I've been focused on behaving, unlike you."

"We are getting you a tattoo and then you are getting drunk."

"No. I don't want a hangover."

"I make no promises, but you are going to have some fucking fun for once in your damn life and I'm going to be there to watch."

"You'll make sure no one drugs me or kidnaps me too, right?"

"I'll make sure you're safe." I sit up.

"Promise?" She eyes me carefully. "You won't ditch me for some hot chick?"

"No. I'm all yours for tonight."

"Then fine. I'll get a tattoo and let you get me drunk."

"You're going to have a great night." I flash her a grin. The idea she trusts me enough to go along with this makes me unreasonably happy. "What tattoo are you going to get?"

"Oh. I don't know. Didn't think that far."

I pull out my phone, sending a text to my buddy Greg, asking him to set aside some time for two tattoos tonight. It shouldn't be a problem. I've sent him enough work that his shop has become one of the more famous ones in town.

"No ideas?"

"No." She shrugs. "What do girls normally get? Butterflies?"

"You are not getting butterflies unless you get them as a tramp stamp, flying out of your ass."

She rolls her eyes. "I just want something small. Somewhere I can cover up, but also show off from time to time."

"Hmm." I grab a napkin from the table, pulling a sharpie out of my pocket. I always carry one in case a fan wants an autograph or I feel like defacing some property. "You are not getting a butterfly tattoo. Or an anchor. Or any of that basic bullshit. If you are going to do this, you do it right." I glance up at her. "If it's going to be an act of rebellion and on your body forever, it deserves to be beautiful."

Staring up at her, then back at the napkin, I ponder all the things that would be fitting for her. To the whole world she looks like a normal rich girl. Well-behaved. Good student. Perfect trophy wife material. But I know better than that.

Uncapping the sharpie, I take to drawing the only thing that seems fitting for a girl like Prue.

She may look like an angel, but underneath that halo rest two horns that desperately want to be unleashed.

I plan on helping them come out.

THIRTEEN

Prue

BEN'S HAND MOVES ACROSS THE NAPKIN. EVEN AS THE server brings our food, setting it on the table, Ben just sighs, flips over the napkin and scribbles away. His hand moves quickly, forming lines and curves until an image of a set of horns surrounded by a broken halo appears.

I had no idea he knew how to draw. It's beautiful. Simple, but well done.

He sits up straight, glancing up at me, before turning the napkin toward me.

"My guy will make it better, but what do you think? I mean it's just an idea." He shrugs.

"It's perfect." My voice is full of emotions I can't name.

Sliding my plate in front of me, he grabs a fry off his own.

"You are a good girl trying to be bad. Might as well have the mark to show it." He smirks.

I wish the way he teased me didn't make me feel safer than I've ever felt before. It's like he doesn't care if his words cut me, because he assumes I can take it. With him I can. I know he is just playing around, teasing me in a way no one else ever has.

He doesn't see me as fragile, even after everything he has witnessed. It's like seeing me freak out or watching Charles put his hands on me didn't affect how he sees me. Ben doesn't let the things I've been through warp how he views me.

I wish I could do the same. I wish I didn't see myself as weak and pathetic. I desperately want to be the girl Ben sees me as. Tough. Bitchy. Mean.

"Eat," he says, lifting his own burger to his mouth.

"My mother would have a stroke if she saw me eating a burger this big."

"Why?" he asks before taking a bite. A sound like those he makes when his cock is in my mouth comes out. Never thought I'd be jealous of a burger. My pussy clenches, wishing it was me making him make those sounds again.

"It's a lot of calories."

"So, she is one of *those* mothers." He shakes his head, wiping at the corner of his mouth, where a bit of sauce sits. "Trust me. You could stand to gain a few pounds. I wish more girls would embrace being curvy."

"Says the man with zero body fat." I laugh, taking a bite of the burger in front of me.

"I wish I was thicker." He smiles. "I got called a twig my whole life."

Biting into the burger my mouth is full of one of the best tasting things I've ever had. The mixture of the juicy meat, toasted bun, melted cheese and just a tiny bit of sauce has my tongue exploding with flavor.

I rarely eat burgers. My mother thought burgers were too messy for proper young ladies to eat. I grew up on fine dining, using forks and spoons, never eating with my hands. I've been missing out.

"Wow. This is really good."

"Isn't it?" He grins. "Happy you have more to eat, huh?"

"Yes." I laugh. "Though I'm not sure I'll be able to finish the whole thing. Which would be such a waste."

"Just enjoy as much as you can. I promise to bring you back here again."

I smile at the idea, even if deep down I doubt he means it. The idea he is thinking about doing something in the future with me gives me hope that whatever is going on between us has a longer shelf life than his other hook ups.

We eat in silence for a few minutes. He glances at his phone a few times. I try not to read too much into it. He made plans with me. I don't think he would ditch me now that I agreed to get a tattoo and get drunk with him.

I eat over half of my burger and most of my fries. Stealing sips of the strawberry shake between bites, before giving up. I'm fuller than I've ever been in my whole life.

Sitting back, I watch as Ben devours his burger, slowly, like he is savoring every bite. Right now, he doesn't look like the sexy bad boy the media paints him as. He is just some cute guy, enjoying his food and my company.

Sighing, he picks up his phone.

"Hey," he says into it, annoyance causing his brows to scrunch. "Fine, but can we make it Sunday? I think I have plans tomorrow." His eyes focus on me, and I glance down on the napkin with my future tattoo on it. "Oh well, fuck me for having a life, I guess. You all get to blow me off for yours, but the minute I have something going on..." He rolls his eyes. "Okay, fine. I get it. I'm the asshole so I'll just adjust my plans to fit your life. No need to be so fucking dramatic, Aaron." He shakes his head. "That's a little rich coming from you. Jesus. Fuck. Fine. I will meet you for lunch tomorrow. Is Stacy coming?" Pausing again, his eyes roll. "I'll send her a fucking fruit basket, but can't it just be us this one fucking time?" Sighing in defeat, his shoulders slump. "Okay. Okay. God. I'm not heartless. See you tomorrow."

He drops his phone to the table, groaning as he pushes his palms into his eyes.

"Trouble with the misses?" I ask. His hands drop, revealing his eyes and a small smile on his face. "He sounds lovely."

"Just for that, you're coming to lunch with me tomorrow."

"No. I'm going to be hungover, aren't I?"

"You'll be fine. I'll teach you all my tricks." He grins. "Please, Prue? Just come with me."

"Maybe."

"I can work with maybe."

The server comes by a moment later, setting the bill on the table. Ben throws down his card before picking up another fry.

"Do you bring all your girls here?"

"No. I like this place too much." He leans back, staring at me. "But since you won't let me fuck you, I figured it was safe to bring you." He smirks.

"So, if I asked you to fuck me in the bathroom right now, you'd say no?"

"No. I like this place a lot, but I want to fuck you more."

"Why?"

"Like I told that prick earlier. I like a challenge."

The server passes by, and Ben holds out the bill to him.

"Thank you for that," I say softly, looking at the table.

"Don't thank me for being a decent person. I know the bar is low, but I hope it's not that low."

My stomach tenses. I'm still not happy with the fact he saw me in the situation. It makes me feel too vulnerable and exposed. Part of me wishes I knew more about him. That I could see him in the same kind of state too.

He's seen me at a low, and in turn I'd see him in one of his own.

"You said you were abused. By whom? Your dad?" I peek up at him. Hoping whatever confession comes out of him will even the playing field.

He tenses for a moment. His eyes drift to stare at something behind me. I regret asking the question now.

The check is dropped on the table, and Ben reaches for it, signing it and adding a tip.

"Sorry," I whisper.

"I'm afraid the ship has sailed on that secret," he says, glancing up at me. "But no, it wasn't my dad. My father was a good man. I think if he knew what was happening to me, he would've killed the person responsible, but I never told a soul about it." Slipping his card into his wallet. "Even mentioning it to you was a once in a lifetime confession. One I would appreciate you forgetting."

I nod.

"Now, let's go get you a tattoo." He smiles, as if the conversation never happened at all.

We stand inside a tattoo parlor. His guy, Greg, gives us paperwork to sign, while Ben hands him the drawing he made.

"I'm sure you can make it better," Ben says.

"Where does she want it?"

Ben glances over at me, raising his eyebrow.

"Oh. I don't know." I glance down at my body. "My ankle I guess."

"No. That's a very boney area. I don't know how you're going to handle the feeling. That is not the best place to start," Ben says.

"I can handle a little pain." I roll my eyes. "I want it on my ankle."

Ben looks over to Greg, but Greg just shrugs.

"If that's where she wants it, that's where I'll put it."

"Fine." Ben shakes his head. "But don't say I didn't warn you."

"Remove your shoes and socks," Greg says. "I'll go set everything up. Have you decided what you're getting?"

Ben looks at me. I shrug.

"Still deciding," Ben says.

Ben stands as I sit on the bench, removing my shoes.

"What side should I get it on?"

"Whatever side you want." He shrugs. "You should be more concerned about what you are going to have me get."

"A dick. I'm having you get a nice giant penis."

"Okay. Where?"

"Face."

"No. Try again."

"You'd get a dick if I told you to?" I ask, sliding off my socks.

"Sure, but I draw the line at a face tattoo."

I look at him. He is insane. He doesn't care what I pick for him. I'm pretty sure he would get anything I tell him to get without a single complaint.

"Do you even have space for another tattoo?"

"Probably not on the arms, but maybe on my back or legs."

"And you really don't care what I make you get?"

"Not at all." He grins.

"Okay. I won't make it a dick, but you don't get to know what it is until it's done." I cross my arms over my chest.

"You are so bossy." He smiles. I shoot him a look. "I said bossy, not the other b-word."

"Only because we are in company," I shoot back, walking over to where Greg sits, setting up. "Do you have any paper? I need to draw something for him to get tattooed."

Greg glances at Ben. He waits until Ben nods before passing me a piece of paper and pen.

"Here you go. Now sit here. I need to clean the area and place the stencil."

I sit on the bench, holding out my left leg toward him. He grips it, spraying it with some stuff, while I look at the blank piece of paper.

Too many ideas are swimming around my mind. Part of me wants to draw a butterfly just to be a bitch. Or maybe a heart with some random girl's name in it just to ruin his life. But once I put the pen to paper all I manage to draw is a set of devil horns attached to a broken heart.

If he is giving me a broken halo, I think a broken heart is fitting for him. I fold the paper in half, so Ben can't see it. Glancing down, I watch Greg place the stencil on my ankle.

"Is that good?"

Ben looks over his shoulder. I have no idea if it looks right or not. When Ben's eyes meet mine, I stare back, trying to gauge what he thinks of the placement. He nods to me.

"Yes," I say, holding out the piece of paper to Greg. "And this is what he is getting. But he doesn't get to see it until after."

Ben closes his eyes as Greg unfolds it. When Greg laughs, Ben just shakes his head.

"It's a dick, isn't it?" Ben asks. "At least tell me it's an impressive dick."

"It's not a dick. Just fitting." Greg laughs again. "Where is he getting it?" Folding it back up, he slides it on his table.

"Placed like a tramp stamp." I grin.

"Ha!" Ben laughs. "That would be something."

"I honestly don't know. Take off your shirt." Ben's eyes snap open, looking at me. "It's not like there aren't pictures all over the internet of you shirtless. Plus, I've already seen you naked."

"I like her." Greg smiles.

"Glad someone does." Ben smirks, slipping off his jacket. He drapes it over a nearby chair, moving closer to me. Pulling his shirt over his head he tosses it at me. "Happy?"

"Turn for me." I swirl my finger, as Greg starts up the tattoo gun.

"Stay still," Greg says. "If it hurts too much, let me know, but once I get going, you'll either have to let me finish or end up with a fucked-up line, got it?"

"Yeah," I say as Ben slowly turns around, letting me look over his body. I spot a decent size empty space on his left shoulder blade. "Left shoulder blade. He will get it on his left shoulder blade."

"Okay." Greg nods. "I'm going to start now. Ready?"

I nod as Ben turns around. He steps toward me, offering me his hand. I don't take it. I'm determined to not need it. It can't be that bad if so many people are covered in them. I can handle this.

The first stab of the needle makes me gasp, but it repeats so quickly I don't even know if it's the first one or the hundredth now. It doesn't hurt, not really. It feels more like getting scratched than anything else. I glance at Ben whose eyes are glued to me.

"You okay, baby?" His voice is low.

"Yeah. I think so. It just feels weird."

"I like the feeling."

"I might too."

It's weird and a bit uncomfortable. Also peaceful. Out of all the pain I've felt recently, this bit of discomfort is going to lead to something beautiful, instead of just misery. So I'll endure it.

I relax, letting my head fall back against the chair, Ben rests his hand above my head. I can feel his eyes still on me, but I turn my attention to what Greg is doing to my ankle.

I know I'm getting his artwork on me. That would probably mean something to other people, but my act of rebellion is mine alone. The art he could own, but the tattoo itself is all mine. My little act of defiance.

Greg moves the needle to a higher part of my ankle, and I wince. He is now working over the bone which is a bit more painful than peaceful. My hand reaches up, on its own, seeking Ben's comfort. I don't have time to pull it away before Ben takes it.

"He won't be there long," he whispers in my ear as he draws circles in my palm. "You are doing so well. I bet you'll be back in this chair soon, needing another fix."

"No," I say softly. Not because it hurts, but if I get any more, my parents would disown me for sure.

Greg moves away from the boney part of my ankle, and I relax again.

"That was the worst of it," Ben says into my ear again. "He just about finished with the horns. You could stop now if you want."

I shake my head.

"Good girl. I knew you could take it."

My stomach flutters at his words and I try to keep my composure. I don't need him getting the wrong idea. I highly doubt I'm going to be able to fuck him any time soon, if ever.

After a little longer Greg finishes, setting the gun on the table beside him.

"Fuck. Okay," Ben says suddenly. "I swear I always block this part out. I'm so sorry."

"What?" I look up, just as Greg sprays something on my skin and presses a towel over it.

It stings and burns. I gasp in agony as he pats the cloth against my sore skin.

"I am so sorry, but it's over now. Only lasted a second."

"I should've made it a dick!" I slap at his arm.

He laughs.

"Everyone hates that part," Greg says, as he starts to wrap plastic around my ankle. "You can wear your sock and boot for the rest of the night but be sure to air it out. Ben will show you what lotion to put on it. Don't use any soap or lotion with scent on it for like a month, okay?"

"Yeah." I swing my leg over the side of the table. My ankle aches a little. I glance down to see Ben's design inked into my skin, and it feels worth it.

Ben helps me up, taking my place. I walk back to the front area to put my shoes back on.

When I walk back over, Ben is lying on his stomach on the chair. His head rests on top, while his eyes are shut.

"Did you let him see it?" I ask as Greg sets up a new needle on his gun.

"Nope. He didn't even ask to look at it, but this asshole never gives a shit what he puts on his body. He draws the dumbest shit and says put it on me. Though he has never gotten someone else's art done before."

"All your tattoos are your own art?"

"Yeah." Ben shrugs.

"Ready?"

"Yes." Ben's lips twitch into a smile as Greg starts the gun, leaning over his body.

Ben relaxes as Greg moves the needle against his skin. In fact, I think he is more relaxed than I've ever seen him before. He almost always seems relaxed, though. Still his whole body flattens, and his head turns to the side. Peace stretches across his face, even as his eyes stay closed.

I wish I knew what he was thinking. How can getting poked repeatedly by a needle make him this serene?

My hand reaches to touch him after a bit. Just to see if he is still alive. He sighs as my fingertips brush his arm.

"Greg?" he speaks suddenly.

"Yeah?"

"Have you ever given a tattoo to someone while they were having an orgasm?"

"No. Can't say I have." Greg laughs.

"Well then, politely tell this naughty girl to stop touching me before I cum on your table."

I snatch my hand away, feeling my cheeks turn bright red.

"You cum on my table, you buy me a new one." Greg shakes his head.

"That's all?" Ben asks. "In that case, Prue, please *don't* stop touching me." His eyes snap open to stare at me.

"You are such an asshole." I cross my arms, rolling my eyes.

"You know that, so why does it continue to surprise you?"

"Why do you keep being blown away when I'm bitchy?" I counter.

"Oh, did you just admit to being a bitch?" Ben lifts a little. Greg pushes him back down.

"Stay still," Greg snaps.

"I'm not a bitch," I huff out.

"No. You are not a bitch at all." Ben smirks, letting his eyes roll shut again.

I watch as Greg finishes up the tattoo. It looks good. Greg barely changed a thing about it. Something about knowing the famous Ben Parker is going to have my artwork on his skin forever makes me feel warm inside. He may not be able to see it, but my mark will be there forever.

When Greg grabs the spray bottle, I reach for it.

"May I?" I grin.

"Uh." Greg freezes.

"Just let her do it," Ben says. "She likes to inflict her fury on me from time to time."

"And you like it," I snap back, as Greg passes me the bottle. I point the nuzzle at the fresh tattoo and squeeze.

Ben hisses and I grin, giving it another squeeze.

"Jesus." Ben chuckles.

"That's enough." Greg laughs, wiping down the tattoo.

Ben groans as Greg pats it dry. He tapes a layer of plastic over it.

"You know the drill," Greg says as Ben sits up.

"Sure do." I watch as Ben tugs on his shirt and slips on his jacket. "Now let's keep the rebellion rolling and get you wasted."

I roll my eyes, even as a smile tugs on my lips. I'm really enjoying my night out with Ben. It may not have started on the best terms, but he has found a way to improve what could've been a really bad evening.

I fear I'm starting to like the person I am with him. I might not be able to go back to the Prue my parents expect me to be. Ben might have done what he set out to do.

Released the wild girl who lives inside me.

And maybe, just maybe, I like being her.

FOURTEEN

Ben

I GET US INTO THE CLUB EASILY. I KNOW THE BOUNCER, so he doesn't even check our IDs. He lifts the rope for us to cut in, much to the anger of the people waiting to get in, but I don't really care about that.

Prue keeps her hand on me as I lead us to the bar. Squeezing past people who do double takes when they see me. I haven't been to The Galaxy in a bit, sticking to more low-key bars where I can hear myself think. For getting Prue drunk I thought a club would be better, and this one is one of the best.

It's loud here, so she would be less likely to mouth off. Even if she did, I wouldn't have to hear it. Instead, I could get her to focus on having fun.

I order shots of Jameson, two for her and two for me. I don't plan on getting too wasted myself. I want to make sure I can keep a good eye on her. I promised her I'd look out for her, and I meant it. She deserves to have a good time without having to worry.

She takes the first shot and makes a face, her little nose scrunching up as her lips pucker up. I hand her some water. The best chaser is water, not soda. Water keeps you hydrated. Soda just adds sugar to the mix which is how hangovers happen.

The second shot she holds in her mouth too long, making the burn worse. I can't help but laugh at her inexperience.

"Rookie mistake. Never let it sit in your mouth," I whisper in her ear. "Swallow it quickly, like you did my cum."

A light blush floods her cheeks as she rolls her eyes.

"Let me try again then," she snaps, so I pass her my last shot.

This time she throws it back and swallows quickly. Watching her neck bob as she swallows makes my cock stiffen just slightly. I have no plans on fucking her tonight. No plans on letting anything sexual happen. I'd want her sober for that.

It doesn't take long for the alcohol to set in and Prue to loosen up.

I have us tucked away in the corner of the club, not wanting any attention to come my way. I do not need girls trying to make moves on me while I entertain Prue. I don't doubt she'd flee if she even thought there was a chance of me abandoning her.

So, I keep us as hidden as I can, letting her sway to the music. It's a sight worth a thousand words and then some. Her hips swirl, as her hands rise above her head, stretching her tight turtleneck in a way that makes my cock throb.

I fight the urge as much as I can, but as we do more shots and the night goes on, I give in. Pulling her against me, I let my hands drop to her hips. She continues to roll them, grinning at me with an evil look in her glossy eyes.

I'm sure she has never had this much alcohol in her system before. Five shots are probably a lot for a girl her size, even spaced out. They seem to be affecting her, because for once she looks happy.

Her arms wrap around my neck, as her body sways against mine.

"See," I say into her ear. "Already much more fun."

She laughs, playfully shoving me backwards, before stepping back against me.

"I've been fun for you before," she mumbles in my ear. "When my mouth was wrapped around your cock, remember?"

Her mouth latches onto my earlobe, sucking softly. My cock stirs once more.

What the fuck have I done? Did I unleash a monster? And can I say I don't care?

I'm going to end up with blue balls tonight, but it will be worth it. If she comes out of this night, realizing she doesn't have to be Miss Prim and Proper just because that's what's expected of her, I will suffer through the agony of blue balls.

"I can be fun too," I whisper back. "You just won't let me."

"No." She shakes her head, smiling. Her body turns, and she leans back, pressing her ass against me. Grinding herself into my body as I try to think of anything but how close her ass is to my cock. "You don't get to fuck me," she says over her shoulder, resting the back of her head against my chest.

My hands wrap around her front, pressing her harder against me. Fuck it. If she wants to tease, I have no problem teasing right back.

"Ever?"

"Maybe." She shrugs.

"What if I don't want to fuck you?" She freezes against me. "What if I just want to make you cum? Can I do that?"

"Maybe," she says again. "Maybe if you are a good boy." She turns again, facing me and placing her hand on my chest. "Will you be a good boy?"

"For you? Yes." I grin.

Eventually she asks to use the restroom. I lead her to it, waiting outside for her. I keep my eyes pinned to the floor, so I don't have to deal with any of the drunk girls stumbling out of it noticing me.

"Ben." Someone slaps me on the back. "How are you, dude?"

I glance up to see Patrick Oswald staring at me. My blood runs cold. He probably shouldn't be out at a club. He should be home with Wes's ex-girlfriend who he happened to knock up. It's no surprise he is out partying instead. He will probably be a horrible father. The fucker raped Abbey after all.

"Remove your hand before I remove it for you."

I don't hide my distaste for the guy. I never liked him. He knew Wes longer. They were real good friends for quite a bit. Then Wes started spending more time at my house and we started our own band. Patrick hated me for it, not that I cared much for him either. Once we got big, it became apparent that Patrick wasn't friends with Wes for any reason but to use him.

He was a dick who spent more time putting Wes down then doing any favors for him. Asking for more than he deserved. He also liked to fuck Wes's girlfriends behind his back too. Also raped girls in bathrooms, apparently.

I should beat the shit out of him now that the opportunity presented itself, but with Prue bound to come out of the bathroom at any moment, I try to cool my temper.

His hand leaves my body. "Is Wes with you?"

"Don't say his fucking name," I say through my teeth. He is only hoping Wes is here to ask him to take pity. Probably beg him to pick up his bar tab.

Prue picks now to walk out of the bathroom, skipping out with a smile on her face. She pauses when she sees Patrick beside me. I instantly don't like her reaction. My fist ball up. I'm starting to think a night in jail for beating his ass doesn't sound so bad.

"Prue!" he says her name. "Long time no see!"

Her lips turn back into a smile. A fake one, but I doubt he can tell or cares.

"Patrick," she says, walking up to us.

"You know him?" I ask.

"Uh. Yeah, kind of. Cameron's band went on tour with him a few times."

"If you tell me you fucked him, I may kill myself."

"No," she says. "I didn't fuck him."

"Oh. Did you and Charles break up?" Patrick asks.

"I..." I watch as the mention of the name Charles make her eyes dim. I didn't bother to learn her prick of an ex's name.

Judging by her reaction, I can assume that's who Patrick is talking about.

"Patrick, you have ten seconds to get as far as fucking possible from me before I beat the shit out of you." I keep my eyes on Prue. "And if you ever, and I mean ever, come near Prue again, I will cut your tiny fucking dick off and make you eat it, okay?"

"Jesus. You are worse than..."

"Finish that sentence and I will end up in jail and you in the hospital."

"Okay then. Good night," he says.

I wait until I feel him walk away, before moving closer to Prue.

"Did he ever hurt you?" I ask, cupping her face and searching her eyes. "Ever lay a finger on you?" She shakes her head, as tears threaten to spill from her eyes. I push her out of the way of people exiting the bathroom. "You can tell me," I say softly. "I know how that jerk is."

"He kissed me once," she says softly. "While Char... my ex watched. He kind of liked to see me uncomfortable." She pauses. "I guess the signs were there for a while."

I watch as she pieces it all together. I sigh, pulling her tightly against me. This night took a very unpleasant turn.

"Can we go now?"

"Yes," I say. "Let me just close out my tab."

I drag her with me to the bar. I fear if I let her out of my sight, she will bolt. I know her flight and fight response is all fucked up. After everything she has been through, it's expected. Now as her mind starts to slip into the dark places it's bound to come out in full force. My only hope is to get her home and try to distract her there, before she freaks out and tries to push me away again.

When we are outside, I keep my hand around her waist as I smoke a cigarette waiting for our car to show up.

"You don't have to stay the night with me," she says softly. She keeps some space between us but allows me to touch her.

"I do fucking too," I say, bending down to put out my

cigarette. "I'm not blind, Prue. I know a downward spiral when I see one."

"I'm sorry," she says after a moment. "I know you wanted to have a fun night. I keep ruining things for everyone around me. I should've just gone to the stupid party with him and just left you..."

"Prue, stop," I say, moving in front of her. "Look at me." Her head lifts, but her eyes stay pinned to the ground. "Look. At. Me," I repeat myself, this time her eyes snap up to mine. "If I didn't want to be around you, I wouldn't, okay? Do you really think me, the giant fucking asshole, would do anything I didn't want to?"

"You just want to fuck me. Once you fuck me, you'll never talk to me again."

"Not true. I mean I'm not saying I'll be your fucking boyfriend, but I'd like to think we could be friends."

She laughs. "Highly unlikely."

"Well, that's just mean," I say, happy to hear her laugh, but not pleased with the reason. "I can be friends with a girl."

"Even after you fucked her?"

"As long as you don't get clingy, I see no reason why we can't be friends, who maybe, time from time, fool around." I shrug.

Laughing again, she shakes her head. "Me? Clingy? You are the one who can't leave me alone."

"I can't leave you alone out of fear you'll get yourself hurt."

The minute the words leave my mouth I know I fucked up. I may have seen her in a vulnerable state, but implying she is weak is going to cost me.

"I can take care of myself," she snaps. "I don't need you to take care of me."

"Need, no, but you did call me." I shrug. I'm not good at not saying the wrong thing. I learned that years ago, so I don't even bother trying once I fuck up. Failure can never be righted, so I always choose to fail some more.

"My apologies," she snaps. "I'll never call you again. Ever."

She tries to pull away from me, but I reach out, grabbing her wrist.

"Oh Prue," I say, pulling her closer to me. "You keep saying that and yet we keep ending up together." I let my other hand graze her cheek. "I think you secretly like me." My thumb traces over her lip. Something about the way she gets angry makes me feel things. "And you know what, I may even like you too."

If my words hold any meaning to her, she doesn't show it. It feels like a gut punch. Maybe she did only reach out to me because she was desperate.

Shoving at me, she tries to break free of my hold. Unfortunately letting her go is not an option. I made a promise to take care of her tonight. I don't care how mad she gets or what she says to me, I'm not breaking that promise.

"You don't get to be my knight in shining armor. You're the furthest thing from a hero. I bet in everyone else's story you are the villain, or worse the victim." She hurls insults pretty well. "I bet whatever abuse you suffered isn't even that bad, but you use it as an excuse for your shitty behavior. I'm not surprised your band doesn't want to play with you anymore. You're so mean."

I keep my face neutral as she hurls her insults. My first action with anyone else would be to attack back, but that's not what she needs. Prue needs someone to take her beating, and I'm happy to be that person for her right now.

"I'm mean?" I ask, as our car pulls up. "I want you to really think about who's being mean right now." I pull her with me toward the car. I grip her hand tight, as she slides into the back of the car. I'm worried if I let go, she will bolt. I don't trust her not to do something stupid right now. "Unfortunately for you, I made a promise and I keep my fucking promises. So, for the sake of both of our sanities, don't say another fucking thing until we are back at Cameron's, okay?"

She looks away, fixing her gaze on the window as the car pulls off. I relax my grip slightly.

Her words sting as they bounce around my head. I've said

them to myself enough to not completely fall apart when hearing them, but they still aren't great to hear.

My desire to keep her from falling apart outweighs my need to self-destruct. Probably the first and only time that will ever be the case. I promised not to ditch her, so I'm staying put. Though the idea of letting myself spiral into my own dark memories sounds very tempting right now.

I try to focus on my surroundings, grounding myself in the present before I can slip into the well of memories that continuously try to kill me. There is no need to go there at this moment. I can't deal with my spiral and hers.

Prue's pulse races where my fingertips wrap around her wrist. Each breath of hers comes out heavy, almost like a huff. The way her body vibrates lets me know she is trying not to cry.

I wish I could think of something to say to help her, but I'm lost in my own mind. Trying to avoid stepping on a land mind that will bring both of us down.

The music playing in the car is some overplayed pop song that I don't hate but would rather never hear again simply because of how much it's been overplayed.

The heater is on because the temperature outside is under 60 and to people in LA that's freezing, but the heat isn't helping my body relax. I crack the window for a moment, hoping the cold air will settle my thoughts.

I'm not that person anymore. I'm not weak. I'm not pathetic. And I am not a victim. *She* can't hurt me anymore. I am completely safe.

I am safe. I let myself repeat that in my head a few times. Over and over, like a mantra.

Prue shifts beside me, moving closer to me, but I can't look at her right now.

I'm never vulnerable. Not with anyone. Maybe Wes has seen me with my guard down, but never like Prue has. Never how I feel right now. And Prue has proven why I don't let people see me like this.

She threw all my secrets in my face. I can't blame her for it. I haven't exactly been nice, and she is kind of going through it, but the lesson remains.

Don't open up to anyone. Ever.

"Ben?" she asks softly.

When I finally glance over at her, she is peering at me with concern written on her face.

"What?"

"You're clawing at your neck."

The moment she points it out, I feel it. My nails cutting into the side of my neck. The sting that's sure to leave red marks behind, hits.

It's a habit I developed as a child. When I got nervous, or the memories floated to the surface. Or whenever *she* came around, stalking me like I was prey, I'd start clawing at my skin to relieve some of the tension from my body.

My hand drops to my lap.

"You're bleeding a little." She points to my neck.

"So what?" I shrug. "Or more so, why the fuck do you care?" I raise my eyebrow at her.

"I don't know." She shrugs. "I don't know why I keep snapping at you. I'm sorry." Her eyes drop to her feet.

I dab at my neck, wiping away the small drops of blood on my pants.

"You're hurting," I finally say, watching her eyes dart up to me. I let my fingers rub circles on her wrist. "You're trying to mask it under this idea you're strong and capable of anything, but you are hurting, Prue. And I've been there. I get it. I'm the safest person you can lash out at right now, so I'll take it, but Jesus." I sigh. "You know exactly what to say to fuck me up."

"Oh God." She gasps, burying her face in her free hand. She sobs and I just let her, stroking her wrists softly. "He ruined me."

"No. He didn't ruin you. He killed a version of you, but now you have the freedom to become someone new." She glances over at me, tears pouring down her face as she processes my words.

"You don't have to be who everyone else wants you to be, Prue. You can get tattoos, get drunk, and have fun. Find a passion or three. Have wild, kinky sex, preferably once or twice with me, or become a nun if you want. You spent too long being good so your brother didn't get any heat, but now, guess what, you have a chance to be whoever you want to be."

"He raped me." Her voice is barely a whisper. "He beat me then he held me down and raped me."

"Oh." Is all I can say, as I'm suddenly reminded that the version of me that exists today is the outcome of what happened after years of someone raping me.

I wanted better for her.

FIFTEEN

Prue

I sob into my one free hand as Ben continues to rub circles into the wrist he refuses to let go.

If my confession shocked him, he doesn't show it. Admitting it out loud has broken something inside me. I can't handle the pain anymore. I thought unloading it would free me, but it just reminds me how ruined I am.

He pulls me gently from the back of the car when we get to Cameron's apartment building. Leading us through the maze of stairs and walkways, until he gets me to the front door.

I unlock it and immediately throw myself onto the couch. Covering my face, I just let the tears continue to fall. The weight of everything that has happened over the last few weeks has come crashing down. It's overwhelming. All the awful things I said to the one person who has been trying to help me makes me hate myself even more.

Ben drops on the floor in front of me. I peer through my fingers to see him taking sips from a bottle of alcohol that belongs to Cameron. His eyes meet mine and he lifts a glass of water towards me.

I sit up, gulping down half the glass as tears still drip down my face. The mess I must be now will surely put the nail in the coffin on whatever could have happened between us, if the confession of my rape didn't already do it.

That's probably for the best, though. Clearly, I'm not good for him.

"I owe your brother a bottle of whiskey. Only I plan on making it much better than Jack Daniels. Jesus Christ, the guy needs to grow up and get the good stuff."

"Hey!" I snap. My mind is so used to defending Cameron, it does it on auto pilot at this point.

"I'm just saying." He sighs, leaning back on his palms. "Take your boots off. Your tattoo needs air."

"I almost forgot about it," I say, reaching down to slip off my boots. I kick them off and then pull off my socks.

Ben watches my movements. His eyes skim over my bare legs, as more of my skin is revealed from how I sit. Eyes wide with desire, despite the fact I'm still a crying mess. It makes my stomach flutter when he stares at me like that.

"Have you cum since?" he blurts out and then shakes his head. "I didn't mean to ask that." He laughs, taking a long gulp from the bottle. "I apologize."

"No," I answer anyways. "I think I'm too scared to try."

He nods. "It isn't so bad. The first time is hard. If you push through it, soon it's like regaining a semblance of control."

"How would you know?" I start to laugh, but then it hits me. He said he was abused. And his reaction to my confession. The comment he just made. It all starts to make sense now. "Ben." I gasp, covering my mouth. He doesn't say anything, just takes another drink. "When? Who?" I ask, sitting up. "I'm so sorry. I said all those things... I didn't know... I didn't think..."

"That a guy could be raped?" His eyes look up at me.

"No. Not that." I swallow the lump of guilt that sits in my throat. I was so cruel to him, and he suffered just like me.

"I'm not sure many people would call it rape. Maybe morally wrong, but guys would probably make fun of me for not liking it." He shrugs.

"Ben. I'm so, so, sorry."

"I never told anyone," he says, his eyes dropping back to my legs. "It's easier to keep it to myself than explain how I could be fucked up because some woman played with my dick."

"How old were you?"

"I think that's the problem. If I was younger, it would be sick, but it happened at an age that makes it weird. I was young, but just old enough that I could've enjoyed it."

His face is blank as he speaks. I wonder if he even realizes he is speaking out loud. How long has he kept this inside? The way he talks shows he is miles away, lost in thought, but how he has a response to every question lets me know he has probably wanted to talk about it. He has probably thought about it often, but never said anything.

"I didn't, though," he adds after a moment. "I tried a few times, you know? To convince myself I wanted it, that it was okay, that I was lucky. Some days I still try to think about it like that."

I let my hand rest on his arm, trying to remind him of the present. His eyes drift to the connection, but he doesn't acknowledge it otherwise, taking another sip from the bottle before letting out a dry laugh.

"God if Wes knew." He shakes his head. "If he knew every night he stayed at my house when she was there, he was saving me, I think he would finally understand why I would literally die for him. I spent those nights wide awake though. Scared she would still try something, or worse go after him." He pauses for a moment. "I wonder if there were others. I think it's nice to pretend I was the only one, but that's just not the reality. Which probably makes me an accomplice, huh? I didn't say anything, so she thinks she can get away with doing it to others. I probably deserve some jail time for that." He laughs.

"No. It doesn't work like that. It's not your fault if there are others. It's not your fault at all."

"Think about it, Prue. I never told a soul. Maybe not going to the police would be one thing, but not saying a fucking word to anyone, ever? That makes me just as guilty."

"No, it doesn't," I say sharply, hoping to get through to him. "Ben, you were raped. You are a victim. It's not on you."

"You're a girl. It's a lot different when you are a guy. It's not like she fucked me in the ass or anything. That people would understand me not coming forward about but putting her mouth on my cock. Riding my dick? That should've been a wet dream come true, not something that makes my skin crawl. And it's not like she was ugly. Not by a mile, on the outside at least." He jerks away from me. "I'm pathetic for being upset about it. Honestly, like you said, it probably wasn't even that bad. I'm just playing victim."

"Ben, I was just being a bitch, okay? I didn't mean it."

"I know." He nods, looking at me. "I know you wouldn't have said that if you knew what happened. I'm just a good punching bag." He laughs. "Someone you can safely hit, and might I say you are really good at hitting me where it hurts."

Taking another sip from the bottle, he glances around the apartment as if he's suddenly aware of his surroundings again.

"What are the odds your stupid ex comes back to night?" he asks, focusing on me again. "How sober do I need to be?"

"You really don't have to stay. I can handle him myself."

"Maybe, but you shouldn't have to. I won't let you," he adds more firmly. "Just let me be your white knight for tonight, okay? It would make me feel a little better about myself."

"Okay." I nod. "On one condition."

"What are your terms?"

"Agree first."

"No." He laughs. "I don't trust you."

"Then leave," I counter. Now it's my turn to find a way to comfort him. To force him to stay instead of run, like all those times I did. And I have an idea how to pull us both out of the darkness. I just have to hope he is up for it. And that I can actually do it.

I don't know what it is about his confession, but I feel extremely connected to him now. Maybe it's how it mirrors my own pain, or the way I know he can understand how I'm feeling, but his confession almost makes me feel better. Less alone even. I don't think I ever felt this close to someone who wasn't Cameron before. I may not even feel this close to Cameron.

A low sigh leaves his lips as he runs his hands through his hair. "I only agree if it isn't you asking me to leave you alone after tonight or sex."

"Hmm." I tap my chin, studying him. "What if it's sex adjacent?"

"You or me?" he asks.

"What does that mean?"

"Are you getting off, or am I?"

"Both is a possibility, but I was thinking I'd get off for a change." I smirk down at him.

A flash of desire dances behind his eyes as he sits up. It's like every ounce of pain just left his body. I wish I was able to do that. Maybe he will teach me.

"Baby, I've been wanting that for a while. I accept your terms. We have a deal."

"You don't get to get me off," I say firmly.

"Wait, what?" he stutters. "Then what did you have in mind?"

"Help me. You can help me get myself off." The mere thought of touching myself makes my body tense, but with his help, it might not be so bad.

"I can do that." He nods as a grin spread across his face. "But I'm going to warn you." He leans closer. "You might not be able to stop yourself from begging to have my mouth buried between your legs. Or my cock."

And God, I hate to admit it, but he might be right.

SIXTEEN

Ben

I TRY NOT TO THINK ABOUT THE FACT I JUST CONFESSED my deepest, darkest secret to Prue a second longer once she asks me to help her get off.

The fact my abuse doesn't make her look at me as some kind of disgusting piece of shit makes knots in my stomach unravel. Tension leaves my body as she stares at me, processing my last statement.

I can't fuck her tonight. Well, I don't think I could, but as she looks at me, sky-blue eyes pooling with lust, I'm not so sure I could say no to her when she eventually begs me to.

Which she will and I won't even have to touch her to get her there. The last fucking thing she is going to think about is her ex, all her attention will be on me and that's going to make her want me in ways she doesn't even know yet.

"I thought sex wasn't on the table," she finally says.

"I prefer the bed." I smirk, and she rolls her eyes. "I didn't want you to touch my dick, but your pussy, I don't know if I could deny her anything."

"Oh, good to know you value my pussy over the rest of me."

"I don't value your pussy over you, I'm just more inclined to be nice to her."

"And if she doesn't like it nice?" She smirks.

"Then I'll be mean, really, really mean."

Her face softens, as her eyes sparkle with a mixture of want and fury.

"I don't want your cock," she says, though her voice hints that she is already lying.

"Yet." I wag my finger at her. Moving the bottle to the side, I lean forward, letting my fingers skim over her leg. Goose bumps rise over it. "You feel so soft."

"I... Wait," she mutters. I instantly freeze, still touching her but not moving any higher. "I want to get myself off, I just may need..." Her voice trails off, as her eyes drift to the side.

"Help." I nod, removing my hand from her leg. "I won't touch you, not until you ask me to," I reassure her. And I mean it. I won't lay a hand on her until she is ready. I can't wait until she is ready, though.

"This is a bad idea." She sighs, pushing herself up and forcing me to scoot backwards. "Like really stupid." She shakes her head.

"It's not stupid. It's smart," I say, standing up. "The first time is hard, getting some help is a good idea."

"What if I can't do it?"

"Then you try again another night." I walk up to her. "Do you trust me?"

She shrugs, and it stings a little, but I get it. Hard to trust anyone once you've been broken like *that*.

"Let's just have fun with it, okay? We can climb into your bed and just have some fun? I won't touch you, but we can talk. I'm really good at dirty talk." I smirk.

A small smile spreads across her face as her eyes do loops. "Okay."

She leads me to her room before ducking into the bathroom.

My eyes dart around the room. It lacks personality but I guess part of that is due to the fact she just recently moved in with her brother. A part of me wonders how she would decorate it if she had the freedom to. Would posters of my band line her walls? I bet after tonight she would want a little reminder of me. Perhaps I'll send her a headshot.

I smirk to myself at the thought of her touching herself to the memories of all the pleasure I'm going to show her.

My mind is buzzing with excitement. I drank a little more than I should've while bearing my soul to her.

I didn't expect her to ask for my help when it came to getting herself off. I wish I could help her in other ways, but I'd settle on dirty talking her sweet cunt to pleasure. Let her see I can get her off without even touching her. Impress her a little.

My cock aches at the thought of watching bliss fall over her face. I wonder what she sounds like when she explodes. My balls are throbbing at the mere thought.

I strip down to just my boxers before crawling into her bed. I eye the door, waiting for her to return.

When she does walk in a moment later, she moves to her dresser, opening and closing drawers.

"What are you doing?"

"Looking for a pair of sweats," she snaps back.

"Why?"

"To wear."

"You don't need clothes for what you're about to do."

"Yes. I do."

"Prue, I promise you, whatever you are hiding, I've seen worse."

"Ha." She turns to glare at me. "Good to know." She reaches under her shirt, tugging off her bra. The sight of her breasts barely sagging makes my mouth water. Perky tits are hidden from my view, but I know when I see them, they are going to be a sight.

She sighs, closing her eyes for a moment, before snapping them open to look at me. I offer her a smile and she rolls her eyes, before letting her hands drop to the side of her skirt. She unzips it, letting it drop to the floor at her feet, revealing her tiny black thong. My cock seriously aches now.

Her hip bones are so defined. Her thighs too. They look firm, even with a tiny gap in the middle, perfect for my head to fit between.

Resting her hand on her stomach she stares at me, and I force my eyes to glance up to her face.

"Most of the bruises are gone but there are a few that still..."

"If you think a few bruises are going to lessen your appeal, you have no idea how fucking hot you are."

Her face turns pink, but her fingers move to the edge of her turtleneck. Quickly she pulls it off and over her head, dropping it to the floor behind her.

Just as I thought, her tits are perky and round. Her nipples are peach and pointy, and I want to stuff my mouth with them. Folding my hands in my lap to keep them from reaching forward to feel her tits, I bite my tongue to keep myself from speaking.

Her stomach is flat and smooth. Her collar bone stands out, and I want to trace my fingers over it, maybe even bite into it. I ignore the few faint bruises that sit on random spots on her body, so I don't start plotting a murder.

She is fucking beautiful. And my mind is jumping through all the many things I want to do to her. It's not like I haven't slept with the same woman more than once on occasion, but I could fill a whole calendar with all the things I want to do to her.

"Um... Can I leave this on?" She pulls on the straps of her thong.

"If you want," I say, clearing my throat.

She nods, moving toward the bed. She climbs up beside me, lying flat on her back a few inches from me.

"How do we start?" She glances at me.

"What do you like?"

"Like? Oh, I don't know. I'm not very picky. I like sucking, which you know." Her lips twitch up. "But when it comes to my body, I don't really care. I take whatever is given."

Jesus. The men she has been with haven't been doing their job. She must be so used to settling on whatever makes them feel good.

"You like giving pleasure?"

"Yes." She nods.

"You know," I start, turning on my side to face her. Her eyes are open and staring at the ceiling. "You're the only girl who has ever taken my whole cock in their mouth."

"Really?" she asks, her eyes darting over to me. "It wasn't easy, but it felt so good. I like the way my jaw ached after."

"Yeah?" I fight the urge to reach between my legs and touch myself. This isn't about me. It's all about her. "I don't know if I'll ever come that hard from a blow job ever again."

"Mm." She sighs. "I like that I'll leave you with a lasting memory." Her hand cups her bare tit, squeezing it.

"When guys go down on you, do you like their tongue inside or playing with your clit?"

"Oh." She gasps, as her thumb rolls at her nipple. "I don't care too much. I rarely come from receiving oral. Just a few times, mostly if they want a second go and don't mind spending awhile down there." Her fingers tug on her nipples and her mouth parts, but no sound comes out.

"Do you like having your nipples played with?"

"No." She shakes her head. "They are all too rough or too soft. Correcting men gets old." Her voice is heavy as she switches to fondle her other tit. "They can never read my cues."

"Favorite position?" I'm trying to get information to paint a picture for us, but she isn't giving me much to work with. I blame the lousy men she has been with.

"Doggy. Better angle. Top is good too, but men don't let me take my time that way."

"Stop talking about other men," I say, trying to keep my voice soft, but I don't need her thinking of her past lovers right now. "I don't care about them. I want to know what you like."

"Doggy still. Though I fear you'll break me that way." I smile to myself as she lowers one hand to rest on her lower stomach. "I like my hair played with, pulled. And when my hips are gripped, a hand around the throat feels good too. Not choking, just holding me in place." Her chest rises and falls, as her hand slides to the front of her thong.

"How many of your fingers can you fit inside?"

"Two. I've only ever used two." Her hand rests over her pussy now. "Sometimes I put one in my ass, but I don't do that often. Only when I'm desperate."

"Desperate?"

"For a little pain."

"You like pain?"

"Not a lot, just a little. A sting, the stretching, really. I like being full." I watch her hand move, slipping under her thong now. "And filled."

Jesus Christ. I'm going to fucking explode just from the words coming out of her mouth.

"How could a man not worship you?" I say softly.

Her eyes find me, resting on my face. "You'd worship me?"

"I would." I nod, keeping my eyes on her. "Anything you wanted would be yours for the chance to make you feel good."

Out of the corner of my eye I see that her fingers are against her pussy, but the gasp that falls from her lips is even more proof.

"What would you do first?" Her voice is shaky and heavy.

"I'd make you come with my fingers. If only to make sure there are enough juices for me to lap up. But as my fingers strum you like a guitar, I'd have my lips attached to your tits. They are so fucking perfect."

My hand drops to my crotch on its own accord, but I don't let it go down my boxers or touch my cock. This is about her, not me, I remind myself.

"Have you ever done 69?" she asks.

"Yes."

"I think that could be fun." Her hips rock against her hand. "I think I'd like to cum with a cock down my throat."

"Fuck," I groan, as I'm pretty sure precum leaks from my cock.

"Yeah. I think I'd like that a lot," she moans. "Though I fear your cock may make me pass out. Can't imagine what your lips would feel like around my clit. They are so soft." Her free hand takes to squeezing her tit again.

"Baby," I say softly, fighting the urge to touch her. "I wouldn't let you suck my cock while I went down on you. That would be a choking hazard."

"But that might make it more fun." She gasps.

"Yeah?"

"Ben?"

"Yes, Prue?"

"I'm so fucking wet." She lets out a deep breath.

"I'm so fucking hard."

"Touch yourself too," she says, lifting her head and glancing down to my crotch. "I want to see it."

"You want to see my cock?"

She nods. "Helps with the fantasy."

I pull my cock from my boxers, giving it a stroke, as she watches with her mouth hanging open.

"What are you doing?"

"Stroking my clit. I like using two fingers, covers more area." Her hips rock against her hand again. "I wish it was you, though."

"Me too, baby. Me too." I let my hand lazily stroke over my cock, as her head stays turned to watch it.

"Maybe one day?" Her eyes are glued to my hand. I'm stroking it slow because I don't think it would take much for me to cum.

"Yes, baby. One day it will be my fingers and mouth, and then my fat cock stretching you open."

"Further than anyone else." She gasps. "Oh god." The hand on her tit drops to the bed, gripping at the blanket, as her eyes flutter. "I don't think I can take it right now, though. I can barely fit one of my..." Her voice trails off. "Fuck."

"I'd get you nice and loose before I put it in you. It may still hurt, but just how you like it," I say softly. My mind is spinning and I'm trying to keep my eyes open, so I don't miss when she cums.

"I think..." she moans. "You would ruin me."

"Ruin you? How, baby?"

"For anyone else," she groans. "Oh god. Fuck, I want to... I'm so close."

"Get there for me, baby. I want to see you cum. Show me what you look like when you feel good."

"Touch me. Please. I need..."

My hand drops my cock, reaching out to her tit. I squeeze it and she rocks into my touch. I pinch her nipple between two fingers, holding the underside with my other three fingers. I apply some pressure before twisting softly.

"Ah. Yes," she yells out as her back arches. Her thighs shake. I watch her mouth drop open, eyes flutter, chest heaves.

It's the best thing I've ever seen in my life. I thought seeing a crowd of people sway to the sound of my guitar was magical. I thought I've seen beautiful women before. Swore I'd never find a person to be the greatest thing in the world, but watching her cum changes my mind.

Nothing could be better.

When she stills, I release her nipple, as she lays there panting. Her hand slips from her thong, and she wipes them on her thigh. The layer of her arousal sitting on her skin makes my mouth water.

Not wanting to take her out of her daze, I keep my mouth shut for once in my life. She opens her eyes a moment later, looking up at the ceiling again.

"That wasn't hard at all," she says softly. "I thought it would be worse. Thank you. I think I really needed that."

"Any time," I say, rolling on my back.

"Your turn," she says, rolling on her side to face me. "I want to watch how you get yourself off."

I laugh. "I don't even remember the last time I jerked myself off." I let my hand drop back to my cock. "No need to when you look as good as I do."

"Ha. Ha." Her eyes roll. "Do it for me. Please? Consider it a peace offering."

"You just love having control over me, don't you?" I groan as my hand makes steady strokes over my cock. "Do you like when I obey you?"

"Very much," she says, moving so her head now rests on my thigh. Her breath against my cock makes my balls tighten. "It's so pretty."

"What is?"

"Your cock."

"You are out of your fucking mind," I groan. "Pretty? This thing is a monster."

"A pretty monster then." Her eyes do loops again. "Tell me before you cum."

"Why?"

"Just do it," she says, her eyes darting up to my face.

"Fine."

I lie there stroking my cock for her enjoyment, letting it drag out for a few minutes. Taking my time, mostly to toy with her because the truth is I could cum pretty quickly if I wanted to after watching her get off.

Her eyes watch my movement, and I feel each breath she takes against my cock.

"I'm close," I groan.

"How close?"

"So. Fucking. Close."

Her mouth wraps around the tip just as the words leave my mouth. The shock of it makes me lose control and I cum seconds later.

Gripping the bed, I let soft groans escape my lips, feeling her suck on just the head of my cock, dragging out every last drop.

When I go slack against the bed, she finally pulls her mouth from my cock. Climbing over my body she straddles my lap, and my soft cock bobs as she looks down at me. Her mouth opens slightly to reveal my cum sitting on her tongue.

"Jesus," I groan. I press two fingers into her mouth. Her lips wrap around them as I push my cum to the back of her mouth. She swallows and I have to pry my fingers from her mouth to keep myself sane.

"Did you like that?" She grins down at me.

"Too much." My hand drops to her hip. We both stare at where my hand rests.

"Can you get hard again?" she asks.

"I'm already halfway there, baby." I lift my hips up and she gasps as my half hard cock nudges against her thong.

"You're so fucking thick." She shifts against my growing cock. "There is no way it fits. You'll tear me in half."

"You like that idea, don't you?" She nods, looking at me, as she rubs herself against me. "You want me to stuff it in you until you are almost bursting with how much space I take up."

"God. Yes," she moans, her eyes fluttering as she nudges her clit against the tip of my cock. "I'm just scared. What if it all won't fit?"

"We will make it fit, together."

"Yeah." She nods. My hand slides up her body. My fingers tug at one of her nipples. "Yes," she groans. "You do it right. So fucking right," she moans as I twist it lightly. "Ben. I want you."

"So, take me."

SEVENTEEN

Prue

I DON'T LET MYSELF PAUSE TO THINK ABOUT PAST events. Something in my mind has snapped. Have I ever talked like this with anyone before? All my darkest fantasies are pouring from my mouth, and he plays right into them. Are they the same as his or is he just that good at playing along? Do I care?

No, I don't. Not right now anyways. I just want to stay in this bubble of lust and pleasure. Tomorrow when he leaves and never calls me again, I will claim temporary insanity, but tonight, I'm just claiming him.

My hand moves between my legs, and I pull my thong to the side so I can rub my clit for a moment. No matter how wet I am, I know I need to be wetter if I'm going to try to take him.

He shifts slightly, still twisting and pulling at my nipple. It sends ripples of pleasure through my whole body. At least he knows the right amount of pressure to apply.

"Jesus. Prue. You're soaking. Is this all for me?"

"Yes," I moan back, opening my eyes to look down at him. "Just for you," I murmur. This kind of dirty talk only ever lived in my mind. I tried it a few times before with Charles, but it just made him cum way too fast or laugh, but Ben, he encourages it, adds to it. Feels like he enjoys it too. "I need you inside me. Now," I order as firmly as my voice will allow at this moment.

"Put me in then," he says back, a small smirk spreads across his face. "If you're going to use me, baby, fucking use me."

I bite my lip, my clit pulsing, nearing an orgasm just at the words he is saying. How can an asshole like him be this fucking sexy?

I reach down gripping his cock in my hand. Stroking it slowly, I try to use the juices that already cover it from my pussy as lube. Half of me was just playing into the fantasy of his huge cock stretching me to my limits, but there is a real possibility I won't be able to fit it inside me. I could barely handle my finger earlier, but I can't let myself think too hard about that right now.

Lifting my hips, I adjust my body so the tip of his cock presses against my opening. My eyes glance down, and I think about when you are very high up, and they tell you not to look down because holy shit it is huge.

"I can feel how fucking warm you are," he groans. "Prue, baby, do you want this?"

I can only nod, looking up at him. Glancing down again, I push my hips down.

The stretch is instant, as I try to push the head of his cock into me. Trying to relax my muscles I press down harder, before the very tip of his cock pops in.

It burns and tears fill my eyes as a haze of something I don't want to think about dances in the back of my mind.

"Jesus Christ, Prue, are you sure you aren't a fucking virgin?"

I shake my head, letting myself sink a little lower.

"You are so fucking tight. Fuck. Hold on." He grips my hips, holding me still. "I need a fucking second." I whimper as he pulls his cock back slightly, so the tip is barely inside. "This isn't going to work," he groans, lifting me from his cock.

"I'm sorry." I mumble, trying to jerk my body away from him. I want to curl up and die of embarrassment.

"No. Don't be," he says softly. "Look at me, Prue." My eyes

snap to his, trying to seek the comfort that laces his voice. "I will make it fit, but not like this. Do you trust me? Not that asshole you met at the party, but this me, the one who knows how to get you off, do you trust him?" I nod. "Say it," he says, cupping my chin. "Tell me, Prue."

"I trust you," I whisper. And I do trust him, maybe more than anyone else in the world at this very moment.

"Good."

And with that, he gently flips us over so I'm lying on my back, and he is kneeling between my legs. I gasp as he pulls my legs apart, dropping on his arms between them.

"Jesus. Your pussy is stunning. You call my cock pretty, then this is a masterpiece." My pussy clenches at his words.

"You should try drawing it sometime," I reply, breathlessly.

"I might. Only thing I'd consider tattooing on my face." He smiles, tugging my thong down my legs.

He knows exactly what to say to make me drip. I don't think I was lying when I said he would ruin me for anyone else. Who else could say these words and make them sound so sexy? Just Ben fucking Parker.

"Are you just going to stare at it?" I say, trying to come across as demanding, but I know it comes out way too desperate.

"No." He smirks up at me. "I'm going to eat it up, then shove as many fingers as it takes to open you up for my cock. What did you say earlier? You can only take two fingers? Well two of mine are a lot bigger." He wiggles his fingers for me to see. "You're going to feel yourself stretch as I make myself fit into you, even if it kills me."

"What if it kills me?" I whisper.

"That I won't let happen." He grins. "Need you to live to tell the tale."

"I can read the headline now." My eyes rolling in the way only he seems to make them. "Benjamin Parker died because his cock was just too big."

"Ha." He laughs, lowering his head toward my pussy. "I hope they let you write my obituary."

"I'll make them."

His tongue flicks against my clit, forcing a gasp from my mouth. He laps at it for a moment before his mouth drops to my opening. That he instantly starts sucking at. His tongue stabs at it, poking in and out, before pushing in deeper.

I squirm as he fucks me with his tongue. His fingers stroke at my clit, strumming it like I imagine he would play a guitar, on stage for all his fans. It's nothing like what I know, but mixed with his tongue it makes my body shiver.

It's exciting, mainly because I don't think he is actively trying to get me off, he is simply enjoying me. I like that more than I care to admit. I want him to enjoy me, I want him to like messing around with me.

I fear when morning comes, I will be hooked, and he will be over me. It's bittersweet, but I'll deal with that agony later.

He pries his tongue from my pussy, moving his mouth to my clit. Hooking his hand under my leg, he angles my hips, so he has better access. Just as he starts sucking, he presses a finger into my pussy.

He barely lets me adjust to one finger before squeezing a second in. The stretch burns for a second, before his mouth on me overtakes the pain, so all I feel is pleasure.

"Ben. Fuck," I moan and he groans into my pussy as his name leaves my mouth. "You like when I say your name?"

His eyes flash up to me, as he nods with his lips still sealed around my clit.

My hand drops to his head, pulling on his dirty blond hair. He allows me small amounts of control, something I'm not used to, but I'm going to soak it up as much as I can. I keep testing the water, seeing how much he can take.

His eyes light up when I dig my fingertips into his scalp. I rock my hips against his mouth, and his eyes drop back to my pussy.

Increasing the pressure of his lips, he fucks my pussy faster with his fingers.

My eyes flutter as he has me on the edge of an orgasm in record time. I want his eyes back on me, so I pull at the roots of his hair until his eyes fly up to my face.

"Look at me as you make me cum." I once again try to sound demanding, not caring if I fail, because he obeys me regardless.

His eyes stay locked on me as he applies just a little pressure of his teeth against my clit. The shock of pain mixed with the pleasure pushes me over the edge.

I try to force my eyes to stay open as my orgasm hits, wanting to watch him, but eventually they roll shut as pleasure completely overtakes me.

He sucks me through to the very end until I'm trying to buck him off me from how sensitive my clit feels. Taking his mouth away from my clit, he continues to pump his two fingers into me. I'm aware that I'm dripping by the sound that fills the room. I'm not sure I've ever been this wet before.

"Not the order I planned on," he mumbles, planting kissing up my stomach. "But you taste too fucking good." His tongue swirls around my nipple. "Your pussy was supposed to be dessert, but I guess I can feed my sweet tooth with your perky tits."

"Or my lips," I counter. His mouth wraps around one nipple. His upper body presses into my stomach, the weight of it brings me comfort, despite the slight pain from my bruised ribs. "Ben," I groan, letting my hips rock into his fingers. "I'm going to cum again. Oh god." I dig my nails into his back, as he bites into my tit.

The pain comes just as another orgasm hits. The pain and pleasure mix so good I see stars. As I drift back down from the high, I feel the slight burn of him slowly pressing a third finger into my pussy.

"Ah. Ben. Fuck."

"You can take it. Trust me," he says, resting his head in between my tits. "Look at me." My eyes drop to his face. "You are such a good little slut, remember that."

His fingers fit snuggly inside me. I groan as he slowly pushes them deeper into me. Spreading them a little, until my pussy stretches to accommodate them.

"That feels..." I groan. I know I liked the feeling of being stretched, but this is almost too good. I could easily get addicted to this feeling.

"Good, huh?" I can only nod. "Ready to try my cock again?" I nod again. "Want to ride it or do you want me to do it?"

"You," I moan as he pushes his fingers deep again. "Fuck."

"I'll go slow," he says, ripping his fingers from me to kneel between my legs. The loss feels huge and I glance down, just as he brings the tip of his cock to my pussy. He spits into his hand, before reaching down to coat his cock with it. "We will make it fit."

"I can take it."

He smiles up at me. "Yes, you can. Your little pussy may be a little sore after, but then you'll remember my cock in the morning."

"I'll never be able to forget it."

His eyes sparkle at that comment and he quickly pushes forward. My pussy is more open this time, but it still takes a little force for the head to slide in.

I groan and his eyes flash up to mine, searching for a sign I need him to stop. Not finding it, he pushes a little deeper.

The sting makes my mind swirl into a blissful mixture of pain and pleasure. I can only gasp as he slowly sinks into me.

"Yeah, baby, there you go. Stretch for me. I want you to feel me so deep. In those places no one else will ever be able to touch again."

My mouth drops open as he pulls back, his cock pressing into a spot that makes my legs shake. He must sense it because he lets himself push back against it, over and over, never going any deeper, until I'm cumming.

My back lifts off the bed as I explode. He pushes me back

down, holding me by the neck against the bed. Not quite choking me but keeping me still.

"Careful, baby." He smirks. "You wouldn't want to dislodge me, now, would you?"

I shake my head, already on the verge of another orgasm, simply from having his hand around my throat and the way his lips curve up.

"Can you take more?"

I try to glance down, to see how much I've already taken, but he doesn't let me move. I feel like there can't be too much more by how full I already feel, but regardless, I want to take all of him. I nod.

"Yeah. I know you can."

His mouth drops to mine, sealing it shut with his lips, just as he rams his hips into mine, letting his whole cock sink into me.

The pain is searing yet intoxicating. I underestimated how much of his cock was left, because he feels much deeper than he did a moment ago. He swallows my groans, letting his tongue dip into my mouth.

Wrapping my arms around his neck, I grip onto him, as he thrusts into me. The pain is quickly gone as I'm overwhelmed with how full I feel. My walls cling to him. Every bump and curve of his cock is going to be imprinted inside me. I really won't be able to forget him.

I'm struggling to breathe as he pounds into me and fucks my mouth with his tongue, but something about the mixture of sensations feels too good for me to care.

When my pussy tightens from an impending orgasm, he rips his mouth from mine. Grabbing a fist of my short hair, he pulls my head off the bed. I'm sure it hurts, but my body isn't capable of feeling anything but pleasure right now.

"Cum for me, Prue. Cum on my fat fucking cock, like we both know you want to."

My body shudders and my eyes fight to close, but he pulls on my hair once again, lifting my head to let me see his cock disappear inside me, but I find my eyes quickly looking up at his face. I hold them open, trying to capture the sight of the feral look on his face, until my orgasm peaks, forcing them shut.

I scream. I can't hear myself, but I feel the scream coming from my throat.

His hold on my hair loosens and my head drops back to the bed underneath me. He drives himself into me hard and I can't do much more than take it. Nor do I want to. Every part of my body tingles with pleasure.

"Fuck. Baby. Your little pussy is going to break my cock. Fits like a fucking glove. Jesus. I'm going to have bruises. Bet you like that, huh?"

"Yes," I moan, barely able to breathe. I'm still reeling from how intense that last orgasm was.

"Little markings will be etched on to my cock for days. Maybe I'll have Greg tattoo them on. Keep them as a reminder of how fucking good you felt cumming around me."

"Oh. Fuck. Ben," I yell out as another orgasm is fast approaching. My body thrashes underneath him, too overwhelmed by the intense feelings he is creating.

He pins my hip down with one hand, while grabbing at my breast with the other. Squeezing it as he pumps into me.

"I think you're going to make me cum with you," he groans. "Would you like that? Me filling you up as you cum? Our juices mixing, until they are one.

"Yes!" I moan out.

"Tell me, baby."

"Please. Fill me up. I want every drop. Ben. Fuck." I shudder as my whole-body jerks as the first wave hits.

He thrusts fully inside me, grinding himself against me as I explode.

A groan falls from his mouth as he erupts inside me. The feeling drags out my orgasm until I'm sent into another smaller, but just as intense one.

He drops his head to my chest, as he sucks in deep breaths. I pant underneath him, covered in sweat and exhausted.

My pussy throbs, as he holds his thick cock inside me until every last drop is drained. Even as he softens, the thing feels huge or maybe I'm just that sore, either way I enjoy being full of him.

He slips out, dropping to the side of me, and rolling on his back. His arm slides under my neck, pulling me against him.

"Jesus, Prue. I didn't think anything could ever feel that good." I press my head into his side, as his hand rubs along my back. "Are you okay?" I can feel his eyes on me but can't find it in me to look up at him.

"Yeah." I plant a kiss on his side. He laughs, so I keep going, kissing a little pattern into his flesh until he squirms.

"That tickles." He laughs again but doesn't push me away or move. I bite into his flesh. He yelps. "Fuck. Ow."

I shove at him when he doesn't move, trying to pry myself from his hold as my mind struggles to know what to do now that I just had him, but can't keep him. Memories tug at the edge of my mind, trying to surface, but only creating a dark haze.

I'm caught in a tug-a-war of emotions. Bliss fights against agony, anger, and resentment. Part of me wants to put distance between this man who has shown me more kindness than my own parents, while the other part wants to melt into him.

He grabs my hand, yanking me closer and placing my fist on his chest.

"You can push me away in the morning. The sex was too good for you to fall apart now," he says, squeezing me tightly against him. "Save it for the morning, Prue." I try to pull away again, but he keeps me in place. "You're safe, baby. It's okay. I promise, you can relax. All those emotions will be there in the morning, but right now you're safe."

His words cut me deep to my core. They slice me up like I'm butter, yet somehow, they also make my heartbeat slow. Relaxing my fist, I let my hand flatten against his chest, as I bury my head into his side again.

Part of me wants to cry, but my body won't let me, too high on the multiple orgasms he just gave me.

"There you go," he says softly. "Sleep. I'll be right here for you to punch in the morning."

I don't like the idea of hurting him, but the promise of him being here in the morning sedates me. I allow myself to just enjoy the warmth of his body, and his cum dripping down my thighs, as my mind drifts to sleep.

EIGHTEEN

Ben

Prue curls herself into me as she lets sleep overtake her.

I'm content, on a level I never thought I'd reach in my life. I've been happy before, but this feels... *better*.

And I don't like it.

Sex wasn't something I should've let happen between us tonight. There is too much damage between us.

Not the damage we are doing to each other, because that feels good. Even though my cock aches from how fucking tight her little cunt is, whatever the hell is going on between us feels good.

But the damage we both carry inside is what isn't good for us. It's like water and gasoline. If we mix the two there is surely going to be an explosion. And if that explosion is anything like the sex we just had, well I'd take it, but I doubt either of us will survive it.

The sex has to be a one-time thing. If we let it happen again, it's only going to cause more problems for us both. I'm already feeling the pull to stick my cock in her again, and if I do that, well, I'm pretty sure I'll become addicted. If I'm not already.

She already tried to fight and fly right after. When morning comes, she will most likely lose her fucking mind. I can already feel the glare she is bound to shoot me. The sting of whatever verbal abuse she plans on throwing at me is going to leave a scar inside my heart.

I knew that would be the case from the minute she laid down beside me in nothing but a thong, but I couldn't stop it from happening. The moment she put the tip of my cock inside her, I lost whatever control I had. What was I supposed to do? I gave her every chance to stop it, handed her control of the situation, and she wanted me. How could I deny her when she wanted me just as much as I wanted her?

As I tighten my grip around her, forcing her cold body to press firmly against me, I block out all other thoughts.

And not just the bad ones, but the ones that give me hope too.

A loud banging jolts me awake. My surroundings are foreign for a moment until I see that short brown hair and pale skin squirming against me.

"What is that?" Prue groans, her eyes opening and staring at me.

The confusion on her face would be cute if it wasn't for the loud banging coming from somewhere in the house. I try to make sense of the situation, but Prue's bare body is very distracting.

Slowly, my mind pieces things together. The sound is coming from outside the room. Probably the front door. Yes. Someone is pounding at the front door.

"And what time is it?" she mutters, pulling her body from mine. The noise continues, only now I'm pretty sure someone is trying to kick the door in. I don't need to guess who it is. I wasn't born yesterday.

Jumping from the bed, I pull my pants and shirt on as she crawls to the edge of the bed, watching me. I don't doubt she is piecing the situation together too, unless I did manage to fuck her brain-dead last night.

"You stay here," I order.

"You don't live here." She crosses her hands over her bare chest and despite the fact I'm positive her ex is at the front door, my cock throbs.

Part of me wants to throw her on her back and make her cum while her shitty ex bangs on the door. Let him hear her scream my name so he knows she will never want him again.

But I don't.

"Prue. Just stay here," I say, opening the bedroom door. "Does this door lock?"

"No."

"Don't come out. Okay? Stay put."

She nods and I wish I could believe that she will listen to me, but I don't.

I rub my eyes once out in the living room. The banging turns into thuds. He is trying to break down the fucking door like a God damn psychopath.

Prue sure knows how to pick them.

I open the door and Charles stumbles forward, almost landing on his face, but catching himself at the last minute on the side table. He is wearing the same suit from earlier tonight, but he smells like a fucking bar.

After fucking Prue, I have a bigger hatred for him than I already did. It makes what he did feel more personal. And little sense. How could he have had her and not want to worship the ground she walks on?

"Ever heard of knocking?" I ask as he straightens himself.

"Where is the little whore?" he snaps.

I glance out into the hallway. Another guy in a white dress shirt and navy slacks stands outside, glaring at me.

The odds are not in my favor tonight, but I don't care. I've never been scared of taking a hit because I learned how to hit back harder.

"I don't know. Where does your mother live?" I shrug, taking a step back as he shoves his way forward to the space between the living room area and kitchen.

"Prue!" he shouts her name, and I hate the way he makes it sound. The disrespect he shows her makes my blood boil. "Get your fucking ass out here now."

"If she is a good girl, she isn't going to do that."

He flashes me an evil glare, stepping toward me as his friend slips into the apartment.

"Did you fuck her?" His spit lands on my face as he presses his hand to my chest, shoving me into the wall behind me.

"That's not really any of your concern, now, is it?"

"Prue!" he shouts again, keeping his hand firmly against my chest.

"Buddy, I'm going to kindly ask you to remove your hand from my body before I ask not so kindly."

"You think this is some joke?" he barks into my face. "If I don't marry that stupid bitch my parents won't give me my fucking inheritance."

Hearing him call her a bitch makes me vow to never call her that again. I hate the way he makes it sound like a bad thing. I've become rather fond of her bitchy attitude but hearing him use it as an insult makes me angry. So angry, I shove him back.

He stumbles, surprised by how much force I use.

"She isn't going to marry you. In fact, she is never going to be with you again," I snap, grabbing his shirt and tugging him closer to me. "She's gotten a taste of a real man now. She'll never want you back, Charles."

His fist connects with my face in seconds. My eyes snap shut for just a moment, opening just in time to see his fist rise again.

I take another hit to the face before shoving him back.

"Good to know you don't just hit women," I snap, rubbing

my cheek. The feel of blood under my fingertips doesn't even phase me.

"Prue!" he screams again, turning his back to me.

Her frame steps out of the room, and I groan in frustration.

"Why can't you ever listen," I mutter.

"You slept with him?" he shouts, taking a step toward her. She doesn't speak, doesn't move. I slide alongside of him. I don't want him getting any closer to her. "Answer the fucking question!"

"Yes," she responds this time. "And I fucking loved it."

My chest swells with pride. Not just because she admits she loved it, but because she is standing up to him.

I slip in front of him before he can close the space between him and her. His arm is already lifted in the air, but when he realizes he won't be able to hit her, he brings it down on top of my head.

The pain is a little overwhelming, and I bite the inside of my mouth to keep from dropping to the floor.

His other fist slams against my rib. Over and over until I manage to push him back. I get a punch in, straight to his nose. As blood drips from it, he lands another one in my side.

"Stop!" Prue yells. "Charles. Stop."

I hate hearing her say his name. It's the last thing I ever want to hear her say again.

He lands another punch to my side, forcing a groan from my lips as it makes all the air leave my lungs. Shoving me to the side, as my legs wobble. I reach forward, despite the pain radiating through my body, grabbing his arm. He tries to tug free, but I dig my nails in.

"I'm going to fucking kill you," he snaps at me. "But first I'm going to show little Prue here what happens when she doesn't behave."

"I'll marry you," she says quickly. "I'll behave. do whatever you say, just stop. Please," she pleads. And I hate it. I don't want her to beg for my safety. Don't want her to offer herself up to try to save me.

"Shut up," he snaps at her. "You're going to do that regardless."

He breaks free of my grip, marching toward her. In a moment, he is pushing her against the wall, raising his fist in the air.

And I see red.

NINETEEN

Prue

One second, I'm bracing myself for Charles' fist to hit me, the next he is being pulled backwards.

Ben's arm wraps around Charles' neck, yanking him back. His fist connects with Charles's rib, over and over until Michael, Charles' friend, springs to action. He grabs Ben, making him wince, but he doesn't let go of his hold on Charles. I can't see much from where I stand frozen, but Michael yells out in pain suddenly.

"I have no beef with you, other than having shitty taste in friends, so consider that a warning," Ben snaps at Michael. "Stay out of this."

Charles is gasping for air, struggling to break free of Ben's hold. Michael slinks away from them both, like a coward.

"Charles," Ben says his name likes its pure evil. "I need you to listen to me very carefully."

"Fuck you," Charles chokes out.

"That's not listening," Ben says, landing another punch to his gut. "You see that beautiful girl right in front of you?" he asks, gripping Charles' face, making him stare at me. "Take a good long look, because you're never going to see her again, okay? If I ever hear that you even came close to her, I will fucking kill you, and it won't be quick. Do you understand?"

"Fuck you," Charles spits out again.

"Wrong. Fucking. Answer." Ben drops Charles' face and next thing I know he has a pocketknife in his hands. He unfolds it. "Let's try this one more time." He holds the knife in front of Charles' face. That gets his attention. "If you ever come near Prue again, I will gut you like the fucking pig you are. Understand?"

"I'll press charges. That's a threat. I have a witness."

"And I have money," Ben counters. "If you think a jail cell will keep me from finding a way to kill you, think again."

"Fine," Charles says. "Have her. It's not like I can't find another cheap slut anyways."

Ben doesn't release him, instead he forces him to turn toward the door. His hand still wrapped around his chest, while the other holds the knife at his neck. He motions for Michael to exit first. He does, keeping his head low. Charles isn't going to be very happy with him.

Ben shoves Charles out the front door, slamming it shut behind him and doing up the lock. He folds the knife back up, slipping it into his pocket, before resting his head against the door.

"Are you okay?" I ask after a moment of silence. I find myself unable to move from the wall. Everything that just happened bounces around my head. It's too much to make sense of right now, so I try to keep myself grounded, focusing on Ben instead of the onslaught of emotions that threaten to break me apart.

"Are you?"

"Yes," I whisper, though I'm not so sure that's true. I don't feel any pain, but I don't feel much of anything right now.

"Liar," he says, turning his head toward me. His cheek is busted and bloody. I think I'm broken beyond repair because part of me finds it sexy while the other part wants to magically erase the damage my ex caused.

"At least I answered." He laughs, pulling away from the door.

Taking a step toward me, he pauses, wincing in pain. "We should get you to the hospital," I say, pushing myself from the wall to move toward him.

"I'm fine. I've taken worse." He grins. Hugging his side, I can tell he is barely keeping himself upright. Memories of the way I felt after Charles beat me surface, but I shove them away. Now is not the time to dwell on that.

"I've been on the other side of his rage. I know the damage he can inflict."

"Don't remind me," he groans. "I'm this close to going after him and ending his sad existence as it is."

"Please don't," I say. "Just sit." He nods, sliding to his knees on the ground. Groaning as he leans forward pressing his head to the wooden floor. "I meant on the couch," I whisper, dropping to my knees beside him.

"I just need a minute," he mutters. I can tell it hurts him to breathe. I remember how long it took for it not to hurt for me.

"He cracked my rib, probably did the same to you." I touch his head and he hisses. "You might even have a concussion."

"Baby," he groans. "I'm barely keeping from flying off the handle. Please stop talking."

"Okay." I fold my hands in my lap.

I want to curl up and cry. Let myself fall to pieces, hide under a dozen blankets and forget I exist.

How did I get myself into this mess? And why did I drag Ben into it with me? He didn't ask for any of this. I just piled it on him without thinking. It was very selfish of me.

What was I thinking even getting involved with Ben? I knew Charles' family wanted him to marry me. They had a lot riding on our union. They want my family to join their fold, so they had control over their money and company. My parents didn't see anything wrong merging businesses, they hoped it would make their empire bigger. I knew his parents were pressuring him to fix things with me. I didn't think they would hold his inheritance over his head, but it makes sense.

It's not like either of our families play fair when it comes to earning their loyalty or love.

I shouldn't have made a big deal about Charles cheating on me. Shouldn't have threatened to break up with him. If I just played my part, pretended to not know, none of this would be happening.

Sure, I would've missed out on getting to sleep with Ben. And the sex was really great, great enough to almost make it worth all this. Almost.

But come morning, Ben is going to leave and never call me again. I will be left to beg Charles for his forgiveness. Take whatever abuse he dishes out and marry him. I'll have to go back to being the girl everyone expects me to be and put on a happy face, like I'm not miserable.

Ben lifts his head, looking at me. "I told you to stay in the room."

"I'm sorry. I was worried about you."

"I had it under control," he says, slowly lifting his head off the floor. "Mostly. Fuck." He grabs at his side. "It's been a while since someone punched me. I forgot how much it hurts." He laughs, then wheezes.

"You really should go to the hospital."

"What will they do? Put me in a wrap and hand me some pain pills? I don't need any of that bullshit," he says, resting on his knees.

"What if you have internal bleeding?"

"I probably do," he groans as he pushes himself to his feet. Walking gingerly toward the couch he picks up the bottle from where he left it earlier. "They will just monitor me for a few hours and then send me a check for half a million dollars." He takes a sip from the bottle.

"Drinking is probably not a good idea right now."

"Nothing is a good idea right now." He plops down on the couch and curses in pain. "Sit where I can see you."

"Why?" I ask, but move to the couch, sitting on the other end of it. I think if he touches me right now, I will fall apart.

"I don't trust you not to bolt. You're a minute away from throwing yourself at the prick's feet and begging him to take you back because it sounds easier than this." He waves his hand in the air.

How does he seem to know me so well? No one has ever been able to read me like Ben does and it makes my stomach tense up. I don't like him knowing me like that. It makes me feel too exposed. Too vulnerable.

"It is easier," I whisper, tucking my knees against my chest. "I'm sorry I dragged you into this."

"Do you really think you could drag me into anything?" He looks over at me. "You could barely take my cock." He smirks, taking another sip of alcohol. "I got involved because I wanted to."

"You felt compelled. Obligated."

"Ha. You really haven't caught on, have you?" He stretches his legs out, groaning in pain. "I don't do anything unless I want to."

"Sure. You only ever do whatever it takes to get what you want. Now you've fucked me, gotten what you wanted and when the sun comes up, you'll be gone and never talk to me again."

"I said we could be friends." He cocks his head at me. "Didn't I say that? I'm not going anywhere, Prue. You are stuck with me." His eyes shut and the bottle rests in the crook of his arm. "Better get used to it, baby."

I don't know what to say to that, so I stay quiet. Slowly his breathing evens out and I realize he must have fallen asleep. I move forward, taking the bottle from his arm and he sighs, dropping on his side and groaning.

"Lay with me," he says, holding his arm out for me.

"You're hurt."

"Yeah, but holding you might heal me."

I carefully lie down beside him, trying not to press my back into him, but letting my head rest on his arm. He sighs before pulling me against his chest. A small gasp leaves his mouth before his breathing evens out again.

I don't want to be stuck with him. I won't. Tomorrow I'm going to do whatever it takes to get him to hate me. To push him until he wants nothing to do with me. Then I will return to the weak girl I've always been.

Go back to being pathetic Prue, the person my parents want and Charles' future wife.

TWENTY

Ben

I WAKE UP IN AGONY. MY HEAD THROBS, MY RIBS FEEL like they've been hit with a steel pipe, my cheek feels like it's twice the size as normal, and my cock is digging into Prue's ass in a way that makes my balls ache.

"Do you always get hard in the morning?" Prue asks when I shift.

"I don't normally wake up with a nice ass grinding against my crotch."

"I'm not grinding. I'm trying to get out of your death grip." She pulls at my arm. "Let me up."

"No," I say, tightening my hold on her. "I'm almost better."

"I need to pee." She sighs, going still. "So, unless you want me to pee on you, you need to let me up."

"I'm not really into water play." I nuzzle my head against her neck. "But if the alternative is having to let you go, I might have to deal with it."

"Ben. Please."

"Fine," I groan, releasing her. She gets up walking out of sight.

I roll on my back, trying to assess the damage to my body. Letting my hand lightly touch my side, I wince from the sharp pain. Jesus. He probably did break a rib. Not the first time, but it's been a while. I feel the top of my head. There isn't a bump yet, just a spot that is tender to touch.

Glancing at my knuckles, I notice a few bruises forming. I've stopped punching people when we got signed. Didn't want to break a finger and risk missing a show, but since my band is pretty much over, I didn't care last night.

That's not even true. I think even if I knew I had a show to play tonight I would've punched Charles. I'd do worse if Prue wasn't around. She didn't need to witness just how unhinged that man could make me.

Prue comes back a moment later, standing above me. Her eyes study me and I plant a smile on my face to try to hide the pain.

"Bet you wish you had those pain pills, huh?"

"No." I force myself to sit up. Biting the inside of my mouth hoping not to show an ounce of pain, I keep my lips curved up.

"Just lay back down. I'll make you breakfast." She rolls her eyes, resting her hands on her hips.

"No need to make it." I smirk. "I'll just have what's between your legs."

Her eyes do another loop. "I'm afraid my pussy isn't on the menu."

"Special request and you know, it's good for business to honor a request given by a famous rock star."

"What do you like? Eggs?" she says, marching to the kitchen.

"What time is it anyways?"

"Like ten. We slept in."

"Shit. I have to go get ready for lunch with Aaron and his fiancée." I push myself to my feet, trying not to puke from the pain.

"Right." She nods. "Should you still go to that? Your face is a little..."

"He has seen me worse. And you should go change, unless you want to go like that." I eye her light pink lacy shorts and tank top. "I know I wouldn't complain if you did." I smirk.

"I can't go. I have plans." She doesn't look at me as she talks.

"Bullshit." I march over to her, without letting an ounce of pain show across my face. My body is throbbing, and I can barely see straight as my feet slam across the wooden floor. "I did not take the fucking beating I took for you to lie to me, Prue. I did not threaten to kill that fucker for you to go running back to him because you're worried, I'm in over my head." I grab her chin, forcing her to look at me. "So, I'm keeping you by my side, until I'm convince you won't go back to him the second you are out of my sight, understood?"

"Or what?" She glares at me. "You'll put a knife to my throat?"

"Never." I grin. "I'll put my cock down it."

"Joke's on you then, because I like that."

"Oh. I know you do." I smile, releasing my grip on her chin. "Now go get changed. I'm not letting you freeze to death."

She sighs, marching off to her bedroom. I follow her after a moment. Each breath feels like I'm being stabbed but I know if she sees an ounce of pain on my face she will be overwhelmed with guilt, and her flight or fight response will activate.

I take to sitting on her bed, watching as she digs through her drawers. A turtleneck is laying on the edge of the bed. She tosses a pair of black jeans beside them.

"You don't need the turtlenecks anymore," I say, picking it up. "Though they've kind of grown on me."

Her eyes roll, as she pulls off her tank top. Her tits are mouth wateringly perky. And her nipples stick out just taunting me, begging me even, to pinch and pull them.

"My eyes are up here," she snaps, quickly sliding on a bra. "You act like you've never seen a pair of tits before."

"None as nice as yours."

"Now who's the liar." She laughs. "You've been with porn stars and models, with perfectly made tits."

"Ah. Don't be jealous," I tease.

"Should I get tested?" she asks, sliding on a pair of cute pink cotton panties. "We didn't use a condom."

"I'm fairly confident you are safe."

"Fairly confident isn't a no." She grabs the yellow turtleneck from my hands. "If you gave me an STD, I will murder you."

"God, that would be a sight to see." I smile as she tugs on her jeans. "I'd love to have you put me out of my misery. Would you fuck me first? Try to cut off my cock with that tight little pussy of yours?"

"No." She shakes her head. "I'd smother you with it."

"Even better."

"You are so annoying," she huffs, sitting on the bed. "Can't even have a normal conversation. Always having to be cocky and arrogant. Does it ever get tiring?"

"Does rolling your eyes?"

"Yes, but I only seem to do it when I'm around you."

"Good to know." I laugh. "I like knowing I have a one-of-a-kind effect on you."

She laces up some black converse before standing up. She grabs her purse from last night, dumping the content into another purse before turning to look at me.

"Are you ready?"

"Yes." I smile, sliding off the bed.

It's pure agony to move right now, but I refuse to let her ass of an ex fully kill my band. Just like I refuse to let her go back to him. I'd die before letting her return to that situation, before I'd let her be in danger.

TWENTY-ONE

Prye

Ben leaves me in his living room as he goes into his bedroom to change. I wander around his condo, skimming over the bookshelves full of books and knickknacks. A small snow globe of Salt Lake City sits on one shelf, and I pick it up, shaking it and watching the glitter snow fall. I stare at a picture he has framed of his band. They look much younger and stand outside a brown, beat-up van.

Behind it is a picture frame of a man with his arms around Joan, Ben's mother. Another woman is crouched down with her arms around a young Ben. He looks to be 7 or 8. Everyone is smiling in the picture. The trees and tents in the background let me know it was probably some camping trip or something.

"What a happy family, huh?" His voice makes me jump.

"Who's that?" I ask, pointing to the woman with her arms around him.

"The devil," he says. "Let's go."

I set the photo back down, knowing in my gut that whoever she is, is the one who hurt him.

Why he keeps a picture of it makes no sense. I already deleted all the pictures I had of Charles and me, and part of me knew I'd have no choice but to take him back but seeing him makes me ill.

More so when he has his arms around me, but knowing Ben, it's probably some kind of self-punishment.

I never thought someone who walks around acting like such a big asshole would secretly hate himself as much as Ben seems to. It makes me sad to think about how he carries around his pain in silence.

Part of me is jealous, because it's becoming increasingly hard to carry mine quietly, and he seems to have it down to a science.

Ben weaves through traffic with such ease while I grip onto the door handle, hoping he doesn't kill us both. He has music playing through the speakers, not so loud that I couldn't talk, but loud enough to imply he doesn't want me to.

That should make me happy. My plan is to make him hate me, but the idea he might without me having to do anything stings a little.

He is in pain, I tell myself. That's why he wants silence. I can tell he is in a lot more than he wants to admit. It's clear from the way he leans himself against the seat, trying to keep the seatbelt from touching his ribs. His cheek is black and blue. The gash is small, but the way his skin is raised makes it look worse.

"Aaron is the other guitarist?" I ask finally.

"Yes," he says. "His fiancée is Stacy. I like her, she doesn't tag along with us on tour very often, which means I don't have to see her very much, but we recently all went to dinner, and I may have picked up on the fact she is pregnant and ruined the surprise."

"You're such an asshole."

"Yes." He nods. "I've apologized but they want me to grovel, so thus this lunch. And I'm just pathetic enough to do it."

"Would you grovel for me?"

"Yes," he replies quickly, and it makes my stomach tense. "Told you last night I'd worship you. I wasn't lying."

"Ben," I say, and his eyes dart to me for a moment. "This doesn't end well for us."

"What doesn't end well?"

"This. Us. Whatever we're doing."

"We are just friends who fucked, Prue. Don't confuse my desire to worship you as more than a desperate plead to make sure you don't do something stupid and reckless. Plus, your pussy is really fucking good."

"You are lying."

"How so?"

"You like me." I smile smugly at him. His eyes dart to me, lips pressed in a firm line. I'm hoping to push him away with my accusation, but part of me also hopes he admits its true.

"You aren't wrong," he says, eyes drifting back to the road. "That's why I'm making you my friend."

"No." I laugh. "You like me, like, like like me." I keep my smug smile on my face, hoping he takes the bait. Daring him to push me away. There is no way, playboy Ben is going to stick around when I accuse him of having a crush on me.

"What do you want from me, Prue?" he asks. "You want me to say no and tell you you're out of your fucking mind? That a guy like me doesn't fall for a girl, ever? Want me to freak out and suddenly create some distance between us? Like I'm so fucking scared of the idea of commitment that I rather never talk to you again than have you thinking I like you?"

I shrug, taunting him with my eyes. He may be able to read me well, but can he resist his playboy ways?

"Because that is not happening. So what? I like you. Doesn't change the fact I don't do commitment. Doesn't change the fact I'm not going anywhere and doesn't mean we can't be friends."

"So, we are just friends, right? Meaning I'm free to fuck whoever I want?"

"Yes." He nods. "Meaning we can both fuck whoever we want." He side eyes me. "But lucky for me, you only want to fuck me right now." His lips curve into a smug smile of his own. "Don't think I couldn't tell that you've never cum so hard as you did last night with my fat cock buried deep inside of you. You want to try to push me away? Do your best, baby. I told you before and you've now seen it firsthand. I know how to take a punch."

Turning my attention to the world outside as Ben continues to weave through LA traffic, I sigh. Getting rid of Ben isn't going to be easy. He is more determined than I thought, but he underestimates me. I'm not going to just let him stick around. I'll push him to his breaking point if that's what I have to do.

Anything to release him from the burdens I bring to the table. Because logically he should want nothing to do with me. He should be running for the hills after last night.

It feels good that he hasn't yet, but it's not fair to either of us. I was dealt a role in life, just like him, and sadly for the both of us, our roles don't mix.

So, I will not stop pushing until Ben disappears from my life completely.

TWENTY-TWO

Ben

I SMOKE A CIGARETTE OUTSIDE, IGNORING THE FACT Aaron has called me twice and we are ten minutes late.

Prue hasn't said much after trying to egg me on in the car and failing. I didn't really want to confess that I had a thing for her, but whatever. Part of me was hoping she'd get the fucking hint and stop trying to push me away, but I know that's not going to be the case.

She has herself convinced that she needs to go back to that jerk and now all I can do is try to keep her from doing that, just long enough for her to come to her senses.

Her arms are folded over her chest as she stares everywhere but at me.

My phone buzzes again and I see Wes's name blink at me this time. I can't not take his call. After everything he has done for me, I know better than to not answer when he calls. I sigh, hitting answer.

"Hey," I say into the phone, and Prue finally looks at me.

"Where the fuck are you? Aaron is pissed. He thinks you stood him up," Wes says.

"I'm outside having a fucking cigarette. Jesus, it's only like 12:10."

"Ben, are you trying to break up the band? Is this your way of letting us know that if we don't play by your terms, you'll destroy us?"

That is a wild accusation. Insane really. Why would I want to destroy the band I'm desperately trying to hold on to? It's not like I have much else going for me. My eyes linger on Prue, and I realize that maybe the band not touring for a bit would give me more time with her. Though if I had to, I'd take her on tour with me. Drag her across the country so she doesn't crawl back to hell.

I can't say that to Wes, at least not right now. Obviously, everyone just thinks I'm acting out. I'm sure there is a secret text chain where they complain about me.

I've become the problem child. Always have been, but they no longer enjoy my antics.

"No," I say firmly. "I've just had a long fucking night and I need some god damn nicotine before going to take his verbal lashing."

Prue's face drops and I roll my eyes. Mentioning having a long night was the wrong thing to say in front of her. I don't need her feeling any more guilty than she already does.

"You could've answered his calls," Wes says. "Jesus, Ben. Are you using again? I'm growing more concerned by the day."

"Funny way of showing it," I reply before I can stop myself. I do not need to make Wes feel bad for being in love. He has earned himself more happiness than he will ever get.

"Not answering the question isn't helping your case."

"I'm not fucking using. Jesus Christ. What about your pretty little girlfriend? Has she put a needle in her arm recently? What about her fingers down her throat?" He doesn't reply, and I'm losing my patience with everything around me, but snapping at Wes is a new low for me. I'm just angry and tired and in so much pain I kind of wish I was dead. Not to mention the memories tugging at the back of my head that came from seeing that photo in Prue's hands. "I'm sorry, Wes. I'm really sorry, okay? I might have a mild concussion and broken ribs. It has been a really long 24 hours."

Prue nods her head with a smug little smile on her face. I wish that smile didn't make me want to kiss her so fucking bad, but something about the way she looks when copping an attitude makes my insides melt.

When Wes doesn't reply for a moment, I know what I said must have really hurt him. He isn't the kind of guy to snap back, he is more of the type to stew with the anger and come back with a well-adjusted response, which I hate but could really use right now. He is the last person I want to hurt in the world. I can't afford to lose him.

"What is going on with you, Ben?" he finally asks.

"Nothing," I reply. "I'm just an asshole. Sorry you got stuck with me."

"I didn't get stuck with you. I picked you," Wes says. "Saw you getting your ass kicked and decided to take pity on you." He laughs.

"Thank you," I say softly. "I'm sorry. I will go in there and make nice."

"Good. Maybe you can come over for pizza tomorrow. We can talk about music and shit. You can tell me how you got the concussion."

"Maybe. I'll text you."

"I'm still here for you, Ben."

"I know," I say, hanging up.

"Abbey does drugs?" Prue asks.

"No. And if you tell a soul anything you just heard…"

"You'll kill me? Are there some things you hold dear, Ben? Some things you're too scared to lose?" A sly smile forms over her face, making my cock ache. "Do I now have even more power over you?"

Tossing my cigarette to the ground, I press her against the wall she is leaning against, ignoring the pain that shoots through my body. Shifting so my leg is wedged between her thighs, I cup her face.

"I won't kill you. Just myself," I say softly, letting my leg nudge the front of her jeans. "And then you'll never get to feel my cock splitting you open again."

Her eyes light up, as if the memory of me inside her still lingers in her mind.

"The only way your cock ever goes back inside me, is if you get on your knees and beg," she says, ripping her face from my hands.

The cute little demanding voice she speaks with makes my dick throb, and if my whole fucking career wasn't riding on going into this stupid restaurant and making nice with Aaron, I'd drop to my knees and beg right here.

"I'll keep that in mind," I say, pulling away from her body. "Can you just play nice for me right now? Just help me survive this lunch and I will gladly beg when it's over."

"Fine." Her blue eyes spin. "But only because I like your band and would hate for it not to exist anymore."

"You like my band?"

"I might own a shirt or two." She shrugs, following me to the door.

"That's hot. Can I fuck you while you wear one?" I ask, pulling the door open for her.

"God, all you talk about is sex now. It's like you're addicted to my pussy," she whispers as we step inside the restaurant.

"Maybe I am," I whisper into her ear. "It might be the best thing I ever tasted."

I spot Aaron and Stacy in a corner booth and grab Prue's hand, pulling her through the maze of tables. I slide in the booth across from Aaron who glares at me, seeming unaware I brought a girl along or that I have a busted cheek, or maybe he just doesn't care. Hard to tell these days.

"Hello," I say, placing my palms on the table, as Prue slides in beside me. "Did you order already?"

"No," Aaron snaps. "Wasn't sure you were going to show."

"You know me." I grin. "Couldn't be on time if my life depended on it."

"Hi," Stacy cuts in before Aaron can reply. "I'm Stacy and this is Aaron. I'm sure you know this already, but Ben is too rude to do introductions." She smiles at Prue and I kind of regret ruining her surprise, because she is making this a lot smoother for me.

"Too rude to do a lot of things." Prue laughs. "I'm Prue. It's nice to meet you."

Aaron looks her over, studying her before turning back to me. "You're fifteen minutes late and you brought a date?"

"A friend," I correct. "I'm babysitting." Prue's mouth drops open as she shoots me a death glare. "She's Cameron Ward's twin sister. You remember Cam from that band we toured with last summer."

"Great Falls," Prue adds. "His band is Great Falls, you asshole."

Aaron laughs. "I like her. Did she give you that?" He nods to my cheek.

"No," I say firmly.

"In a way I did," Prue says, with a smug smile. I know she is trying to push me to snap.

"No, you didn't. Do not take responsibility for that prick's crime," I say, trying to keep my voice low. "And I thought you were going to behave."

"You said play nice." She rolls her eyes. "Maybe my nice is different than yours."

"Oh, this is interesting." Aaron sits back, taking a sip from his beer. "A girl who seems unfazed by you." He laughs. "Never thought I'd see the day where you couldn't charm the pants off a girl."

"You'd be surprised." I shrug, biting my cheek to keep from groaning in pain. "You have no idea how unfazed she is by me. Utterly unimpressed."

"Not utterly unimpressed," Prue says. "You are good at some things."

"Like?" Aaron asks. "What can you possibly find impressive about his sorry ass?"

Part of me knows he is just playing around. Poking fun at me because of what I did the other night, but part of me knows he does think less of me. I'm the odd one out. They are all my friends, but only because of Wes and the music we make. If it wasn't for Wes, we would've never become friends.

"He knows how to play guitar," Prue replies. "Probably better than anyone else."

"Including me?" Aaron raises an eyebrow.

"Including you." She nods. Something inside me swells. I don't need Prue to think highly of me. I accepted that she thinks I'm an asshole from night one, but it's nice to hear her stick up for me.

"When he isn't drunk as a skunk, I guess." Aaron laughs. "Or being a giant asshole."

"He isn't wrong." I shrug.

When the waiter comes to take our orders, Prue orders a salad and I fight the urge to order her something with some fucking iron. The girl is far too pale and skinny, but I know better than to push her right now. My future is in her hands.

"So, Ben tells me you're pregnant," Prue says to Stacy. "Says he ruined the surprise."

"We were going to tell everyone after dinner, but yes, he just had to ruin the moment." Stacy laughs.

"Well, you know Ben, always causing a scene." Prue smiles at me, and I know whatever she is about to say next is not going to be good for me. "Congratulations. I'm destined for motherhood too. Though probably not for a few years. Charles will want to get settled into the family business first."

"Charles?" Stacy asks, glancing between the both of us. Curiosity rests in Aaron's face now and I hate it.

I grip the booth tightly, trying not to react. She is just trying to get me to snap. She knows how much is riding on this lunch going well, and she thinks if she pushes me now, that I'll walk away from her. Let her go back to him. But that isn't happening.

"He is my fiancé, well... will be soon."

"Prue," I say, my voice filled with warning.

"And he is fine with you hanging out with Ben?" Stacy laughs. "Must be a very healthy relationship. I'm not even sure I trust Aaron around him."

"It has its moments, but I think we are determined to make it last." Prue smiles outwardly, but I can see behind her eyes that the words are starting to sink in. She wants to paint it out to be some kind of fairytale, but inside it's killing her to say out loud. "He is a great guy. Truly, just top notch. He is going into finance and once we are married our families' firms will merge, creating a wonderful empire. He will take good care of me. I'm going to be a great wife."

"I'll kill him before I let that fucking happen," I snap. "I swear to God, Prue. I will end his fucking life before I let you marry that fucking piece of shit." Stacy flinches as my voice raises, and Aaron just stares at me. "You really said all that with a straight face?" I say, turning toward her. "Really? You called him a great guy? A great guy, Prue? Really?" Her eyes drop to the table. "Tell me, Prue. If he is so fucking great, why the hell did I have to hold a knife to his fucking neck to make him leave you alone last night? Huh? Explain that to them."

"Ben," Aaron says. "I don't think making a scene is going to make her feel any better about the situation."

"I don't give two shits if she feels better about it. I want her to feel bad about it. I need her to hear how fucking silly her words sound. Think them over, Prue. Really hear what you just said. You want to make Mommy and Daddy happy at any fucking cost, huh? Who gives a shit if you're happy as long as everyone else is, right? Don't give a fuck about your wellbeing because it's easier to cover bruises than hit back." I push at her to slide out of the booth. She goes easily, standing up and looking at the ground. "It sounds fucking ridiculous. And I'm not letting it happen, okay?" I push myself to my feet, too angry to feel any pain. "Even if I have to glue myself to your fucking side, I am not letting you end up with him."

I take a few steps toward the exit, ready to be out of the cage that is this fucking fancy restaurant. Leave it to Aaron and Stacy to pick a rich place to make me beg for their forgiveness.

Prue doesn't move when I take a step. I groan, ready to rip my hair out.

"We are leaving," I say, grabbing her arm. "I'm not in the mood to grovel for them."

She looks up at me. Tears threatening to spill from her eyes, as she glares at me. "Why should I go anywhere with you ever again?"

"Because." I pause. God, this girl is going to be the fucking death of me. I swear she is going to drive me insane. When she is all better, when she no longer needs me anymore, there is going to be nothing left of me.

And I'm perfectly okay with that.

TWENTY-THREE

Prue

I'M HOLDING BACK TEARS. BEN'S LITTLE SCENE STUNG worse than the tattoo I got last night or the way his cock made my pussy stretch, but when he drops to his knees in front of me, I can't look away.

"Prue," he says my name, staring up at me. "I know I'm an asshole. Probably one of the biggest assholes you've ever met, and I'm sorry. Okay? You didn't deserve that, but to be fair my fucking head is killing me, and I think my rib is trying to stab me in the lung. I know you probably hope it does, but unfortunately for you, I don't plan on dying until you stop being fucking crazy and come to terms with the fact you are not going back to that piece of shit."

"Are you lecturing me or begging?" I raise an eyebrow, folding my arms over my chest and glaring down at him.

Everything about this is hot. He is literally on his knees, in a public restaurant, with his bandmate sitting right there, begging me. Well, more like apologizing, but either way, it does something to me. Makes my stomach tense and my pussy wet.

"I apologize. You asked me to beg, so fine." He closes his eyes for a moment, letting out a deep breath, before looking at me again. "Please, Prue, I need you to forgive me. I desperately want to make it up to you in ways you can't possibly imagine. Last night was just a sneak peek at how good I can make you feel. Let me worship you and your pussy. Allow me the chance to show you that while, yes, I am a huge asshole, I still know exactly how to make you cum."

My cheeks heat up, knowing so many people are hearing this, but at the same time, I like it. Let them see that I can make a notorious playboy, get on his knees and beg for me.

"Doubtful." I roll my eyes. "Your ribs are at the very least bruised, and you probably have a concussion, so I highly doubt you could make me cum now."

"Now? Like right now? Because I have no problem proving how wrong you are with an audience, but I think the restaurant manager might." He smirks that stupid smirk that makes my chest tighten.

"I meant now, like today, asshole."

"I'm sorry." He smiles. "My mistake. But if you think a broken rib or concussion would keep me from worshipping at the alter that is your perfect pussy, you are wrong. It's the least I could do. Let me show you what it feels like to be free of the pressure to please everyone else and just get to enjoy your own pleasure."

I stare down at him. He keeps his eyes on me, full of lust and determination. For a moment, I think he may actually throw me to the floor and devour me right here. A tiny part of me wishes he would.

"Prue, baby, should I go on?" He raises an eyebrow.

"If you have more to say, sure."

He chuckles. "More to say? I could fill a whole fucking discography with everything I want to say to you, but it's hard to think when the blood in my body is going other places..."

"I told you, you had internal bleeding." I cut in.

"Not there, baby. Having you stare down at me while I literally beg to make you cum in a restaurant full of people is making my cock hard."

"Glad to help you discover a new kink."

"Let me help you discover one back."

"Get off the floor. You look pathetic." I roll my eyes.

"Do you not like it when I look pathetic?"

"I do, but I'm pretty sure we are about to be kicked out," I say, nodding to a man in a suit that is making his way quickly toward us. Ben glances over his shoulder and groans.

"God, how many times do I have to get my ass kicked for you?" He pushes himself to his feet.

"How many more times do you have left?" I counter, smirking at him.

"As many more as you'd like."

"Ben," Aaron says, and we both look to him. He jerks his head toward a door behind him.

Ben nods, grabbing my hand and dragging me out the door.

Once outside, I let out a little chuckle as he leads me to his car. None of what he said inside was funny, not before he dropped to his knees or after, but I laugh anyways.

Ben has a way of making me feel alive. Happy. Excited. Desired. I have no idea how I'm going to live without those feelings once I go back to my old life.

"Did you enjoy that?" he asks, flashing me a smile. He unlocks his car, opening the door for me. I slide in, flashing him a grin.

"Yes. I enjoyed that very much."

"I'm glad," he says, shutting the door.

When he climbs into the driver's seat, starting the car, I can't help the big smile plastered on my face. The plan doesn't change. I still need to push him away, but it's nice to know Ben Parker is willing to do pretty much anything for me.

TWENTY-FOUR

Ben

PRUE EYES ME AS I DRIVE. I CAN FEEL HER STARING BUT can't bring myself to look her way.

It's not lost on me that I literally fell to my knees for her. If it was only in front of strangers that would be one thing, but I did it in front of Aaron, my friend and bandmate. That changes everything. There is no way he doesn't run and tell the others.

I have lost my fucking mind.

They are used to me pulling stupid shit, but never like this. I've never lost my cool over a girl before. My ability to be rational when it comes to Prue is non-existent apparently, and now she knows it.

"I'm sorry," she finally says.

I didn't expect an apology. She knew what she was doing. Her intention was to push my buttons. I can't blame her for her behavior these last few days. She is going through a lot and I'm more than willing to take whatever she dishes. In fact, I'm growing to like it.

I should've handled myself better. Losing my cool wasn't okay. I should've kept myself together, for her sake, and not taken the bait. It's just the idea of her being with him triggers me in ways I can't explain.

I'm trying to tell myself it's all about her being safe, but deep down I know there is another layer to it. I don't want her to be with him because he isn't me. That part fucking scares me.

"For what exactly?"

"Making you mad."

"Was it not your intention to upset me?"

"No," she whispers.

"Don't lie," I reply playfully, so she sees I'm not upset with her. "You might be able to lie well to others, but I see right through it."

"Okay, so I was trying to push your buttons, but you didn't need to fly off the handle like that," she snaps back.

"You're right," I say, glancing over at her. Her mouth drops open, as she processes what I just said. "I'm sorry, Prue. Losing my cool like that wasn't very nice of me. It wasn't my place to say that stuff in the company of others. I'm truly sorry, which I hope I made very clear when I was on my knees, begging for your forgiveness."

"You did a pretty good job." She scoffs. "Though it didn't need to be so vulgar."

"Didn't it?" I flash her a cocky smile.

"Not in public." She sighs. "I think I'm losing my mind."

"You don't say?" I laugh.

She pushes at my arm, and I grip the wheel tighter, sucking in a labored breath that I hope she doesn't notice. The sudden movement makes my side ache.

"Really, Ben. What the hell am I doing?"

"Processing. It's going to take time to become someone new, Prue. Time and effort. It doesn't happen overnight. The struggle between staying with what you know and changing is hard. Learning to live with the pain takes time. Trust me, I know. But you'll get there."

"What happens when I do?"

"Huh?"

"When I'm someone new, what happens? Will you stop bothering me? Finally leave me alone?"

"If that's what you want, sure. Or we can stay friends." I shrug.

I don't like her asking that question. I don't want to think that far ahead. The idea of not being around her feels *wrong*. It's only been a week of having her in my life. Not even a full week at that, but she has managed to make a mark on my life. I don't know what I'm going to do without her now.

It's stupid really. Insane. I shouldn't feel like this after only a few days. Shouldn't be spilling all my secrets, making scenes or getting my ass kicked for her, but here we are.

I'm in way too deep and liking it too much.

"You'd still be my friend? Even after everything I've done and said? I've been a real bitch."

"I'd like to stop using that word to describe you," I say, pressing my lips together at the memory of the way Charles called her that.

"Bitch? I thought it was your favorite thing to call me." She laughs.

"Not anymore."

"Since when?"

"I don't want to talk about it."

"Okay." She laughs again. "So, what would you like to call me now?"

"Mine."

The word comes out before I can stop it. Luckily for me, the car in front of me slams on their brakes. As I slam on mine to avoid hitting him, I hope she didn't hear what I just said.

The car jerks, making the seatbelt tighten around my sore ribs. My hand swings to the side to keep her from hitting the dashboard. It has become my first instinct to keep her safe at all costs.

"Fuck," she yells.

"Sorry. This idiot just slammed on his brakes for no reason. Are you okay?"

"Yes. Asshole. Learn to drive better." She laughs.

"I'll get right on it." I sigh, grateful she didn't hear me.

What the fuck did I just say? Mine? Am I having a fucking stroke? Jesus Christ. I need to get my shit together. Mine? I'm an idiot. Fucking stupid.

There is no world in which Prue can be mine. There isn't a chance in hell that ends up well for either of us. I don't do commitment and she deserves more than I can ever offer.

Prue Ward is never going to be mine.

And that hurts more than any bruise could.

More than the memories I pretend don't exist.

TWENTY-FIVE

Prue

Ben stops by a drug store. He makes me go inside with him since he is convinced I'll bolt if he doesn't have eyes on me at all times. It's a little annoying to be treated like a child, but I probably deserve it.

He is right too. I would bolt if left alone. I need to get far away from Ben before I do something stupid. Like fall in love with him or something that will lead to more pain for the both of us.

He grabs some lotions and a bottle of aspirin. I toss in a bag of overpriced chocolates and a box of tampons trying to annoy him. He doesn't say a word or react in any way. I throw in a box of condoms and a bottle of lube, hoping that will irritate him. Still, he doesn't react, so I grab a pack of adult diapers, going to drop that into the basket he carries.

"Want an enema too?" he asks, raising an eyebrow.

"Do you need one?" I counter. "I'd be happy to stick something up your ass."

"I'll make you a deal. You can stick something up mine if I can stick something up yours." He smirks.

Sighing, I put them back on the shelf. Next, I return the condoms and grab for the lube. He wraps his hand around my wrist.

"Leave it. In case you take me up on my offer." He winks.

I roll my eyes but drop the lube back in the basket. I leave the other items too, because free tampons and chocolate are not things any girl would pass up.

When we slide back into the car, he rests his back against the seat for a second, taking slow breaths. Clearly, he is more pain than he feels like admitting.

"Want me to drive?"

"No. I just need a second, okay?"

"I don't mind."

"No one drives my car but me. Ever," he says, opening his eyes. "Might be the only rule I have." He sighs, wincing as the air leaves his lungs.

"Let me drive."

"No. I'll give into almost every other whim you have, but I draw the line at you driving my car. That isn't happening."

"I'll let you finger my ass." His eyes drift to me, the slightest hint of desire fills his gaze, under a layer of pain. "I've only ever taken one of my fingers. Never let a man play with me back there before." I smile at him. "You'd be the first to do it and all it would cost you is letting me drive your car."

"Jesus," he groans. "No." He shakes his head, but his hand reaches for the door handle. "No. Nope. Not happening. No."

"One in my pussy, one in the ass. God, can you imagine how hard that would make me cum?"

"Prue." His voice is full of warning, and just a spark of lust.

"Or would you put it in as your cock was buried in my pussy? I mean it might not fit. It would be a tight squeeze."

His door opens and I smile, watching him slip out of the driver's seat. He walks around the front of the car, pulling my door open. I slide out, smiling smugly at him.

"If you crash my car, my finger isn't the only thing going in your ass."

"Oh, that sounds tempting," I say, walking to the driver seat.

Slipping in, I go to adjust the mirrors. "But I think that will cost you more than you can afford."

"When you think of a price, let me know," he says, leaning his head against the back of the seat.

"Where should we go now?" I ask, starting the car.

"Where do you want to go?"

"Want to meet my parents?"

"Yes." He flashes me a grin.

This is a stupid idea. I didn't think he would agree to it. Driving to my family's mansion in the Hollywood Hills, I take my time. Part of me keeps waiting for him to change his mind.

"Tell me more about dear ole Mom and Dad," he says after a bit of silence.

"My father comes a well-off family. His great-grandfather started a finance business and slowly bought up a lot more. Since then, that's all my family did. Now the company is worth a few billion. My parents met in college. Harvard. My mother's family is well off too, and once they married my grandfather on her side signed over his wealth management company to my father so he could retire and see the world."

"Sounds like money is very important to your parents."

"Money. Status, their kids doing what they say. Cameron gave up trying to keep them happy young. I decided to take on all the pressure so he could be free."

"Do you have any happy family memories?"

"Happy? I don't know. I think each memory is laced with unspoken burdens. Each birthday was a chance for them to invite their friends over and try to impress them. Each family vacation was to show off what we could afford. We didn't eat dinner as a family unless we had to for a party or function. We don't share stories about our days. We barely talk at all to be honest. Most conversations I have with them are just full of instructions. How they want me to act, how I should behave. What they need me to do for them."

"That's really fucked up. I'm sorry," he says softly. "My family was close. My parents loved each other a lot. Shining example of a happy couple. They wanted more children, but my mom lost her parts due to an early bout of cancer. And so, they settled on just having me, and taking in Wes eventually. But we talked, we went on vacations, had dinner together. I have more happy memories with them than sad. I'm really sorry you missed out on that."

"But they don't know what happened to you?"

"No," he says. "Only you do. And I'd like to keep it that way."

"I won't say anything," I whisper.

"I believe you. I think even you have a line when it comes to hurting me." He laughs. "Probably would kill me before you would spill that secret."

"You make me sound evil."

"You are a little evil, but I like it." He laughs. "Did they really disown Cameron?"

"Nothing official or whatever, but they cut him off. Well, he more or less told them to. They expected him to go to college and straighten up, but when he didn't graduate, they came home ready to strangle him but he was gone. Left a note and all his credit cards, saying he was done being their puppet. He has more guts than me."

"He left you to the wolves, Prue. That's not having guts, that's chicken shit."

"He would've taken me with him if I asked, but I stayed. It kept my parents from going insane. At least they had one child to parade around. And if I stayed, I could help Cameron survive. I give him money sometimes."

"Jesus. Prue. You are far too selfless for your own good."

"This is a bad idea." I sigh. "They aren't going to like seeing you with me."

"Oh, come on. They are going to adore me." He laughs. "What is there not to love? All the tattoos, the bruised face, the fact I made their daughter cum her fucking brains out. I'm a fucking catch. They would be so lucky to have me on the arm of their only daughter."

I laugh. He has no idea what he is walking into, but something tells me he doesn't care.

"You know how people think some girls have daddy issues?"

"Oh no. Prue, do you have daddy issues?" The amusement in his voice makes me roll my eyes.

"No." I glance at him. "But my father has issues. He doesn't take well to anyone who doesn't worship the ground he walks on. After disowning Cameron, he more or less pretends he doesn't exist. They will invite him over, but it's only a formality. Cameron knows better than to come. As far as my father is concerned, he only has one kid. I know the reason Cameron hasn't gotten signed yet is because of him. He can't live in a world where his son is a famous rock star. It would look bad for business."

"Woah. Wait a second," Ben says. "There is bad parenting and then there is crushing your kids' dreams out of spite. That is beyond fucked up."

"He has issues. They both do. My mother, she has impossible standards. She loves Char—"

"Don't say his name."

"My ex, but that was all because of what his family could bring to the table. She'd hand me over on a silver platter, wrapped in a bow, if it meant my family could double their money. She pretty much told me to give up my virginity to the boyfriend before him. I was 13, and he was a senior, but from a very wealthy family. She said if I didn't fuck him, he'd leave me. He left anyways, off to college on the East Coast. But she blamed me for not keeping him interested. She tracked what I ate all throughout my youth. If she found out I ate anything not on her list of approved items, I'd have to run five miles on a treadmill. She hates me but can't afford to lose me."

"Prue," Ben says, and I steal a glance at him. "If we do this, you'll have to fully embrace the change. I won't be able to contain myself when I know how shitty these people are. There will be no going back."

"They are my family."

"Sorry, baby, but your family is horrible."

"Besides Cameron."

"I like Cameron, but he let you carry the burden of your parents' pressure too fucking long. If you take me to meet them, I will be a wrecking ball that destroys it all."

"And after? Will you still be my friend?"

"Yes," he says. "I'm not going anywhere, Prue. Ever."

I nod. "Okay. Let's go see my parents."

As I pull up to my family's mansion. I don't know what the outcome from this will be. I know he is right. If I take him inside there, it ends badly. They won't be happy with me. When they say the wrong thing, Ben will make a scene. I'll have to pick. Him or them.

The problem is, I have no idea which one to pick.

I either find a way to finally get Ben to leave me alone or I end up disowned just like Cameron.

And I don't know what outcome will hurt more, or which one I want.

Ben follows me inside the house. I glance around. Nothing has changed, but the space feels different. Still makes me feel small and nervous. Ben puts his hand on the small of my back and some of the tension in my body leaves. I glance back and he offers me a smile, like he knows this place crushes my soul.

I press the intercom button. "Mom. Prue is here," I announce myself.

"We are in the den, dear." My mother's voice carries over the speakers.

I grab Ben's hand, leading him through the maze of hallways. The den is my parents' favorite place to gather.

He locks our fingers as I lead him. I can't look at him right now, not while my fate is hanging in the balance. The outcome of this is going to change everything. I don't need my feelings for him swaying my decision.

When we enter the den, I drop Ben's hand. My mother lounges on the couch, feet tucked under her knees. Her blonde hair draped over the arm of the chair. She is high on one prescription pill or maybe two, who knows these days.

My father sits by the fireplace, a whiskey glass in hand. The flames from the raging fire make shadows dance over his clean-shaven face. His face looks nothing like Cameron's or mine. Sharp, where ours is round. Hard, while ours are soft.

The TV is on, but his eyes have been on me since the moment we entered the room. I feel myself straighten up, like I always do under his gaze. The need to impress him crawls up my spine. His expectations are like a weight around my neck.

"Hello." I force myself to speak, stretching a smile across my face.

"Prue, dear, you didn't mention you brought your brother along," my mother says, sitting up slightly. Leave it to her to not be able to tell the difference between a stranger and her own child.

"That's not Cameron," my father says. His voice is loud, as if he needs to assert dominance. I've never been on the other side of that voice. He reserves it for Cameron and people who he wants to put fear in.

"Oh. I just saw the shaggy hair and tattoos." my mother says.

"This is Ben. He's a friend."

"Of yours? Or is Cameron in some kind of trouble?" Mother asks, with a sigh. "That boy is nothing but trouble."

"He is a friend of both of ours."

"I didn't know you two shared any friends." My mother's eyes zero in on me. The look on her face is sharp enough to kill. Clearly, she is conveying that sharing friends with my brother is not acceptable.

"Hello," my father says, stepping toward Ben. He extends his hand and I watch as Ben grasps it back. "I'm Calvin Ward, and this is my wife, Betty. Ben, was it?"

"Yes. Ben Parker." Ben nods, shaking his hand for a moment before dropping it. My father stares at his hand. No one has ever let go of his hand first. Ben might as well have slapped him across the face.

"Nice bruise you got there, kid. Should I see the other guy?" my father asks, trying to save face.

"If you find him, please let me know," Ben replies with a grin.

"Ha," my father says, sitting back down. "Sit you two."

I slide into the loveseat across from my mother. Ben drops down beside me. I shift so we aren't touching. The more space between us the better. My parents might be acting nice, but it's all fake. They aren't happy with me. I can feel the tension in the air. Sense their disappointment in my gut.

"What brings you here, Prue? I thought you were enjoying being at your brother's. Have you finally grown tired of that dump?" my mother says, tucking her hair behind her ears, and shooting me another pointed look.

"No. We were just in the neighborhood. I thought I'd show Ben where I grew up."

"Why would that matter to him?"

"Obviously, Ben must mean something to our little girl," my father replies. He eyes me as he speaks. "She clearly wanted to show off for him."

"Prue has no need to show off for me," Ben says. "Not a damn thing about this place could impress me, more than she, herself, does."

"Do you fancy my daughter?" My father laughs. It's clearly a fake laugh. To him, the idea of Ben liking me must be the most amusing thing he has ever heard. "Because you should know she is already off the market."

"Dad," I say softly, "I told you. Char—" Ben's hand touches my thigh, squeezing it. "We broke up."

"Prue, sweetie, kids do impulsive things. I'm sure you two will patch it up in no time. You know your absence at the Hilton last night sure made a fuss, but I know Mr. Davenport is willing to ignore that. Headaches happen, but you do have an obligation to attend these things. Especially when a man like Charles invites you." My mother uses her lecturing voice as she speaks.

Ben's fingers dig into my thigh at the mention of Charles' name, but his face doesn't change. A polite smile is spread across it, but his eyes dance with rage.

"I didn't have a headache," I snap. Ben's rage is fueling my own.

My parents don't care about me, but I have someone who literally took a fist to the face for me. He is sitting right beside me, ready to go toe to toe with the people who should love me more than anything. It hurts and feels good at the same time.

"Prue, dear, don't raise your voice. It's rude, especially in front of guests," my mother says. "Even if they are your brother's friend." Her eyes glance over him for a moment, before turning back to glare at me.

"Yes, Mom," I say back softly.

"You know the Davenports are hosting brunch tomorrow. I think that's the perfect place for Charles and you to patch things up," my mother adds.

My mouth opens to speak, ready to agree to go and drag Ben out of here. There is no sense in trying to reason with them. It's best to just agree to their terms, and not follow through. Before I can speak, Ben's hand flattens against my thigh.

"I'm afraid I can't let that happen," he says, patting my thigh.

"Excuse me?" My father's voice is laced with shock.

I glance up at Ben, who smiles at me. "I told you, I'd be the wrecking ball."

My eyes roll the way only he seems to be able to make them, but I smile too. He warned me and I still brought him here. Maybe I knew my choice this whole time. Maybe this is what I needed. Let Ben destroy my life for me. Then I'll have no choice but to become someone new.

"You can't let that happen? Why do you think you have any say in this?" My father's voice grows louder, much like his heartbeat must have since he saw me walk in with Ben by my side.

"I'm bound by the morals bestowed upon me, of not being an abusive prick to stop your daughter from getting back with that piece of shit."

"What filthy language." My mother gasps. "Extremely rude."

"Oh, right. I forgot this is the upper class where we ignore bruises and force our daughters to do our bidding. I'm so fucking sorry." Ben scoffs.

"Young man." My father jumps to his feet. Ben rises too, staring at him. "You need to leave right this minute."

"Gladly," Ben says, holding his hand out to me. "Prue."

"She's not going with you," my father snaps. My eyes dart to him. He glares at Ben, threateningly. When I look back at Ben, his eyes are on me.

"Come on, Prue," he says.

"What has gotten into you?" My mother shakes her head. "This behavior is so unbecoming. We raised you to be better than this. Given you everything you could've wanted. Promised you a good life, and you decide to act out with this boy."

My eyes drop to the ground. I don't know what to do. Leaving with Ben will destroy my whole life, but if I stay, I'll end up back with Charles, who will be far too happy to cause me pain and misery.

"I'm sorry," I say after a moment.

"Don't apologize to them," Ben says.

"Not them. You," I say, looking back up at him. "I shouldn't have brought you here. You should go."

"Not without you," he says, reaching his hand toward me.

"Do not touch her," my father snaps, taking a step closer to him. "You are to never go near my daughter again. What you do with Cameron is one thing, but you won't soil my daughter."

"Ha." Ben laughs. "Should I tell them it's a little too late for that, or do you want to?" My face turns red, as does my father's, but for two separate reasons. "Prue. I'm like a minute away from getting my ass kicked, once again, for your honor. Can we please go?"

I stand up without putting much thought in it. Ben has proven he cares more about me than anyone else I've met. I'm not letting him get hurt over me again. I can't. So, if leaving here with him keeps him from harm, I'll go, but I'm not sure I won't come back.

I don't trust my father not to destroy Ben's career just to hurt me.

My father steps between us, blocking me from Ben.

"You will not go with him, Prue. Do you hear me?" he shouts in my face. "You will fix things with Charles, marry him, pop out a few kids and fulfill your duties to this family. Let's hope Charles never finds out about what you did with this boy. God help us if he does."

"Oh. He knows. I made sure of it last night when I kicked his ass," Ben chimes in.

My father raises his arm, and for a moment I think he is going to hit me. My heart skips a beat as I wait for him to strike, but he turns, slapping Ben across the face.

Ben laughs, openly laughs, rubbing his cheek. My mother gasps. I blink back tears.

"You vile little shit." My father grabs at Ben's shirt, yanking him forward. "If you ruined the business deal of a century for me, I will cut off your tiny dick and feed it to you for dinner."

"I see where Prue got that insult from." Ben chuckles, shoving my father back and breaking free from his hold. "But I gladly proved to her my cock is big enough to feed a family of six."

My father shakes with anger, balling up his fists. "Get out now!" he shouts.

"Prue?" Ben says, ducking his head to the side to look at me. "Hey, baby, it's okay. Let's just go, okay?"

"She isn't going with you. I'll call the cops. They will be here before you make it down the driveway."

"And what will you tell them, Calvin? That the man you assaulted took your bargaining chip away? Have some class. Don't make a scene. Wouldn't want anyone thinking you're anything like me." Ben smirks. "Prue."

"Excuse me, Dad," I say, trying to get by him.

He grabs my arm tightly, yanking me back. His grip hurts my arm. The very act of him yanking me floods my mind with memories of Charles, the very man he wants me to marry.

"Let her go," Ben snaps, taking a step forward. "Because if you don't, I'll have no choice but to do something drastic, like I did with Charles last night."

"Please, Dad." I look up at him, tears in my eyes. "I can't marry Charles. He hurt me. I'll do anything else you want, just don't make me marry him. Please."

"He wouldn't have hurt you if you just looked the other way, dear," my mother says. "Men have affairs, you just have them buy you something expensive and move on."

"God that is disgusting," Ben groans. "Let. Her. Go."

My father tightens his grip on my arm, and I wince. Ben's eyes widen as if the sight of me in pain makes his anger double. He reaches into his pocket, pulling out the pocketknife from last night.

I shake my head, pleading for him not to do anything to make this situation worse.

My father laughs when he sees it. "Going to stab me, kid? Jail is a better cage than you deserve."

"Oh no. I'm not going to stab you. That would be counterproductive." I watch as Ben unfolds the blade, pressing it to his shoulder. "Buddy, just because I fucked your daughter, doesn't mean you have to stab me." Ben presses the blade until it cuts through his hoodie, and keeps pressing, until I see him bite his lip. His eyes never leave my father's face.

"What the fuck are you doing?"

"Me?" Ben questions, as the blade slips deeper into his flesh. "This is all you."

"No one will buy it. I have witnesses," my father counters.

"Prue won't defend either of us, and I'm willing to bet your wife's medicine cabinet has plenty of reasons to make her an incredible witness. Regardless, it's not really the court of law I care about, but the court of public opinion. I don't think it looks very becoming of the CEO of some huge company knifing some guy."

Ben pulls the blade back. It's coated in blood. He presses it back in. My body jerks forward to stop him, but my father keeps me in place. Ben is insane, and it's kind of hot. "And who would think I'd stab myself? That's such a crazy thing to do. In my guitar holding arm, nonetheless? That's just fucking insane. Now. Let Prue go."

I squirm against my father, trying to break free of his hold. Ben stares at him, letting the blade pierce through his shoulder. A wet spot is forming through his hoodie.

My father releases me, shoving me forward. Ben's hand flies out to steady me. Tears fill my eyes, and Ben pulls me against him.

"Are you happy, Prue? Going to destroy the family business all because some trashy rock star has you convinced his dick is enough to keep you warm at night."

"I'm not good enough for your daughter. I don't think that at all. She is far better than anything I could ever have. I'm just brave enough to show her that," Ben snaps back.

I reach up, pulling the knife from his shoulder.

"Fucking have her. Take the slut. I never want to see her again."

I wince at my father's words but keep my eyes on Ben. He takes the knife from me, folding it shut.

"Come on, baby. Let's go."

I'm quiet as Ben drives. I have no idea where we are going, and I don't care. My whole life has just fallen apart. I knew I was nothing more than a pawn to my parents, but this confirms it.

My eyes dart to Ben. The sleeve of his hoodie is wet and getting more so by the minute. The hand that grips the steering wheel has blood on it.

"You need stitches," I say, and he glances at me. "You're still bleeding."

"It will stop."

"Or you'll bleed to death."

"I didn't go that deep." He shrugs.

"You stabbed yourself for me. Are you fucking insane?"

"Obviously. I kind of thought you figured that out the night we met." He laughs. "But I had no idea you'd turn out to be a bigger mess than me."

"My father almost killed you!"

"Eh." He shrugs again, wincing. "He wouldn't be the first to try. Though he'd find out I'm awfully hard to kill. Trust me, if a needle didn't get the job done or a razor blade for that matter, I don't think he could."

"Ben! My parents just disowned me. I'm disowned. Tomorrow all my accounts will be frozen. They will cancel my college fund. I'll have nothing."

"What about Cameron?"

"Cameron can barely take care of himself. I've been helping him stay afloat for years. Oh God. I just ruined both our lives. You have to take me back. I have to fix this."

"Over my dead body," Ben says. "I can help. I have more money than I know what to do with. And Cameron is a big boy. Now that I know your father has been cock blocking his band, I can solve that problem for him."

"I can't take your money."

"Just until you get your feet on the ground. Let me help you, Prue." His hand touches my thigh. "We're friends after all."

"We can't be friends if I'm indebted to you."
"Marry me then."

TWENTY-SIX

Ben

My shoulder is still dripping blood as we both fall silent. My words hang in the air. Words I never thought I'd ever say to a woman. Words I never even thought about.

I'm blaming the blood loss. Though the idea of Prue as my wife doesn't completely disgust me. Marriage is a legal binding cage, but I don't think I'd mind being in any cage with her.

Still. Why the fuck did I say that out loud?

"Jesus, Prue. I'm not serious, but if it means you will take my money." I shrug, trying to gloss over how appealing the idea is becoming.

"I'm not taking your money," she repeats, not addressing the proposal of marriage at all, which I'm grateful for. "Just take me back to Cameron's so I can cry in peace."

"You can't stay at Cameron's tonight. Not alone. Maybe not ever," I say. My plan was to take her back there to grab some things before taking her back to my place.

"Why?"

"Do you think that piece of shit ex of yours isn't going to come back? I'm pretty sure he is putting a bounty on my head as we speak. If not him, your father."

"They aren't that crazy." She folds her arms over her chest.

"Not crazy enough to stab themselves. Mr. loves his car so much doesn't seem the slightest bit concerned about bleeding all over it," she counters.

"It's used to having bodily fluids in it." I smirk. She leans over, pressing her palm over my wound. "Jesus," I hiss. "Give a guy some warning before you cover his bleeding wound."

"Give a girl some warning before you decide to ask her to marry you."

"I was joking."

"I've had a long day. I just want to lay in my bed, watch stupid chick flicks, and cry." She sighs. "Alone," she adds, leaning back in her seat. Some of my blood sticks to her hands, and I'm pretty sure if I wasn't bleeding out right now, my cock would be hard.

Never knew I had a blood kink, but it seems she is creating new ways to get me hard.

"You can lay in my bed, watch all the shitty movies you want, and cry, while I sleep on the couch."

"No. My bed."

"No. Mine."

"You'll have to tie me up because I'm not staying at your place any other way," she snaps.

"Okay." I nod. "Have it your way. Lucky for you, I already have the handcuffs."

"You don't," she says, her mouth dropping open as she studies me. I just grin. "You wouldn't."

"I do. And I most certainly would."

My plan to take her back to Cameron's died the moment she decided to push back against my plan on keeping her at my place, so instead I head straight to my condo.

There is no way I'm leaving her alone. I don't trust her father, her ex, or herself to not cause problems. She is safer by my side. I don't give a shit if she wants to watch movies and cry. She can do that in my room, but I'd have to be dead to let her be completely alone right now.

I'll grant her space and grace, but she needs me around right now.

When we pull up outside my condo, she reaches for the handle, pulling on it. I was fairly sure she would try to make a break for it the moment she could, so I switched on the child safety locks.

Smiling, I slip out of the car, grabbing the bag from the store, before walking to her door. I yank it open and take ahold of her hand before she can even think about bolting. I'm in no mood to chase her right now.

"I'll make a scene," she says as I pull her from the car.

"And I'll make a bigger one." I shrug, leading her to the lobby.

I keep my grip on her wrist firm, but not tight as we take the elevator to my floor. She keeps as much distance between us as possible. When the door opens, she tries to plant her feet, but I'm stronger, even hurt, so I just tug until she gives in and follows beside me.

I gently push her into my condo the minute I unlock it, doing up the half a dozen locks I have on my door. It buys me time if she tries to run. Gives me a chance to stop her.

"I was hoping to take you back to Cameron's so you could get a few things, but I didn't trust you to leave there without kicking and screaming, so here we are."

"Smart." She glares at me. Her arms folded over her chest, as her hip sticks out.

"Please make yourself at home." I wave my hand around. "But first, let's get some lotion on your tattoo. We should've done that hours ago."

Sighing, she plops down on my couch, kicking off her shoes and pulling off her sock. I grab the lotion from the bag. I kneel before her, taking her foot in my hand.

She just watches as I apply lotion to it. I blow on her skin after, to help the lotion dry into her freshly inked skin. Her ankle looks good with my art on it. Her body relaxes, even if her eyes keep glaring at me.

"I'd ask you to do mine, but I'm pretty sure you'd dig your nails into it." I laugh.

"I won't," she whispers.

"What did you end up having me get anyways?"

"Not telling," she snaps. She takes the lotion from me, and I tug off my hoodie and shirt, wincing as the wet fabric yanks from the sore skin around the stab wound. "You'll have to ask the next girl you fuck."

I laugh, sitting on the ground in front of her. Her hand slaps over my tattoo. The sting of her slap and the cool of the lotion create a pleasant feeling, making me groan. I lean into her touch as she presses her fingers into my fresh tattoo.

She leans forward, pressing a kiss to the back of my neck. I sit still. There isn't much I wouldn't let her do to me right now. Her teeth scrape against my flesh one moment and then she is biting into the shoulder I stabbed myself in. Digging her teeth into my sore flesh and sucking.

I groan again. The pain she inflicts is becoming intoxicating. I would endure all of it just to keep her safe and by my side.

Her hand slides down my side, pressing into my ribs. A whimper escapes my mouth, as she keeps sucking on my shoulder.

The bleeding has stopped, but I haven't had a chance to clean off the dried blood yet. If it bothers her, she doesn't show it.

When her mouth breaks away from my skin, her hand drops to the front of my jeans. I shift, granting her better access. My cock is stiff, has been from the moment she bit me.

"Do you want me to touch it?" she whispers in my ear, before letting her mouth wrap around the lobe.

"No," I counter, and she pulls back, but I grab her hand, keeping it in my lap. "I need you to touch it. Please." How I've become so willing to beg for it, I'll never understand, but I'm desperate for her.

"If I touch it, if I make you cum, will you let me leave?" she asks.

"No. Not happening," I say, jerking forward. I push myself to my feet. "I much rather have you stay here, where you are safe, than I would cum, but good try." I stroll to the kitchen. She is evil. A vixen from my worst nightmare. My cock aches for her, but I'm not playing whatever game she is playing. "Now I'm starving. How about a frozen pizza?"

"Then that's the deal."

"What?" I counter, looking back at her as she sits back on my couch with a smug smile on her face.

"As long as I'm trapped here with you, you can't cum." I stare at her, processing her words. The idea is pure agony, but she has my back against the wall. "Like at all. Not from my touch or your own. Or even involuntarily. You cum. I leave. Deal?"

"You'll stay here as long as I don't cum?"

"Yes. I won't try to run. I will stay put like a good girl, as long as you don't cum."

"Fine," I groan. "I accept your terms."

Have I ever cared for anyone as much as I seem to care for Prue? I highly doubt it. The extremes I'm putting myself through to keep her safe and sane are pathological.

I wouldn't even do this shit for Wes, and I feel like I owe him my life, so what does that mean I owe Prue? My soul? And why? Why do I care about her so much? What has she done other than cause me a shit ton of problems, deep throat my cock and cum so hard around it that I still feel her pussy like a phantom limb.

Now she is torturing me by dangling good behavior in front of my face. I can't cum and she will stay put. Should be easy enough given the amount of pain my body is in right now, but as she strips down to just her underwear, curling up on my couch with a plate full of frozen pizza in her lap, I think I'm going to have to chop my balls off to keep from exploding.

She eats slowly, groaning with every bite like it's the best damn thing she has ever had, despite the fact it was just frozen thirty minutes ago. But right now, she would probably eat grass while moaning just to make me suffer.

I'm not normally into being tortured. Light manhandling has happened in the bedroom, but nothing compared to what she does to me. My shoulder still throbs from where she bit me, and I stabbed myself in front of her father like a fucking psychopath.

"I've never had frozen pizza before. It's disgustingly yummy," she says, putting the plate on my coffee table and her feet in my lap. "Ever gotten a foot job?"

"No."

"Want one?"

"I can't cum, remember?"

"I didn't say cum, but a little light edging might be fun." She grins.

"You're evil. Pure, evil."

"And you like it." She laughs, nudging my hardening dick with her toes. "Come on, I've never given a foot job before and with my new tattoo, I bet it would look so hot."

"Prue. I'm exhausted. I doubt I could cum if I was allowed to."

"And you aren't allowed to. Not as long as you want me to stay put." She flashes me the evilest smile that makes my cock even harder. "I, however, get to cum as many times as I want."

"Jesus," I groan. My phone buzzes in my pocket, and when I pull it out and see Wes's name, I get even more annoyed. I answer it anyways, if only to distract myself from the fact Prue is half naked on the other end of my couch, with her foot in my lap. "Hey," I say into the phone.

"So, I heard this interesting story from Aaron today."

"I don't want to talk about it, Wes."

"Who is she?"

"Her name is Prue and I'm pretty sure she's the devil in pink panties and a white bra."

"Not for long," Prue whispers, and I get to helplessly watch as she undoes her bra.

"How did you two meet?"

"I called her a stuck-up bitch at a party and have been trying to make up for it every day since."

She slips off her panties, taking a seat on my coffee table directly in front of me. Spreading her legs apart, letting me get a good look at her perfect little pussy. My cock leaks in my jeans.

"Seems like you're doing an awful job," Wes says on the other end of the phone.

"Yeah, just fucking terrible," I mutter as Prue cups her tit. "Apparently, a busted cheek, crack ribs, mild concussion and stab wound haven't been enough."

Prue rolls her eyes as she pulls at a nipple.

"Jesus, dude," Wes says. "What the fuck?"

"It's not from her," I clarify as Prue's other hand drops between her legs. "She hurts me in much worse ways."

"Does it hurt?" Prue asks softly, circling her clit. "Your cock claims otherwise."

"You're doing drugs again, aren't you?" Wes asks for the second time today. "Fuck, Ben. We've been through this before. Was Janet not a big enough lesson for you? You had to go find another girl to shoot up with?"

"Janet has nothing on her." I laugh. "I honestly can't believe I let that girl convince me to do heroin. I would do far worst things for Prue."

Prue's mouth hangs open as she rubs her clit. Her juices seep from her opening and my control is slipping.

"Are you fucking high right now?"

"No. Just in extreme agony."

"Do you need help? A hospital? The cops?" Wes's voice is laced with concern, but I have no idea how to reassure him everything is fine right now, as my eyes focus on Prue naked in front of me, touching herself.

"No," I say softly. "I think... I think I'm in love with her."

TWENTY-SEVEN

Prue

I can't hear what's being said on the other side of the phone, but when he mentions another girl's name as I'm naked before him, I see red for a moment.

I have no right to be jealous. I know he has gotten around. Read the proof and can't blame any girl for wanting a piece of him, but it still sucks to have another girl's name leave his mouth when I'm touching myself for his eyes only.

Of course, I'm doing it to be mean. Trying to get him to break. I'm not really sure why. I know he is right, being at Cameron's dangerous, but being with him is starting to take its toll too.

Not in a bad way, but in a very good way that makes me want to flee. I do not deserve the kind of attention he gives me. The power he lets me have is almost overwhelming, but extremely erotic.

I may be addicted to it even. I crave the thrill of watching Ben submit to me. The fact he is willing to suffer for me is not something I'm used to. It makes no sense, but I enjoy it.

My body rocks into my fingers, as I stroke my clit. It's only when he says that he thinks he is in love with me that I refocus on him.

Before I can even process what he just said, he tosses his phone to the ground and slides on his knees in front of me, for the third time today.

"Jesus, baby, keep going."

"Make me," I whisper, trying to keep control of the situation before either of us has a chance to soak in the words he said moments ago.

"Make you?" His eyes look up from my pussy. "How?"

"Use your hand to move mine."

"Fuck," he says, reaching for my hand. Gripping it, he places his fingers over mine as he guides them over my clit. He applies more pressure than I'm used to, and I suck in a breath. "You go too soft."

My toes curl as he moves my hand. Small circles, at a slow pace, with just enough pressure to hurt in the best way possible.

"Should I put a finger inside?" I ask, my voice shakes by how turned on I am right now.

"Yes," he says, prying one of my fingers from my palm and lowering it to my pussy. He keeps my other finger moving against my clit as he pushes both our fingers inside of me. "Oh baby, you're so tight."

"Fuck," I groan as he works both our fingers in and out of me. "Ben. Please don't stop."

"We're just getting started, baby."

"I want to cum. Make me cum."

"You want me to do it?" he asks softly.

"Yes," I yell out as he hooks our combined fingers up, stroking the best part of me. My head rolls back. "God. Fuck. I'm so close."

"I know, baby. I can feel it. Your pussy is squeezing our fingers." He goes faster, grinding my fingertips into my clit as he does. "If I can't cum, I need you to cum for me."

"Yes." I nod. "I will. Fuck. God. I will. Just like that."

I'm cumming before I finish my sentence. My eyes shut.

Sparks dance behind them as my hand abandons my pussy. His stays, however.

He adds another finger of his, making me stretch to accept them, as his lips wrap around my clit. I yelp, still sensitive from the orgasm he just gave me, but not willing to move from him.

"Your lips feel so fucking good."

He groans into my pussy, sucking even harder at my clit.

"Are you hard?"

He nods, refusing to release my clit.

"I bet it's throbbing. I bet you cum without even touching it and I get to spend the night in my own bed after all."

He pulls his body from mine, and I feel the loss in my toes. Sliding back onto the couch, he rests his head against the back of it. His cock is nearly bursting through his jeans, but he doesn't touch it or free it.

"You're mean," I groan.

"I'm mean?" He scoffs. "I'm getting blue balls as we speak."

"Who is Janet?"

"No one important." He reaches for the remote to his side.

"She was apparently important enough to make you do heroin."

"Convince me to do it. No one made me do it."

"What was so special about her?"

"I was young and stupid." He shrugs. "I thought love could heal my wounds, and she was around. Not that she cared to know anything about them. She said she didn't want to hear about my pain, because hers was enough. So instead, she said we should forget about our troubles and get as high as we could. But eventually we always came back down. Then I was offered a chance at something, and a really good friend was depending on me not to fuck it up."

"Wes?"

"Yes." He nods.

"But you never told him you were abused?"

"No. I told you, only you know. And I keep waiting for you to use it against me."

"I'm not that cruel."

"My cock begs to differ."

I climb off the table, crawling into his lap.

"I can make it up to him."

His hands grip my hips, rocking me against his body. The rough fabric of his jeans rubbing against my clit makes me gasp.

"God. I want that so bad," he groans as I roll over his hard cock. "But I'm not falling for it." He pushes me off him, and I land softly on the couch beside him.

I get up, resting on my knees. "It was worth a try." I smile.

"You really want to go that bad?" He glances over at me.

"I don't like being kept prisoner. I didn't leave one controlling guy for another."

He puts his hand to his mouth and lets out a scream into his palm. The sight is unsettling. His hand drops from his mouth, and he pulls his hair as tears roll down his cheeks.

"Ben," I whisper, crawling back into his lap. "Hey. Ben. I'm sorry, okay? I didn't mean it."

He pushes his hands into his eyes, groaning as his body shakes underneath me.

"Babe," I say softly, testing the waters. He has called me baby countless times and I'm hoping if I call him something sweet, he will snap out of whatever mental breakdown he is having. I pushed him way past his breaking point. I know this is my fault, and while I did want to push him away, seeing him like this makes my heart hurt in a way I didn't expect. "Babe?" I repeat.

He takes a deep breath as his arms drop to his side, his eyes looking into mine.

"I'm sorry," I say again.

"No. I'm sorry."

"For? I'm the one being a bitch."

"I don't like that word anymore," he says, pressing his face into my neck. "If anyone, even you, calls you a bitch again, I'm kicking their ass." His lips plant kisses along my jaw. "I can never make it up to you, can I? I screwed it up from the first night." His mouth travels up my chin, until his lips rest, barely touching mine. "You can go. I won't keep you but fuck, I don't want you to leave me right now."

His lips press against mine as if he hopes they can convince me to stay. I melt into them. Letting him guide the pace, hoping surrendering some control will make him feel better.

Because he doesn't know, but I stopped wanting to leave the moment he said he might love me.

TWENTY-EIGHT

Ben

A WALL INSIDE OF ME IS CRUMBLING. I'VE BEEN AWARE of the cracks for a while, but I didn't expect it to break at the hands of a cute brunette in a turtleneck.

Prue wraps her arms around my neck, deepening the kiss. When her tongue invades my mouth, I try to think about anything but my throbbing cock. It's a hard task when she is practically humping me right now. Her bare pussy is dripping onto the front of my jeans.

I gave her permission to leave and have no way of knowing if she will take it. I don't like the idea of her being somewhere I can't protect her, so I'm determined not to cum and give her a reason to try to leave.

When she compared me to her controlling ex and father, it broke me. The idea of her seeing me in the same light as them made me want to sink through the floor. Disappear from existence. I can't stand the thought of her seeing me like that. Being compared to them might be the lowest anyone has ever made me feel. But I know I can't tell her that. I won't use pity to try to make her stay.

I can't say I blame her. I don't even hold the pain against her.

She is right to feel how she feels. I am holding her hostage in a sense. It's for her own good, but that doesn't change what it is.

I think watching me break down made her feel bad. Guilty even. It's probably the only reason she is pushing her tongue down my throat right now. She is trying to make up for the wounds she's been giving me, not knowing her simply existing is repairing far worse wounds, made by far worse people. Her punches hurt in different ways, but I'd take them over my own any day.

She pulls back, keeping her arms wrapped around my neck, as her blue eyes meet mine.

"Babe?" she questions for the third time.

"Did you call him babe?" I raise an eyebrow.

"Did you call her baby?"

"No." I shake my head.

"Oh." She tilts her head. "Benny?" She tries that but her face scrunches up. I try not to wince at that name. It's a pet name only one person has ever used, and that makes bile rise in my throat. "Handsome. No." She shakes her head. "What should I call you?"

"Don't call me anything," I say, letting my hands slide up and down her sides. "I rather hear my name coming from your lips than anything else."

"Mmm." She smiles. "Ben."

"Yeah. I like the way that sounds best."

"Ben, would you please fuck me? Fill me with your big cock and then your cum?"

"No."

"Why not?" She pouts. "I won't leave. You can cum and I'll stay."

"I don't trust you." I plant a kiss on her collarbone. "You're evil and cruel and I'm not falling for your trap."

"It isn't a trap. I promise." She pulls back again, staring into my eyes. "I'm really sorry I was so mean. I didn't mean it, not really. I'll stay. I just want your cock in me, please? It makes me feel better."

She is far too good at getting what she wants from me. Part of me is determined to not cave this time. Let her see how it feels to be tortured, but I don't have it in me to do that to her.

She shifts slightly, letting her cunt guide around the outline of my cock. I'm about to give in. About to throw her on the floor and fuck her senseless when the door shakes from someone pounding on it. Both our heads snap to the door.

She turns back to me, eyebrows raised.

I shrug as she slides off me. She scrambles for her clothes, and I try to will my cock to go soft as the pounding continues.

The possibilities of who is on the other side are endless, but none of them are good.

I hope beyond reason it's Wes coming to check on me. I didn't exactly give him a reason not to be worried when we spoke moments ago. It would be in his nature to come try to save me, but something tells me my confession at the end would give him pause.

He would be the first person to say love makes you do crazy things. But I doubt he thought I'd ever be this far into it.

I'm grateful Prue hasn't brought up my words yet. Maybe she didn't hear them. Too busy touching herself to notice the word love come from my mouth, but she did bring up Janet, so maybe she is just choosing to ignore it.

That would be best for both of us. We do not have a chance in hell at making whatever this is work. Too much pain and drama exist, and I don't know the first thing about being a boyfriend. Let alone loving someone.

"Benjamin Parker," a voice on the other side shouts. "Open up." I'm overly aware by the authority in their voice that I'm about to be arrested. I'm not exactly sure what the charge will be, but either way this isn't good.

Sighing, I turn to Prue as she steps up beside me.

"Who is that?"

"I need you to listen to me. Okay? I know you have a habit of not listening to me, but this time I need you to follow my orders." She nods. "Stay here." I pick up my phone from the floor and thrust it into her hand. "Call Wes. Tell him I've been arrested. He will get me a lawyer, but I probably won't be out until Monday. I need you to stay here. My wallet is somewhere, buy whatever you need, use it for anything, but just don't go back to Cameron's unless he is home. I need you to stay safe for me, okay, baby?"

"Ben, what are you talking about?"

The pounding starts again, and I sigh.

"Either your piece of shit ex or your shitty father called the cops on me," I say, walking to the door. "Can't be sure what the charges will be, but regardless, I'm going to be spending the night in jail." I swing open the door.

Two police officers stand there. One is tall but balding, the other is short with greasy hair. Their name badges read Ortiz and Babcock.

"Benjamin Parker?" Ortiz asks. His bald head shines from the hall lights. Matches Babcock's greasy hair.

"Good evening, officers, how can I help you tonight?"

"Are you Benjamin Parker?" Babcock asks.

"In the flesh."

Ortiz reaches for my arm, pulling me out the door and spinning me around.

"You're under arrest," Babcock says.

"For what?" Prue says, coming into view. "What are you arresting him for?"

"Assault with a deadly weapon," Babcock replies.

"Oh. Spicy." I smile before pressing my finger to my lip, signaling to Prue to not say anything, while Ortiz yanks my other hand behind my back. The pain in my side and shoulder makes me see spots, but Prue's face brings me back to the moment.

"Where are you taking him?" Prue asks, hands on her hips, glaring at them. It's hot, and the idea of her glaring while I'm being handcuff turns me on.

"To jail," Babcock replies. "Any weapons?"

I'm so glad I tossed the bloody pocketknife in the sink earlier. I do not need to give them anything to use against me.

"Nope. Just my massive penis."

"Do you want that on the record?" Ortiz asks.

"That I have a giant penis? Fuck yeah, I want that on the record. I'd love nothing more than to prove that to a jury of my peers."

I'm slightly disappointed when Prue's eyes don't do a loop after my comment. I thought for sure that would get a reaction from her, but she just stares, a worried look etched into her face.

Ortiz laughs though. "That smart mouth of your is going to be a problem, isn't it?" he asks.

"Ask her. My mouth can get me out of a lot more trouble than it creates." I smirk. This time Prue's eyes do roll as she shoots me a pointed look. "I'll see you soon, baby." I wink.

This isn't my first time being arrested, but it is the first time it's gone to the point of getting my fingerprints and mugshot taken. I'm usually let go, but I haven't been arrested since high school, so this is new to me.

I've gotten much better at not getting caught or the people I fought weren't dumb enough to press charges. Of course, I've taken to verbal assaulting people more than physical.

Leave it to Prue to cause me to stray off track.

She is worth it though. I could spend my life in prison if it meant she was safe. And I have a feeling that's going to be a real possibility.

Assault with a deadly weapon? What a load of crap. It was a pocketknife, that was sharp enough to pierce my shoulder, but still. Charles is pathetic for calling the cops on me. No doubt he is teaming up with her father now.

They couldn't just let her be. Which, trust me, I get it, but given how neither of the pricks really care about her, I don't understand why they can't just get in bed together and leave her out of it.

What does it matter if Charles marries her? If the two families want to go in business, why does marriage have to be involved? This isn't the olden days for crying out loud.

I sit in a questioning room, waiting for someone to come ask me questions I have no plans on answering. It would only do me harm to talk to anyone without my lawyer present.

"Mr. Parker." A female detective walks in with her male counterpart behind her. "We got some questions for you."

"I have one answer for you, dear." I smile.

"And that is?"

"I'm not speaking without my lawyer present."

"Is that really the road you want to take," the male counterpart speaks.

I nod.

"All we want is some information on what happened. He says one thing, you say another, maybe we find out this is all a big misunderstanding," the woman says, playing good cop. They sent in a woman undoubtedly thinking the playboy rock star would be more willing to speak to a chick.

I shrug.

"Come on, buddy, give us your side of the story," the guy says, folding his arms. "The guy is like twice your size, I'm sure you didn't have much choice on how you decided to fight back."

I stare at him. They haven't said Charles' name, most likely hoping I bring him up, and that sets me at the scene. I'm not stupid. I watched enough TV to know how this works.

"Well, you know, it's Saturday night and most lawyers don't work on weekends, so looks like you will be spending some time in a cell."

"Cool. But I do get a phone call, right?"

"Eventually."

I just nod.

My only hope is that Prue has called Wes and stays fucking put. Not knowing is probably going to drive me crazy and keep me up all night, but I have little choice at this moment.

Whatever happens from here on out, I just have to hope Prue realizes she is worth more than either of those dicks have to offer her. Hopefully my sacrifice will be enough to convince her to let herself be happy.

TWENTY-NINE

Prue

I CALL WES THE MINUTE THEY HAUL BEN AWAY, USING his phone. I don't question why the guy doesn't use a pin to lock his phone, because I highly doubt he ever lets anyone else touch it.

"Hey, you good?"

"No. He is not good," I say into the phone.

"I'm going to guess you're Prue."

"Yes. Ben has been arrested," I blurt out. "He told me to call you. Said you could get him a lawyer."

"Arrested? For what? What did you get him into? Drugs?"

"No. I didn't get him into drugs," I snap back. "He got arrested for assault with a deadly weapon."

"Damn it. That guy, I swear. What happened exactly?"

"Two cops showed up at his door and arrested him."

"I mean, did he do it?"

"I'm not going to answer that."

"Great. He is guilty. Fuck. Okay. I'll call my lawyer, but chances are nothing can be done until Monday."

"Oh God," I whisper.

"Listen, I don't know you, or what is going on, but if Ben is willing to do everything I've heard about for you, you matter to him. That means you have to trust me. I've known him longer, I care about him more, and I know him best. Let me handle this, and take care of yourself, got it?"

"If you care about him so much, why haven't you been around?" I snap.

"If you care about him at all, you'll let me handle this," he counters. "Trust me, Prue, I'm going to take care of him. He's like my brother."

"Fine," I mumble. "Call me if there are any updates."

"I will. If he wants me to, that is."

"He will," I counter. "Bye."

I fight back a scream when I hang up on Wes. He has no reason to trust me, and I have no reason to tell him what happened. Unfortunately, I do need to let him handle this, because Ben told me to. I'm not happy about it, but for Ben's sake, I will let him get the lawyer.

And I'll stay put. At least until Cameron is home.

After washing the bloody pocketknife and tossing it in a random drawer, I pace Ben's apartment, over and over. I turn the picture of him, his parents and the lady I'm sure hurt him around. I rearrange his little trinkets. Moving the snow globe from one shelf to the other. I organize the books he has a few times over before I accept that I'm not hearing from Wes or him tonight.

Giving up, I head to his bedroom. The walls are a dark gray. His furniture is basic and dark. His bed is huge, and the blankets are thrown about. Guitars hang on his walls. Six of them. All different colors and makes. An acoustic guitar sits on a stand next to a chair. He has a few awards on the walls as well. Clearly music does mean a lot to him.

I use his on-suite bathroom, eyeing his shower and smiling at his tea tree shampoo and citrus body wash. He also has facial moisturizer on his counter. Sexy rock star comes at a cost, apparently. I plan to tease him to no end about this.

I wash my face in his sink before stealing some of his mouthwash. It's odd being in here without him. His absence hurts and I don't know how to deal with that. We haven't been together that long, but he has become a permanent fixture in my life already.

There is no way of knowing what is going to happen next, but all I know is I can't lose him. I'll take just being his friend, I'll take whatever he is willing to offer me, because as much as I hate to admit it, I need him.

I strip down to my panties before grabbing a shirt lying across his bed. I don't care if it's dirty at this point, I just want to feel his presence somehow.

As I tug it over my head, I soak in the way it smells like him. Clean, smokey, and like the earth after rain. My heart aches knowing where he is right now, and I know it's all my fault.

I don't know how I'm supposed to get any sleep tonight, but once I curl up under his blanket, wrapped in fabric that seeps his scent, my eyes feel heavy, and sleep overtakes me.

When I wake up, the first thing I do is call Wes. He tells me his lawyer is going to call Ben today but won't be able to see him until tomorrow. It's concerning that Ben hasn't called Wes or me yet, but I highly doubt he knows my number. And if he did call Wes, I doubt Wes would tell me.

Cameron calls me around noon, asking where I am at and that's when I decide I can't take another second being trapped in Ben's condo without him.

When I walk into Cameron's apartment, he is sitting on the couch, watching tv. He glances up when he sees me.

"How was your weekend?" He smiles. "I see you did some drinking." He nods to the bottle of whiskey on his coffee table.

"No. Ben did that. He says he will replace it."

"Ben? Like Ben Parker?" he asks, and I just nod. "He was here? Are you sleeping with him, sis?" Cameron studies me, surprise written all over his face.

"I took him to meet Mom and Dad," I say instead of answering that question.

Cameron burst out laughing. "No way. Without me? God, I would've loved to witness that. How did it go?"

"Terrible. They disowned me." I leave out the fact Ben stabbed himself. Cameron doesn't need those details.

"No. You're the golden child. They aren't disowning you over hanging out with Ben."

"Yeah, pretty sure they are. If they didn't over Ben, then they will when they see the tattoo."

"You got a tattoo?" His jaw drops. "Holy shit. What happened while I was gone? Did hell freeze over or something?"

"Something like that." I shrug.

"I want to see it."

"It's small and on my ankle," I counter as Ben's phone buzzes in my pocket. I answer it without looking, figuring it's probably Wes. "Hello?"

"How sweet of you to answer my phone for me, baby." Ben's voice instantly makes my chest tighten.

"Ben?"

"Yeah. I didn't remember your number, so I thought I'd try mine and at least leave you a message. Lucky for me you have no problem invading my privacy."

"Oh. I'm sorry. I didn't think. I thought maybe it was Wes."

"Relax, Prue. I'm just playing around. Where are you?"

"Cameron's."

"Is he there with you?"

"Yes. I slept in your bed last night, like I promised."

"I'm sad I couldn't be there for that," he says softly. "I would've rather fucked you before letting you sleep, but as it would seem I'm in major fucking shit right now."

"Ben. I'm so sorry."

"For?"

"This is all my..."

"Shh, baby. Now is not the time for that. I'm just calling to let you know I have court tomorrow. Wes's lawyer says they will probably offer me bail if I surrender my passport. I'm having Wes bring it down tomorrow so I can get that squared away quickly. If all goes well, I'll be out before noon."

"On bail."

"Yeah," he says. "Listen, I need you not to show up tomorrow, okay? I'm pretty sure we can guess who is to blame for all this. If not one, then the both of them are teaming up. I have an odd feeling one or both will show up tomorrow and I can't risk something happening to you when I'm unable to do anything about it."

"Ben, this is all…"

"Shh, baby. I'm trying very hard to behave right now, can you please help me out? I will make it up to you, however you see fit, but just don't come down here tomorrow, okay? Can you do that for me?"

"Okay."

"I have to go, Prue, but I'll see you real soon." The line goes dead before I have a chance to say goodbye.

I stand there, blinking back tears as Cameron stares at me.

"Prue, what the fuck is going on?" he asks.

I sigh, sinking into the spot beside him on the couch. I don't know where to start. Cameron is normally the one who comes to me with a wild story, but lately it's been me relying on him. It feels strange, but when he stares at me with those same blue eyes as mine, I remember how close we were as kids. And how much I know I can trust him.

"It's a long story," I start. "You know I met Ben at that party Monday."

"Yes, but I didn't know you guys got close."

"We didn't then. He ran into me at the coffee place by school. His mom taught one of my classes last year, he was meeting her or whatever." I shrug. "He saw Charles talking to me and how upset it made me, so he followed me, and from there it's just been him annoying me and defending me."

"Charles talked to you? Why didn't you tell me he was bothering you?"

"I didn't want you to get involved."

"Prue. You are my sister. The only reason I didn't kick his ass because you told me not to, but I want that man dead more than you know."

"He wanted me to go to an event with him Friday, but I couldn't. Ben gave me his number, so I called him up since you were gone."

"I would've come back if you asked me."

"I know, but I never want to put your dream in danger."

"Prue. You are more important to me than my dying dream. I can miss a show if you need me to."

"It doesn't matter now. Ben showed up after Charles and got him to leave."

"Charles came here?"

"Twice. And Ben, well... he did some damage."

"Kicked his ass?"

"And got his ass kicked."

"Fuck. I owe that guy. How can I help?"

"You can't. I think Dad and Charles are working together on this. We don't stand a chance." I shrug, fighting back tears. "He got into it with Dad too. Dad is set on me marrying Charles, even after everything."

"I know," Cameron says. "They've been trying to pressure me into sending you back there, but I told them to fuck off."

"Oh. You did that for me?" It's hard to picture Cameron standing up to my parents on my behalf.

"I'd do it for free, but gladly do it for you." He shrugs. "You aren't going back there, Prue. I won't let you, and apparently neither will Ben."

"What if I don't have a choice?"

"You will always have a choice as long as you have me. And you have me until the end."

"Yeah." I nod.

"I'm going to be a better big brother going forward. I know I kind of abandoned you, but I thought it was what you wanted. Maybe I knew it wasn't deep down and I'm just a coward, but either way, I'm sorry. I promise, from now, you have me however you need me."

"You're only five minutes older," I tease.

"Doesn't matter. I'm still your brother. It's my job to protect you and I failed. I'm sorry."

"Thank you, Cam."

"Always, Prue."

I'm curled up in bed watching a sad chick flick and trying not to cry. It's hard not to think about how Ben is spending another night in jail while I'm in a comfy bed. It makes me feel extremely guilty.

I have been nothing but mean to him and he has done nothing but take care of me. I owe him so much after all this. I fear his kindness may end at getting arrested, but something tells me that's not who Ben is. If he has gone this far, there is little doubt he will go even further if he has to.

No one has cared for me like this. Not even Cameron, who may be the only person up until now who cared about me at all. Even if he was doing his own thing, I knew deep down that Cameron cared for me, but I never relied on it. Still don't feel like I can, but with Ben... he doesn't give me a choice.

I mean he gives me tons of control but steps up to defend and protect me without question, without me needing to ask, even when I don't want it. Like it's just instinct for him. Just something he has to do.

And he said he thinks he loves me. We haven't gotten a chance to talk about that. I don't even know what to say to that. Ben Parker loving me is insane. I don't see a world where we end up together, definitely not before this past week.

Even now it seems unlikely, but just knowing he feels so

strongly about me makes me all warm inside. It shouldn't. We are obviously bad for each other. He is reckless and willing to almost kill for me, and I am cruel to him for some reason. But both things feel really good.

It feels amazing to be with him.

And the sex. The sex is beyond words. I don't know if I'll ever find someone as good at making me cum as him.

At some point my phone buzzes. When I glance down and see Charles' name, my heart stops. I know I can't answer it. Ben wouldn't want me too. Cameron would tell me not to, as well. Answering it brings nothing but trouble.

But when it rings again and again and again, I know I don't have a choice.

Ben and I never end up together. That's a given. He is a famous rock star, and I'm a girl who grew up among the rich. We would never be able to make it work. I have my responsibilities and he has his.

I knew that from the start, didn't I? That I have no choice but to go back to the life I had before. Sure, Cameron has promised to protect me, and Ben has proven he would too, but ultimately they can't.

But I can protect them.

I close my eyes, trying to push all the good feelings Ben has shown me from my mind. I don't need to be reminded of what I'm about to give up.

"Hello," I say softly into the phone. Ben would be livid with me right now, but I have to try to fix my own mess, to save him.

"You finally answered," Charles says.

"What do you want?"

"I have an offering."

"What kind of offering?" I counter.

"A diamond ring, a family merger and dropped attempted murder charges, all for the price of your pussy belonging to me for the rest of your life. Of course, there will be mild punishment to make up for the hell you put me through, but I think we can work out a way to keep the pain minimum and non-scarring."

"If I agree, you'll drop the charges against Ben?"

"Yes."

"Why should I believe you?"

"I really don't have time for a lawsuit, Prue. Plus, Ben has proven to be a loose cannon. I don't have a clue what kind of shit he would pull in court."

"You mean you don't want to risk him telling everyone how you beat and raped me?"

"Prue, you shouldn't say those things about your future husband, not unless you want to see Ben rot in a prison for a few years."

"Fine," I grumble. "I will marry you, be your good little housewife, take your beatings and lousy fucking, so long as you drop the charges against Ben."

"Good. Now get your stuff together and I'll drop you back off at your parents. Your father would like a few words with you, and I would like you to stay there until I'm ready to have you back at my place."

"I'm not going anywhere until tomorrow when the charges are dropped," I say firmly. "I'll be submissive and sweet, better that I was before, never say a word while you fuck other women, but not until Ben is free."

"Fine," Charles says. "We can meet at the courthouse then. I'd just love to watch his face when he realizes you came back to me after all."

"We can meet at my parents' house."

"Courthouse or nothing, sweetie."

"Fine. I'll see you at the courthouse tomorrow."

Ben asked me not to go. I said I wouldn't, but I already broke my promise to him in worse ways. He knew they would set a trap for me, but the thing is the trap was set the minute he got arrested. Now this is the only way out for us.

THIRTY

Ben

I sit behind some guy named Kevin who was arrested for petty theft. There are about half a dozen of us, waiting to see the judge before lunchtime. My lawyer said I'd probably be offered a deal, but it wouldn't be a good one. Assault with a deadly weapon often gets upped to attempted murder. If I'm lucky, it would be a year behind bars and a few on probation.

Unfortunately for me, I pissed off some powerful people. They may be willing to settle this outside of the courtroom, but the deal they would offer would be far worse than a year. It might be better than going in front of a jury, but not by much.

I don't care about any of that right now. I'll deal with the punishment later. Now I just need to get out of here and make sure Prue doesn't do anything stupid. If I know her half as well as I think I do, the guilt of me sitting in jail is probably getting to her. It shouldn't, because it's my actions that got me here. I did this to myself.

For her, but nonetheless, this is my own fault.

I'm more than happy to explain why I did what I did to a room full of people, but I already did that once and ended up on my knees begging for Prue's forgiveness. I highly doubt I could pull that off in front of a judge.

So, I sit as patiently as possible, waiting for my chance to plead for bail. Wes is out there somewhere, with a bunch of money and my passport. Ready to buy my freedom, much like I was when he got arrested. His charge was for far less, and everyone knew it was justified. That is not the case for me.

I take some comfort in knowing I'll be the reason my band breaks up. Or maybe they will just replace me when they finally decide to start touring again. Either way, I do enjoy being the cause of my own ruin.

Well, I used to, now I would much prefer Prue be the cause. Her cruelty is like a drug to me. That pussy of her is heaven and I would spend forever on my knees praying to it if I could. The amount of time I'll have on bail is not going to be enough to feed my craving, but I'll soak up as many memories of her cunt as possible.

They will be the only thing to get me through my time trapped in the cage. After as well, because freedom will come after a few years, but by then I'll be a distant memory to her, and she will be a constant reminder that I'm an asshole.

"Benjamin Parker?" a guard by the door calls my name.

Raising to my feet, I walk toward the door leading to the courtroom, preparing myself to grovel for mercy to authority, which I hate. But there isn't much I wouldn't do for Prue.

"No. This way," the guard calls and my head snaps to the back.

"Huh?"

"The charges have been dropped."

"No," I say as my stomach drops. What did she do? "I think there is a mistake."

"Nope. Just got word the charges were dropped. Guess they got the wrong guy, or the price of the lawyers weren't worth it. Either way, you're being released."

"Fuck," I groan.

"Never seen someone upset about dropped charges before." The guard laughs.

"That's because this time it comes with a cost. One I don't want to pay for."

Wes is waiting at the top of the stairs outside the courthouse for me.

"Lucky day," he says with a soft smile. "Let this be a lesson. Play stupid games…"

"Shut the fuck up," I snap, scanning the area for her short caramel hair. My head whips every direction. I know she is here. I feel it. She never fucking listens.

"Who are you looking for?"

"Who do you think?" I snap, looking at him.

"You told her not to come."

"Yeah, but clearly she never fucking listens to me."

"Maybe given how serious the situation is, she finally did. I know it took me getting arrested for Abbey to come to her senses."

"Unlike your girl, my girl is actually insane," I reply. "And news-fucking-flash, I'm a free man. You don't think that just happened by some miracle, do you?"

"What even happened? She barely told me anything," he says, shoving his hands in his pocket.

"Good," I say, spotting Prue at the bottom of the stairs. She is wearing tight blue jeans and s white turtleneck under a long tan coat. Her hair is clipped up, and she glances around carefully. An arm wraps around her waist, and I'm about to fucking rip it off. "Go home, Wes. I'm about to commit far worse crimes." I start down the stairs.

"Ben." He grabs my arm as he follows me down the stairs. "Is that the guy you may or may not have threatened with a deadly weapon?" he asks, pulling me to a stop.

"Wes. I swear to God." I tug on my arm. "Let me go. Please."

"No, because whatever you're thinking about doing is only going to end badly for the both of you. Think it through for a moment. You go over there right now, not only do you risk her safety, but you will also be assaulting the dude in front of about a dozen or so more cops. She will pay the price after you are arrested for a second time."

"No, she won't because I won't stop until he's dead."

"Ben. Fuck." He curses when I yank my hand free. He grabs me by the shoulder, and I wince from the pain. "You pulled me off the jerk that hurt Abbey. You kept me from killing him. Why do you get to kill him for her? What did you tell me? Murder is a life sentence. You can't be with her when you are serving a life sentence."

"Yeah, something like that," I say, staring as a car pulls up and Charles pushes Prue toward it.

"So, the same thing applies here."

"No. It doesn't." I glance at him. "I don't get her either way, Wes." When I glance back, she is gone and I'm ready to scream. "God damn it."

"You need to calm down. You're making a scene."

"I don't give a fuck," I yell at him. "I really don't care about any of these fucks." I wave to the people who are glancing our ways. "The person I care about just sold herself for my freedom and I'm not fucking okay with that."

"I know." Wes nods. "She told me to give you this when you weren't so mad, but I think it may help you more when you are."

"What?" I glare at him. "You saw her? You knew she was here?"

"She is very good at blackmail and apparently you have a big mouth."

"Give it to me." I hold out my hand. He places my phone in it. "My phone?" I groan, ready to toss the thing into the fucking street because I don't give two shits about my fucking phone right now.

"She said she left you a message in it." He shrugs. "I don't know what exactly. She didn't give me much to go on, but said she hoped it would make you feel better."

"Nothing is going to make me feel better. No message is going to change the fact she left me." My voice cracks as the words hit. She left me.

"Yeah, I know." He sighs. "And I know you well enough to know it's not going to stop you from doing something stupid, so do whatever you have to do. You know I'll support you, even if that involves hiding a body, or just talking."

Wes knows me too well. He cares about me too much. I know he really would help me hide a body or do anything I needed him to. He has proven that time and time again.

"I'm sorry. I'm sorry I'm such a piece of shit."

"You aren't so bad."

"Go home. Abbey needs you more than I do right now."

"She is fine. I'm here for you now."

"Wes. Go home. Please. I didn't get it before, you know? I didn't understand how you could pick a girl over me, but I do now. And for Abbey's sake, I'm not about to drag you into this. Go fuck that sad girl silly and fix all her wounds, because she needs you and you need her. Leave me to do what I have to do to save my girl."

"Well then." He sighs. "You know it's going to kill me to have to replace you."

"It will hurt me more to be replaced, but for her I'd do anything. Let her pick my replacement, okay?"

"Yeah?" He chuckles. "Sounds good. She must be a good judge of character if she picked your sorry ass."

"No. She is an awful judge of character, but she at least knows I'm good at guitar."

"I hope to see you soon, Ben."

"I make no promises."

He nods before walking away.

I'm left alone, with no idea how I'm going to fix this. My

heart hurts too much to come up with a plan as I stand on the courthouse steps. Once I get home, I'll think of something. I'll do whatever it takes to set Prue free, to keep her safe. Even if it lands me in prison for the rest of my life.

THIRTY-ONE

Prue

I DIDN'T GET TO SEE HIM. THAT'S THE ONLY THING I can think about as Charles grips my thigh as we drive back to my parents' house. I didn't even get to see him one last time.

Tears sting my eyes, but I know I don't have the luxury of crying right now. If Charles even thinks I'm crying over Ben, he will not be happy.

"So here is how this is going to work. Everyone has agreed to just pretend your little outburst never happened, but you're going to have to play extra nice for a little. You know, lay it on thick with the girls. Let them get their way for a bit. Not too long, after all, once we are married, you'll be the queen bee, but for now, just let them see how sorry you are for this whole mess."

"Yes." I nod.

"With me things are trickier. Outwardly I'll be completely forgiving, but you know it's going to take some work on your part to make me truly forget about everything you put me through."

"Yes."

I love how he says everything I put him through, like he wasn't the one who hurt me. Like he was the one who ended up in the hospital.

"Are you even sorry at all?" he snaps, digging his fingers into my thigh.

"I'm very sorry," I whisper.

"If anyone finds out you fucked him..." His voice trails off, but the tone paints a picture of what would happen then. "Let's just hope that doesn't happen."

"It won't."

"Good. Now before I even think of touching you like that, you'll need to get tested. I'll want a copy of the results sent to me directly. I assume you wore a condom, but you can't be so sure who that punk has been with."

"True." It's easier to just agree to whatever he says than speak too much.

"In the meantime, I'm going to be screwing around. Not a lot, but enough. Only fair, right?"

"Yes." I nod. My soul feels like it's being crushed with each agreement, but I have no choice. "I understand."

"It won't be forever, though I may pick up a girl here or there, but overall, the sex with you is pretty good. When you're pregnant, I'll probably have an affair or two, but I'll be discreet. Though we should probably get on the baby making quickly. I figure I'll propose around Christmas. We can have the wedding in June and get to getting you knocked up."

"Makes sense."

He has my whole life planned out for me. He gets to do whatever he wants, and I just have to sit there with a fucking smile on my face. It makes me want to scream, but all I can do is play along. Ben's freedom depends on it.

"I'm so glad to see you getting on board. Your father thought you'd put up more of a fight, but I knew you'd respond well to the bait. You are a smart girl after all."

"No." I laugh. "I'm not smart at all."

"Maybe smart is the wrong word, but either way, I'm glad you've returned to me. Even if you've been a real bitch."

My father spends an hour screaming at me. I don't absorb his words. They hold no meaning. They can't hurt me anymore than the mere fact he is willing to hand me back to a man who beat me.

After, my mother spends a good few minutes ripping me apart, she tells me how being a whore will get me nowhere and I should be ashamed for letting myself sink so low. I fight the urge to tell her to fuck off.

I don't mention the tattoo, but I'm sure Charles will when he sees it. The only saving grace is I get a few days before he expects me to fuck him. I'm going to avoid that as much as possible. I much rather him cheat now then stick his dick in me. All it would do is remind me of what I'm missing out on.

Ben has called me repeatedly. Left me voice messages I can't bring myself to listen to and text messages I can't bear to read. Eventually I take to blocking his number. It's easier this way. He will get over it, and I will relive every moment we shared together for the rest of my life.

When Cameron calls, I answer, only because I want to avoid him coming over here and causing a scene.

"Prue, what did you do?" he says when I answer. "Why did you go back there?"

"I had to do it, Cam. For Ben."

"Ben doesn't want you there. He much rather be in prison than have you back with Charles."

"It's fine, Cameron. I will be fine."

"Prue. Please? Don't do this to yourself."

"I didn't have a choice. It was either him or me, and it's better that it's me."

"He is going insane. You have to know he isn't okay with this."

"I know, but he will get over it."

"What about me? What happens when they tell you that you can't see me anymore?" His voice breaks a little, and it makes my heart crack. "I won't get over it."

"That's not going to happen. I won't let it."

"But you'll let him hurt you?"

"He won't hurt me if I behave."

"You sound just like Mom, you know? I don't want that for you, Prue."

"It's how things have to be. Life isn't fair, we both know that. Out of the two of us, I'm more than willing to be the one dealt the bad hand. Just promise you'll keep focusing on your music and not worry about me. I can handle myself."

"Yeah, but you shouldn't have to."

"I love you, Cam. I'll be fine. Please tell Ben that too."

He laughs. "If you think Ben is going to believe that any more than me, you have no idea how crazy that man is for you."

"Please try to convince him to leave me alone?"

"I'll do my best. Love ya, sis."

"Love you too. Talk again soon."

When I hang up, I lie back on my childhood bed, staring at the ceiling. I'm perfectly okay being the sacrificial lamb for Cameron and Ben. I can survive whatever hell is in store for me, so long as both of them are out there living their lives.

Everything will be okay. Charles will inflict some hell on me, but if I take it well and behave from here on out, there shouldn't be any more problems.

I can survive this.

God. I *hope* I can survive this.

THIRTY-TWO

Ben

She blocked my number, moved out of Cameron's and told him to tell me to leave her alone. She also happens to be under her father's roof, while back together with Charles. These thoughts swirl around my head for the rest of the day as I pace my condo, trying to figure out my next move.

I debate going to her parents', but I doubt that will go over well. I'd probably end up arrested, and she'd end up beaten. So, I can't very well do that.

I have to think. Have to be smarter. Plot better, but I refuse to let her stay there. I will do whatever it takes to get her out of this.

The next morning, I tuck myself into a chair in the corner of the coffee shop by her college the minute it opens. Sitting, I hope she stops in here before class.

It takes two hours, but she finally walks in. Two girls stand on either side of her. Some blonde in Uggs and a short brunette in pink sweatpants.

They talk to each other while Prue just nods along. She is wearing a light blue turtleneck and jeans. My stomach knots, scared there might be new bruises for her to cover.

They order and she turns, resting on the wall by the pickup counter. She still just nods along to whatever the other two are babbling about. Clearly, she is trying to seem interested, but her face tells me she is miles away. She glances around. Her eyes skim over me, dart away, then come back to me. I watch as her face drops and eyes widen.

I offer her a smile, beckoning her to me with my finger. She shakes her head, quickly looking at the girls beside her. That's how she stays until their drinks are ready and they disappear out the door.

I shouldn't be surprised she couldn't get away to talk to me, but it still makes me mad. If her father and Charles think they can keep me from her, they are wrong. I'm not letting them control her fate. That should belong to her.

So, plan B it is.

I sit in my mother's office, waiting for her to finish up her next class. I eye the picture frames on the wall. So many of her with my father and with me. And of course, her sister, my Aunt Martha.

Judging by how few of these pictures are of me older than the age of 10, I know I should be a better son. I should spend more time with her, but she should've picked up on the fact that once I hit eleven, I suddenly wanted nothing to do with the family. That didn't just happen for no reason.

I glare at the copy of the photo I have in my apartment. Knowing that is the reason makes me sick.

"Ben," my mother says when she walks in. "It's good to see you."

"I need a favor," I blurt out, turning toward her.

"What kind of favor?" She studies me. Her eyes take in the bruise on my cheek, but she won't ask.

"I need you to find out what classes Prue Ward has and have one of her teachers ask her to stay after class." Her face scrunches up as she tries to make sense of what I'm asking. "Then I need to use that time to talk to her."

"I don't understand," she says. "You want me to get a teacher to keep some girl after class just so you can talk to her? Why?"

"Because it's the only way, I can be alone with her that doesn't end up with a dead body."

"A dead body?" My mother gasps. Her concern is apparent. I've done my best to keep her out of the dark parts of my life, unfortunately for the both of us that ends now. "What is going on, Benjamin? Are you in some kind of trouble?"

"No more than usual." I shrug. "Though I did spend the weekend in jail."

"Jail?" She is stunned, shocked, terrified. "For what?"

"Don't worry about it. The charges were dropped."

"What is happening?" She sits back on her office chair. "You weren't always this wild."

"Yeah." I nod. "You should ask Aunt Martha about that. I'd be curious what she has to say about my wild behavior." Her name feels like poison on my tongue, but I'm in too much agony to care right now.

"What does she have to do with this?"

"Good question. Ask her that too."

"Ben," my mother says, staring me in the eyes. "Just tell me what's going on, please?"

"I met a girl who has an abusive ex, who I happened to beat up, with or without a deadly weapon, and this girl decided to trade her freedom for mine. That doesn't sit right with me, so I need to talk to her, without her prick of a soon-to-be fiancé finding out so he can't hurt her before I have the chance to end his miserable existence."

She sighs, her eyes dropping to a picture frame on her desk.

"I can't help you," she says, glancing back up. "You had me for a moment until the last part. I'm proud that I raised you to take care of people in need, but I can't let you kill a man to protect her. I won't help you if it puts you at risk of ending up hurt. As your mother, I just can't do that, Ben. I won't fail to protect you, even if that means someone else's daughter has to suffer. That will be my burden to live with, but I won't fail you."

"Already have, Mom," I say, walking to the door. "Ask Aunt Martha about that too. Or don't. She probably wouldn't tell you about it anyways, but I would like her to know I haven't forgotten. Can't forget."

"Forget what, Ben?"

I glance back at her as I open the door. Her face is etched in worry, and a kind of love only a mother could have. She deserves a better son, one who doesn't stress her out. One who isn't about to destroy her whole world like I am.

"That she is a fucking rapist." I shrug, turning and walking out of the room.

She didn't deserve to find out like that, but if I'm going to start pouring gasoline on everything I love, why not start at the top?

I stalk Prue for two days from afar. I lurk the hallways of her college, hang out in corners while she is in class. How I don't go insane anytime Charles is near her, touches her, or plants a stupid little kiss on her cheek, is a miracle.

I keep telling myself I need to keep my anger in check for her safety, for my plan to work.

Wes is not thrilled with my plan. Less thrilled about keeping things from my mother. He is a mommy's boy. She called him after our little chat, asking him questions. Lying to her will probably haunt him for the rest of his life, but what are brothers for?

She is deeply concerned, as is he. Only difference is he knows he would go to the same length as I am for his girl.

I'm surprised when Prue takes a seat outside my mother's office. Waiting for my mother to finish up with the student she is talking to. Her eyes dart around the hallway. I'm glad she can't see me from where I lurk.

When the student exits and my mom steps into the hallways, spotting Prue, she sighs.

"Prue."

"Hello, Mrs. Parker," Prue says, standing up.

"You're not in my class this year." My mother holds the door open, ushering Prue inside.

The minute the door shuts I walk over, standing to the side of the small window, I press my ear to the side of the door, hoping to hear their conversation.

"What brings you here?" my mother asks.

"Ben."

"Yeah. I figured as much, though he made it seem like getting you alone would be much more difficult."

"No one knows you're his mother. I told them I was asking about a TA spot for next semester."

"And what's the real reason?"

"I need you to tell Ben to leave me alone."

My mom laughs lightly. "Do you not know Ben? He doesn't listen to anyone, least of all me. I didn't understand why that was, but I'm starting to piece it together." She sighs.

"I just need you to convince him to stay away. I made my decision. This is what I want. Tell him that. Tell him I'm okay and that I want this."

"I'm not lying to my son. You don't want this. Don't get me wrong, as his mother I'm very thankful you saved him from a prison sentence, but as a woman, you don't want this."

It would be wishful thinking to think my mother could convince Prue to give up her plan. I know Prue better than that.

"It was the only way."

"No. It wasn't. Ben would've spent a lifetime behind bars for you. He still might. If you think me lying to him on your behalf has any barring, I hate to disappoint. He has always done what he wants, regardless of the consequences. He never listens to reason, and I think when it comes to you, it's ten times worse. I've never seen him care about anyone like he cares about you. He has no problem getting his hands dirty, but for you, I think he'd burn the whole world down."

"Please," Prue pleads. "I just need him to know I'll be okay. If he does anything, he will only make things worse for both of us."

"I know that. Wes knows that and deep down, so does Ben. The problem is, I don't think he cares."

Prue sighs, like she knows this has become a lost cause. "Who's the other woman?" she asks, and I can only assume she is asking about my aunt.

"That's my sister. Martha."

"Is she still alive?"

"Yes," my mother says. "She spends a lot of time with us."

"Next time you see her, tell her I hope she dies," Prue snaps, turning toward the door.

I move, knowing I have one shot at this. I duck into the janitor closet, keeping the door cracked to wait for her to walk by.

Prue marches out of my mom's office, turning toward where I stand. She strolls toward me and just when she steps in front of the door, I yank her inside with me, clasping my hand over her mouth.

She jerks against my hold, squirming and kicking at my shins. Her teeth bite into my palm and I hiss. My cock stiffens despite the fact this shouldn't be hot.

"Stop. It's just me," I say into her ear, holding her tightly against me. She relaxes into my embrace. "You went to see my mom?" She nods, and I release my hold on her. She turns, facing me. "Why?"

"To tell her to make you leave me alone," she snaps. "Ben, are you crazy? You need to stop. Just let me go. I made my decision."

"It was a stupid fucking decision," I say. "I'm not letting you sell your soul for me. Trust me, I'm not worth that much."

"Maybe I didn't do it for you," she says, putting her hands on her hips. The space is tight, but her movement makes her tits push forward and I'm so close to giving up my plan just to slide my cock into her again. "Maybe this was all just me throwing a fit and acting out. Maybe I actually love Charles and you just got caught in the crossfire of one of our little spats."

I laugh. "Jesus, Prue. You think I'm that dumb?" I press myself against her, holding her against the door. "You don't love him." My lips dip to her neck. "Probably don't even love me, but I don't need your love. I just need you to be safe." I plant kisses along her neck. "And sadly, that means I have to do some terrible things."

"Like what?" she asks softly, her breath increases with each kiss I place along her flesh.

I pull back, grinning. "Like kidnapping you." Her eyes widen. "The more you resist, the easier it will be to sell. So put on your best act, baby. Our lives are on the line."

I pull Prue from the supply closet, and she squirms, kicking my leg again. Part of me wants to believe she is just doing as I ask and trying to sell this as a kidnapping, but I know she never listens to me, so chances are she is just unhappy with my plan.

Why she thought I'd listen to her desperate plead for me to let her go, is amusing. But I guess I've spent the better part of the time we've known each other bending to her whims, so of course she'd think I'd obey her with this. Even though my desire to please her is sky high, it has its limits.

Like not letting her be unhappy for my own safety.

Jesus, I'm out of my fucking mind for this girl.

She opens her mouth to scream, as I drag her down the hallway, but I quickly cover her mouth with my hand again.

"If you don't bite me, I promise to make you cum before I'm done with you," I whisper in her ear.

She mumbles something against my hand that sounds a lot like asshole. I walk us both toward the exit. I can see Charles hanging around the corner with some of his jerk friends, waiting for her to finish up her meeting with my mother. Idiot didn't think twice about her meeting a lady with the same last name as me. I'm glad. It means my mom will be left out of this for the time being.

I parked my car in a handicap spot, not that I can afford more bad karma, but desperate times. I hope whatever karma police are watching understand I'd never do that under ordinary circumstances. Lucky for me there are plenty of other handicap spots open.

She puts up a good fight in my arms as I pull her toward my car. Her elbows dig into my ribs, making me see white spots. Her teeth nip at my hand as her head bumps back against the stab wound on my shoulder.

I yank open the passenger side door, pushing her into it. The moment I take my hand off her mouth, she lets out a scream. I slam the door and watch for a moment as she struggles to open it. Grinning as she realizes she can't get out, I walk around to the drive side and slide into the car.

She kicks at the door as if her tiny, little body could do any damage to my car.

"Ben. Don't do this. Please. He will kill you."

"I don't really care if he does." I shrug, starting up the car.

"What about me? He will kill me, Ben. Do you want him to kill me?"

"He won't get the chance," I say firmly. "Because I'm going to kill him first."

The fear on her face is quickly replaced with anger. "Ben! Let me go! Please. Let me go!" she screams, thrashing around in my car.

People start to look over at us, and I know I'm running out of time before Charles realizes what is happening.

"Prue!" I yell back. "Stop." The level my voice hits makes her freeze and my heart break. I don't like yelling at her.

"Please," she whispers, her voice shaking.

"You should've just listened to me."

"You should've just left me alone."

"Yeah. Probably. But I didn't want to."

Prue cries as I drive down the highway. Sobs so hard she

shakes. I pass her napkins, which she snatches from my hands, glaring as she cries.

"Has he touched you?" I finally ask.

"No. He won't fuck me until I get tested. Wants to make sure you didn't give me anything," she snaps.

"Has he hurt you in any other way?"

"Not really," she says softly. "A few rough grabs, but mostly he hasn't touched me at all. My punishment comes when the test comes back."

"Good. I'm glad you haven't had to endure any more pain, and I don't have to extract any more revenge than I was already planning."

"What is your plan?"

"Lock you up somewhere safe and kill him."

"You're really going to commit murder?"

"Yes." I nod glancing at her. "I was hoping to just murder his reputation, but you took that opportunity away."

"You mean when I saved you from prison?"

"Yes."

"You do know if you got sent to prison, he'd come for me after, right?"

"No, because I would've killed him while out on bail."

"So, your plan has always been killing him?" she snaps.

"I don't fucking know, okay?" I bark out. "I don't know what to fucking do. I have no clue if any of my plans are going to work, but if I don't try something to keep you from a miserable life of pain and unhappiness, I will kill myself."

"Ben..."

"I don't need you to be happy with me, Prue. I don't care if I spend the rest of my life in a cage, if it means you get to be free and a chance at happiness. I'd give it all up for you. Not that I have a lot going on anyways, but still. The stage, the feeling of a guitar in my hands, the fame, my freedom. Fuck, I'd give up cumming for you. I just can't let you give up anything for me. I don't deserve it, Prue, but you do."

"I don't want to be with him." She sobs, pressing her hands into her face. "I don't want any of this."

I take the next exit, pulling into the first parking lot I can find. Putting the car into park, I reach over, prying her hands from her face.

"Look at me, baby. It's going to be okay. I'll find a way to get you out of this mess."

"No, because if you kill him, I can't have you either," she whimpers, pressing her head into my chest. "Oh God."

I stroke her back as she cries into my chest, ignoring the pain in my ribs.

Her words are nice to hear. Really nice in fact. I like that she wants to have me. Unfortunately for the both of us, I'm not sure that's going to be possible. I'm not sure there is a way for us both to be free.

If all goes according to plan, there is no way this ends with us together.

A buzzing from her pocket has her pulling back from me. She slides out her phone from her pocket, staring at the name on the screen. I don't need to see it to know who it is. Taking it from her hand, I hit answer.

"Hello," I say.

"You," Charles yells into the phone. "Did you not learn your fucking lesson?"

"Nope." Prue looks at me, tears still pouring down her face. Her tears remind me why I'm picking a fight with a man whose family is worth a billion dollars.

"You want me to get the case back open? Have you arrested again, add kidnapping to your rap sheet?"

"Kind of. But I'm hoping we can make a deal."

"What deal do you think you could possibly offer me? I have all the power here."

"Not really. What's your master plan? Keep Prue as your little housewife to make Mommy and Daddy happy? Beat her in secret, force her to take your small cock and just get everything you ever wanted?"

"Yes. Pretty much. I was hoping I wouldn't have to beat her too much, but judging by how she keeps running off with you, I'm thinking it's going to take like six or seven times to get the message through to her."

My blood boils and I take a moment to study the shape of Prue's face. The bruise from the first night we met is gone, but I still remember the way it looked sitting below her eye.

"She didn't run away with me," I say. "I took her. She put up quite a fight too. Wouldn't shut up about how much she wanted to stay put and marry you, but I'm just so damn crazy about the girl. I couldn't stand it, so I took her."

"So, you're admitting to kidnapping her." Charles laughs. "Going to angle for mentally unstable?"

"No need to angle for it. Anyone who knows me can see I've clearly gone insane for her." Prue stares at me, biting her lip. "But that's not the fucking point." I sigh. "You don't deserve her, you know that, right? She is far too good for either of us, but if you're who she wants." Prue shakes her head, pressing her hand to my chest. I cover it with my own. "Then I guess I have to let you have her, but I have conditions."

"Conditions?" he snaps.

"You can't beat her. Violence isn't how you control a girl like Prue. She response better to pleasure. She'll do anything you ask after you make her cum a half a dozen times. I'm sure that's going to be a bit of a struggle for a guy like you, but just buy her a vibrator and I'm sure she will find a way to reward herself."

Prue's eyes do one loop, almost against her will, before resting back on me. A single tear rolls down her cheek.

"You are such a piece of shit," Charles mutters.

"You can't hurt her, okay? If I ever find out, and I will find out, that you laid a hand on her, I will come and cut off the micro penis we both know you have and make you eat it."

"So, if I promise to never beat her, you'll give her back, just like that?"

"If you promise to never beat or rape her, I will drop her off at her father's doorstep in an hour."

"Fine. Deal."

"I need to hear you say it, Charles."

"Fine," he groans. "I will never beat or rape her…"

"Who?"

He groans again, "I will never beat or rape Prue, again."

"Hmmm. So, you admit you did it before?"

"Fuck you," Charles yells. "Yes, okay? The little bitch couldn't just let me have my fucking fun, and I beat her. I hurt her bad too. You should've seen her. It was fucking great, watching that little slut bleed and scream in pain. Then I fucked her. Just tore that little pussy up."

I'm glad Prue can't hear what he is saying. I don't want those words running around in her pretty little head. It's bad enough she had to live it.

"Woah there, buddy," I say, cutting him off before he can say anything else. "Almost sounds like you're going to have a hard time keeping your end of the deal."

"You fucking asshole!" he screams. "You're just dicking me around, aren't you?"

"Trust me. I would never dick you around. You're not my type."

"You fucking piece of shit. When I get my hands on you, they won't be able to identify you from anything but the blood that soaks the earth I kill you over."

"Kinky," I say, hanging up.

"You're going to take me back?" Prue asks, softly.

"No. Afraid not, but I am going to take you somewhere."

She has no idea what my plan is. I know by the end of it she is probably going to hate me, but it will be worth it. She wanted to go to extremes to protect me but has no idea the levels I am about to go to save her.

THIRTY-THREE

Prue

Ben drives for two hours before pulling up to a hotel. He makes me wait in the car while he gets us a room. The child locks are on like he still thinks I'd try to escape. Which to be fair, I haven't done the best job proving he can trust me.

He still hasn't told me what his plan is. Part of me thinks that he doesn't even have a plan and is just shooting off the cuff. I don't really mind that plan. I'd go anywhere with him. Run for a lifetime with him if that's what it takes for us to be together.

The ride has been quiet. He turned on music but didn't say a word for the whole two hours. If my confession of wanting to be with him meant anything to him, he has a funny way of showing it.

Seems he is willing to go to great lengths to keep me safe, but not necessarily to keep me.

When he comes back from the hotel lobby, he walks to the trunk. I glance back as he takes out two backpacks and then opens my door for me. I eye the bags. One is purple with white flowers on it, much like one I have.

"One of those is mine?" I ask, staring at it.

"Cameron packed it with some of the stuff you left at his place." Ben shrugs.

"You brought Cameron into this?"

"Let your brother help you for a change. He owes you. Plus, the shiny new record deal he is going to land in a few weeks will be more than enough to keep him safe from whatever backlash happens."

"You got him a deal?" I don't know how Cameron is going to feel about that, but the idea that Ben is willing to not only help me, but my brother, stirs emotions in me.

"No. He will get himself a deal. I'll just make sure your father doesn't mess it up."

"Thank you," I say softly, as tears fill my eyes. I can never repay Ben for any of this. Nothing I do will ever show him how much I appreciate all he has done for me.

"Come on. We have three flights of stairs to climb because their shitty elevator is down and I'm exhausted." He holds out his hand, helping me from the car.

"Are you still in pain?" I ask, as he leads me to the stairs.

"I haven't not been in pain since I was ten, Prue," he says, carrying the backpacks up the stairs as I follow behind him.

"Is that when it all started with Martha?" He flinches at her name, pausing for a moment. "Your mother told me her name. She is your aunt."

"Prue. I have a lot going on right now, can we not talk about that?" he says, marching up the stairs.

"So, I'm supposed to just let you in on all the details of my misery without getting a word about yours?"

"You've gotten plenty words out of me. More than anyone else in fact, so please, just let that go. I'm kind of busy saving you right now."

"Will you tell me after?" I ask as we come to a stop outside a door. He jams a key into it, unlocking it.

"Tell you what exactly?" he asks, looking at me. "What do you want to know? The details? The timeline? What does that do for you? Paint a clearer picture that you aren't the only one who's broken? Have I not made that abundantly clear to you?" He swings open the door, stepping inside the room.

"No, you've made that very clear." I fold my arms over my chest, glaring at him.

"So, what else could you possibly want to know?" He drops the backpacks on the floor, standing in the doorway, waiting for me to come in, but I don't move.

"Do you love me?"

"Only completely."

"Say it."

"I love you, Prue. Happy? I said it. I love you and it's driving me fucking crazy. Jesus," he groans, pulling at his hair. "I love you and I don't know how to love anyone. I've never felt like this before. It's maddening and I keep fucking it up. Jesus Christ, I'm so fucking bad at this. But I really fucking love you."

"You love me." I smile. "Benjamin Parker loves me."

"Yes!"

I step into the hotel room, kicking the door shut behind me. Walking up to him, I press my lips against his.

He doesn't hesitate, wrapping his arms around me and pulling me closer against his body. His tongue pushes its way between my lips, darting around my mouth like if he doesn't map out every detail of it, he'll die.

I don't know what's going to happen. There are more questions than answers right now, but I don't care. Just for this tiny moment, I want to pretend everything is going to be okay and we can be together.

My fingers tug down the zipper of his hoodie, pushing it off his shoulders as he just lets it fall off his body. Wincing into my mouth as his arms wrap back around me. I tug at the bottom of his shirt, and he finally pulls himself away from me.

Sighing, he rubs his bottom lip with his thumb, staring at me for a moment. I wait, expecting him to make the next move. He just stares at me for a moment before marching over to the bed.

"It's been a long day. We should sleep," he finally speaks.

I'm stunned as I watch him kick off his shoes before plopping down on the bed. The lights aren't on, but I can still see his outline from the lights peeking in through the window. He is far too sexy for his own good, even in the dark. It's not fair how badly I want him.

"Sleep?" I ask, walking toward the bed. "You confess that you love me, force your tongue in my mouth, and then suggest sleep?"

"Yeah." He nods. "I even got us a room with two beds. Wouldn't want to sleep next to a girl who has a boyfriend."

"I can call him and break up with him if that helps your guilt."

He laughs. "Oh, it's not guilt keeping me from sticking my cock in you."

"Then what is?"

"Fear mostly," he says softly. "Fear if I fuck you again, I'll chicken out of my plan."

"What is the plan?" I sit on the edge of the bed he is lying on.

"The less you know, the better."

"I disagree."

"I can't shield you from all of it, but enough to make sure you don't end up in your own cage. You are an unwilling participant in all of this."

"Not all of it." I smile, climbing up the bed. "I'm not unwilling in all of it."

"I'm glad to know if I did fuck you, it wouldn't be rape. Glad I'm not that much of an asshole."

"I think you only pretend to be an asshole. I think deep down you're a big softie. Inside of you lives a gentleman, just waiting to come out. To buy a girl flowers and take her to dinner and make her cum countless times."

"Maybe the last part." He shrugs, peering down as I kneel beside him.

"You wouldn't buy me flowers?"

"Going to be hard to buy you much of anything after I buy you freedom."

"You don't have to buy me freedom." I swing my legs over his chest, settling my hips against his lower stomach. He groans, "We could just never go back." Rocking my hips against him has his hand dropping to my hip, rubbing small circles into the bone. "Run away together."

"Running isn't freedom."

"I don't need freedom, Ben. Not if the cage fits the both of us."

THIRTY-FOUR

Ben

Jesus Christ, Prue does not play fair. Never has, probably never will. At least with me, that is.

I'm not sure what the version of her was like before Charles hurt her, but I never want to meet that doe eyed creature. I'll take this evil version of her any day.

She grinds her cunt over my growing erection. Our pants keeping our flesh from touching, but the friction is still overwhelming. My resolve to just go to sleep is melting by each flex of her hips.

My plan did involve sex, at least a little. I wanted a goodbye fuck before getting sent to prison for the rest of my life. Then she had to bring up a certain name I didn't like to think about and force a confession from my lips. Telling her I love her was something I was trying to save. I wanted it to be the last thing I said to her, but it should've been apparent.

Maybe my lack of experience in that department and her messed up history with relationships made her miss the signs, but it should've been clear as fucking day that I'm madly in love with her.

It's also not lost on me that she didn't exactly say it back. Saying she wanted me is enough to let me know she cares, but the words I love you have yet to fall from her lips. I'm not an idiot. I know there is a good chance she doesn't love me. She needs and wants me, but loving me is different.

I don't need her to love me, though. I want to, sure, but I'm going to save her regardless of her feelings for me. I love her too much not to.

That's why I can't fuck her right now. If we have sex, I won't be able to leave her. Sadly, that's the only option we have. No matter what happens from here on out. If Charles doesn't die, he'll be out for blood. I couldn't care less if he killed me, but I don't think he stops with just me. My plan has to go right or else she is still in danger.

Prue reaches under her shirt, undoing her bra and pulling it out of her sleeve. She tosses it on the other bed with a wicked grin on her face. Peeling off her shirt, my eyes watch as her tits are revealed. My hand on her hip squeezes, as my self-control is dying by the second.

Grabbing my other hand, she brings it up to her chest. She wraps it around her tit, holding it against her flesh as her hips continue to grind into my throbbing cock.

"Ben. Please fuck me." Her voice is all breathy and full of desire. I'm going to go insane. "I want to feel my pussy stretch around your fat cock again. One time is not enough."

"Yeah? Will two times be enough, baby?" I thrust my hips forward and she groans.

"No." She shakes her head. Short caramel strands of hair swish in the air. "It will never be enough."

"Too bad," I say and gently push her off me. She lands on her back beside me.

"What the fuck is your problem?" she huffs, sitting up. "Does falling in love make your dick limp?"

"Think we both know that's not the case."

She crawls off the bed, yanking her shirt off the second bed and pulling it over her head.

"I'm leaving. And you're an asshole."

"You are not leaving," I say, standing up.

"What are you going to do if I try?" She glares at me. "Make this an actual kidnapping?"

"Technically, it always has been." I shrug, walking to my backpack. Sadly, for her, I came prepared for her fight-or-flight instincts, pulling out a set of handcuffs I hold them in the air for her to see.

"You wouldn't," she states as her eyes widen.

"I beat the shit out of your ex, stabbed myself in front of your father, agreed to not cum, spent the weekend in jail, kidnapped you and confessed my love for you. Do you really think I won't handcuff you to the bed?"

"If you handcuff me to the bed, I'll never forgive you."

"Just like I don't need your love, baby, I don't need your forgiveness." I take a step toward her, and she takes a step to the side. "I've accepted my role as your punching bag and martyr. Now it's time for you to accept your role as damsel in distress."

"I never asked you to save me." She takes another step toward the door. She is going to have to find a way past me if she plans on getting to it. That's not going to be easy. "And I'm not a damsel in a distress."

"Oh baby. You did and you are."

"When did I ask you to save me?"

"You called me that night."

"You called me first."

"True. And you answered." I smirk, as her eyes dart to the door. "And then when you needed saving, which you did, you called me. You called me and I came."

"Quite literally," she snaps back.

"Yeah." I nod. "Filled you up nice and deep. Since then, I've been saving you nonstop."

"So, stop."

"I don't want to." I shrug. "What part of that don't you get? I like saving you. I'm not sure I could stop trying if I wanted to, but the fact is I don't want to. I'd spend the rest of my life saving you if I could. Unfortunately for the both of us, I only have one shot at it."

"Marry me," she blurts out.

"What the fuck would that solve?"

"That's not a no," she says. "Marry me. We can go to Vegas right now and get married. Then they will have to leave us alone."

"I'm not marrying you."

"Why not? Is that level of commitment too much for you?"

"Baby, any level of commitment is too much for me."

"Is that it then? You off my ex so you don't have to become my boyfriend?"

I laugh. What a silly thought. Murder to avoid being her boyfriend? Even I'm not that crazy.

"I'm going to kill your ex because he deserves to fucking die."

"There isn't a little part of you that's glad you'll get off the hook? You can confess you love me, save me and never have to commit to me."

"Jesus," I groan. "That has nothing to do with it. Is this all not enough for you? You want a fucking diamond ring too?"

"I don't like diamonds," she shoots back.

"Or listening to me," I add, taking a step toward her. She tries to sidestep me again, but I just grab her by the waist. "Now because I need some fucking sleep and I don't trust you not to try to run, I have to do this."

I slap one handcuff on her wrist and the other to mine. She stares at where the cuff links us together. When she looks up at me, she has a cute little shocked expression etched on her face.

"What..."

"You said if I handcuffed you to the bed, you'd never forgive me, so I had to improvise." I shrug.

"What if I need to pee?"

"I guess I get to watch."

"I'd rather die."

"If you need to use the bathroom, I'll walk you to the door, undo the cuff and let you go, just to reattach it when you are done." She opens her mouth to speak, but I cut her off. "The bathroom doesn't lock, and if you think for a second you can try hiding out in there, I'll drag you out."

"You're being an even bigger asshole than normal," she snaps, tugging at the cuff.

"And you're being extra difficult. Glad we are both at our best. Now let's get some sleep."

THIRTY-FIVE

Prue

There is something about watching Ben sleep right now that breaks my heart. The last time we slept next to each other, he had his arms wrapped around me. This time he has us cuffed together but keeps his distance.

His face moves as he sleeps. Little lines form across his forehead and his eyelids scrunch up. Words form on his lips, but no sound comes out. His body is perfectly still. He doesn't toss or turn, just lays flat with his chest facing the ceiling.

My body craves his embrace, even as my actions try to push him away. My body and heart want his affection. And my pussy desperately wants his cock.

The fact he won't give it to me is frustrating. I thought my threat of leaving would be enough to break him after begging and teasing failed, but all it got me was handcuffed to his side. I don't necessarily hate it. There is something kind of hot about being literally stuck to him, but still, I want him to want me.

I slide closer to his body slowly, trying not to wake him with my movement. When he doesn't show any signs of stirring, I rest my head gently on his chest.

"Prue." He sighs.

"Sorry," I whisper. "I didn't mean to wake you."

"It's fine," he says softly. "Try to get some sleep," he murmurs.

Once his breathing evens out, I nuzzle into him, glancing up to make sure he's still asleep.

"I love you too," I whisper.

Ben wakes up first. I only know this because when I wake up, I can hear him talking quietly into the phone.

"No," he says. "That is not happening." Pausing to listen to whoever is on the other side of the phone, he bites his lips, but his fingers stroke my back.

It's then I realize he has removed the handcuffs.

"Don't even think about it," he whispers, looking down at me, with the phone away from his mouth. "I'll cuff you again, if I have to." I smirk up at him. "Naughty little girl."

"So punish me."

"No," he says back into the phone, though he yanks his hand from around me. "That's not happening either. I don't trust him." His hand rolls me onto my back though. His fingertips stroking my nipple through my shirt. I bite my lip to keep from moaning. "I'm not risking her safety." He glances down at his phone as his finger rubs circles around my nipple. "I got to go. If they are tracking my calls, I am way over the time limit. Don't worry, Wes. I have it all under control."

He hangs up the phone tossing it to the side, before rolling over on his side to look at me.

"So, you want a punishment?"

"No. I want a reward, but I figured you'd be more inclined to punish me."

He laughs, pulling on my nipple. "No. I'm more inclined to worship you."

"But not fuck me."

"You still want my cock?"

"Yes. Have I not made that clear." I mock his voice.

"You haven't made a lot of things clear." He shrugs. "Go shower. We have a long day ahead of us."

"Careful, Ben," I say, pushing myself up and swinging my legs over the edge of the bed. "If you don't fuck me soon, I might get desperate enough to go back to Charles. Sex with him was nothing compared to sex with you, but it is better than no sex." I grin with my back to him, waiting for him to react.

His hand is on me in a flash. I knew that my words would upset him. I'm very good at doing that and just desperate enough to push him.

"You didn't just say sex with the man who beat and raped you is better than no sex," Ben says. His voice low and full of anger. I could take a hate fucking.

"I did." I nod, not turning to look back at him.

He yanks me backward though. Gently. He has this way of manhandling me in the softest ways. Like he wants to strangle the life from my body, just to bring me back to life again.

Pushing me onto the bed, he straddles me, staring down at me his dark blue eyes light up. He wants me. I can tell that by his eyes and cock stiffening in his pants. For whatever reason he is trying to fight it, though.

"Are you that fucking horny?"

"Yes. Got a taste of your cock and haven't been able to think of much else since." I smirk up at him.

"Other than running back to your ex," he grumbles, gripping the edge of my shirt. He tugs it over my head. "You want my cock that bad?"

"Yes." I nod frantically as his hand presses softly into my lower stomach.

"You need it?"

"I need you," I correct him.

And I do need him. I need him more than I care to admit,

more than I want to. I didn't think I ever needed anyone. I only needed to be something for them.

The good girl. Their dutiful girlfriend and daughter. The loyal, supportive sister. Those were roles I played to make everyone happy, but I didn't need anything in return.

Now here I lay with Ben's body over mine, promising me safety. Willing to kill for me and I realize I need him.

God. I need him so bad. And I don't want to lose him. Not to a prison cell, not to save anyone else. I can't be without him now.

If that is a weakness, it sure doesn't feel that way as he stares down at me. His eyes light up at my statement as his hands react fast to unbutton my jeans. They are off my legs, and he is back to straddling me in record time.

His head dips to my collarbone as he plants kisses against my flesh. His hand parts my legs and grips my inner thigh.

"Ben," I mumble. "Maybe we should..."

He pulls back. "Oh what, now you don't want my cock?" he says, using this moment to unbutton his own pants. "You're sending me mixed signals, Prue."

The outline of his erection has my mouth watering, but I need to know he won't do anything stupid. I want him to tell me he will stay and be mine.

"I want your cock, but..."

"But what, baby?" he cuts me off again. "You want to pause so we can talk about your little confession? You need me. You get me."

"All of you?" I question.

"As much as you can fit." He smirks.

"Ben. Wait."

He freezes all movement, staring at me.

I don't know what to say. How do I explain to him that I want more than just sex? How do you tell a known playboy, rock star that you want him to commit himself to you? To not murder your ex or go to jail. To not leave you.

"I'm waiting," he says after a moment.

"Don't you think we should talk about things?"

"Talk about what? I love you. You need me. I'm going to kill your ex-boyfriend. I think that pretty much covers everything."

The fact he doesn't want to alter his plans makes me irrationally angry. How is he not getting it? I don't want to lose him.

"So, you just fuck me, kill my ex, and then abandon me?" I snap, pushing at his chest.

"It's not like you'll be alone." He shrugs. "You'll have Cameron, and a girl like you will find another guy to toy with in no time. I'll be a distant memory in six months or less."

He thinks that little of me? Can he not see how much he means to me? Did I hurt him so much that he thinks I could just move on from him so easily?

I squirm, trying to get free of him. My heart feels like it's snapping. I find someone I can actually rely on and he wants to leave me.

"I don't want some other guy," I snap, shoving at his chest. "If you don't want to be with me just fucking say it."

His hands wrap around my wrist, prying them from where I push against his chest.

"I want to be with you, Prue. I want nothing more than to spend the rest of my life being tortured by you."

"Then don't leave me," I say, letting my voice break and tears fill my eyes. "Please don't leave me." I cover my face as tears spill down my face. "I don't want to be without you. I need you, Ben."

"Hey, baby," he says, pulling my hands off my face. I blink out tears, looking up at him. "Jesus, baby. I'm not leaving you because I want to. I'm leaving cause it's the only way." His head dips down, pressing kisses on my cheeks. His lips brushing away the tears that still fall from my face. "I'd stay with you forever and a day, if I could." He pulls back. "Fuck, I'd give up my band for you. Touring. Other women. Everything. I'd give up everything to be yours, Prue."

"So don't do it. Don't kill him. Find another way." My lips tremble, and he traces it with his thumb.

"Okay." He sighs. "Okay. I'll find another way."

THIRTY-SIX

Ben

Prue presses her lips against mine the moment I tell her I will find another way. I let her take control of the situation because I don't like lying to her. It tastes like poison on my tongue. Lying to her may be the worst thing I ever do and I'm about to kill someone.

Funny how hurting the person you love feels worse than murder.

She pushes my shirt up my chest and I let her tug it over my head. Her hand is struggling to find a way to get my jeans off without having me move. That's going to be impossible, so I pull back. Pushing my jeans down my legs and letting them bunch at my ankles.

Her hand slips into my boxers, as I wedge myself between her legs. I can't help but groan as her hand wraps around my cock, pulling it out the front of my boxers. She licks her lips at the sight of it, stroking me until I'm so hard I think I may black out.

"Fuck. Prue. Let me put it in you. Please, baby?"

"Now who's begging whom?" She smirks that smirk she only seems to show me. And fuck, if it isn't one of the best looks in the world.

"Me. I'm begging you," I groan again as her thumb swirls around the head.

"And you'll stay?" she questions.

Jesus Christ. She is going to be the death of me.

If I lie to her and fuck her, that's rape. I know that. How many times has that happened to me? How many times was I promised this would be the last time, but it never was. How many times was I told it would just be a look, a touch, a second for it to be worse? But if I don't fuck her, then she knows I lied and knowing her, she will do something that will get us both hurt.

"Ben?"

"Fuck. I can't fucking think straight," I groan. It's not a lie. I can't think straight right now, but it also doesn't answer her question.

She laughs at that, dropping onto her back. Her legs spread as she smiles up at me.

"Worship me then."

Is it a lie if I never answer the question? My self-control is snapping as she stares up at me, bare chests and just in her panties.

I move forward, not bothering to take off her panties, just pulling them to the side. Her pussy is too fucking pretty.

I rub my cock against her opening, then up her clit. Despite her tears from just moments ago, she is dripping wet. I let her arousal coat my cock as I rub myself between her lips and clit over and over.

"Put it in me, Ben. Stretch me open and make me cum," she moans.

I can't do this. I'm not a fucking rapist. Taking advantage of her is not something I can do and live with myself after.

She reaches down, taking my cock back in her hand. She moves the head, so it presses against her opening, as her sky-blue eyes lock onto mine.

My balls are bound to fall off at some point, but the look on her face seals my fucking fate. I can't fuck her on a promise I don't intend to keep. While her crying and begging me not to leave shattered my soul into a million pieces, breaking her trust like that would kill me.

I pull back, cursing to myself. I climb from between her legs, almost stumbling on my pants as I stand to my feet.

"What are you doing?"

"I don't fucking know!" I groan.

"Ben?"

"We need to go. If they are tracking my phone, then they know where we are. So, we need to go."

"What does it matter now? I'm not going back to him, and you aren't going to kill him. We are finding another way to deal with this."

"Prue," I snap, pulling up my pants. "We are still at risk of being in a lot of trouble. The Davenports and your family for that matter, have the kind of money to rid the world of their problems, and right now we are a big fucking problem for them."

"You're more afraid of dying than getting blue balls?" She smirks at me and for a moment I almost give in. Throw her back down and fuck her until I can convince myself there is another way out of this mess for us.

"I'm more afraid of you dying."

"Uh. Fine." She sighs, rolling her eyes. "Where are we going next?"

"North," I reply. "We'll drive a few more miles north and find somewhere to hide out."

"And then you'll fuck me?"

"Yes." I nod. "Then I'll fuck you."

It's another lie but better than fucking her when she is under the impression, I'm not leaving her.

She is going to hate me in a few hours, but that's better than her being hurt or worse, dead.

We drive for a few hours. It's the most peaceful my time with Prue has been. We listen to music as we drive along the coast side. She asks me random questions like she is studying for a quiz. It's oddly comforting to know she wants to learn things about me.

She tells me stories about her life, not knowing that every detail she gives me just cements the fact there is no other way for me to solve this situation than to kill Charles.

She deserves so much better than her family gave her. Better than Charles can promise her, but they won't let her go without a fight. I'm more than willing to finish the war for her.

We take bathroom breaks and eat cheap fast food as we drive. She is behaving far better than I thought she would. Perhaps the promise of my cock was all it took to make her be good, but more so it's the idea that I'm not abandoning her.

It's bittersweet. I love the fact that us being together makes her happy, but knowing it has a time limit hurts my soul.

When I pull up outside the Hilton, I booked just outside of San Francisco, she grins.

"Fancy."

"I'm not going to have to drag you to the room, am I?"

"Not unless you think it will be good foreplay." She smirks.

"You are very lucky you're hot."

"And you're very lucky you have a fat cock." She sticks her tongue out at me. It makes me smile instantly. I love this version of Prue just as much as the evil vixen who tortures me. This version of her is cute and fun, and I could spend the rest of my life soaking up the beam of her smile. Too bad I'm on borrowed time.

"I'll be right back," I say, getting out of the car.

I pay for the hotel and slip the young lady at the counter a wad of cash. She eyes it, then me, then it again.

"Do you know who I am?"

"Yes," she replies. "What is this for?"

"Listen. In about two hours I need someone to go into my room and unlock the beautiful woman I'm about to handcuff to the bed. The key will be in the front pocket of the backpack on the floor. Can you make sure that happens?"

"Are you trapping her up willingly?"

"Yes," I lie. No way is Prue going to let me handcuff her willingly, but this lady doesn't need to know that. "It's the leaving part that isn't willing."

"Got it." She eyes the cash again. "I can make sure that happens."

"Great. Thank you." I pause, grabbing the pen on the counter and a piece of paper. I scribble a note for Prue on it, and hand it to the lady. "Can you make sure she gets this too?"

"A breakup note. How nice."

When I walk back to the car, Prue is sitting in the passenger seat, waiting for me. I grab our bags out of the car and open the door for her. She jumps out of the car, following behind me as I lead us to the elevator.

"How long are we here?"

"Haven't decided yet." I shrug.

"San Francisco could be fun."

"It could be. But I think anywhere would be fun with you."

She smiles at that. As silence takes over the elevator, I watch the wheels in her head spin. I should fill the silence so she doesn't start questioning me, but I don't know what to say.

I lead her down the hallway to our room. Opening the door for her, she steps in, but turns to look at me. I drop the bags on the floor, not bothering to turn on the lights. There won't be any need for that.

"I love you, Prue."

"Why are you saying it like that?"

"Like what?"

"Like goodbye."

"It's not a goodbye." I offer her a smile.

I feel the walls closing in as I sit on the bed. She stands, watching me. I'm extremely happy that she seems capable of reading me so well, but I know that doesn't work in my favor right now.

"So, what's the plan now?"

"What do you mean?"

"Do we just hide out forever?"

"No. I'm still working on figuring out my next move. Maybe we hide out here for a few days, maybe we keep moving. I don't know yet."

"You're lying," she says, folding her arms over her chest. "You are keeping something from me, and I don't like it." She walks over to me, standing in front of me. I wrap my hands around her stomach, as she rests her head on top of mine. "Just tell me."

"No." I shake my head, kissing her stomach. "I'm not ready yet."

I grab her, tossing her softly on the bed, before pressing my body against hers. She doesn't fight me, not even as I plant kisses up her stomach, collarbone, and neck. She rocks into my touch. It's probably cruel of me to be teasing her like this, but I can't help myself.

Her hands drop to my head, and I grab her wrists, pinning them above her head. I picked this hotel for a reason. I stayed here once, so I knew they had headboards with slacks in them. Easy to handcuff someone to.

"Fuck me, Ben. Please."

"I'm afraid I can't do that," I say, my lips less than an inch from hers. "I really want to, Prue, but liars don't deserve to go to heaven."

I don't give her a chance to reply to that before pressing my lips against hers. I have to make this kiss count. I highly doubt I'll ever get to kiss her again.

As my tongue dips into her parted lips, she melts under me. Her lips move with mine, as her body presses up against mine. I let myself get lost in it for a moment, even as I grip her wrists with one hand.

It's only when I see her eyes are still shut that I do what I need to. Pulling the handcuffs from my back pocket, I clip one to her right wrists, quickly sliding it through the slant in the headboard and attaching it to the other.

The second click gets her attention, and she bites at my bottom lip.

I pull back, climbing off her body.

"What are you doing, Ben?" She pulls at the cuffs. "You said you wouldn't leave me."

"I lied," I say softly, staring at her, willing my cock to go soft. Nothing about this is sexy, only the fact the girl I love is handcuffed to a bed... but the reasons aren't desirable. "It tasted like poison. I'm sure I lied before, but it's not in my nature to lie. I'm going to pay for it greatly, but the worst part is knowing you'll never forgive me." I grab my backpack. "Don't worry. You won't be trapped for long. Consider this the last few hours of being in a cage. Soon you'll be free."

"Ben. Don't do this. Please," she begs, pulling at the cuffs. "There has to be another way."

"Maybe." I shrug. "But not one I'm comfortable with."

"I'll never forgive you. Ever. You don't get to trade your life for mine and then expect me to be grateful."

"I don't need your love, forgiveness, or your gratitude. Just knowing you're safe will be enough for me."

"I won't be safe," she snaps. "I'll live dangerously and recklessly. I'll drink and drive. Fuck everyone I meet. Shoot up heroin."

I laugh, what a funny thought. "No, you won't."

"Yes. I will. Anything to make you pay."

I shrug. "As long as you're doing what you want for a change, I'll be okay with it. Have fun," I say, walking over and pressing a kiss to her forehead. "I love you, Prue. You may never forgive me and that's fine, but when I kill your ex, please take it as an act of love not abandonment." I straighten up.

"Ben. Please." She cries now. "Don't do this. I'm begging you."

I walk to the door. Knowing I have very little time to get to the airport if I don't want to miss my flight back to LA.

"Now this is goodbye." I open the door.

"Stop. Ben. Please," she continues to beg. "I love you," she blurts out, right before I'm about to step out.

I smile back at her.

"You're way better at goodbyes."

When the door shuts behind me, I stand frozen outside the room. My feet refuse to move. My heart is begging me to go back in there and beg for forgiveness in the form of countless orgasms and more self-mutilation.

But while I've spent most of my adult life being selfish, I've seemed to have adopted a hero complex since meeting Prue. Saving her is looking like a full-time job. The time clock will be the jail cell I'm going to be sentence to, but a job done well, is a job well done.

The flight back to LA takes less than two hours. So when I land, I know it's just a matter of time before I'm putting a bullet in the head of Charles Davenport. If all goes well, that is.

There is a good chance he kills me first. I made sure to leave a small trail of breadcrumbs to let him know where he can find me. Laying out a trap, but I'm not entirely sure if he is getting caught or me.

I might have been making it seem like my plan is to kill him, and it is. But I failed to mention the part where my plan could cost me my life too.

Best case is I get to kill him. Worse case, he kills me and gets to rot behind bars instead of me. Either way works for me, so long as Prue gets to live a long and hopefully healthy life.

I have to admit her little threat to do more harm to herself than good almost had me, but I know her. She isn't stupid. It was just her last attempt to get me to change my mind. Just like saying she loves me as I was leaving.

It was nice to hear it, but I don't buy it for a second. She needs me, yes. At this time in her life, she needs someone to take her lashings and show her what freedom feels like. I'm very grateful I got to be that person for her, but she was always going to outgrow me.

Lucky for us both, I'm sparing us that misery.

I know at this moment she is probably free of the shackles that trap her to the hotel bed and one step closer to whatever life she desires. She may pretend like that's me, but it isn't.

Wes meets me in the airport parking lot. He leans against his car, smoking a cigarette.

"I was half expecting Prue to be with you."

"That wasn't part of the plan."

"Thought you might've changed your mind."

"You know me better than that." I flash him a grin.

"Wishful thinking, I guess." He shrugs, climbing into the car.

"Thank you for picking me up," I add after sliding into the seat beside him.

"Yeah." He nods. "Not really sure I should take you home, though. Part of me thinks a mental hospital is more fitting."

"Ha." I smile. "Just drop me off at my condo, Wes. There is nothing for you to worry about."

"You're like my brother, Ben. Of course, I'm worried." But he starts the car regardless.

"Can I tell you something?" I ask, looking at him through the corner of my eye as he drives.

"You can tell me anything."

"You know my Aunt Martha, right?" Her name feels like acid on my tongue.

"Yeah."

"Well, I should've never let you spend the night when she was there. I was selfish. Using you as a shield to keep her from...

hurting me." I pause for a moment. "But I put you at risk by having you there and I'm sorry."

"Hurting you?" He glances at me.

"You don't want the details and I don't want to give them."

"Fair enough."

"But regardless. I'm sorry."

"Don't be. There isn't a lot I wouldn't do for you."

"I know." I nod. "And I love you too or whatever."

Wes laughs. "Just do me a favor."

"What?"

"Make it count."

"That's the plan."

I'm only half surprised to find my front door unlocked. I'm a little more surprised to find all the lights on and the place a wreck, though.

However, when I see one guy lounging on my couch and the other sitting at my kitchen table, I'm not surprised in the slightest.

"Rookie mistake, leaving the door unlocked and lights on," I say dropping my backpack on the ground.

"Where is she?" Charles says, standing up from the kitchen table.

"Right now? Probably desperately trying to get a plane ticket at the San Francisco airport."

"And you're here, because?"

"She got a little too clingy for me." I shrug.

"You got bored of her?" Charles laughs. "He got bored of her," he says to his friend who laughs with him. The guy looks terrified to be here, but he is going along because that's what you do when your rich friend asks you to. Why Charles is doing his own dirty work is beyond me.

"The question is why are you two here?"

"To follow through on a promise." Charles grins. "I said I was going to kill you so I'm here to kill you."

"Oh, come on. She is surely going to come crawling back now that she knows she can't have the best thing to ever happen to her. Can't we just wrap this up in a rug and toss it into the ocean like they do to dead bodies in the movies?"

"No. But thanks for the tip." Charles laughs. "I much rather watch your body go up in flames, though. Maybe I'll slit her throat over your ashes."

"Little violent don't you think?"

"Violent? You held a fucking knife to my throat."

"And you broke my rib. Let's let bygones be bygones or whatever they say."

"I rather piss on your corpse."

"Jesus. Kiss your mother with that mouth?"

"You're such a piece of shit." He throws a chair in my direction. It misses, crashing into my TV, which shatters.

"I'm made of rubber, you're made of glue, whatever you say bounces off me and sticks to you."

He answers that by hurling another chair at me. I have to duck so this one doesn't hit me. A shiver runs down my spine as it crashes into the wall behind me. I'm starting to doubt my odds of surviving this, but hey, dead or alive, Prue will get her freedom.

"Charles," his friend says, standing up. "You don't want someone calling the cops before we're done with him."

"I wouldn't mind if someone called the cops," I chime in.

Charles marches over to me. Since I'm not a chicken shit, I keep my feet firmly in place. His fist connects with my jaw with enough force that I'm pretty sure another hit like that has me drinking out of a straw for the rest of my life.

I have enough sense to shove him back. He stumbles two steps backwards, stunned again by my strength.

"Grab his arms," he barks at his friend. "I don't want him to lay a finger on me."

"All give and no take. No wonder Prue found you to be an inadequate lover."

He punches me in the gut as his friend walks up. His friend grabs both of my hands, yanking them behind my back.

This could've gone better. I probably should've walked in with a gun in my hands and shot Charles in his stupid fucking head the moment I saw him. Though that would've been harder to sell. It would've looked like cold-blooded murder instead of man slaughter. I really didn't expect him to be this unhinged. I'm a fucking idiot apparently.

His elbow smashes into my stomach, so hard I almost vomit from the impact. Another hit lands against my side, followed by more to the ribs.

"Jesus," I groan when he steps back. "How did you not kill Prue? I'm impressed she survived with her brain still intact."

"Obviously she didn't if she went and ran off with you." He spits in my face as he shouts.

"Are you going to fuck me or kill me? Kind of sending mixed messages."

He rewards my witty remark with an elbow to the head. I'm seeing stars made up of Prue's face which makes the pain a bit more bearable.

As another blow lands against my rib, I gag, spitting up mucus or blood. Hard to tell what color it is as my vision is blurred and my body in pure agony. I'm glad I walked in here thinking my life was over already, or the fact I'm about to die might suck.

If life really does flash before your eyes when you go, I hope it slows down at the short time I got to have Prue's attention.

"You know it's sad, really. Your band isn't half bad. Maybe they'll be even better without you in it."

I want to say something snarky back, but my air supply seems to be a little limited at the moment, so I focus on trying to breathe instead. Part of me is desperate to survive this, if only to make sure he gets locked away and isn't able to hurt Prue again.

"That's enough," his friend says. "If your hands are bruised, they could pin this on you. So just finish him and let's go."

"Bruised hands are the least of his concerns," I mutter, laughing as more spit, blood or vomit dribbles out of the corners of my mouth.

"Lucky for me I have an alibi." Charles laughs, punching me in the side again. He takes a few steps backwards. I allow my eyes to shut for a moment. When I hear a gun cocking, I open them. His friend pulls at my arms tighter, lifting my chest up more. "Any last words, fuck face?"

Well, I can't say I'm surprised he brought a gun of his own. It's not like he didn't know I may have a weapon. Only mine is stashed in a drawer in the kitchen. Not my smartest moment, but I was hoping for the element of surprise.

I'm not going to survive this, but Prue will. He doesn't know it. Charles believes he can get away with this, but he won't be able to for long.

"Yes," I say, trying to get a good view of the gun that is about to kill me before my eyes dart to the corner of the room. "I love you, Prue."

The words barely leave my mouth before the sound of the gun going off fills the room. A sharp, ripping feelings spreads through my chest and if it hurts, I can't feel it. The only thing I can feel is my head hitting the floor.

Sparks light up behind my eyes. Sky blue sparks with pin prick pupils that dance with desire, fury and maybe a hint of love.

Hopefully, the cameras were able to pick up the last thing I said. I want Prue to know she was the last thought that went through my mind before I died.

THIRTY-SEVEN

Prue

When the cleaning lady finds me handcuffed to the bed, she doesn't seem the slightest bit surprised. She fishes the key from the backpack Ben left behind as if she had been instructed exactly where to find it.

Once she frees me, she hands me a note and leaves the room like this is a completely normal situation for her.

My heart feels like it's been ripped out of my chest but I'm too angry to cry. I crumble the note up without reading it, tossing it across the room before thinking better of it and walking to get it.

I smooth it out, looking over the words. Clearly it's Ben's handwriting, because there is a little doodle of a broken halo on the top of it and a broken heart on the bottom. He knows the tattoo I drew for him. Other than those two markings all it reads is 'Plane ticket waiting for you at SFO airport.'

I rip the note to pieces and throw them all over the room. It's childish and dramatic but I don't care. They obviously knew I was tied to the bed for the last two hours.

Grabbing the backpack off the floor I call myself a car as I march out of the hotel room. I don't want to spend another second here any longer.

By the time I get to the airport and pick up the ticket back to LA that is waiting for me, it's been almost four hours since Ben left me.

I've been calling and texting him nonstop. Everything from calling him names, to begging for him to not do it. He doesn't respond to any of them, and it only makes me crazier.

I scroll through my phone not sure who else to call. Cameron is a theory, but I don't want him involved in this anymore than he already is. When I get to the end of the list and see Wes's name programmed into my phone, I know who I need to call.

It rings twice before he answers.

"Hello, Prue."

"Where is he?"

"I dropped him off at his condo about thirty minutes ago, so I assume he is either on his way to being a murderer or dead."

"And you just let him do it?"

"He'd let me if the roles were reversed."

"No. He wouldn't. He would've done it for you."

"That's probably true," Wes says softly. "And I would've helped him had he let me."

"You should've taken him anywhere else. Anywhere but there. What kind of friend just lets..."

"Prue. Listen, I love the guy, probably more than you, so trust me when I say that there was no way I could've talked him out of this. I tried."

"Should've tried harder." I choke back a sob. "I can't lose him."

"You barely knew him. Imagine how I feel."

"So, go back there and stop him!"

"I have my orders. Pick you up from the airport and keep you safe until everything settles. That means more to him than his life. I will honor those wishes."

"God," I breathe out, letting the tears stream down my face.

"I'll see you at the airport when your flight lands."

When I land in LA, I spot Wes by the baggage area waiting for me. I quickly bolt the opposite way. I don't care what Ben asked him. Right now, I just need to find Ben and stop him from whatever he is going to do if he hasn't already done it.

I start marching toward the exit when a thin, pale, black-haired girl steps in front of me. I know who she is right away. It's impossible not to know the great Abbey Dark.

"Prue?" she says softly.

"Leave me alone."

"I'm Abbey." She smiles, even though she looks extremely nervous. "Ben told Wes you were difficult, so I was put in as a backup. I mean I kind of owe Ben. He helped keep Wes from murdering someone." She wraps her arms around her stomach.

"I'm glad Ben decided to be the better friend," I snap. "And if you think this makes you even with him, you are so wrong. He did more for Wes and you than you can ever repay."

"Hello, Prue," Wes says from behind me. I turn to look at him. "I understand you're upset, but please don't take it out on her."

"Oh, I'm so sorry." I roll my eyes. "I should be nice to your girlfriend that you get to be with because mine decided to keep you from going to jail for life after you just let mine..."

"Take a bullet to the chest for you."

"What?" My voice cracks.

"At least that's what the news is saying." Wes shrugs. "We can find out more when we get to the hospital."

"He's alive?" I ask as tears slowly slip down my face.

"I don't know." He sighs, his eyes drifting toward Abbey. "All I know is they found him with a gunshot wound to the chest."

"Oh God."

Abbey doesn't come with us to the hospital. She takes a car home. Didn't want to take up any of the attention. Personally, I just think she hates hospitals and knows I'm not going to be easy to be around.

When we get to the hospital it's pure chaos. The police almost didn't let us in, but Wes seems capable of talking his way into anything. Charming bastard couldn't convince Ben not to do it, though.

It's a media circus outside. It's all over the news how Ben Parker got shot in the chest inside his condo. The press are outside causing a shitshow as we sit waiting to find out if he is alive or not.

Wes sits beside me as cops stand down the hallway talking. They're waiting for more information like us. Wes tried to get the nurse to tell him anything, but apparently, he isn't his emergency contact. I beg. I offer the nurse all the money in my account, but they still won't tell us a damn thing.

I sink into a chair as Wes calls Joan to come down, hoping she might be able to find out more as his mother.

I stare at the clock. We've been here for an hour, and no one is telling us anything. For all we know Ben is dead right now. Wes doesn't speak either, just stares at the wall.

When his phone buzzes, we both jump. He glances down before getting up and disappearing down the hall. I want to follow him, but I can't move.

A hospital waiting room has become my own personal hell. I've never felt so hopeless, scared or alone.

When Wes returns a few minutes later, Joan is hanging onto his side, crying. Wes keeps his arm wrapped around her shoulder, comforting her.

It never dawned on me that Wes was that close to Ben. Or that Wes would be that close to Ben's mother.

"Wes, is my son dead?" she asks, standing in front of me.

"They won't tell me anything. We were hoping they might tell you," he says.

"I highly doubt they will tell me anything if they didn't tell you."

"Worth a try," Wes says.

I watch as they stand at the nurse station. Joan becomes very animated as she demands information. Wes just keeps his arm around her the whole time.

When my phone buzzes in my hand and Charles' name flashes across the screen the realization that Ben took a bullet for nothing makes me throw my phone at the wall. It crashes into the wall and hits the floor as I bury my head into my knees.

Ben is probably dead, while Charles is still a free man. He's going to come after me and I'm going to be trapped for the rest of my fucking life.

"I think it's toast," Wes says, holding my broken phone out to me.

"I'm not staying here." I stand up. "He did it for nothing. Charles is calling me. He is going to show up at some point and try to get his revenge. He did it for nothing."

"Don't worry about Charles. He won't be a problem much longer."

"Why?"

"Don't worry about that right now." He sighs. "You're his emergency contact," he says, staring at me. The disbelief on his face lets me know he was unaware of this part of Ben's plan.

"What?"

"Not sure when he changed it, but they won't tell Joan or me anything because you're his emergency contact."

"Me?"

"Yeah."

"Oh."

The lady looked over my ID for a full three minutes before finally taking me back to a smaller waiting room. I tried to convince them to let Wes and Joan come with me, but they wouldn't let them join me, so I'm forced to find out this news by myself.

They just left me in this tiny room all alone. I fear any moment they are going to tell me Ben is dead, and I'll have to find a way to tell Wes and Joan when all I'll want to do is cry.

My heart is pounding in my chest so hard I barely hear when the doctor walks into the room.

"I'm Dr. Richardson. You're here about Benjamin Parker?" I simply nod. "He came in with a gunshot wound to the chest. Just a few inches above his heart. He lost a lot of blood, and by the time they got him here, he already coded once. They were able to get his heart started in the ambulance, but he did code once more on the operating table. It took a moment, but we were able to bring him back. We don't know if there will be any lasting damage from that, but he seems determined to live. He has a long road to recovery ahead of him. Nerve damage, three broken ribs, a lot of internal bleeding, and a concussion."

"But he's alive?" My voice comes out as a whisper.

"He's in critical condition, but yes, he is alive."

"Good. Because I'm going to kill him," I say as tears pour down my face.

Lucky for me the doctor has a sense of humor and doesn't forbid me from seeing Ben after threatening to kill him.

They currently have him in the ICU but hope to move him to a private room once he is more stable. I can't go in the room, but they allow me to stand outside. My eyes are glued to him through a small window.

I watch as his chest rises and falls, with help from the tube down his throat. There are so many wires going from his body to different machines. A monitor displays his heart rate, and the repetitive beating sound brings me a little more peace.

He is in tough shape, and it terrifies me. I keep waiting to wake up and find out he isn't alive after all. The damage is severe. No one knows for sure if he will fully recover. Talk of brain damage or lasting nerve damage has me fearing the worst.

He risked his life for me. I have no idea if it even worked. Charles could've covered his tracks too well to get caught. This might not be the end of trouble for us, but just the start.

Wes doesn't seem concerned, but I'm not sure he fully realizes the situation.

They finally make me leave after close to an hour. It's hard to walk away. Leaving Ben alone is hard to do, but I don't have a choice. I need to go update Wes and his mother anyways.

When I walk back to the waiting room, I find Wes and Joan sitting side by side. He holds her hand, comforting her. Both of them look so distraught it makes me feel bad for being gone so long.

This whole time Ben felt so alone, but these people did care about him. They are his family. He risked leaving them to protect me. It makes me feel worse to know that it's my fault. I never should've dragged him into this.

"Hey," I say softly, and they both glance up at me.

"You were gone so long," Wes says. "What's the news?"

"I'm sorry."

"Oh god." Joan gasps and covers her mouth.

"No. Wait. I mean, I'm sorry I didn't come to tell you sooner. He is alive, barely, but alive." I quickly try to correct myself.

This woman who I barely know jumps to her feet and wraps her arms around me. She grips onto me tightly, crying into my shoulder.

Wes nods his head, but his eyes dart to the hallway. When he stands, he touches Joan's back gently.

"Hey Joan. I need a minute with Prue, okay?"

She nods, still crying, but seeming more at ease as she sits back down. Wes places his hand on my arm, guiding me away from her.

He tucks us against the opposite wall, as I notice two police officers headed our way.

"They are going to want to talk to you. I'm not sure exactly what they will ask, but I can assume it will involve Charles and probably your relationship with Ben."

"What do I say?"

"The truth, but you know, maybe not the whole truth," Wes says softly. "I know you probably aren't happy with Ben right now, and lying isn't smart, but maybe just leave out unnecessary details."

"Should I say Charles, did it?"

"I don't know if you need to. I'm sure they have all the evidence they need."

"What evidence?"

"You really don't listen, do you?" He laughs.

"What evidence, Wes?" I push back.

"Before kidnap... taking you to San Francisco, he had his apartment fitted with hidden cameras. You know, just in case someone decided to break in and steal his guitars or something. And just maybe, they are very well hidden," Wes says quietly. "And maybe they caught the whole thing, and the police are collecting the data as we speak."

"He planned to get caught."

"He planned to make sure it didn't fail. If the blood was on his hands, yeah, it wouldn't be good for him, but if something happened to him, they'd be able to pin it on Charles."

"Ben is insane."

"Insane and alive."

"Until I kill him."

"Yeah?" Wes laughs. "And when do you plan on doing that?"

"Oh. I plan on making it take a lifetime."

THIRTY-EIGHT

Ben

Everything hurts. That's the only thing I can feel as my eyes blink open and close. That, and the lights burn.

I must be in hell, because I'm pretty sure something sharp is up my cock. Each inhale feels like being stabbed, and each exhale feels like being choked. This is pure agony. The only rational conclusion is to assume I died and went to hell.

Whatever sins I'm going to atone for better have been worth it, because the pain is intense.

"Ben?" The voice is low and familiar. I was not expecting this next part of my torture to be so painful. "Asshole, I know you hear me."

Using her to make me suffer is truly unfair. Though I'd take it, if only so I get to see her face again. I hope they got her eyes right.

My eyes snap open, searching for the demon version of her in the far too bright room.

I thought hell was supposed to be all fire and brimstone, but this feels sterile and clean. My head tries to turn, and the agony radiating from my body increases. If they are going to use her form to make me pay for my sins, I'm going to enjoy every fucking second of the pain.

Her face comes into view toward my right. Soft, caramel hair, just to her shoulders, sits in mellow waves. One side is tucked behind her ear, while the other side falls forward as her head is bent toward me. Her pouty lips are a light pink and pressed into a thin line as her sky-blue eyes glare at me.

She is wearing a yellow top and a little black skirt that shows off her pale legs. A hoodie that looks a lot like one of mine sits over her shoulders.

She looks too beautiful to be a creature of hell. I'm honestly kind of impressed. Everything I learned from the brief time my mother tried dragging me to church painted God as all powerful, but if the Devil can make her look this real, I'm not sure we are praying to the right deity.

"Can you speak?" she asks. Her voice makes my head swoon. Literally, it feels like it's been turned to mush. I can't help but smile. "What are they giving you?" She shakes her head, and brown locks go every direction, creating a sparkle effect in their wake.

"I don't know, but whatever is in my cock needs to be removed before I get a fucking boner, from a demon bitch no less."

"I thought you didn't want to refer to me as a bitch anymore?"

"That's her, not you."

"You think I'm not real?" She raises an eyebrow.

"I'm in hell. Of course, you aren't real."

Her eyes roll and she moves to perch on the side of the bed beside me.

"Hate to break it to you, Ben, but you are very much alive. Until I decide how I'm going to kill you, that is."

I blink, taking in the fuzzy background behind her, but not letting my eyes wander from her.

"Where the fuck am I?"

"A hospital, you idiot. You went and got yourself shot, trying to be a hero. It's kind of pathetic really. Most guys buy the girl they love flowers, but not you. You get yourself beaten up, stab yourself and almost die to prove you love her."

"Well not almost die." Wes's voice fills the room, but I still don't let my eyes leave her. I'll stare at her the rest of my life if she lets me. "He did code twice, so technically, he did die."

"Leave it to you to try to make his heroic act seem more impressive," Prue says, shooting him a glare. My hand reaches for her. I desperately want her eyes back on me. I groan as more pain shoots through my body. "Stop moving so much," she snaps. "You have like a million different wires connected to you and an incision the size of my forearm."

"Then don't look away from me," I say, biting my cheek as I let my hand graze her leg. The pain is worth the way her body feels under my fingertips.

"How are you feeling?" Wes asks. I'd look at him but I'm never taking my eyes off the beautiful girl that sits to the side of me.

"I have a tube up my dick. I've never felt better."

Prue rolls her eyes again, but grins. Obviously, she doesn't mind me suffering a little extra, given everything I did.

"Hey!" Wes exclaims. "Good to know your brain didn't suffer any lasting damage."

"Was that a concern?" I ask, studying Prue's face.

"Only a little." She shrugs. "Your heart really did stop twice." She blinks back tears and I squeeze her thigh, ignoring the pain once again. "He almost shot you in the heart. Two inches lower and you'd be dead."

I laugh and then groan in the agony that has made a home in my body.

"It's not funny," she says, shifting her leg away from me.

"Don't move," I groan. "Please." I soften my voice and she moves back, lifting my hand and placing it back on her leg. "Thank you."

"It is a little funny," Wes adds.

"You always defend him." She shakes her head.

"Baby, he had a point-blank shot and missed. That's hilarious in my book. The fucker couldn't even kill me."

"He should've never had the opportunity to try."

"Is he in jail?" I ask.

"Yes. Judge denied bail due to his father's connections. Attempted murder is quite the charge," Wes says.

"He deserves to spend the rest of his life in a cage," Prue snaps. "I hope he gets stabbed in there too. Icing on the fucking cake if you ask me."

"Speaking of cake." I smirk. "When can I fuck you?"

Her cheeks pinken as her eyes spin in circles. She is playing it off like she is so annoyed by the question, but I know her better than that.

"You're going to have to earn that."

"Is a gunshot wound not enough?"

"Enough for kidnapping me, handcuffing me to a bed and abandoning me in San Francisco? Not sure there are enough bullets in the world to make up for that."

"Ha." I laugh, grunting in pain. Why do I keep forgetting that my body is in agony? "Lucky for you, it looks like I'm a masochist."

"On that note," Wes pipes in, "I'm going to go. Just stopped by to drop off some food for Prue. You know she hasn't left your side for a second."

Prue shoots him another glare, and I dig my fingertips into her thigh until her eyes come back to me.

"I meant what I said. Don't move."

"God. You are such an asshole." She rolls her eyes again.

"I'll be back later," Wes says, patting my foot. "Hopefully, you'll be in one piece."

"Not likely," I say, grinning like a crazy person.

One should not be so happy to be in the amount of pain I'm in, but I'm fucking ecstatic. I didn't die. Charles is in jail and Prue is by my side. What reason do I have to be unhappy right now?

"How are you?" she asks, once the door shuts. "Like really? If you're in a lot of pain, I can ask the nurses to bring you something. They said sky's the limit when it comes to pain management for all your wounds. I mean it was iffy if you'd even wake up. They didn't even know if you'd be able to function."

"I'm fucking fantastic."

"Ben, you should see your chart. It's a miracle you're even alive."

"You're the only miracle I see."

"God," she groans, shifting her leg away from me. I reach forward, digging my fingers into her leg. She definitely is a little bit of a demon. "Sorry. I keep forgetting." She moves back. "It's just what you did was incredibly stupid."

"But effective."

"Not worth it. I'm not worth it."

"Prue, baby, you are worth far more than one gunshot wound to the chest."

"You're insane." She sighs. "I should have them transfer you to a mental hospital."

"Probably." I nod, instantly regretting it. "Your piece of shit ex has some really boney elbows."

"You have a concussion."

"You have a concussion," I groan back, letting my eyes close for a moment as I try not to vomit.

"You need more pain medicine." She starts to move, but I grip her thigh again. "I'll be right back."

"No. You aren't going anywhere."

"So, you get to abandon me, but I have to stay put?"

"Yes," I say. "But rest assured, baby, I am never abandoning you again." I let my eyes open to look at her again. "As long as you let me, I'm staying by your side."

"Let's be honest. Even if I told you to go, you'd never leave my side."

"Not true. If you tell me to go, I'll go and finish the job your ex-boyfriend started." I smirk.

"Does that make you my new boyfriend?"

"Woah. Hang on for just one minute. No one said anything about being your boyfriend. I don't do commitment, you know," I joke.

She hits my arm, sending sparks of pain through every corner of my body and a loud groan from my lips.

"Oh. My. God. I'm so sorry, Ben." She quickly leans closer, checking where her hand hit me for any signs of damage. "Are you okay? God, I'm such a bitch."

"No."

"What do you need? How can I help? I'll go get a nurse."

"No. I mean you aren't a bitch," I say softly. "I'm going to have to spend the rest of my life trying to make up for calling you that, aren't I?"

"It's just a word, Ben."

"A word he used."

"I don't mind it coming for you."

"I much rather call you mine."

"I do like that better." She smiles.

"Me too."

"Say it," she says firmly.

"You're mine." I laugh.

"And you're mine, right?"

"Yes, Prue. I'm yours."

"Good." She grins, pressing a soft kiss to the side of my head. "But if you ever get shot again, I'm going to kill you."

"Yeah. I know."

"I love you, Ben."

"I love you too, baby. I love you too." I chuckle.

I never thought an asshole like me would ever fall in love, but at last here we are.

EPILOGUE

Ben

THE GUITAR FEELS HEAVY IN MY ARMS. I'M TRYING TO pretend it's not taking all my effort to keep holding it up, but it feels like it's made of two tons of iron. My fingers strum it with little thought. That part doesn't hurt. My fingers have gotten plenty of practice ignoring the pain that came from flexing them playing with Prue's tight little pussy almost every night.

I'd ignore death to get to touch her.

She sits on my brand-new coffee table, naked, watching me.

It's hard to care about the fact I nearly died on the floor to the side of her, when she looks so fucking hot, watching my fingers strum over the strings.

I've been avoiding practicing. Too scared that after three months of recovery and physical therapy, I'd have lost my touch. Not trying meant I'd never know if that was true or not. I'd rather not know that my whole music career is over than have to face it.

But my little torturer saw right through my avoidance. She laid the terms of her conditions out at dinner. A meal she cooked, as she continues to try to learn life skills she didn't think she'd ever need. All of which she is good at.

The terms were simple, she was going to strip down to nothing, but I couldn't touch her until I spent at least thirty minutes practicing.

So here I sit. An erection is growing beneath my sweatpants, my favorite guitar is pressed into the scar across my chest and the girl I love naked in front of me. I try to focus on moving my fingers in the correct position to a song I've played a thousand times.

My mind does most of the work, but I'm too lost on the sight in front of me, the contentment in my bones, and the blood flowing to my cock to care if I make a mistake or not.

"You aren't even looking at your fingers," Prue says, rolling her eyes for the billionth time since I met her.

"My fingers are hideous compared to you."

"You are so fucking cheesy." She laughs. "Now, the terms were you have to practice guitar for thirty minutes before you can touch me."

"I'm well aware of the rules my evil girlfriend laid out."

"But I never said I couldn't touch me." She smirks.

"Why do you enjoy torturing me?" I groan as she lets her fingers rub circles around her peach-colored nipples.

"Because you let me." She shrugs.

"Fair point," I say, letting my fingers fall into the rhythm of some cheesy song Wes wrote for some girl that isn't his girlfriend or mine, but fits the moment regardless. "Can I finally fuck you?"

"I don't know, can you?" She raises an eyebrow, letting her other hand drop between her thighs, stroking her little pussy.

She has been withholding sex, choosing to ride my face or suck my cock. She says it's because the doctors say I'm not ready for strenuous activity, but I'm not buying it. I swear it's some kind of punishment for the fact I let her ex shoot me while she laid handcuffed to a bed in San Francisco.

Apparently, finger fucking her and eating her pussy doesn't count as strenuous, nor does choking her with my cock.

So, I have yet to feel her pussy again. I'm dying to have it wrapped around my cock, but I'll wait as long as she desires, simply grateful she lets me touch her at all.

"I like this song," she moans softly, making my cock throb. "Who is it about?"

"Some girl Wes used to date."

"Oh." She gasps as she slides a finger inside her cunt.

"You can take two of mine, add another."

She eyes me with a wicked grin. "Doesn't matter how many I take, just thinking about your cock is enough to get me close."

"Not close enough to actually let me fuck you, though."

"Fuck," she groans, grinding herself against her hand. "But I want you to. It's just the doctor…"

"I survived a bullet. I think I can survive your tight little pussy."

She moans, her eyes opening to look at the clock. "You still have 19 minutes."

"Then I can fuck you?"

"Then you can touch me." She smirks.

"You're cruel," I say, letting my fingers play a different melody. I just wrote this one a few weeks ago, while I was still lying in a hospital bed, but haven't had the chance to hear how it sounds.

"That's pretty," she moans.

"Yeah." I smile.

Wes likes to do most of the writing, but I'll be damned if he doesn't let me write at least one song on the new record, whenever we get back into the studio. Prue deserves a whole fucking discography written about her, but I highly doubt the band would allow that. Wes gets to have Abbey on the album, and half a dozen songs about her, but I'll probably get lucky just to get an occasional song about Prue thrown in.

"Fuck," she groans, fucking herself a little harder. "Play me something to cum to." Her eyes zoning in on me. "Then I'll let you fuck me."

"You had me at play something to cum to." I smirk, strumming a nice, sexy melody for her.

Prue and I may be two completely broken people, with a lot of damage to sort through, but there is no one else in this whole fucked up world I rather do it with than her.

After my little hint about my aunt, my mother asked me to go to therapy with her. I see no use in it, but she wants to know what happened and understand why I didn't tell her. She blames herself, despite my desperate pleads for her to blame the only person responsible.

I told her under no circumstances would I be talking about it further and then Prue tortured me into submission. My mother has no idea my relenting to therapy had anything to do with getting to cum on Prue's pretty little face, not will she ever. She's just content I agreed to go.

Prue's parents don't speak to Cameron or her anymore. The damage of Charles' arrest still lingers. They deny him bail repeatedly, which is smart. Daddy Davenport would have him out of the country before the handcuff indents were gone.

He has good lawyers though, and despite Prue insisting that I did not take her against her will, they are using that as motive. He will most likely get attempted manslaughter and spend a few years behind bars. Hopefully, by the time he is released, Prue and I are far from his reach, on a sandy beach, living the good life.

Prue dropped out of college, despite my offer to pay. Now she is trying to find herself and I couldn't be happier, so long as she doesn't find herself far away from me.

"Fuck. Ben," she groans, her eyes focused on the way my fingers move over the strings, much how they move against her clit every time she lets me play with her.

"I love when you moan my name."

"I love you," she moans back, letting her eyes roll shut as her orgasm overtakes her.

"I love you too, Prue." I smile, tossing my guitar to the side, ignoring the lingering ache, and dropping to my knees before her bare pussy.

Somehow, I'm always on my knees for this woman, and I couldn't be happier about that fact.

I lean forward, prying her finger from her still spasming cunt and letting my tongue take over the job.

It hasn't been thirty minutes, so she probably won't let me fuck her tonight, but I just couldn't take one more moment of not touching her. I'd gladly take whatever punishment she gives me for that. I'd endure a lifetime of torture for her. And she knows it.

Who knows if we will be together forever. Once her internal wounds heal, I'm not sure she will have much use for me, but I'll never regret what I did for her, not even if Charles comes around and finishes the job. Until she chooses to leave though, I'm going to enjoy every second with her.

I'm not sure how I got so fucking lucky, nor do I think the scar from the bullet I took for her shows it, but fuck, if I'm not the luckiest asshole in the world.

THANK YOU FOR READING!

I hope that you enjoyed reading *A Broken Melody* as much as I enjoyed writing it. If you have a moment, please hop online and consider posting a review! As an indie author, I depend heavily on word of mouth and the feedback and support of readers like you.

Thank you!

ACKNOWLEDGMENTS

I couldn't have done this without my husband, Matthew. His endless support, constant encouragement, and very warranted pushing are what got me here. Before him, my stories were unfinished and unpublished, but through his unconditional love, I found the courage to get them out of my head and onto the page for the whole world to read. He is, and always will be, my dream come true.

My family has put up with my wild stories since I was able to talk. They encouraged my creativity by playing dolls and Barbies with me, and I would not be the weird, strange, and slightly deranged person I am today without them. For that, I'm forever grateful. They never tried to silence me or dull my light, and I am incredibly lucky to have them.

My writing friends have kept me going when I felt like throwing in the towel. Their encouragement throughout this entire process made sure I never gave up. Their support means the world to me, and I'm beyond thankful for every single one of them. Having fellow writer to talk with, vent to, and brainstorm with, is something every author needs. When you aren't alone, writing becomes so much easier. Their support is something I will carry with me forever.

A huge thank you to K. Jaspersen for the beautiful cover, wonderful formatting and all the other help she gave me.

Ramona Mihai did a great job editing and proof this book. Thank you!

To the readers, I want to express my deepest gratitude. My works may not be the next great American novel, but the fact that you took the time to read any of them means more to me than I can say. We live in a time overflowing with incredible books, and you chose to pick up one of mine. Thank you.

This book would not exist without Abbey Dark. She is the first character of mine to receive a finished story. *A Dark Melody* is where this entire universe was born. Without her, Ben, Prue, and The Melody Universe would not exist. What was meant to be a single story turned into something so much bigger, so a huge shout-out to her and Wes.

That being said, I need to acknowledge past Sam. She never thought she'd publish a book, let alone two. As much as she loved writing, publishing didn't feel possible, but she kept going anyway. And here we are. I wish I could go back in time and show her just how far we've come.

To anyone who has read this far, **thank you**.

I hope my story entertained you.

—Samantha

ABOUT THE AUTHOR

Samantha Butterfield is a Bay Area author who has lived there her entire life. She has been writing stories and poetry since she was young, always finding comfort in words. She loves crafting deep, emotional poetry and creating complex characters in drama-filled worlds.

Drawing from her own personal struggles, Samantha has published several poetry collections that explore the hardships of mental illness. Her storytelling doesn't stop at poetry. She also writes full-length novels, using her emotions and experiences to create raw, unique characters and emotionally driven stories.

When she isn't writing, Samantha can usually be found reading or listening to music with her cat, Hemingway, curled up beside her, finding inspiration in quiet moments and the melodies that shape her work.

Consider subscribing to Samantha's newsletter, Sam's Soundtrack, for all the latest new regarding future projects.

Newsletter: https://www.samanthabutterfield.com/sams-soundtrack

Website: https://www.samanthabutterfield.com

Follow on social media for sneak peaks on upcoming books.

- instagram.com/s_butterfieldauthor
- tiktok.com/@sbutterfieldauthor
- youtube.com/@Sbutterfieldauthor

OTHER BOOKS IN THE MELODIVERSE

A Dark Melody

Abbey Dark is the biggest star on Veritas Records, but fame has its dark side. Wes is the lead singer of Haunting Memories, who happens to be on tour with Abbey. When they meet, sparks fly, but friendship is what Abbey really needs. Will they be able to maintain their friendship or will their chemistry and fame destroy everything?

Available Now!

A Broken Melody

Ben is the lead guitarist for a famous band. Prue is a rich girl trying to escape her fate. When their paths cross, they learn their broken pieces might actual fit nicely together.

A Tragic Melody (2026/2027)

Tuesday Blue is an up-and-coming singer. Wyatt James is a freshly sober guitarist. When they head out on tour together, drama unfolds. What could've been a working relationship, turns into a battle for glory. With these two enemies find a way to survive the spotlight together, or will they become just another tragic story?

A Bitter Melody (TBA)

A Twisted Melody (TBA)

www.ingramcontent.com/pod-product-compliance
Lightning Source LLC
LaVergne TN
LVHW091706070526
838199LV00050B/2299